THE RESERVOIR

THE RESERVOIR

· A NOVEL ·

JOHN MILLIKEN THOMPSON

OTHER PRESS · NEW YORK

Production Editor: *Yvonne E. Cárdenas*
Text Designer: *Simon M. Sullivan*
This book was set in 11.25 pt Caslon by Alpha Design &
Composition of Pittsfield, NH.

10 9 8 7 6 5 4 3 2

LIBRARY OF CONGRESS CATALOGING-IN-PUBLICATION DATA
Thompson, John M. (John Milliken), 1959-
The reservoir / by John Milliken Thompson.
p. cm.
ISBN 978-1-59051-444-3 (trade pbk. original) —
ISBN 978-1-59051-445-0 (e-book)
1. Richmond (Va.)—Fiction. 2. Virginia—History—19th century—
Fiction. I. Title.
PS3620.H68325R47 2011
813'.6—dc22
2010040659

FOR MARGO, EVAN, AND CLAIRE
AND FOR MY PARENTS

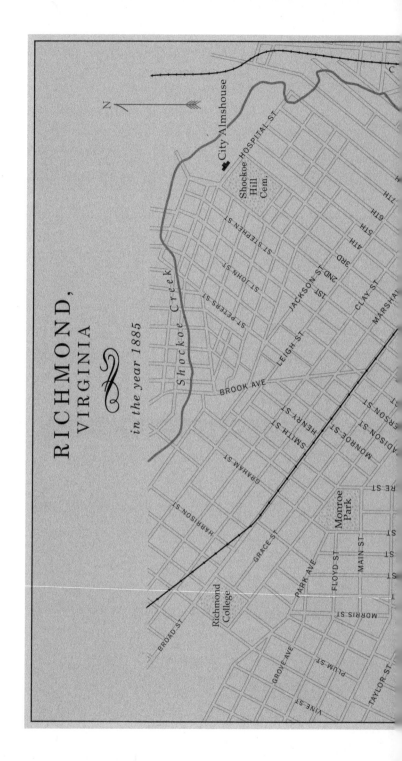

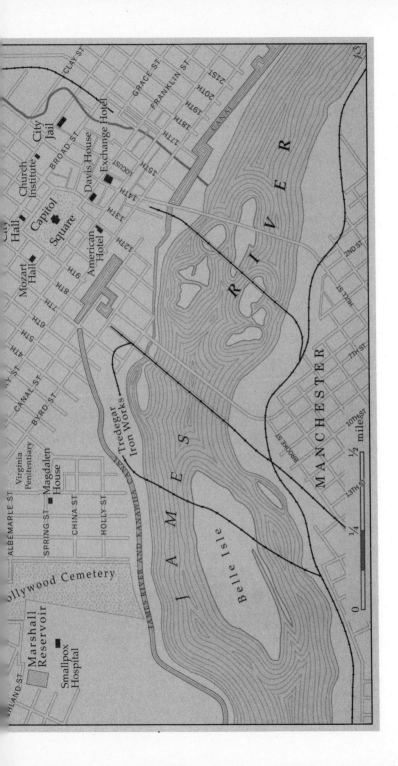

THE RESERVOIR

The way it floats in the water so serenely in the moonlight and the sunlight you would have thought it was meant to be there. Pure and unyielding and as solid as silk. She floats there, a mystery as deep as the moon and the mind of God. What does it mean? A pregnant girl floating in the city's drinking water?

CHAPTER ONE

ON MARCH 14, 1885, a body is floating in the old Marshall Reservoir, in a light snow, and then under a waxing moon.

In the morning the superintendent of the reservoir, Lysander Meade, discovers a furrowed place on the walkway that he does not remember seeing the night before. Someone has crawled through the fence again—early in the year for youngsters to be out cavorting at night. He glances down toward the water and sees what appears to be a dress. It's floating along the edge of the water, where the embankment slopes down to a picket fence. He's seen a lot of oddities in his years—rubber condoms and smutty books and the occasional sack of puppies—but never a dress. He tries to imagine the scene. Mighty cold last night for such carryings-on. Except now he sees it isn't just a dress, but a whole person. A woman. And a dead one at that, or what appears to be. Never has he found a dead woman, nor man neither for that matter.

So down he goes for a better look. Who would not want to see a dead woman? Could she be something to look at? Could she be a fine-looking lady, or might she be one of your more common sorts? Mr. Lucas comes up from the pump house where he has been repairing a stopcock, and helps Mr. Meade with his speculations. They stand there together, Lucas a head taller, loose-limbed and slack-jawed, with stick-out ears, while Meade, wearing thick eyeglasses, bends rigidly forward at the waist, his navy jacket stretching across his back, his neat mustache crin-kling as he sniffs the air. All they can make out at first is a gray wool dress with flounces at the bottom and hair hanging like dark weeds about her head. "The grappling hook's the thing," Mr. Meade says.

Mr. Lucas comes back presently, hook at the ready. But now Mr. Meade is not so sure. He nudges the body closer to the shore. Then he stops and yells. "Hello, ma'am? Hello, miss? Hello?"

"I expect you'll have to yell louder than that," Mr. Lucas suggests.

Mr. Meade nods. "Yep, dead sure as I'm standing here. Dead as dirt." But now he thinks that Mr. Lucas should go fetch the coroner. "Let him decide what to do."

So off goes Mr. Lucas again. And now it's a long wait. Mr. Meade stands guard with his hook like a spear hunter over his kill, thinking of all the time this is going to take, when he would be nearly finished with his morning walk and inspection by now and heading back to the warmth of his house. The girl's legs swing out, the gray woolen skirt going with them, and Meade reins her back to the edge. A lock of hair has come loose from her combs and curls lazily across her forehead, her eyes look-ing glassily heavenward. Her prim little jacket looks so digni-fied against the dishevelment of her condition—as if she were only momentarily delayed here on the way to some important engagement.

And then Lucas returns with Dr. Taylor. He's wearing his black coat and carrying his medical bag. Balding and wall-eyed, he appears to survey both men at once. The three of them ma-neuver the body to the little gate in the picket fence, which Mr. Meade opens. Mr. Lucas goes out onto the narrow grassy ledge and, because the water level has dropped during the night—what with people drawing from the pipes—has to lie on his belly, Mr. Meade holding his legs, and take hold of whatever he can, which happens to be the woman's right arm. It's up and stiff. He takes it at the wrist. It's like cold gutta-percha, and the hand is clutching mud. He tugs and she comes right up, dripping water. Smaller than he thought, like a child, but round-faced and strangely stout.

"Could be one of your German women, from over in Manchester." He nods toward the industrial section across the river.

Dr. Taylor pays no attention. He's feeling for a pulse, examining her eyes, pushing at her skin, unbuttoning her coat. Mr. Meade is not looking at the girl at all. But Mr. Lucas can't take his eyes away from her. She looks like a perfect little doll, and now he wishes he had found her and could take her home with him. What an odd thought to have, he tells himself. "Why would she come all the way over here to do herself in?" he says. "When the river's right there?"

"Mr. Meade," Dr. Taylor says, "would you mind lifting her head just so?" But Mr. Meade cannot seem to make himself touch the girl, and so Mr. Lucas obliges. It's not every day, he tells himself, that a dead girl washes up in your very own reservoir. And now as sure as anything they'll be wanting him to drain it out, but as for himself he doesn't see how a girl like this could unpurify the water. He wouldn't mind drinking it himself. Not at all. He is on the verge of telling this to Dr. Taylor, when Dr. Taylor slaps her between the shoulder blades and water trickles from the corner of her mouth. Mr. Lucas keeps her head off the ground as if she were a sick child, and he is reluctant to let go when Dr. Taylor turns her onto her back again.

By now onlookers have begun making their way up to the embankment, which rises like an earthen fort above the reservoir grounds. It's a pleasant Saturday morning in Richmond, with a hint of spring in the air, and news of something going on at the reservoir spreads abroad like pollen. Here comes Detective Wren, his greatcoat unbuttoned and flapping as he lumbers at an angle up the embankment, then pauses to get his bearings. In his mid-thirties, he is large, bulldog jowly, sideburned, and pink-faced, with a divot in his chin; he gives the impression of worldliness, gaining respect by appearing to know what others have just discovered. Mr. Meade fills him in and points out the footprints. "Has anybody else walked up here?" Mr. Wren thunders, moving toward the footprints. Mr. Meade is not sure but says he can find out, and Mr. Wren shakes his head in exasperation and in a surprisingly high, yet commanding voice tells everyone nearby to please step off the walkway. Mr. Meade obeys and, unsure how much authority Wren really has and how well he knows Meade's boss at the waterworks, decides just to try to avoid this meddlesome bear who has intruded as much as the dead girl on his morning's routine. He rejoins Dr. Taylor at the water's edge.

Then, under Mr. Wren's direction, Mr. Lucas removes one of the girl's shoes and brings it up to the walkway so that Mr. Wren can compare it with the footprints. Mr. Lucas is delighted to be of assistance. The shoe feels tiny in his big hand. He places it delicately within the footprint and finds that it fits. But there are some bigger ones as well, half-prints really. "Do you think she was here with someone?" Mr. Lucas says, as though to himself.

"Could be," Wren says. "Could be." Taking the shoe from Lucas, he holds it to his large nose and inhales.

"But why would she come out here with somebody when she was planning to do herself in?" Lucas wishes he had thought to smell the girl's shoe.

"She might not have been planning any such thing atall," Wren says, taking notes, looking around, sniffing the air as though for clues. Mr. Lucas nods, trying to imagine the girl coming out here with a companion, who then left her alone—at which point she climbed over the picket fence, or else found the little gate on the south end. But Mr. Meade always keeps the gate locked at night.

Now a young reporter from the *Dispatch* has arrived and is down by the picket fence where the body lies covered on a stretcher, lately brought by Dr. Taylor's assistant. The reporter is talking with Dr. Taylor and Mr. Meade, so Wren goes down to avail himself of the opportunity for free publicity. He pushes his way into their circle, to Meade's relief and Taylor's annoyance—though both use the opportunity to get back to work—and introduces himself to the reporter, telling him that he's unofficially investigating the case. The reporter eagerly takes note. An actual *case*. An *investigation*. "Do you not subscribe to the suicide theory?" he asks Wren.

"Let's just say there are some unexplained circumstances. Such as the presence of two sets of footprints, one larger than the other. One would naturally like to know to whom does that second set belong."

"Any ideas yet about the identity of the girl?"

"That is a mystery yet to be solved. But Jack Wren does indeed have some ideas. I can crack this case in three days." He tilts his chin in a knowing way.

Mr. Lucas comes down from the walkway with the girl's shoe, surreptitiously smelling it. As he puts it back on the girl's foot, Dr. Taylor winks at him. "There's something those two would be interested to know." He nods toward the detective and the newsman, standing a little ways off. "The girl was pregnant."

Lucas's eyes grow large. He looks back at the body. "Going to have a baby?"

"That's the kind of pregnant I mean."

Lucas shakes his head. "That's a shame," he says, somehow a little disappointed now in his drowned angel. "She's a pretty little thing, though."

Dr. Taylor waits until he's asked—by the newsman—if there was anything unusual about the body. At first he says no, then mentions the mud in her hands. "Oh, yes," he says, "and she was with child." The newsman scribbles away, while the detective merely nods, as though he'd suspected as much all along.

When it's time to take the body away, Mr. Lucas insists on helping. "No trouble atall," he says, lifting the foot of the stretcher. "She's light as a feather." The assistant takes the head and they proceed up the embankment, then down the walkway to the steps at the far end and out the gate where Dr. Taylor's ambulance is waiting, its blinkered horse standing patiently. The sheet covering the body has worked itself up to where the feet are visible. Mr. Lucas notices. Such dainty feet in their little shoes, and her stocking-covered ankles. Her foot had been stiff to his touch when he removed the shoe for Mr. Wren, but now they look so lifelike that he cannot resist the temptation to touch one as he helps slide her into the back of the ambulance. "Good-bye," he says.

◆

It's late on Friday the thirteenth, the night before the discovery of the body. A young man, pale and slender, stands on the embankment atop the reservoir. He looks down into the inky water a final time, but in the darkness it's hard to distinguish smooth water from human form. There's no sound of any struggle. What more is there to do except to pick up her hat and gloves, here on the gravel walkway. But why not just leave them here? Would a suicide leave her things lying about? He tries to think, but his head is throbbing. "O dem golden slippers" comes to mind, though he couldn't say why. He can find only one glove, and her scarf—was she not wearing a red scarf? It's nowhere, and yet he cannot swear she wasn't wearing it when she went in the water. He can't think straight.

Now his heart is beginning to thump blood through his ears. He has to get out of here. He picks up her clothes bag, pulls his hat down tight, and very nearly trots down the embankment to the hole in the plank fence, where not thirty minutes earlier the two of them came in. He crawls through and then heads out the opposite way, cutting across the Clarke Spring property and past the smallpox deadhouse. And here he stops and does a curious thing. The deadhouse hasn't been used for years—the few sufferers at the smallpox hospital are simply buried over in the little plot by the hole in the fence. Lillie just now said something about the graves, but what it was he can't bring to mind. One of the deadhouse windows is broken, so he tosses the hat in and continues on. Won't be found for days, he thinks, and by then if any connection is made, it will simply be, "She was in a state of mental distress, not aware of what she was doing."

He wants to get rid of her bag, but where to hide it? Now he sees that he has dropped the glove. He scans around for a minute, but every instinct is screaming at him to get out now. So he skirts the little hospital building and heads for the tall outer fence, where another hole should get him free. He peeks through, then shoves the bag out. It's a tighter fit than he remembers, though he has never been here wearing a winter coat. A button pops off as he goes through, but there's no time to look for it—there's someone on the other side of the street, coming this way, singing.

Has he been seen coming out? He picks up the bag and walks briskly, as though he has been here all along. The man on the other side steps into the street and Tommie feels himself go limp with fear. Yet now the man is weaving and singing even louder.

"A drunk negro," Tommie says to himself. He practically laughs in relief. But the strange thing is what the drunk negro is singing: "O dem golden slippers! Don't 'spect to wear 'em till my weddin' day." Could he have heard Tommie singing this? But he wasn't singing it, was he? Could the negro have heard it in Tommie's head? And now Tommie wonders if he's not more than a little crazy.

He turns right and heads down Cherry past Hollywood Cemetery to the little cart bridge over the canal. From there it's a quick scurry over the railroad tracks and down to the river. The clanging from Tredegar ironworks arises several hundred yards downstream. He looks around, sees no one, and heaves the bag out into the current. A skinny little splash and it's gone.

Now he's nearly a free man. Back up to Spring Street and thence to Main, where he joins with the after-theater, late-supper crowds. In fact, was he not just now coming from the Dime Museum, the evening performance of *The Chimes of Normandy*? Of course he was. He saw it this afternoon—his friend Bernard Henley saw him there—and liked it so much he decided to go back this evening. Nearly convinced of his clever alibi, he stops at Morgenstern's for a glass of beer and a plate of fried oysters.

He takes a seat near the back, against the wall. His mind is a blur of images and sounds and fatigue. *O dem golden slippers!* Goddamn it. *Shall we gather at the river.* But why would he be thinking of that song and of his baptism in the pond with his brother so long ago?

"Huh?"

"No appetite after all?" repeats the waiter, a young blade with a curling mustache.

Tommie brings himself back to the world. "Of course I do," he says. "I just—I'd prefer to take these back to my hotel." The young man says he'll box them up in a jiffy, and sweeps the plate away. Tommie wishes he had just paid and left. Now he has to sit and wait, and stare at the mud he's just noticed on his overshoes. Best not draw attention to himself, he thinks, by cleaning them here.

Then back out into the street, where a boy offers to shine his shoes. Goddamn it all. Tommie smiles and thanks the boy, who touches his finger to his hat. In a quiet eddy of amber gaslight, he stops and wipes the mud off with his handkerchief. Calm yourself, he says inwardly. The boy noticed nothing—he offered to clean my shoes, not my overshoes, and he wouldn't remember it as unusual anyway. I've been seen by scores of people already, and not one noticed me in any particular way. Too bad I haven't seen somebody I know. Just in case. Might have to prove I was here along Main Street the whole evening.

Back at the Davis House, he greets Mr. Davis with as warm a hello as he has ever given. Davis looks up from his newspaper suddenly, as if he doesn't recognize the voice. "It's me, Tommie Cluverius. How are you, Mr. Davis?"

A walrus of a man, Mark Davis nods, his hand going to his large, hairless chin. "You go to the show?"

"As a matter of fact, I did. I went to the afternoon show and liked it so much, I went back again just now."

"It's just letting out?"

Why are people so curious about matters that don't concern them, Tommie wonders. "No," he says, "I stopped by Morgenstern's for fried oysters, and had some fixed up for my lunch tomorrow." He holds up the box. "Could you call for me at five in the morning? I want to catch the early train."

"Find a young lady to take out?" Not looking as he jots down Tommie's wake-up time.

Tommie smiles pleasantly. "No, unfortunately not. But I did enjoy the show."

Mr. Davis leans back in his chair and tells Tommie to have an apple. "You look wide awake," he says. "Might as well sit and talk a few minutes. Get your mind off your troubles."

"I don't have any troubles," Tommie says, taking the apple. He stands and begins eating it, eyeing Mr. Davis. But the innkeeper appears only to want company.

"What was the show about?" he asks.

"I thought you said you didn't go in for opera," Tommie says.

Mr. Davis laughs. "I surely did," he says. "But I don't mind hearing the story, if it's a good one." Tommie starts in telling him about the French nobleman and the little girl rescued from the sea who becomes his ward. Mr. Davis yawns and asks him if there were any pretty girls in the show. "Yes," Tommie says, "one or two. A blond and a brunet."

Mr. Davis perks up. "A blond and a brunet, huh?" He crunches deep into his apple.

"Yes," Tommie says. "The blond was prettier. Her hair was pulled up off her forehead and hung long in the back. She was a fisherman's wife. She had a round, pretty face and a loose blouse, low-cut." Davis licks the juice from his chin and stares into space.

Tommie has a hard time going to sleep that night. His mind is swirling with the events of the day and how they led to the evening and whether he has forgotten to do something crucial that could mean his life is now changed forever. It doesn't seem possible, none of it does. He says the Lord's Prayer softly into the darkness and thinks about the play he saw this afternoon, willing himself to believe he went back to the night performance, instead of meeting with *her* at the American Hotel.

He is sound asleep when the bellboy knocks on his door at five past five. He jerks awake, and for a moment he is still Tommie Cluverius, rising young lawyer from King and Queen County, Virginia, not a stain on his name, nor a care in his heart.

❧

CHAPTER TWO

POLICE JUSTICE DANIEL CINCINNATUS RICHARDSON is sitting down to his midday dinner when his servant informs him that an officer is calling on an urgent matter. Richardson excuses himself to his wife and daughters and goes to the door. The officer briefs him—white girl found dead at the reservoir, suspected suicide, pregnant, no identification, Dr. Taylor taking the body to the almshouse.

Richardson tells the officer to keep him informed, then closes the door. He strokes his long sideburns, which join to his beard. He has a whalelike forehead, but otherwise handsome, craggy features, with penetrating hazel eyes, and he is possessed of a Lincolnesque stature. "Lord," he says, shaking his head, then goes back to his dinner. One more year before he retires, and he hopes to God he doesn't have anything more serious than drunk negroes, knifings, and dead babies to deal with. Running Union blockades off Cape Hatteras was child's play compared with some of the things he has seen as magistrate. As he sits down he pictures a dead girl in the reservoir and takes a close, loving look at his daughters. To their questions he tells them what he has just heard, leaving out the pregnant part.

"I'll never go up there again," his older daughter says. She is thin-faced like her mother, and as cautious.

"It's perfectly safe," Richardson replies. "But nobody has any business up there at night."

"Oh, Daddy," says the younger, who has his dark coloring and his curiosity about the world, "everybody knows you can get through the fence. They board it up, and the boys pop it back open."

"Well, you don't have any business knowing that."

"I didn't say I'd done it."

Richardson gives her a half-stern, half-amused glance and changes the subject to the upcoming cotillion at the governor's mansion. His wife, silent on the previous subject, now takes over, and when the conversation turns to dresses Richardson mentally drifts away, eating his Saturday roast while thinking of simpler times, growing up by the river, spending whole days fishing and swimming with a companion or by himself.

Late in the afternoon the policeman returns to inform Richardson that a river pilot found a woman's linen traveling bag floating along the coal docks. It contained women's underwear and a change of clothes. A pair of underpants had a label bearing the name F. or T. Madison.

Earlier that morning, Tommie Cluverius is on the seven o'clock train heading east toward the rising sun. The scratches on the back of his hand hurt, but, more to the point, they are ugly and very noticeable. What can he say? He somehow caught his hand up in his watch chain getting on the train. Or reaching for the rail as the train lurched on the tracks. Yes, that's better. He puts his hand in his pocket to see if it's possible to do such a thing. But, he tells himself, he's worrying for nothing—no one will notice anything. Now that he has nothing to do for the next hour, he sits there thinking about what he will say when he gets home. This morning he spoke to an acquaintance on the platform, then moved farther down, as though he wanted a car more toward the rear, when in fact he just wanted to avoid speaking. Mr. Davis is the only person he's had a real conversation with since last night, and he noticed—how did he put it?—that Tommie was wide awake. What did he mean by that? Did he not mean agitated? Scared to death? Because that's how he felt.

Now he pushes down a rising welter of dread and stares out at the farms flashing by, the cows swishing their tails without a care, the colored boys waving at the crossings. At a stop, he watches an ancient, gray-headed negro patiently repairing a stone fence, while nearby a handful of boys burst from a shack throwing rocks at birds feeding on freshly broadcast seeds. He cannot give in to his exhaustion just yet—he has to be cheerful until he can get back to Aunt Jane's and get some sleep, or at least try to. He has business on Monday in Tappahannock, which gives him a couple of days to gather his wits. If only there were somewhere to go and hide for a few weeks, until it was safe to come out. Perhaps he should have headed west this morning, and kept going all the way to California. Certainly they could use a young lawyer out there. "Not since the Garden of Eden," went the real estate ads, "has there been such an opportunity."

When he arrives in South Point he debarks and heads over to the steamship terminal. His plan was to take the *R. E. Lee* up the Mattaponi to the landing at Clifton, but now he sees a friend at the dock and deviates down to the ferry landing. A few minutes later he's across the river with his valise and is hiring a buggy to drive him the twelve miles to Little Plymouth. He'll be home in a few short hours and then he can hide his face from the outside world.

Yet when they pull into the village, the old men sitting on the store porch, thumbs tucked in their overalls, have nothing better to do than holler to every passing vehicle, person, or animal. They're friends of his father's, and, in fact, one of them *is* his father. Tommie pays the driver and alights. "I can walk from here," he says.

"Speak of the devil," one of the men says. "Your pa was just bragging on you."

Tommie grins sheepishly and shakes hands all around. And right off his father notices. "What did you do to your hand, son?" he asks.

Tommie glances casually as though he hadn't noticed a thing. "I don't know," he says. "I must have caught it in my watch chain getting on the train. I didn't notice anything at the time."

One of the old-timers arcs a stream of tobacco juice across the porch into the dirt. "How's business, Tommie?"

"Fine, just fine."

"I'm gonna get me up to Richmond now the weather's better. Find me a young lady. The wife's gettin' old and wore out. 'Spect I'll have any luck?"

"If anybody would it's you, Mr. Taliaferro. You want any help selling that property, you let me know."

"I will, I will, Tommie, when I get around to it. But if I was a young man like you, I wouldn't concern myself with business all the time. How's that lady friend?"

"Nola's fine."

"Well, you court her too slow and she'll be gone. She's a fine young woman too. Hm mm." He murmurs appreciatively, the breeze lifting a gray lock.

Tommie's father takes him aside and asks him to please stop and visit his mother on the way up to Aunt Jane's. Tommie was planning on going over there later in the day, but he says of course he will. His father's eyes droop and seem cloudier than the last time Tommie noticed them, his frame more gaunt and hunched, his beard longer and thinner. Since they lost the farm—after losing their youngest son—his parents have steadily declined. But at the same time his father's spirit seemed to have been let loose, as though taking on the role of the defeated Southern farmer had freed him to become the rocking chair sage he had always wanted to be.

He takes his son's hand and examines it. "Ask your mama to put some salve on that, son. And get some food while you're there. She'd love to feed you a meal. Let her fuss over you just a little."

Tommie promises his father that he will, then takes his leave and turns down the dusty street at the end of which stands the little house his parents moved into when they sold the farm nine years back. Tommie was fourteen then, and he and his brother went to live in their aunt's farmhouse. His father had sold off bits of their property, before and after the war, just to be able to keep it. He had often reminded his wife that many a man had lost the works, yet she could not help thumbing back through the years to find little weaknesses in his husbandry, a bit of inattention here, a failure to gamble on an opportunity there—a running tally that when one of the "dark spells" came on she could lay at his door, in her mind if not in language, and say, "This is why I've come to this pass."

During the war, there were blue-clad soldiers on the loose, intent on meanness after their Colonel Dahlgren was killed in an ambush. His men came back and burned everything they could set a match to—the courthouse, stores, clerk's office, even the jail, which made no sense to anybody. But there were good times too in those days. Weeks would go by with no news of anybody hurt or killed, not a hint of war along the Mattaponi. And just the sight of morning dew on the cut cornfield or a twist of smoke from the chimney was enough to make your heart full. Mr. Cluverius would come in for his morning coffee and often as not slip his strong arm around his wife's waist and tell her there was a new day coming—the farm was going to look better than it ever had, with a wide front porch, maybe a portico with columns and a balcony. She would laugh and shake her head, "I don't need all that." But picturing it nonetheless. So what if depredations on the garden were commonplace? Life was still good.

A year after Charles died, Mr. Cluverius hurt his back carrying a sack of grain. He cut back on his workload, and seemed to have less and less desire to get up in the mornings.

Now Tommie's mother takes her time answering his knock, but then hugs and kisses him and tells him she hasn't seen him in the longest time. The sweet scents of bourbon and soap issue from her crinkled face. "Just a week, I think," Tommie says.

"Come in and I'll get you some dinner," she says. "Or are you expected at Aunt Jane's?" It's an old routine—he'll eat a little something, even if only some cold biscuits and last year's canned peaches. It's just after noon, and though his stomach is gnawing him, the idea of eating anything makes him feel nauseated.

"I am a little bit hungry," he tells his mother. He sits at the square table in the kitchen and pushes a stack of papers and books out of the way to clear a space. A broom leans against the other chair as though she has been cleaning just now, yet the dust and dirt seem little changed since the last time he was here. The water stain in the ceiling looks bigger.

Tommie's mother sets a plate of cured ham and applesauce in front of him. "I wish I had some coleslaw to go with it. I know you like it. But I can put a pot of beans on. I just have to light the stove. The wood's already in there."

"No, Mama, don't. This is all I want. I don't have a taste for beans right now."

"I have to put them on for your father's supper anyway. You're so thin, and you work so hard. Let me just look at you." She leans back and peers up at him through the half-light. Her hair is still a rich chestnut, her eyes clear and filled with love for her favorite son.

Tommie shakes his head and inquires after her health. She removes a pile of clothes from the other chair and sits down and starts telling him the details of her last bout of illness. "And your father's joints are mighty cruel to him. I expect it's rheumatism. The doctor says it's gout, but look at how thin he is. The liniment is some benefit, but the pills don't help much."

Tommie has heard all this before; he picks up a carved wooden object on the table and asks his mother what it is. She laughs and shakes her head. "I don't know," she says. "Something your brother carved. I think maybe it's a bear. He says it's a mythical animal. What do you think it is?"

Tommie studies it a moment. "Could be a boar, or a bear. A mythical object?"

"Willie says he's taken to carving things when he feels like his mind is wandering away from him. I thought that was a curious thing to say. I don't think he's been the same since he broke off with Fannie Lillian."

Tommie stares at the carved animal. "That was years ago," he says. "He's had lots of girls since then."

"Lillian was what they called her. Wasn't it?"

"Yes, that's what they call her." He does not take his eyes off the figurine, and it seems to him to be changing shape there on the table, sprouting horns and moving toward him. He feels suddenly so tired he can barely keep sitting up.

"What is it, son?"

"What?"

"Looks like something's bothering you."

Tommie shakes his head. He flashes to an image—ripples on the dark surface of the water. "No, I'm just a little tired." He can hear the clanking of heavy machinery. Where?

"Go on back to the bedroom and take a nap. Nobody'll disturb you."

Tommie tells her that Aunt Jane is expecting him soon, and his mother smiles sadly. "Thanks, Mama," he says. He kisses her good-bye and tells her he'll be around in a few days and that he'll get Willie to bring her some wood and fix her roof.

When he heads out the bright day has suddenly gone cloudy and cold the way it will in March. It's a mile up the Trace, along fields and woods, to the turnoff for Cedar Lane; a buggy driver stops and offers him a ride, but he politely declines. He and his mother used to look at catalogues and picture books together and fantasy what it would be like to live in a big city or sail to a foreign capital and visit the castles and museums. He knew he was her favorite, and after Charles died she seemed to become even more attached to him, as though she could make up for the lost love by loving him even more. His brother, Willie, was happier working in the fields with the horses and machinery, but though they had grown to care about different things, Willie never, since the death of their little brother, ceased to take responsibility for protecting Tommie—the hard kernel of guilt born in Willie was countered in Tommie by a sense of unburdened freedom from guilt. Tommie would stand with his brother in the general merchandise store in Ayletts, sucking the sweetness out of a piece of penny candy and staring at the Currier & Ives lithograph of elegant, long-necked ladies with glittering jewels and parasols strolling with fine gentlemen. Since then he had been to balls in Richmond, seen elegant ladies walking dogs on leashes, and patronized saloons and houses of bad repute. But all through law school he dreamed of more—of travels to Washington and New York and beyond, of those dazzling lives he and his mother had imagined were out there waiting for them. His mother had kept her heart young with a stone-ware jug her husband kept filled for her. Tommie alone of the family was left to carry out some as yet unfulfilled promise.

As he turns up the cedar-lined drive, he sees a girl in a white dress scurrying in front of him and disappearing through a break in the trees. He almost calls out for her. Then his heart leaps. He was going to call "Lillie" because that's who she looked like, her brown ringlets bouncing off her shoulders when she came to live with them—when? Has it been seven years already? He tries to remember. She was almost fourteen, he sixteen, and when she got used to him she would jump out and scare him or try to get him to chase her up the drive. If he refused, she would laugh and say he was an old grump—she poked her lower lip out and stumped along, hands in pockets, mocking him. He hated her making fun of him. But it was worse when she ignored him, even when she did it to get his attention.

Now he hears high laughter, and it is so like Lillie's he feels the hair on his neck stand. He darts through the trees looking for the child. "You there! Come out! Come on out now, I won't hurt you." He looks around, goes over to a clump of English boxwoods, and peers in. No sign of anyone.

He heads back to the drive, keeps walking, then turns around suddenly. He had thought perhaps to catch her this way, but no one is there. He hurries up to the porch and goes in, calling out for Aunt Jane.

As he expected, Mr. Lucas is ordered by Mr. Meade to drain the reservoir so that no one can complain about the sanitation of the water. "Foolishness," Mr. Lucas says to himself as he turns the valves in the pump house. "I've found more dead animals in there than anybody wants to know about, but never mind that.

Water's so low, won't take but ten or twelve hours to empty." In the meantime Mr. Lucas goes back up to the embankment and down to the picket fence surrounding the water. He lowers a pole to measure the water level; in an hour he'll check to make sure it's dropping. The mid-afternoon sun feels good on his back. Police officers have come and departed, and now most people have gone home to their dinners. A few curiosity-seekers are strolling the embankment, pointing out where they think a body was found. They stay respectfully at the top, and Lucas is thankful he does not have to answer any more questions.

He heads back up the slope to the top of the embankment. He's not sure why he walks on the grass instead of the steps, nor why he keeps his eyes down, unless it's that he might find something belonging to the girl—some token of her last night alive that he might take for a souvenir. It's not likely, the police having thoroughly searched every inch of the place and turned up a glove and a piece of shoelace on the walkway, a matching glove and a veil outside the reservoir grounds, and a hat in the deadhouse.

Now he heads down the other side and to the hole in the outer fence. He lifts the loose board and pokes his head through, imagining the girl crawling in on her hands and knees, poor little thing. He goes out, so that he can come back in just as she did. The sun is winking through the trees at the verge of the small-pox cemetery, casting the fence in sharp relief. As he lifts the loose board again, the sun angles in and a yellow glint catches his eye. He hurries through, reaches into the thick wire grass, and pulls out an inch-long watch key. The tube-shaped key has fancy little curlicues around its bulging middle and an open heart for a crown, attached to which is a metal loop, presumably for a watch chain. The loop is somewhat sprung out.

Lucas looks around. No one appears to have noticed him. He pockets the key and continues his search of the grounds. After a while he goes back and finds that the water level is dropping apace. He reaches into his pocket and pulls out the key. Could it have been hers? She had no watch that he could remember. And yet he feels that it must be hers. Perhaps she caught it somehow going through the fence. But then it would have been on the other side. Ah well, he tells himself, it could still be hers—maybe it fell out of her pocket.

In the evening he walks back to his little row house in Oregon Hill. His mother lived with him for ten years until she died; for the past six years he has lived alone. He never married and doesn't expect he will now, he supposes because of his funny jug-ears and his clumsy way around women. He has his work, and in his off hours he takes long walks and does odd jobs for the neighbors, mostly plumbing, and if they can't pay him—and most can't— he happily accepts a meal. Now he does something strange. He takes the key out and puts it in his mouth. He closes his eyes and pictures the girl; in his mind she is holding the key in her hand shortly before she died. It's a comfort to him having something that she owned and touched, though he wishes he had a piece of clothing or a lock of hair. The key will have to do, and since it's not necessarily an article belonging to a woman, there's no need to tell anyone of his discovery. He takes it out of his mouth and attaches it to a cord, loops the cord around his neck, and tucks it into his undershirt.

In the morning Mr. Lucas heads back early to the reservoir so that he can refill it. In the terra-cotta muck at the bottom he spies some old cans and long-buried stones. He's inclined to go down in there and start looking around to see what wonders might be revealed. But he would have a hard time explaining to Mr. Meade why he was knee deep in mud when he was only supposed to open the supply valves. Reluctantly, he heads back to the pump house and turns on the water.

On the same Sunday morning Mr. Richardson arises at nine, dresses for church, and after breakfast heads over to Grace Street Baptist with his family. Reverend Hatcher is preaching on Malachi 3:6, "For I am the Lord, I change not; therefore ye sons of Jacob are not consumed." The constancy of the Lord is soothing, but on the other hand there's the refiner's fire, and the Lord will be a swift witness against sorcerers, adulterers, false swearers, and those that oppress hirelings and widows. There is but a narrow path one can tread on the way to righteousness and thus to heaven. Strange how meek and friendly Hatcher seems man-to-man, while up on the pulpit he's God's own scourge. He can make you remember every bad thing you've ever done, said, or thought, and wish you could take them back. Richardson tugs at his collar and pats his wife's knee; she ignores him.

His mind goes away from the sermon and out to the reservoir, where a pregnant girl was found yesterday. It was odd. Why would she go out there on a cold night to kill herself? There has never even been a drowning there that he knows of. Plenty of suicides all over town during his time—hangings, shootings, a few train-track messes, a couple of poisonings, lots of drinkings-to-death, and even a self-inflicted stabbing. And there have been drownings, accidental and on purpose, but they were all in the river. God may be unchanging, as Hatcher was saying, but the human heart is mutable and unfathomable. He wants to keep sitting here with his family, but something tells him he needs to pay a visit to Dr. Taylor. After the sermon he excuses himself and slips out the back.

The city almshouse stands not quite a mile away. Richardson heads up toward Shockoe Hill Cemetery, across from which rises an imposing triple-bayed brick building that, like so many others, was a Civil War hospital. At sixty-four, he moves with almost the same alacrity as he did as a naval captain. Losing his young wife to a brain fever just before the war, he joined up early, not caring what happened to him so long as he could forget. After the war, he married again; the present Mrs. Richardson had given him standing in society, two lovely daughters, and several years of wedded bliss. You couldn't ask for much more than that.

Inside the almshouse, Richardson is directed down a long white-brick corridor, past large rooms in which indigents with various maladies lie on narrow beds, voicing their dismal humanity in outraged utterings and feckless garbled complaints, pierced here and there with the bitter laughter of final comprehension. He finds his way to the examination room at the end of the hall; Dr. Taylor's assistant tells him to come in. The odor of formaldehyde punches him in the nose. Taylor is just finishing the autopsy. The girl is splayed open from sternum to pubis, her glistening organs neatly arranged beside her. Gullies on the sides of the steel table channel blood to buckets on the floor. Richardson glances at the viscera, then focuses on Taylor, who is slick to his elbows in blood and yellow-gray slime. His young student towels him off as he addresses Richardson. "Almost finished here. Four foot eleven female, one hundred twenty-five pounds. About twenty years old, approximately eight months pregnant. Fetus was female." He taps a purple mass in a ceramic bowl on an adjacent table, but Richardson only nods, keeping his attention on Taylor's wide-set eyes, one of which strays off as though examining something on a shelf. He imagines Taylor is about his same age, but unlike himself Taylor still seems to enjoy his work.

"Strangely small amount of water in the lungs. But you see"—and here he squeezes some lung tissue—"that froth indicates death by drowning. As does the serene look. About a handful of food in her stomach, partially digested. I'd say she ate about four to six hours before she died. Death occurred between ten o'clock Friday night and two o'clock Saturday morning. The air was around the freezing point that night, the water temperature about forty-five, which may have played a role. But the interesting thing is the marks on her head."

Now Richardson looks. There is a pinkish knot an inch or so in diameter, above and to the right of her right eye. "The swelling," Dr. Taylor says, "is from an extravasation of broken blood vessels beneath the skin. It appears to have come from a light blow."

"A blow?" Richardson raises his eyebrows.

"Could have been. It's possible she hit her head on the bricks when she went in, but I don't see how."

"Could she have struck it on something when she was pulled out?"

"Not to leave a mark like that. Besides, she was face up. Women usually float face up—pregnant women always do."

Richardson nods. "What about this bruise on her lip?"

"Curious, isn't it? It was not so noticeable yesterday. But bruises darken like that after the body begins decomposing." He lowers his hand toward her mouth, then goes around behind Richardson and does the same. "A hand held tightly could leave a mark like that."

"Suppressing a scream?"

"It's possible."

Richardson points to a line of stitches in her scalp. "Your handiwork, I assume?"

Taylor smiles for the first time. "I lack the undertaker's artistry. Yes, I examined the brain. Would you like me to reopen the skull?"

"I don't think that'll be necessary."

"I found a small infusion of blood on the surface beneath the upper left side of her forehead."

"Another blow?"

"Possibly, but since there was no corresponding mark on her forehead, I'm inclined to believe it was a counterstroke of blood settling opposite to where the original blow was struck, above her eye. These other little nicks and abrasions on her face don't indicate anything in particular. They could have occurred during a struggle or well before."

Richardson stands by while Taylor directs his assistant to detach the viscera for temporary storage and begin sewing the body back up. The young man carefully places the organs into glass jars that he has labeled "Reservoir drowning." An air pocket pops as the large intestine sloshes into the jar, and Richardson turns to glance at the fetus—a fully formed little baby, its hand at its mouth and its eyes closed.

"So you've changed your mind about the suicide?" he asks Taylor.

"I believe so. The marks on her forehead could indicate a blow that might render her unconscious. I would say she died from drowning preceded by partial or complete insensibility."

"What was used to make the blow?"

"I couldn't say. Possibly a fist, or some blunt object."

"And you think someone threw her in?"

"I think I'm going to have to convene an inquest jury."

Richardson nods. A sad affair, a working girl and her lover. There would be an investigation. Probably Jack Wren was already digging—possibly it was Wren who got Taylor thinking murder instead of suicide in the first place. Richardson almost wishes Taylor had just stuck with suicide. But justice had to be served—if there was a guilty man at large, he had to be brought in. Anyway, in a week, perhaps two, it would all be over.

CHAPTER THREE

THE MORNING TOMMIE RETURNS FROM RICHMOND, Willie is out cutting timber down near the river. For some time now he has had his eye on the trees that have grown up in the empty fields all around since the war. Owners will like as not let you take the trees just for the service of clearing the field, and plenty of them are good enough size to float down to the sawmills. At the moment he and a short colored man named Biggs are wrestling a felled and roped black gum around a stubborn little pine. The horse stands switching its tail, waiting for them to finish.

"Snagged a fair," Biggs observes, "mought have to chop it."

Willie pulls his hatchet from a belt loop and begins chipping downward into the pine's trunk. Biggs turns his back on the proceedings, having lost over the years half a finger to a steampowered mill saw and one eye to a flying splinter. Willie follows the cuts with several quick cross strokes, and within half a minute the obstruction is out of the way. Biggs slaps the horse's side, hollers "Gow," and the animal, its ears twitching, strains against the harness and continues dragging the black gum.

"You member that time we tucks yo brother out to cut wood?" Biggs says. He is graying at the temples and fond of reminiscing. Willie can work all day without saying more than it takes to get the job done, but he understands that there are people who work better if they have something to think about and that some people think better out loud.

"Last summer was it?" Willie replies.

"Yep, and we do just like dat. We chaup de trees outen de way. And dat Tommie," and here Biggs gives way to a belly-deep, low-pitched laugh while continuing to lead the horse, "dat Tommie cussed dat little tree so it liked to fall over daid. You member what he say?"

"Not exactly," Willie says. "What did he say?"

"He say, ''Fyou don move out de way, I'mon chop yo damn haid off.'" Biggs laughs again, his blind eye tearing up. "Den he tuck de broadax and smack dat tree right in de middle. I jump outen de way, and the tree just bend over. Didn't do nuffin. Den Tommie gets good and fired up, and he strike dat tree down in three strokes, growlin' at it like a wolf. I never saw de beat. Den he tuck a hol of it and hoist it over his haid and start in singin' bout how he a mighty woodchopper. Dat Tommie's a sight."

"He does like to sing," Willie says. "His teacher said he could be a professional singer." Ahead, Biggs shakes his head as though Willie is missing the point, yet Willie won't concede to Biggs or anybody else that his brother is strange in any way other than in smartness. To Willie, it's just his little brother acting his normal half-crazy, or, as Aunt Jane puts it, "eccentric," self. When a schoolmate mocked Tommie's highfalutin speech after Tommie had spent the previous day with his nose in *Gulliver's Travels*, Willie took the opportunity to let him and everyone else in the schoolhouse understand that to pick on his little brother was to risk getting a bruised cheek.

Since the death of their youngest brother, Willie has looked out for Tommie, though he probably would have done so anyway. It is in his nature to protect what he feels to be his own. At home he could beat his little brother up, but in public an insult to Tommie was an insult to himself. As they grew older, they fought less and less—Tommie could almost always win with words, and Willie could hammer Tommie to a whimpering jelly. There were, however, times when a few quiet words could beat Tommie's crafted argument; then the tables turned and Tommie, his temper gone, would try for a quick tackle, pin, and sock in the gut. If a rock were handy, he might throw that as well, though he would inevitably miss and then have to endure Willie's wise and patient remarks on the value of keeping one's temper.

Willie Cluverius was the one whose ambitions lay all around him, in the land that his forebears had worked for generations. While Tommie dreamed of wider fields for his many talents, Willie saw himself as the kind of man his father had fallen short of being—a farmer and landowner who would take the measure of himself not just by how much land he held but by how well he cultivated it. His ambition did not gnaw at him the way his brother's seemed to. His brother's book-learning was a source of great pride to Willie, but he could see that Tommie's striving to be a person of substance was often a trouble to his mind.

Hauling timber now with Biggs, Willie thinks back to that day last summer. It seemed that they finally were not competing anymore, that Tommie was on his own path as a country lawyer and that his struggles were with the world rather than with his brother and his own self. That they had been in love with the same woman seemed a thing of the past. He does not remember Tommie singing that day, but he can picture it after Biggs's story, and he laughs quietly.

"Now you recollects it," Biggs says, laughing as well.

"Yes, I think I do," Willie agrees.

When Tommie comes downstairs in the late afternoon, his aunt is in the parlor with a teapot and a plate of Maria's almond cookies. She pretends to be reading instead of waiting for him. "Oh, Tommie," she says, "were you able to sleep at all? You looked so tired, you poor dear. Come sit down. You're working yourself to the bone." Once a great beauty, she still has bright eyes that go into crescents when she smiles, but despite high cheekbones, her face sags in a sad way. Her hair is still a lustrous gold, and she keeps it long and piled up the way her husband always liked it. She likes to use her hands when she talks, and the way they float like a dancer's hands has always fascinated Tommie.

He helps himself to a cookie, though he has no appetite. He has only been gone two nights, but he has to leave again on Monday for business. His brother is away at least as often, which means Jane is alone much of the time and on an unpredictable basis. Her companion, Rosa Hillyard, who divides her time between Jane and two nieces, is currently away. "I'll go take a cookie out to Willie," Tommie says.

"Oh, he's liable to be way off by the river now. He's looking at some woods to buy. Time he gets through he'll've chopped down every tree in the county. Are you sure something's not troubling you?"

Tommie says no. He stands, scratches the back of his neck, and goes to the window to see if Willie is coming.

"There was an article in the paper about a man in California found with his head chopped off," Jane tells him. "Two Indians did it for eight dollars apiece and buried the head seventy-five miles away. And there was another one about a man right up in Richmond who hanged himself and went to change his mind, but his daughter couldn't get him down in time—"

"Thanks, Jane, I'm not in the mood for news right now."

She chuckles. "I was only trying to get your mind off your problems. Maybe you need to hear something more cheerful."

Again, he envisions concentric ripples on the water. "I think I'll go for a walk. Did you see a girl in a white dress out in the front yard before I came in?"

Jane says she didn't, but that it could be one of the neighbor's cousins, visiting from Gloucester. He goes outside and walks along the cornfield, shielding his eyes with his hurt hand and scanning the long afternoon shadows for what he can see.

When he gets to the Trace and looks down the road that leads to the river, his brother appears on horseback, as if summoned. They wave to each other, and for a moment Tommie feels safe again. He stands there waiting while Willie's bay takes its time. After he crosses the road, Willie dismounts and they walk together to the house. "You just get home?"

Tommie nods. "A little while ago."

Willie is taller and broader in the shoulders than his brother, his skin more tanned. Tommie's features are the more delicate and symmetrical, his lips the envy of many a girl. Willie's thin line of a mouth barely hides a snaggletooth, yet his rugged good looks have served him plenty well. He wears a wide-brimmed straw hat and dirty boots; a spear of meadowsweet hangs from his mouth. His eyes are dark and deep set and he pauses to think before he speaks. "Find any business up there?"

"I looked into that acreage for sale in the bankrupt court out near Oakwood Cemetery for Mr. Bray."

Willie strokes his horse but doesn't say anything.

"You remember I told you about that," Tommie says.

"Yeah, you find any good timber up there, let me know. If it's cheap."

"What's the matter?"

"Not a thing in the world, brother." They walk a few more steps in silence. "You're seeing somebody up there, aren't you?" Now a sly smile creases Willie's face.

"What makes you say that?" Tommie sighs in relief. Then he has the distinct feeling that he is being watched by someone.

"You seemed all nervous and flustered before you left. I had to lend you a collar—how often has that happened? And you went off unshaven."

"I got a shave in Richmond."

"And you come back looking like a cat got you." At first Tommie doesn't understand; Willie has not even appeared to glance at him.

"You mean the hand? It's nothing. An eruption of some kind."

"Well I hope whoever it is is worth the trouble. You've been in a botheration for I don't know how long. She's not married is she?"

Tommie snorts. "The only women I see in Richmond are at Lizzie Banks's house, and I haven't been there in months."

"You're not still keen on Lillie are you?"

"Lillie Madison?"

"You know who I mean. Yes, cousin Lillie."

Tommie waits but Willie says nothing, and the sound of high laughter comes so clearly from behind that Tommie jerks around. All he can see is the sun glinting through the tall pines across the road and a lone osprey winging toward the river. It feels colder than when he started out. "No, I'm not keen on her," says Tommie. "Why?"

"Her father was asking about you."

"Her father? When?"

"I saw him over in King William, market day. He thought I was you, or else he got our names mixed up. He said, 'You been shunning me, Tommie?' And I said I'm Willie, the older brother. Tommie's the ugly one. But he's not much on funnin'— he just gave me a squint-eyed kind of look and said, 'Well, you tell your brother he's mighty high on his horse. If he thinks he's too good for me and my daughter, he's wrong. It's the other way around.'"

"That old coot. I don't know what he's talking about. I haven't seen her since, gosh, it must've been last fall, before she went off to Bath."

Sunlight glances off the sides of their faces as they walk up the field, their lungs filled with the smells of manure fertilizer and freshly turned earth. "But you've heard from her," Willie asks.

"Nothing more than the letters she sends to Aunt Jane. Honestly, I don't know anything more about her than you do. You know I was sweet on her for a while there after you and she . . . but nothing came of it. Nothing at all, and then she went off up to the mountains. I don't know what her father means. Maybe she wrote him something, but she never says boo to him. You know that." Why now, Tommie thinks, when they never talk about her?

Willie shields his eyes with his hat brim, trying to see into his brother's eyes. "Shad are running," he says, just to say something, though doubting he'll get much interest.

"Maybe I'll go out with you," Tommie says. The brothers walk on together, Willie talking about how he's gotten all his beets and carrots and potatoes planted but hasn't quite finished the oats yet on account of a bent harrow. All around, the cultivated fields running to the lines of woods have a serenity and a timeless feel that give strength and confidence to Willie—the solid ground underfoot is reassuring in its promise of work and food. A barred owl makes a scratchy echo out in the distant woods, and clouds are gathering from the west.

"What is it?" Willie says, looking at his brother. "Goose fly over your grave?"

"No, that owl gives me the shivers."

Willie laughs, slapping his brother in the shoulder. "Four years of college and you're more superstitious than I ever was."

In the morning Tommie takes Aunt Jane's dappled gray to Upper Oaks to call on the Brays. It doesn't seem so long ago when he rode along here in Lillie's company, before he was engaged to Nola Bray. He was going up there to court Nola, and Lillie was still living at Aunt Jane's. She was heading off to her tutoring when Tommie overtook her in the road. He had just returned from law school and Lillie was saucy with him, not nearly as respectful and awestruck as the girls at church for instance. Of course, by then she was almost like a sister, but she could annoy him in ways he thought no sister could have. He does not remember what she said now, only that he seemed to have offended her in some way and that as she, flush-faced, trotted away from him he noticed how her blouse stuck with sweat to a spot on her back and the ribbon on her hat bobbed as she posted. While visiting Nola that time he could not stop thinking about Lillie, the spot on the small of her back and the curve of her calf visible through her skirt.

Now he lets himself in the front gate and rides up the horseshoe drive, past the white pillared portico, where the stableboy takes his horse. And he beholds again the finest house remaining in the lower part of the county, its Georgian symmetry and grace a statement of aristocratic refinement since well before the war. The Brays' butler ushers Tommie back to Mr. Bray's study, where Tommie dutifully reports that the land is available for two dollars an acre but he may be able to get it cheaper if he waits. Mr. Bray asks if he's going to church with them, and Tommie tells him that, no, he's off to Tappahannock in the morning and wanted to see Nola before he left. He goes out to wait for her in the garden. Presently she comes, wearing an overcoat. She has put on some weight in the last few years, giving her a less severe appearance. "You're really very lovely," he says to her.

"Thank you, Tommie. Isn't it a little chilly for a garden stroll?" She closes her eyes an extra beat as she addresses him—the habit has always slightly unnerved him, as though she half-expected to see somebody more interesting when she opened her eyes.

"Yes, but it's our favorite place, and I wanted to see if there were any blooms yet besides the redbud."

"You're a romantic, Tommie." She lets him take her hand. "Was there some reason you wanted to talk with me this morning?" Since the death of her mother in December she has seemed less critical of Tommie, but also less patient, less willing to laugh at frivolities. He told her recently that this spring he expected to find himself in a promising financial situation and that he had his eye on a house in Little Plymouth. What he hadn't said was that he hoped to be disentangled from a rather pressing problem.

Again last night he could not sleep well. Now he hears bells. He knows the sound is only in his head, but they ring clear like cathedral bells in some old European capital, or like all the church bells in Richmond clanging at once. How precious life is, he thinks. What a miraculous gift. "The sun feels good," he says.

"Yes, but it's going to rain today, which we need. Did you just want to walk?"

"Yes, I think so," he says, gripping her hand tighter and thankful she is not as perceptive as his brother, as attentive to his moods. Once upon a time he hardly dared to think of himself as her suitor—she seemed so much more sophisticated and better positioned. But when he became a law student with a future, coupled with his aunt's connections and money, he was somebody. She also found him handsome, and he could make her laugh about the books and music she had studied so devotedly. He was a breath of fresh air to her, and if she was a little prudish for his tastes she was nonetheless the older of two daughters and hence the heiress to one of the few intact estates left in the county.

"I got a letter from Lillie," Nola says.

"When did she write?" He pretends to be interested in some dogwood buds, but his head is throbbing.

"Only a few days ago. She told me she was going to Old Point Comfort to help take care of a friend's sick aunt. She's awfully sweet to come all the way across the state on an errand of mercy like that, don't you think?"

"Yes," he says, noncommittally. "What else did she say?"

"Well, I don't remember . . ."

Think, Nola. Did she mention me? Tommie feels himself going slack in the neck and the legs, as if the blood is leaving his body and draining into the ground.

"Oh, she said her teaching was going fine, but that it was very cold and they had lots of snow up in the mountains. She has a new coat and asked me to send some material for her to work a hatband. It must be so beautiful there and she has a wonderful way of making friends. I'd like to go out and visit, though I don't want to intrude. What do you think? It's thanks to you that we became such good friends, you know. Tommie? Tommie, are you listening?"

"Yes, I—yes, of course I am. You wanted to know about visiting. I don't know. Only if you want to."

"Yes, but she hasn't specifically invited me, you see. And Daddy depends on me now—I'd hate to leave him for very long."

There must not have been any more to the letter than that, he thinks. "I have to go now, Nola," he says. "They're waiting for me to go to church."

He kisses her on the cheek and, though she appears to want

something more from him, he turns and lets himself out the gate. It *is* going to rain. He can feel it in the air.

All afternoon long, people come by the almshouse, tracking the floorboards with mud and water from the rainy streets. Rich and poor, black and white, farmers, bankers, laborers, factory workers, prostitutes, and entire families dressed in church clothes—all file through for a look. The Sunday paper had carried a story about the dead girl; word went around. She lies in an open coffin, a clean white shroud up to her neck. The almshouse workers have combed the red dirt out of her hair and washed her face.

Detective Wren has positioned himself in a corner of the chapel where the dead girl lies, studying the people who study the girl. Every so often he will approach one of the gawkers and ask a few quiet questions. Did you recognize the girl? It seemed as though you knew her. Just curious, huh? Richardson has decided to let Wren stay, as long as he does not appear to be scaring anybody off.

People are quiet, respectful, as though viewing a dead body were part of their regular Sunday ritual. Some people remark on how small and pretty she looks. Others shake their heads and say what a pity it is, her dying like that and no one here to claim her. Quite a few comment on the bruises and wonder how she came by them. By dark, no one having identified the woman, the almshouse superintendent closes the door to further visitors. Several people continue to knock during the evening and are told to come back tomorrow.

First thing in the morning Dr. Taylor impanels a jury of inquest, composed of the usual half dozen officers and medical experts. In the meantime, people keep coming by to view the body. Finally a woman with a squinty eye swears it's the body of Harriett Mays, who used to live in her boardinghouse. The superintendent asks her if Harriett Mays had long hair, and she says, "No, it was short and brown, just like hers." Since the young woman's hair is mostly pinned behind, the way it was when she was found, the superintendent is dubious. Standing with the squinty-eyed woman, an unshaven man, his jacket out at elbows, says he'd bet his life on it being Harriett Mays. He saw her himself a week ago last Friday. He wants to know if there will be a reward.

Richardson takes a police ambulance out to Harriett Mays's address in Manchester. From an alley the mingled odors of cooking greens and stale urine assail him. He ducks under a laundry line, his tall leather hat dripping rainwater onto his shoes, and climbs a rickety flight of stairs. He knocks on a thin, cracked tenement door. "Is there a Miss Harriett Mays here?" he asks.

"You're looking at her," says a shock-haired woman with no eyeteeth.

"Harriett Mays," Richardson says. "I hate to inform you, but you're dead."

Her eyes bug out. "I ain't either," she insists.

Richardson explains the situation and asks her to come with him up to the almshouse for a few minutes. When she arrives, the crowd makes way for the suddenly revivified Harriett Mays. She stares at the corpse, then shyly at the crowd, then back again, as though she has indeed cheated death. On her face is the biggest smile it has ever known.

A short while later a young woman named Miss Emma Dunstan comes to the almshouse in the company of her younger sister. When she sees the body, she knows it is that of Fannie Lillian Madison of King William County. "We visited her family Christmas before last." Her father, she explains, is from King William, and knew the Madisons quite well. Both Taylor and

Richardson are interested in the Misses Dunstans' opinion. Richardson takes them into a room for further questioning.

"Any distinguishing marks that you know of?"

They both shake their heads.

Richardson touches just above his left breast. "A scar about here?" They don't know of any such scar, but they are ready to swear it is her. The paper mentioned the finding of a traveling bag with clothes marked F. Madison. It got them to thinking. Emma hands Richardson a folded-up red scarf and says her mother found it on their front hedges Saturday morning. Their house happens to be near the reservoir, which seems an odd coincidence. Richardson at first doubts the scarf has anything to do with the dead girl, then he begins to doubt the Dunstans. They don't seem like the type who just want to see their names in the newspaper, but why would the girl's scarf end up at their house? Unless she was going there. "Had she ever been to your house?" he asks.

"Not that I'm aware of."

"What sort of person was she?"

"A high-minded, ambitious sort of girl, I thought," says the elder Miss Dunstan. "But not the sort that would ever do a bad thing or think a bad thought."

Uh huh, thinks Richardson. *Nil nisi bonum.* Don't speak ill of the dead. "You know she was pregnant?"

"I read that." She glances down.

"Anybody she was particularly close to?"

"I didn't know her that well, but you could ask her cousin Cary Madison. He's a carriagemaker. He lives down on Fifth."

Richardson thanks the young ladies and shows them back to the hallway. People are still coming in, eyeing the body, making speculations. The Dunstan girls take another quick look in the coffin as they pass, then hurry back out into the gray rain.

◦◦◦

CHAPTER FOUR

THE FIRST TIME he really noticed her was at his uncle Samuel's funeral. It also happened to be the day he met Nola Bray. Tommie was fourteen and he and his brother had recently moved downcounty to live with their aunt and uncle. Uncle Samuel had been a wealthy merchant who knew nearly everybody in three counties—fine carriages were parked a mile up and down from Mount Olivet Baptist Church. After the service they went back to Cedar Lane, where Aunt Jane in widow's weeds gallantly shook everyone's hand, flanked by her two nephews.

The children drifted to the back lawn with plates of food. Tommie found his brother out by the well talking to an older cousin from King William and two girls from a nearby estate. He stood quietly just beyond the little group until the older girl introduced herself. "Hello, I'm Nola Bray, your neighbor," she said. She spoke with a precision and formality he had never heard in a person his age. Her little sister giggled at him, standing there like a statue, and he blushed. Willie and the cousin went off to the edge of the field, leaving him there with the two girls.

"I'm so sorry about your uncle," Nola said. "And I'm sorry you haven't yet been to Upper Oaks. We'll have to remedy that. I've been away a good part of the summer at White Sulphur Springs. The air is so much better there. A lot of people from Charleston go there. Some of them are nice, but some of them put on airs. Have you been there?"

Not sure if she meant White Sulphur Springs or Charleston, but the answer being the same to both, Tommie shook his head. At that moment a swarm of younger children went dashing by. Leading them was a girl of about twelve who tagged him as she passed, and sang out, "Follow my leader." After standing around greeting unfamiliar people, he was itching to shed his suit and run around like crazy, chasing after the girl. But, damn it all, he'd be thought rude to be carrying on so at a funeral.

Nola was telling him what a good place Aberdeen Academy was and how lucky he was to be going there this fall instead of Locust, where his brother was going. Secretly he was proud that he had been chosen to go to the better school, but he had misgivings about boarding in a place a half-day's journey away. So he pretended indifference. "I'd as soon go to Locust," he said, shrugging.

"Well, you're wrong about that," she insisted, tossing her thin nose. Her face was narrow, and her eyebrows rose with almost everything she said, giving her a haughty look. She made some comment about the heat and the lack of good rain, then took her sister in hand and made her way back up to the house. Her dark hair was braided and twisted tightly to the back of her head; from behind she could be taken for an adult, with her black dress and her proudly erect walk.

Not so the girl who had tagged him. Tommie wandered down to the icehouse, looking for his brother. He peered into the darkness, inhaling the cold vapor that felt so otherworldly on a hot day. The girl came along again, this time by herself, but still running, her brown ringlets bobbing and white dress sliding ghostlike over the clipped grass. She tagged him again and as he turned to say something, his brother jumped out from behind the icehouse and grabbed her by the wrist. She struggled to free herself. "What's the matter with you," Willie said, "running around here like a little hellion?"

"You oughten to cuss." A blush spread across her marble-white cheeks. She almost had a woman's shape, yet everything—her hands, her feet, her features, even her voice—seemed diminutive.

"And speaking up to her elders too," Willie said, letting go her hand.

"You ain't my elders either." She swept a curl off her forehead. Willie laughed. "I know you. You're Fannie Lillian, and almost grown up since last summer."

"Lillian."

"What?"

"It's not Fannie Lillian anymore, it's just Lillian. Or Lillie." She sniffed out, as though challenging him.

Tommie remembered his cousin now—really his mother's brother's granddaughter, which made her and her many brothers and sisters his first cousins once removed. Except slightly more removed, his mother had said, because the brother was a half-brother. She said it in a kind of disparaging way, as though this branch of the family was not one she was proud of.

"Well then, Lillian," Willie said, "What have you got to say for yourself?"

"Nothing to you." She had run off while he was telling her how sassy she was, but not before taking a closer look at Tommie, who said nothing at all. There was a mischievous smile about her lips as she turned and wisped up over the lawn like a spirit. Then he and Willie went and sat at the edge of the hayfield and he told Willie he wished he were not going off to Aberdeen. Willie said not to be stupid—he, Tommie, was the smart one, the one who needed an education. "All I want is right here," Willie said. "And someday my own buggy, and a horse to go with it. Maybe even a wife."

"I want to go places," Tommie said. "See the Taj Mahal and elephants and New York and Paris."

"The burlesque shows?"

"Maybe," Tommie said, blushing.

"You can see an elephant up in Richmond. John Griswold saw one at a circus there." Tommie said it would be nice just to see Richmond.

Before school started, his father took him up to Richmond for a day. Aunt Jane wanted to treat them to dinner at a hotel restaurant, but, not wishing to hurt her brother-in-law's pride, she ended up just giving Tommie a little spending money and packing him a lunch in a paper sack.

Two years later Lillian came to live with them after some unspecified trouble in her home. She had been at Cedar Lane more than a month when Tommie returned home from Aberdeen for the summer. She and Willie had started out shy with each other but had become friends, and sometimes even fought like brother and sister. Now Tommie found himself the interloper in his own home. His young cousin seemed to enjoy tormenting him, mocking him whenever he tried to discuss Plato or Shakespeare at the dinner table. "I guess there's no point in trying to be civilized around here," he said, glaring at her.

She smiled sweetly. "You could learn to be civilized if you tried," she said. "You could say please pass the butter, instead of reaching across the table like a baboon."

Stunned into silence, he wanted to slap her pert little face. Aunt Jane scolded them both; Willie just sat there enjoying the show. After supper Tommie watched through the summer kitchen window as his brother and Lillie went out to grain the horses. He clomped up to his room and tried to read, but found himself staring out the window at the barn.

Later in the summer he saw the two of them walking hand in hand coming up from the back hayfield. He was on the porch rocker and pretended not to have noticed anything. But they didn't leave off holding hands even in the yard, and he realized it was for his own benefit that he was pretending. Willie stopped at the well to fill a bucket, and Lillie dashed on up the stairs, stopping just long enough to say, in mock seriousness, "Hello, old Mr. Tommie." She laughed and disappeared inside. He slammed his book shut and got up to help his brother.

One afternoon when he was walking home from the river, she was lying in wait behind the cedars lining the drive. Instead of springing out at him, she waited until he had passed, then quietly slipped just behind him so that when he realized someone was there he lurched around with a frightened "Whaaa!" He turned back around, trying to ignore her. She asked him where he'd been, and he said, "The river."

"What for?"

"To look at the side-wheelers. Who wants to know?"

"Not even to fish?"

"No."

"You're so different from your brother." She mouthed something, but made no sound.

He kept walking, head down, hands in pockets, not caring if she imitated him. The way to deal with her, he'd decided, was just to let her have her fun, and then she'd grow bored and run off. But this time she seemed to want to talk with him. She asked him what it was like at Aberdeen. She was going off to Bruington Academy at the end of the summer; it too was a half-day upcounty. "Not bad once you get used to it," he told her.

"But don't you miss being at home?"

"Sometimes. But they keep you pretty busy."

"I don't miss my home in Manquin, but I think I might miss it here."

"Why don't you miss your home?"

She thought about this for a minute. "Can you keep a secret?"

"Yes."

"They're mean to me."

"Who?"

"Ma and Papa. Not so much my brothers, and my little sisters hardly ever. But Papa won't let me write or get letters from boys. He tore the lock off my trunk and burned all my letters, from girlfriends too. I said he was the very devil, and he whipped me so hard I couldn't sit down good for a week."

Tommie did not know whether to believe this tale.

"I have a little blister right here," she touched herself above her left breast. "I was sick when I was little and they didn't have enough money for a doctor. That's what Aunt Jane said. She said the girls at school won't take any notice of it. Did you get whipped a lot?"

"No, hardly ever." Tommie thought about his father, too heartbroken to ever raise a hand to him after the death of his little brother. And his mother, kind and gentle, especially so in the evenings after her medicinal doses. He had resented them for letting themselves go to where they'd had to send him and his brother to Aunt Jane's. Of course, they'd said that he and Willie would have better opportunities with Jane than they could provide, and it did not take long for them both to see that this was so. "They whipped Willie some, when he was little. He got in trouble more."

"I expect he did," she said. Again, her lips moved soundlessly.

"Why do you do that?" he said.

"Do what?"

"You say back the words to yourself after you just said them."

She looked at him hard, then blushing, said, "I don't do it as much as I used to. My little sister crosses her fingers whenever she sees a black cat, and my brother spits instead of saying a cuss word."

Tommie looked into her eyes, wondering about a girl who

would want to check her words after they'd been said. They were almost at the house now and she slowed down. "I got in trouble too, somehow. I don't know why." She seemed on the point of saying something else, then she saw Willie around the side of the house and hurried over to him.

By the end of the summer, she and Tommie had become, if not friends, then at least tolerant of each other. And he began noticing her more, the way a lock of hair curled down her forehead, or how she would absently scratch an ankle while reading, and the color that would suddenly come to her cheeks when she was excited or embarrassed. At times she was downright plain-looking, but when she was animated she was almost beautiful. He found himself seeking her out to give her advice about boarding school. During the day when he was out in the fields working with Willie, the new muscles straining in his shirt, he missed the sound of her voice, her trickling laughter. He would listen to her talk about a sick calf a friend had written of, or about some needlework, just to hear her speak.

And then it was time to say good-bye, her school starting before Tommie's. She hugged them all, lingering longest with Willie. Then when Willie went to help her into the cart, Tommie stepped forward too, as though she needed two people, and her hem caught under his foot. She laughed as it pulled loose, and he stood there feeling foolish and awkward and waving to her.

Later that day Aunt Jane told him in private that she thought Bruington would be good for Lillie. "And it won't hurt for her and Willie to be apart for a while. Not that I don't trust them. But between you and me I trust him more."

Word gets around that the girl found at the reservoir may not have killed herself. In fact, a coroner's jury is looking into the possibility that she was murdered. When Mr. Lucas asks Mr. Meade what he thinks about it and Mr. Meade says he thought all along she was murdered, Mr. Lucas is skeptical. But mainly he is worried. In his shirt is a potential piece of evidence. He goes back to his work. At times he takes out the key and examines it. He likes the heart shape at the top and the weight of it in his hand. He has begun to feel it was Effie's gift to him. That's what he calls the dead girl. He has concocted fantasies involving Effie and himself. In his favorite, he comes back to the reservoir at night just before she jumps in. He sees her huddled in the cold by herself, crying softly, and he asks if he can be of service. "Not much good with problems of the heart," he says, "but if it's a leaky pipe that needs fixing, I'm your man." She smiles at his awkward attempt to comfort her, and lets him put an arm around her shoulders. He tells her that something made him want to come up one last time and check on the reservoir grounds—he's not sure what, but now he's glad he came. She has nowhere to go, so she spends the night with him. She ends up staying on, cooking his meals for him, and having the baby in his house. At first he's like a father to her, but eventually—he's not sure how—she comes to love him as a man.

The idea that there was a man with her that night suggests a different story. Now Mr. Lucas arrives during the middle of a struggle. He takes a blow to the head, but Effie is spared and the man runs off and is never heard of again. The rest of the story is more or less the same, except that occasionally Effie will cry for no apparent reason. Yet Mr. Lucas knows that in her heart Effie understands how cruel her young lover was. He takes the watch key out of his shirt and looks at the little heart shape. What he feels now is anger. How could someone do this to such a poor, sweet little girl?

What would his mother want him to do with the key? More important, what would Effie want? He knows, he knows. Yet what could he say to Mr. Meade now? He would have to wait until tomorrow, and then say, "Well, Mr. Meade, I was going my rounds this morning and I came across a curiosity." It would be a lie, but it would be the right thing to do, much better than saying he'd discovered it Sunday.

He finds himself out walking in a drizzling rain, and without his realizing it he is headed up to the almshouse where the body of the drowned woman is being displayed for identification. Just to refresh his memory, he tells himself, in case he gets called up for a witness.

Inside, he takes his derby off and gets into the line of people. The girl is laid out in a dank stone-floored chapel, watery gray light filtering through the arched windows. It isn't right to have her displayed like a sideshow curiosity, Lucas thinks. There is a rumor out that her name is Fannie something. He takes a look, but doesn't recognize her as the same girl he pulled out of the water. She seems smaller and deader, and she has been cleaned up. The bruises around her eye and mouth are more noticeable, or, he wonders, does he just think that because the paper mentioned them? He's disappointed she no longer looks like Effie, just a girl named Fannie. On the one hand he is relieved—he was half afraid he'd want to touch her or kiss her—but on the other hand he wants more than ever now to keep her watch key. He doesn't know why. It just feels like it's *his* now, something she gave him. Leaving the chapel, he touches his hand to his chest—it's his.

On Monday evening Tommie is up in Tappahannock, where he spent the whole day with Brown Evans working on an estate settlement. There's a will to probate, entailments to decipher, piles of papers to dig through, documents to copy, three contending branches of the family to satisfy, each with legitimate claims on a property going back to the 1700s—in short, it's the kind of work Colonel Evans has taught Tommie to seek out and love. "We could be up to our elbows in this for weeks," he says with satisfaction, lighting up a cigar at the inn where they are spending the night. "Not that I want a *Jarndyce v. Jarndyce*." As a friend of the family, he took Tommie on after law school, and Tommie has not disappointed him. The only thing that worried him a bit was that Tommie seemed reluctant for a while to cross the river. Tommie had his own reasons for not wanting to go over into King William, and it had nothing to do with being lazy.

"It's a damn shame they can't get a newspaper out here any quicker," Tommie says, holding a copy of Saturday's paper. Sunday's might have something important.

"What were you looking for?"

"Oh, just wanted to see the news. It's not every day you have a Democrat as President."

Evans smiles. He massages his fringe of graying hair with his thumb and middle finger. Evans has a rotund face that goes naturally into a smile and reminds Tommie of a carnival barker in an orange-checkered suit he once saw in Richmond—though Evans wears dark, restrained clothes, Tommie can't help picturing him sometimes as a pitchman. A case of Bell's palsy half shuts his right eye, except when he's excited about something, and then it becomes apparent that both eyes are equally alert. "Tommie, you never fail to impress me. Politics might be just the thing for you someday. You have a gift for persuasion. Your courtroom locution is coming right along. You're clever too. You know when to be the educated gentleman and when to play the humble country boy."

Tommie adds a polite word about the case at hand, then goes back to his paper. Evans wants to talk. "You know, someday you won't have to wait a day for a newspaper. I'm sure of it. Do you know they're planning on stringing electric lights all over Richmond? Right through a wire, and pop! Light on every street corner. And telephones too. They're opening up a telephone office down in South Point next year. The modern world is coming, Tommie, and you'll be a part of it. But the thing I like best is the cigarette. You ever try one? Of course you did." He laughs as Tommie agrees. "Richmond Gems. Wish I had one on me now. I have another cigar, though." He offers one, but Tommie declines. "And the negro, Tommie. The negro is, per my prediction, proving as educable, in many cases, as the poor white. You mark my words. The black race is very clever. Putting them in office just to make us squirm was hypocritical foolishness, but they'll be back. Mark my words, Tommie. Nothing stays the same. If I've learned anything in my life, it's that. And if you can't go along with it, you might as well give up and die. And who wants to do that? A new world is opening up to you, Tommie."

Evans sniffs the air. "Mmm that smells good. I'm so hungry I could eat a horse."

At the same hour in Richmond, Justice Richardson is paying a visit to Cary Madison. The carriagemaker and his wife are distressed to learn that the reservoir girl has been identified as his cousin. He agrees to go over to the almshouse tomorrow; his wife invites Richardson to come sit in their cramped little parlor and have a cup of tea. From Cary, Richardson learns that Lillian (the name she went by) was teaching in Millboro' Springs, Bath County. "She'd just gone up there in the fall, round about October, and hadn't moved anywhere else that I knew. I heard from them—when? I reckon a few weeks ago."

"Who was it you heard from?"

"Her folks, down in Manquin."

Cary Madison strikes Richardson as a modestly educated, hardworking, reasonably honest young man. He works with his hands and has several days' stubble on his face. "Do you know of any particular gentleman she kept company with?" Richardson asks.

Madison thinks a minute, shifting his gaze to the faded hooked rug. "There was a well-driller name of Jenkins she took to for a while. Her daddy sued out a peace warrant to make him behave hisself, and he went away. Last I knew she'd taken up with her cousin, Willie Cluverius from down in King and Queen, but I don't know if that's true. Fact is, she corresponded with lots of young men."

"Oh?"

Madison glances at his wife, then down again. "I might as well tell you, we corresponded for a time, her and me. She was keen on me, but there wasn't much to it. She told people we were engaged, but we never exchanged rings or nothing. I think there were lots of young men like that."

"Were you intimate with her?"

He looks at Richardson. "Naw, not like that. We kissed once, in a friendly way."

"So she had several young men friends in addition to this Willie Cluverius?"

"I believe so, but you better ask her papa."

Richardson thanks him and hurries back to his office to wire the telegraph offices in Millboro' and Manquin.

CHAPTER FIVE

THE WEEK BEFORE he went off to school, Tommie found himself looking for Lillian out on the porch, or in the kitchen, and had to remind himself that she was gone. The wildflowers she put in vases around the house wilted and were thrown out. The last of her jam tarts was eaten. And then he was off in school and busy again with his books and new roommates. But sometimes at night after he said his prayers, he would invent heroic dramas for himself. Her school was less than five miles away, and he would imagine her venturing out into the night to use the necessary and, frightened by a snake or a robber, she would cry out; like Heathcliff he would somehow hear her and come to her rescue.

She wrote him once at school. He wrote back, wondering if her father would disapprove. They were friendly, cousinly letters. She told him her news and of her dreams of teaching or nursing in an orphanage in Richmond someday. Her teacher had been a nurse in a private Richmond hospital during the war, and it sounded like such a brave, romantic thing to do. She also told him that "Nola Bray has spread false rumors about me."

He sat down to write a response, but the letter came out sounding too stilted and sententious, full of precepts borrowed from the Bible and his pocket Shakespeare quotations. He crumpled the page and threw it away. He took out another piece of paper and wrote, "Dear Lillie, How I long to see you, just to stare into your brown eyes. At night I imagine coming to your rescue and holding you and kissing your sweet lips. I would press my throbbing chest against yours. Would you let me kiss your soft neck, and stroke your hair? If you said yes, I would die happy. Nola is a prig and I don't care for her." Tommie looked over his shoulder, then wrote, "If I could have one wish before I die it would be to lie with you naked."

He immediately tore the letter into small pieces and threw them in the wastebasket. His final draft was short and neutral. "Thank you for your thoughtful letter . . . I've been busy with Latin and natural philosophy, which I enjoy . . . Your fond cousin, Tommie."

Over the Christmas holiday, he avoided Lillian and sought out the company of Nola. He and his brother and cousin were invited to the Brays' house for a dancing party, but Willie found some excuse to stay behind. Lillian said that she was not good at dancing, and even though Aunt Jane encouraged her she refused to go. As Tommie was leaving she lifted her chin and said, "You look like you're going to Sunday school."

"You could go too, you know."

She looked a little unsure, and he wondered if he should have asked her to go before now. "I know my place," she said. "Anyway I wouldn't want her to think I was stealing her time."

"What, with me? Nola and I are just friends."

"Uh huh." She gave him a coy, lowered-eyelid look.

Tommie rode off by himself, thinking about his little cousin. He had never danced either, but he was willing to learn. He had been to the Brays' a few times, and Nola was always friendly, if a little too up-nosed. There were always other young people there, talking about cotillions and horse races and other things he had no familiarity with. Tommie had done his best to fit in. The Brays' house was bigger, their garden more elaborate than Aunt Jane's, and he wondered what it would be like to own such a grand place.

This time even though there were more people, Nola seemed especially attentive toward him, her eyes sparkling as he told her about Aberdeen. Many of the young men wore white vests with crop-tailed coats and tight pants; their hair was oiled and split in back, their breath perfumed with spearmint. Yet the fact that he wore a simple pinstripe suit and red necktie seemed unimportant to Nola; she took him by the hand and guided him over to a refreshment table laden with hot cider, lemonade, trifle, cakes, and raspberry sherbet in a big silver bowl. "I'm sorry you couldn't get your brother and cousin to come to my little german," she told him. "But you'll just have to make up for them with your own dancing."

"I'm not much of a dancer," he told her.

"It's easy," she said. She was wearing a dark red dress with a tight basque and a loose black bow on the back of her hair. They were in the dining room, with the connecting doors opened onto the sitting room and the furniture cleared away. A few well-turned-out grown-ups—wistful, gossipy, proud, or indifferent—stood along the edges of the merriment like stately pillars from another time. The musicians were stationed in a corner of the sitting room, and when they took up a waltz, Nola showed Tommie the steps. He found that he was not as bad as he thought. Then came a polka, and again he picked up the steps so quickly he thought he must have some special talent, and he was delighted with himself.

"I don't want to monopolize your time," he told Nola.

She pulled back and regarded him with spirited eyes. "Aren't you having a gay enough time with me?"

"Yes," he said, embarrassed but quietly thrilled. He pressed his hand more firmly against her crepe de chine back.

She asked politely about his aunt, then said, "And I hear Lillie is making herself popular at Bruington."

"Where did you hear that?"

"She told me so herself," Nola said. "She and I have become great friends. We trade letters almost every week."

And yet Lillie had told him that Nola was spreading rumors about her. He didn't understand girls at all—could he possibly be an object of both their affections? It was vain to think so, yet he was not a bad-looking young man, he thought. His aunt told him he had nice symmetrical features and that both he and his brother were as handsome as young men could be. He had sandy brown hair, widespread eyes, and full lips that had, at nearly seventeen, never kissed a girl. "Want to take a walk in the garden?" he whispered.

She smiled and shook her head, then after the dance excused herself to go speak with a group of boys milling around the refreshments. He felt ashamed. Of course she couldn't leave her own party and go out in the cold with him; he had sounded too eager, too unrefined. But she hadn't been completely dismissive. She hadn't slapped him or said he was rude. She seemed to understand boys and how to carry herself among people of all ages and stations. Lillie was friendly with Lewis and Maria back home, bringing them leftovers and vases of meadow flowers, but she could never order them around with the simple ease that Nola could. Nola was more sophisticated and grown up than Lillie would likely ever be. She could even play the piano and speak fluent French.

And yet he found himself thinking of Lillie's tiny waist and the way she ducked her head when she was talking about something she was unsure of. She wasn't elegant like Nola, but she was adorable, even if she did sometimes stretch the truth. The contrast between the two girls seemed to give him a window into the nature of his soul; he thought he must be in love with Lillie, but it disturbed him that the way he felt about her was passionate and physical, almost violent in its ability to take over his entire body and mind. It would be so much more pleasant if he were in love with Nola.

He danced again with Nola, inhaling the strange warm smell of her body. She was very lovely and refined, and though he didn't want to crush her against himself it was still a joy to hold her. "You dance like an angel," he said.

Nola gave him a mock smile, flaring her thin, aristocratic nose. "And you learn very quickly."

He rode home in the late afternoon, a waltz still playing in his head. A light snow was falling and he pushed his horse, trying to fit its rhythm with the one in his mind—it would not work, there were too many beats. He slowed down, catching his breath, enjoying the cold stinging his cheeks. When he got home he called out for his brother. Lewis told him that Willie was out cutting wood.

He had not really wanted to see Willie, only to know where he was. Lillie was in the parlor, a piece of needlework in her lap; Aunt Jane was lying down in her bedroom. He stood for a moment staring at the fold in Lillie's bodice as she bent over her work, his throat a dry husk. "You should have been there," he said, his voice almost choked out.

She glanced up. "You have snow on your shoulders."

He just lingered there in the doorway while she laughed at him; she got up and came over. "Lost in thought, Professor?" A curl draped across her forehead as she went up on tiptoe and brushed the snow from his coat, her hand-stitched bodice stretching across her sides and chest as she reached for him.

She laughed gaily while he told her about the party. He hummed some of the music, then put his arm around her and began waltzing her around the room and out into the back entry-way and into the summer kitchen. "See?" he said, "You do know how to dance. You should've come."

And then Willie entered. He stood there a moment, a be-mused smile frozen on his face, his eyes uncertain.

"She's *my* cousin too," Tommie said.

Lillie stopped. "That's enough dancing for me," she said, and she took herself back to the parlor.

Willie bent to unlace his mud-caked boots. "That should be enough wood for the week."

"Been out chopping?" Tommie asked. Willie grunted, and Tommie stood there watching his bare head. "Go on and hit me if you want to."

"Why would I want to do that?" Willie said, standing, chest out. In his stockings he was taller than Tommie. He forced a good-natured laugh, then rapped Tommie on the chest with a fist. "I'd sooner hit myself."

The next fall he was off to the College of Richmond, having kissed Nola twice—once on the cheek and once lingeringly on the lips behind an Oriental screen. She seemed to favor him over all other boys. She admitted that she had kissed boys at camp meetings, but "just for practice" and only "because they were sweet," not boys she would take seriously as suitors, such as himself. He sensed that her logic was somehow flawed, but she sounded so convincing that he never tried to do anything except hold her hand unless she suggested he might do more.

As for Lillian, she and Willie had become such close friends that Jane had quit worrying about them. "I don't know exactly what they're doing when they're gone together all afternoon," she told Tommie, "but I think Willie is very mature and he'll do the right thing by her. He's not too young to marry at eighteen, nor she at fifteen."

A few days before he left for Richmond, Tommie asked his brother what it was like to lie with a girl.

"Why do you ask me?" Willie said. They were standing out under a tremendous multitrunked pine in the front yard, a prestorm wind shivering the needles. Willie's shirt was soaked with sweat from lifting hay bales; Tommie had just bathed, though he had worked as hard as Willie earlier in the day, then gone in and studied for two hours—a habit he had kept up all summer.

"I'm going off to college and I wanted some pointers," he said.

Willie made a puffing noise. "I don't know anything about girls, especially Richmond girls. Though I expect they're about the same as girls around here." He grabbed a branch and leaned his waist into the trunk in a casual way that Tommie admired. His brother had always been a better athlete, a more outgoing and uncomplicated person than himself. But though they were best friends and he knew Willie better than anyone in the world, there were things Willie kept to himself. Tommie suspected that Lillian had become his new best friend and confidante. His brother had all but quit asking him to go out on fishing and hunting jaunts, not that he missed them so much, though he did miss being with Willie and having him desire his company.

"But you've been with a lot of girls," Tommie said.

"Not so many. And only ones that I care about."

"You used to ask me what I thought about her."

Willie nodded. "So you want to know if I've lain with her?"

"I didn't say that."

"Then I won't tell you."

"Well, have you?"

Willie looked out across the oatfield. "Maybe. What about you and Nola?"

Tommie puffed and shook his head. "Nola's not that kind of girl."

"And you think Lillie is?"

"I didn't say that."

"I know some terrible things nobody else does," Willie said. "About her father. Her father's an evil man."

"I know he beat her."

"Worse than that," Willie said. He flexed the muscles in his jaws. With Tommie waiting for him to go on, he opened his mouth, closed it, then said, "He made her feel dirty . . . he came into her room when she was getting dressed."

"You know she tells lies."

"So she fibs sometimes about where she's been, or what she's been doing. That's the kind of fib you'd learn to tell if you didn't want your father to hit you for living."

And that was all that Tommie was able to get out of his brother. He knew that going away to college in Richmond would be different from going off to boarding school. He was fairly certain that both Nola and Lillie would miss him—what he did not know was whom he would miss more. Three days before he was to leave, Lillian had departed for her second term at Bruington. She'd stood on tiptoe and laid her head briefly against his chest. He'd started to pat her head, then stopped himself, his hand suspended awkwardly in the air.

On his own departure day, Aunt Jane kissed him on the cheek. "You're such a man now," she said, beaming proudly at him, her eyes crinkling into crescents; then she turned away a moment so she wouldn't cry. She adjusted his bowler and necktie. "Don't neglect your health in the city," she said, gripping his shoulders.

He shook his brother's hand, endured another squeeze from his aunt, and got into the cart. His father came just in time to see him off and give him a pocket edition of Shakespeare quotes, which he already owned, telling him it was from his mother who was not feeling well. Inside was a folded ten-dollar bill that Tommie knew better than to try to refuse.

He had not been to Richmond since the trip with his father, and the city had been growing ever since. It was after New Orleans the largest city in the South, and it was on the verge of change. The reluctant Confederate capital was still in some ways a war-scarred city, holding on for dear life to its past, with memorials popping up in cemeteries and public squares, and one-legged veterans swinging down the streets on crutches. The trauma of the war years was not easily shaken off. But the bitterness and despair the city had endured under the watchful eye of the conquerors was gone, and the city Tommie was entering was a changed place. Its ironworks were again preeminent in the South, its marketplaces hummed with life, and in nearly every way it was on the verge of industrial modernity.

He caught a horse-drawn omnibus heading west on Broad. At seventeen years old and on his own, he felt constrained in a new way, having to act the part of a man, like the dignified gentleman on the seat beside him. The man had nodded to Tommie when he boarded near the capitol, as though he knew Tommie were green, as fresh from the country as first-cut alfalfa. At the same time, Tommie was so caught up in his excitement at being in the city he could lose himself for blocks at a time in the passing show out the window: all the fine houses, the carriages clipping smartly along.

He took the bus to the end of the line, two miles from the station. The driver helped him with his trunk, and then he was alone, standing there not quite knowing what to do with himself.

He began to drag his trunk toward the largest building he saw. A young black porter with a hand cart came running to help him. "Richmond College?" the boy asked him. Tommie said yes, trying to act as though he knew his way around. The boy nodded and said, "Ryland Hall, straight ahead."

It was a massive new building, Second Empire–style, mansard roofs crowning ornate towers. It was what college should look like, and Tommie liked that it had the same name as his minister back home. The boy stayed with him until he found his room, then Tommie gave him a nickel and thanked him. Tommie's roommate was already there. He introduced himself as Tyler Bagby from Essex. He had unkempt dark wavy hair, an open collar, and a droll smile about him, as if he found the entire world an amusing curiosity. He also had a sharp angular face, shadowed with evening stubble that made him look older than he was. After a few minutes of light conversation, Tyler put his hands behind his head and leaned back. "I think we'll get along just fine, Tommie," he said. "I hope you don't mind if I call you that." Tommie shook his head. "And you should call me Tyler. Bagby sounds too boarding school, and Mr. Bagby too formal. Help yourself."

He tossed Tommie a package of what were labeled Richmond Gems. He watched with amusement as Tommie opened the thick paper pouch and slowly pulled out one of the pencil-thin cylinders. "What's the matter with you?" he said. "Never heard of tobacco?" Tommie nodded and smelled the cylinder. He and his brother had tried cigars, but his aunt disapproved and he himself didn't care for the taste. Moreover, Reverend Ryland had said in one of his sermons that tobacco was an addiction and therefore a vice and had only hurt the farmers who depended on it.

"It's a cigarette," Tyler explained. "Greatest thing this city's ever produced. And when I get myself an education, I'm going to join my brother over in Manchester. He's a floor manager at Allen & Ginter. I worked under him this summer, as assistant floor manager. They have twenty-two women rolling these beauties, which by itself is a good reason to get into the business. We're going to make a fortune, and if you want in on it I could say a good word for you."

He showed Tommie how to smoke it, but since smoking was a vice Tommie had a hard time taking pleasure in it. Still, he enjoyed watching Tyler hold the cigarette between two fingers as he slowly exhaled a cloud of smoke in apparent utter satisfaction.

They started going to church together at Grace Street Baptist, where the college chaplain, Reverend Hatcher, preached on Sundays. One Sunday they met the widow Carlotta Henry, who invited them to a Saturday tea dance. On the appointed day they strolled down Broad to her brick-and-stone mansion, its turreted bay and columned portico making it, in Tommie's mind, a castle. A short lively bird of a woman, Mrs. Henry was a society matron who thrived on the company of young gentlemen; the locket she wore around her neck was said to contain a shard of her husband's shattered thigh bone. She grasped Tommie warmly by the hand and introduced him and Tyler to a group of older students. The women were mostly from the Richmond Female Institute. He danced with a pretty, blond-haired girl, and since he was homesick he asked if he could visit her sometime. She told him matter-of-factly that she was not allowed to go carriage riding with a young man unchaperoned and that anyway she expected to be engaged shortly after her coming-out party in the spring.

Thus schooled and chastened, Tommie rejoined Tyler and a group of upperclassmen who had decided, as soon as the dance was over, to go to a place called Garolami's on Mayo Street. One of the young men, a medical student named Randall Croxton,

had a cousin who worked there. And so Tommie found himself
swept along in the camaraderie of a boisterous group heading to
the east side of town. There was Bobby Valentine, of the Valentine meat juice family, a law student named James Courtney, and
Sid and Harry Aylett from King William.

The farther east they proceeded, the rougher-looking the
people they passed—painted women on corners openly leering,
scruffy men carrying illegal sidearms. It was a cool evening, with
moisture beaded along the bases of gaslight globes; Tommie felt
the growing warmth of his herd. By the time they got to Garolami's it was as if they were well into their third round already.
Bobby's arms were draped around Tommie and Tyler and they
were singing "O dem golden slippers." At the saloon, Randall's
cousin seated them near the back. He wiped his hands on a
dirty apron and told them in a friendly way he hoped they were
all eighteen years old, which Tommie was not, nor was Tyler,
though Tyler, in an offhand way, claimed he was. They ordered
drafts of lager, except for Sid, who asked for porter. Then after
his first sip, he told the group about a cadaver raid on Oakwood
Cemetery with Randall when he was a freshman. "They never
found out who it was, but it was thanks to us that the legislature
finally decided to donate corpses to the medical school. That's
progress, gentlemen!" He raised his glass and everybody cheered.

Then Bobby Valentine told the group about a duel his uncle
fought in Oakwood with a newspaper editor who was against
paying back the war debt to the federal government. "He got hit
in the jaw by a flying piece of somebody's headstone. I believe it
was an Aylett."

"Naw," Sid said, "my folks ain't buried around here."

"Anyway," Bobby went on, "he took it on the chin for Virginia's
honor." This led to another chorus of bellowing in simulated

outrage. Bobby told the group if anybody needed a job at his father's plant, he would see that he got it.

Tommie and Tyler were mostly quiet, listening to the tales of the older boys, though Tommie was able to pitch in a few wry little remarks that got some laughs. Harry, also a freshman, entertained the group with remarkably accurate imitations of their professors. James was the quietest of all, and Tommie saw that he was able to maintain his composure and place within the group without a great deal of effort. Perhaps, Tommie thought, he should model himself after James, who had a dignity the others lacked. He was also the best dressed, and Tommie could picture himself studying law someday and behaving in a similarly modest manner.

A blind negro fiddler was playing at the front of the room, his foot tapping time in the sawdust on the floor. At the table next to theirs a group of rough men were playing cards. The man closest to Tommie had a purple wen on his forehead; he called out, "Play 'Chicken in the Breadtray.'" Tommie looked over and saw him removing his wooden lower leg so that he could scratch his stump. The man shot him a murderous look and as Tommie turned back he heard the cardplayers laughing. His own kind were around him and he felt that never had he known such a fine group of fellows—he wanted to belong to them forever.

Sid told Tommie and Tyler that they would make excellent candidates for the Bell Ringing Society. By tradition, at midnight during final examination week one member of the group would ring bells and holler like mad for a brief time. No one knew exactly who was in the society and where the next bell ringing would occur. Tommie said he would be proud to be a member. Then Sid suggested they all go over to Locust Alley to Lizzie Banks's house. After a few minutes of spirited innuendo and guffaws, Tommie deduced that Lizzie Banks ran a brothel, where you could have the woman of your choice for five dollars. Students were welcome. James and Harry decided to save their money and go on home. Tommie did not have five dollars on him, nor could he afford to spend it, but his curiosity was so inflamed now that he quietly asked Tyler for the loan of a few dollars.

No one but Sid and Randall seemed to have been there before, or to any such place. But the other three were game for the experience, and off they all went, no longer singing, nor quite so boisterous. When they got to the row of jammed-together houses, Sid went up and knocked on one that was indistinguishable from the others. A middle-aged woman, her hair wound into a severe knot, let them in as though she were ushering them into Sunday school. She introduced herself as Lizzie, and offered them sherry from a crystal decanter sitting on a table beneath a winding staircase. A tall mirror stood on one wall, half its silver missing, its carved gilt frame suggesting an opulent past; another wall held a convex mirror that afforded views down the hall and up the stairs.

As nonchalantly as they could, the young men took seats in boot-scuffed wing chairs and sprung sofas artfully covered with antimacassars. They sat drinking superfluous, weak sherry, until presently a group of young women materialized from different parts of the house. The one who came to sit with Tommie had short reddish hair, plump arms, and an upturned nose; she called herself Gretchen. He liked Tyler's girl better, a wispy woman with big sad eyes and long straight black hair. Seeing him looking at her, Gretchen pouted, "You don't like me?" She had a hint of Irish in her accent.

"No," Tommie said. "I like you fine." His voice seemed muffled and far away, but he felt pleasantly free of himself and he took another big sip of sherry. He banished Nola from his mind for the hundredth time, as well as visions of the crucifix, his mother, Reverend Ryland, the flames of hell, Reverend Hatcher, and semi-naked sinners moaning in eternal darkness as depicted in an old Sunday school booklet. In their place he put an image of Sid walking happily up the stairs with a laughing, buxom young lady, and he reminded himself that God expects us to sin, in order that we may be forgiven—a formula that had been lying ready for use in his brain since the day he'd conceived it at a long, otherwise dull revival at the Stratton Parish Episcopal Church.

Gretchen led him upstairs past a red velvet wall hanging with gold tassels. As he passed, he ran the back of his hand along the plushness of the velvet for reassurance that his money was going to a worthy cause. The little room they entered was high-ceilinged and furnished with a low iron bed, a wooden chair, and a nightstand with a ceramic pitcher and wash basin. She went around to the other side of the bed, her back to him, and began unlacing her beaded basque; he sat on the chair watching her in the candle glow. Her back was suddenly bare, the basque hanging from her waist like a carapace she'd emerged from.

She half turned, smiling in a coy way that struck him as artificial. "Need some help?"

"No," he said, pulling off his shoes. His fingers fumbled over his buttons. Finally he was down to his underwear, and, not sure what he was supposed to do, he came over and sat on the close side of the bed.

Gretchen had used the time to strip down to nothing but pale skin and a gold necklace. She twisted half around again and placed a hand gently on his chest. "You're a very handsome man," she told him. No one but his aunt had ever called him a man before, much less a handsome man. Her breast swayed as she stroked him down to his navel. Then she was on the bed facing him, squatting on her heels, and the room seemed full of flesh. He was afraid of disappointing her even as she stroked between his legs and he felt himself swelling. He let her be in charge—let her slip his drawers down, place a rubber condom on him, as though she were a nurse and he afraid to look too closely at his injury. He touched her breast as she worked on him, and she didn't seem to mind. But as she slipped the condom down he could not help letting go. She held him and murmured, "Mm-hmm, junior's excited. That's a good boy, that's a good boy."

She handed him a towel, then lay beside him and told him how strong he was. "Next time," she said, "I'll be quicker. You'll see." She tapped his nose. They lay there awhile, and she told him about how she was going to earn enough money to go to New Orleans by riverboat; she'd had a gentleman customer from there, a man with a white suit, who told her she could have a job as a dancer if she wanted it. But she'd only just come to Richmond, so she didn't want to leave quite yet. She was from Alexandria, and had left as soon as she could because she didn't get along with her aunt and uncle who had raised her, her parents having too many of their own. While she talked, she let Tommie play with her breasts, until he felt the sadness of the world slipping away and desire coming back. He leaned in toward her as she was sitting up.

"My, oh my," she said. "We can go again, but it's three dollars extra."

This hardly seemed fair, seeing as how he had not technically gone even once. But since he was not sure how such things were counted, all he could do was lament, "I don't have but five."

"How am I ever gonna get to New Orleans if I give out special favors?" she asked, as though it were a problem they had discussed for years.

"I could pay you later."

But she was already putting on her underclothes, and he didn't want to beg. "You ask for me next time, hear?" she said. He said he would. "What's your name?" she asked.

"Tommie," he said. "Tommie Merton." It was the first name that came into his head, from church history—Walter Merton, thirteenth-century bishop.

"Well, Tommie Merton, it was a pleasure to meet you." She gave him a sassy little smile. "Now it's time for you and me to get dressed."

᙮᙮᙮

CHAPTER SIX

O N TUESDAY Richardson receives word from Millboro'
that Lillian Madison got on the train on Thursday bound
for Richmond. It was six hours late and didn't arrive until three
o'clock Friday morning. Richardson then learns from the conductor that the young woman was traveling alone and that she
was staying at the American Hotel and expected to meet a friend
in the city.

The American Hotel sits on the southwest corner of Twelfth
and Main in a row of iron-fronted buildings that arose after the
war. It's a white four-story with arched windows and green shut-
ters and decorative cornices—one of the nicer hotels in town,
with its own barbershop and restaurant. The entrance is down
around on Twelfth, with a ladies' entrance to the left. Richardson
steps briskly in and asks for the manager on duty. There were several young women here that night, he is told. While waiting for
the clerk who was on duty last Thursday night, he is shown the
register; running his finger down the list of late-arriving guests,
he comes across one of the last—F. L. Merton of Roanoke City.
He taps it. "This Miss Merton," he asks. "What was she like?"

The day desk clerk doesn't know, but tries to make helpful
suggestions while they wait for Mr. Dodson, the night clerk, who
has to be woken up at his house six blocks away. "She probably
was one of the finer young ladies from Roanoke, visiting a sick
relative or something. Though I don't know her personally."

Richardson nods but is not really listening. He's trying to imagine why Miss Madison would travel to Richmond and register under a false name, if indeed she did. The train conductor supplied him with a fairly good description that matched the reservoir woman—short, stout, brown hair, wearing a grayish dress, he thought, and a black hat with feathers; carrying an oblong clothes bag and a hand satchel. He'd also mentioned a red shawl. The Dunstans' shawl could very well be hers. But best not leap too far ahead, he tells himself. He decides to make inquiries of the bellboys and night watchmen.

The night clerk arrives shortly, nattily dressed for someone who has been rudely awakened. A dandy boy. Baby-faced, late twenties. As soon as he opens his mouth, Richardson knows he'll give a good description but will be nervous and unsure of himself. "Ah, yes," he says. "I do remember her. She arrived on that late train. She was wearing a charcoal-colored alpaca dress and a black hat with ostrich tips and a veil and bugle-gimp beads, I believe. Let's see, a blue jersey jacket and there was a red crochet shawl around her shoulders. There may have been brown gloves. Possibly cotton, but I can't be one hundred percent sure. We see so many people every day."

"You have a very good memory, Mr. Dodson," Richardson tells him. "Now, tell me what else you remember about her." Dodson says that she seemed like a well-bred young lady with good connections. She didn't seem at all out of place. He did not see her again, but she sent a note by a newsboy, a short mulatto of about fourteen or fifteen years. One of the bellboys, Slim Lane, apparently took the note out to the newsboy, but the newsboy could not find the person for whom the note was intended and so Slim returned the note to the desk.

"I went off duty at ten," Dodson says. "The note was there when I came back and stayed there all day Saturday. But the young lady had already left—without paying her bill. So I tore the note up and threw it away." Dodson then asks if this has anything to do with the reservoir girl, though he knows it does. Richardson only says that it might.

Now he has Dodson digging through the trash, which the clerk is fairly certain has not been emptied in the past three days. They take two trash bins back to the clerks' office and sort through handfuls of notes, orange peels, candy wrappers, pencil shavings, and other detritus, Dodson explaining that all manner of refuse gets left on the front desk even though the clientele is generally of the finest quality. Richardson pulls out a crumpled note and three torn ones, or rather pieces, and begins assembling them. Two of the torn notes have names that are not ones he's looking for; the third one is inside three pieces of a ripped cream-colored envelope. The note is unsigned and appears to be torn from a larger piece of ruled paper. It reads, "I will be there. So do wait for me." The envelope, pieced together, is more interesting. There is a name in cursive on the outside.

Dodson says he glanced at the note before reinserting it into the envelope and tearing it up. He is almost certain it is the same note that Slim brought back undelivered. Richardson puts the three pieces of the envelope together on a table and asks Dodson to read the name. Dodson squints and says, "T. J. . . . Clements?"

Richardson nods. He can see plainly what it says, but it's not a name familiar to many people. He strokes his jaw, lost in thought. He and Dodson keep sifting through the trash looking for anything else that might have belonged in the envelope. Dodson cannot remember. The note looks complete in itself, but it's odd that it was torn from a larger paper. Likely she was frugal, Richardson thinks. Probably she had grown up that way—large family in the country, scraping by after the war; she goes across the state to teach when she's barely of age, if that. Even with much on her mind, the habit of not wasting paper was natural. He cannot yet form a picture of Cluverius, her cousin and possible seducer. But why "T.J." when Cary Madison had clearly said "Willie"? Perhaps it was a nickname.

Richardson meets with Slim Lane in the clerks' office. Detective Wren has been waiting outside, but Richardson tells him he'll have to wait a little longer—Wren can be useful, but he has an unfortunate way of bullying people into believing he's in charge of an investigation he may never be paid a cent for. Making him wait is the best medicine.

Slim is skinny and brown, in his mid-twenties, his nose as angular as a white man's. He carries his head back, as though his neck were too weak to hold it upright, and he constantly shifts his eyes right and left in what Richardson at first thinks is nervousness, then realizes is simply a personal tic. Richardson asks him about the woman who was staying in Room 21 on Friday.

"A yellow boy give me a note to take to her," Slim says, darting his eyes right. His voice is nasal, his accent almost as Caucasian as his nose, as though the whiteness in him is concentrated in the middle of his face.

"Who was this boy?"

"Don't know his name. I'd recognize him though." His eyes shift to the left, making Richardson look to that corner of the room, as if for the ghost that Slim sees.

"And what did the boy ask you to do?"

"He said a man give him a note to take to the lady in Room 21."

"So the man knew she was in Room 21?"

Slim's eyes shift back and forth, pausing for the first time directly on Richardson. His Adam's apple bulges. "How do you mean?"

"I mean, did he ask for the note to be delivered to a room or a person?"

Slim shakes his head. "I disremember exactly. The yellow boy might know."

"Do you remember the name of the woman?"

Slim says no.

"Was it Merton?"

"Yessir, I believe it was Murder, Murdon, yessir."

"And what was on the note?"

"I didn't look at it. It was on a little card. I took it to the lady in Room 21, and she said wait, and she handed me an envelope to take back out to the man. I give it to the boy, and a nickel. She give me one too."

"Then what?"

"Then I went back to work."

"Did you see the lady again, or the man that sent the note?"

"Nosir, I never saw that man. The lady went out later in the morning and came back in at dinnertime."

"Did you see her after that?"

"She went out again in the evening. Came back after dark and went out again. I didn't see her after that."

Richardson tries to fix times to her coming and going, but gets different answers each time. Slim describes the woman as short and wearing a dark dress and coat and a red shawl. The last time she went out he believed she was carrying her clothes bag. He remembered that because most folks don't carry their bags out at night.

The night watchman, a black man in his forties named Hunter Hunt, remembers her comings and goings a bit differently. Hunt claims she went out after dark, as did Slim, but says she did not return after that. He agrees that it's possible Slim saw her and he didn't, but that it's also possible Slim mistook her for another woman staying in the hotel. He remembers a short woman with a red shawl leaving Room 21 with her clothes bag. Not long before this, along about nine o'clock, a gentleman called for her by mistake. He said he was waiting for a lady his sister went to school with, and the lady in 21 only looked something like her. So Hunt had him wait in the parlor, but when he looked in a few minutes later the gentleman was gone.

"What did the gentleman look like?" Richardson asks.

Hunt thinks a minute. "He was tall and thin. Had a mustache, a light-colored coat."

"As tall as me?"

Hunt takes his time in answering, trying to judge Richardson's height rather than the importance of the question, as Slim appeared to be doing. "I'd mostly say so, yessuh. But without him here, I don't know."

"So the gentleman left the hotel without the lady?"

"Yessuh."

"And did you see her go out?"

"Nosuh. Round midnight I noticed her door open a crack and the light squeezin' out. I knocked and went in. Looked like she was clean gone. Bed made, no bags, no lady. I turned off the light and closed the door."

"And you didn't see either of them again?"

"Nosuh."

Richardson turns back to Slim. "Anything else you remember about her or any visitors she might have had?"

"Nosir," Slim says, eyes wide right. "I don't remember another thing."

CHAPTER SEVEN

TUESDAY EVENING Tommie and Mr. Evans are back in the sitting room at the Tappahannock Inn. The Sunday paper is there and Tommie helps himself to it. The article is on the front page. He had hoped there would be nothing, but it's right there, staring at him, "Woman's Watery Grave." He gulps it in. It doesn't say much, only that an unidentified young woman was found dead in the old city reservoir. The pregnancy is mentioned, the coroner, an autopsy to be performed, a lonely place to commit suicide, a detective. Why bring in a detective for a suicide? He reads it over again and then scans the rest of the paper. Something more troubling appears in a short paragraph at the bottom of the fourth page. A woman's clothes bag was found at the coal docks; a pair of underwear was labeled F. or T. Madison. The paragraph concludes, "Perhaps the bag may furnish a clue to the mystery of the girl found in the reservoir." How can they leap to such a conclusion, Tommie wonders. It's irresponsible.

He glances up at Mr. Evans, enjoying his cigar, apparently lost in thought. He smiles at Tommie. "Anything interesting?" he asks.

Tommie's blood races. "Just the usual," he says. "Robbery in Manchester, Catholics celebrating St. Patrick's." He peruses the other headlines and passes the paper on to Mr. Evans, who is eager to check on the baseball scores and his railroad stocks. "We should raise a glass to St. Patrick ourselves," Tommie says, brightening. The thing to do is forget about it, to relax, he tells himself.

"Indeed we should, Tommie, indeed we should. Go order us a couple of bottles of lager." As Tommie gets up, Mr. Evans shakes his head. "You see this about the girl found at the reservoir?"

"The suicide?"

"Yes, it's a sad business."

Evans reads from the paper. "Coroner suspects suicide . . . but evidence to the contrary . . . articles of clothing belonging to the woman were found elsewhere on the grounds."

Tommie sits back down. "How do they know they belonged to the woman?"

"Good for you, Tommie." Mr. Evans taps the side of his head, obscured in a haze of cigar smoke. "Where's the hole in their argument? You always have to be alert to these things."

"There's no proof of any connection."

"True," Evans says, one hand going to his paunch. "You know how they write these things up to sell papers. People like a mystery—takes them out of the humdrum. They get credit if they're right. If not, oh well, everybody forgets about it. The language is cagey—they don't come right out and say this bag belonged to her. They just suggest it. That's good courtroom technique." He pokes his side and winces, "Dern bowel flare-up. Forgot to take my powder."

When Tommie returns with the lagers Evans goes on. "Richmond's gotten so big I don't hardly recognize it. Why, you can walk down Main Street and not see a soul you know." He then tells about a cousin of his who killed himself by jumping off a cliff to make it look like an accident. "Said he was just going out for a walk. What he didn't know was that his own brother saw the whole thing."

Tommie nods, smiling, not paying much attention, even though Mr. Evans is a good storyteller. What he's thinking is that since no paper comes out on Monday, he'll have to wait two more days for further news. Unless Tuesday's happens to come on Wednesday. It sometimes only takes a day. Meanwhile, the lagers and forget about it.

Two pints later Mr. Evans is deep into a story about a midget who was the sergeant at arms when Evans served in the state legislature; he stood on a chair and used a megaphone. Then he moves on to telling about when he was an engineer in Cary's Brigade, retreating with Lee to Appomattox Court House. Tommie is amazed at the fund of entertaining stories Mr. Evans has at his command and how they can make one feel that the best years to have lived were the ones he knew. The hum of other conversations fills the room, and a sense of well-being suffuses Tommie's veins.

Slim Lane shakes himself like a dog as he steps out of the clerks' office. Richardson's interrogation has left him harried and suspicious. His eyes shoot left and right, then grow large as he nearly walks into an enormous man wearing a long black coat and holding a notepad that looks about the size of a cracker in his meaty hand. "William Lane?" the man says. Slim nods. "Detective Wren. Mind if I ask you a few questions?" Slim shakes his head. Wren puts a paw on his shoulder and guides him out to the hallway, then just outside into the alley off Eleventh. The clopping sound of carriages from Main is muffled back here, the air sour with the stench of garbage.

"Hunt tells me you carried a note to a girl in Room 21 from a gentleman. Is that right?"

Slim glances down to Wren's shoes. They are as large as boats, and there's mud on the soles. The man wearing them is asking him a question in a quiet, friendly way that doesn't really seem friendly. "Yessir, that's right."

"And she sent one back?"

"Yessir."

"Who was the gentleman?"

"I don't know. I didn't see him. A yellow boy took the note."

Wren widens his stance so that he's eye to eye with Slim. "What yellow boy?" he demands.

"I don't know his name. I've seen him around."

Wren corners Slim's eyes into looking straight at him. "You can find him for me, though, can't you?"

The big man's face is right in front of Slim's; his breath is heavy with onions and some foul kind of fish that white people eat for breakfast. He's nothing like a wren—more like a bear without all the fur, and a skritchy voice like a fox. Slim adds two random numbers in his head to calm himself: 3,586 + 4,567 = 8,153. "I don't know if I can," Slim says. "I'll be working most all the time."

"I'll see about your job," Wren tells him. "Don't worry about that."

Don't get mixed up in white folkses' business, Slim Lane. Don't you do it. Your mama would slap you across the room. He tries to say something, but his mouth won't work.

"If you can get me his name in a day, there'll be something extra in it for you."

Slim sees an opening and dodges his eyes left. "I don't know."

Wren places a hand against the wall right beside Slim's face. His nostrils open up like caves, and Slim imagines running up into one and hiding. He begins to burst into laughter, and pretends to have a coughing fit. Wren waits for him to finish. "Let me put it to you this way, son. You like your job at the hotel, don't you?"

"Yessir."

"Good, I thought so. The manager's a good friend of mine. So's the owner. I do favors for them. You do this favor for me and they'd be mighty pleased. I'm going to speak to both of them about it directly. You take the afternoon off and start hunting for that boy, and when you find him you come running to my office and don't stop for anything until you talk to me. You understand?"

Slim nods, glancing briefly into Wren's sharp eyes. Don't get messed up in no business, he tells himself. But suddenly Wren is gone, and Slim *is* messed up in the very business he wanted not to get messed up in. And not a thing he can do about it.

Tommie and Mr. Evans leave on Wednesday morning, hoping to get home in time for dinner. They make a stop at the Trace crossroads store; the eastbound stagecoach has just arrived, carrying, among other things, mail, freight, and Richmond newspapers. But nothing from Tuesday yet. They head out in the carriage again.

It's warmer out today than it has been. The rank, fecund odors of skunk cabbage and newly plowed earth mingle in the air, and the faint buds of dogwoods are wedding lace along the roadside. The grinding carriage wheels suggest a rhythm. Tommie opens his mouth and begins singing: "Ching-a-ring-a-ring ching ching, ho-a-ding-a-ding kum larkee . . ." He whistles awhile.

Mr. Evans looks up from his paper, inhales the scents of spring, and absently takes up the verse: "Brothers gather 'round, listen to this story 'bout the promised land."

Then together they go. "You don't need to fear if you have no money, you don't need none there to buy you milk and honey." Lustier now, "There you'll ride in style, coach with four white horses, there the evenin' meal has one two three four courses."

Mr. Evans compliments Tommie on his singing and tells him a story about minstrels traveling through King and Queen when he was a boy. "The best music I ever heard. The grown-ups were a little less appreciative—I didn't understand it at the time. They were free coloreds—in the company of a white manager—but folks were afraid it would give the slaves ideas. Of course, we had free negroes in King and Queen, so I don't know why they were worried." Tommie is reminded of his first trip to Richmond. His father took him on the train and showed him the burned-out Spottswood Hotel where he'd seen Jefferson Davis, and when they walked across Capitol Square two old negroes were singing and strumming a banjo. A policeman told them not to disturb the governor, and they moved on, singing more softly, "Why do I weep, when my heart should feel no pain?"

They arrive in King and Queen Courthouse before noon. Tommie bids Mr. Evans good-bye and continues on to Little Plymouth, where Aunt Jane hugs him and fusses over him again as if he has been gone two weeks instead of two nights. An hour later he's sitting down to dinner with her and Willie. She tells him a letter arrived from Lillie. He had forgotten the letter, and for a moment he says nothing.

Jane continues, "She says in it that she's going down to Point Comfort to take care of a friend's sick aunt. Can you imagine? Here I am, with you boys away all the time, and she can't come here and spend some time with me. After all I've done for her. My health hasn't been anything to brag about this winter, as I've told her."

"She'll probably stop by, if she can," Tommie says.

"It would be out of her way," Jane says, shaking her head. "I don't want to be a bother to her, but you'd think if she took the trouble to write she could spare me a day or two. What I don't understand, though, is why she didn't ask me for anything. Not even a dollar. It's strange."

"She probably just wanted to keep you up with her doings," Tommie suggests. Willie glances at him, but doesn't say anything.

"Well, you read it for yourself and see what you can make of it." She looks at him over the top of her eyeglasses, which are secured around her neck with a gold chain. Tommie knows the look as one of worry, but he cannot help reading accusation in it.

He peruses the letter and nods, as though he doesn't already know its contents. Then he mentions the nice weather and asks Willie about the crops, and he repeats a story Mr. Evans told him about a farmer who worked for his father. Animals kept eating the front row of beans, so Mr. Evans's father told him, "Looks like you should quit planting that front row." The farmer nodded and turned, and about halfway back to the field he suddenly got it. He chuckled so hard his shoulders went to his ears.

"You're in a fine humor today," Willie tells his brother. "Lawyering suits you, I believe." He smiles and takes in his brother's entire countenance in a glance, and Tommie knows he is being scrutinized. Did something ring false in his speech or his manner? After dinner he talks to Aunt Jane for a while, then goes out to the machine shop where he finds Willie sharpening mower blades. He likes watching his brother work. Though manual labor never had appeal for Tommie, he takes comfort in the skill and care with which his brother goes about the job.

"Let me take over for you," Tommie says.

Willie looks surprised but yields his stool. Right away, Tommie cuts his thumb on the blade. "I'm out of practice," he says, sucking the crescent of blood. He lights a cigarette to steady his hands, leans back, and mentions the cottage in Little Plymouth he's interested in. If he could just get to that point, he thinks—say, a month from now—then maybe the storm will have passed.

And he's there, smoking a cigarette and talking about the house he wants to buy, when he hears the back porch bell ringing and Jane hollering, "Boys, oh, Lord, boys come quickly."

Justice Richardson heads over to the cheap boardinghouse where Mr. Madison and his brother-in-law have spent the night. He goes in and finds the brother-in-law, Lillian's uncle, finished with breakfast and ready to go. The father seems in no hurry to get out to the almshouse and identify his dead daughter. Nor does he seem particularly distressed. He's a stout man, with a thick sinewy neck, white hair, and a grizzled beard, his hands strong and worn as leather. His wrinkled necktie bunches his collar so that when he swallows, his Adam's apple bobs up as if for air. Walker is thin, clean-shaven, and at least a decade younger than Madison. Both of them wear old, cracked boots.

When they get there, the almshouse superintendent pulls back the sheet. Mr. Madison nods and says it's his girl. The uncle stands back and peeks, while gripping tight to his slouch hat. A kind of strangulated noise issues from his throat like a rusty hinge, and he smears the corner of his eye with a thumb knuckle. Richardson regards them both—you never know how people are going to react to the sight of a dead loved one.

He asks them if they know anything about a scar above the girl's left breast.

Madison nods. "A fever blister when she was little," he says. "Didn't heal properly." He's not inclined to say much more, but Richardson accepts the identification now as complete. He takes the two men into an office, gives them coffee, which only Madison takes, and asks about Lillian. Mr. Madison tells him that she was not yet twenty-one years old. She lived with her aunt Jane in Little Plymouth for about five years starting when she was fourteen. She moved there because she had become "difficult to handle." She went to Bruington Academy for a while, but Mr. Madison and his wife thought it was not good for her, that she was putting on airs, and so they wouldn't let Jane send her back. Then, not quite two years ago, she moved in with her grandfather and uncle, who lived only a few miles from her parents.

While Madison talks, the uncle, George Walker, sits there fiddling with his hat and looking forlorn and out of place. Richardson instinctively trusts him more. When asked about Willie Cluverius, they agree that he and Lillian were fond friends. "And were they intimate?" Richardson asks. Madison seems to take offense at the question, while Walker only looks puzzled.

"Were they sweethearts that you were aware of?"

"Not that I was aware of," Walker says. "No sir."

Madison adds, "She was well brought up. She wouldn't let a man do her just anyway he pleased."

"Are you suggesting she was raped?"

"I'm not suggesting anything."

"I know this is hard on you, Mr. Madison," Richardson says. "But I'm trying to get at what happened. She was pregnant, as you know. The coroner suspects she was murdered." He lets that sink in. Madison sits back in his chair, seemingly unsurprised. Walker tightens his lips as though he's about to cry; he glances toward the door. "Now is there anyone you suspect could be responsible for either getting her pregnant or wishing her dead, or both?" The two men shake their heads, Madison with his hat still on. "She was not romantically involved with anyone you know of?"

"I don't know of anybody except that Tommie Cluverius."

"*Tommie* Cluverius?"

"Yeah, he wudn't particularly fond of me. Seems like he took every opportunity to shun me. He's high and mighty with me. I don't know why." He suddenly looks irritable, the broken veins on his nose going purple and his Adam's apple bulging.

"Her cousin Cary mentioned a Willie Cluverius. Is this the same person?"

"No, that's the brother. Tommie's the lawyer."

"Do you know his middle name?"

"Judson."

Richardson takes some notes, then directs his attention to Mr. Walker. "Were they sweethearts, Miss Madison and this Tommie Cluverius?"

"No sir," Walker says, looking puzzled, "not as I know of. Many a night he spent at air house on court days. I'd say they was good friends, but I can't speculate on the rest."

"So there was an opportunity for a seduction to occur?"

"She slept in a room by herself," Walker says. "He slept with me when he stopped by air place. There was a empty room between."

"Locked?"

"No. It has the old string latches, but 'twasn't locked, ever." Walker thinks a minute. "I remember twiced he got up in the middle of the night. I don't remember him coming back to bed. In the morning he said he had bowel trouble."

"I see, but were they alone together?"

"They might a went out walking together once or twiced, and I believe they went riding once, with a picnic. I wasn't a-watching them every second of every day and night, but I don't think he'd a-done such a thing. He cared too much for her."

"All right, thank you, Mr. Walker, and was there anyone else who saw her that you know of?"

Walker glances at his brother-in-law, then at the hat in his hands. "Not that I know of. But she did write to some fellers." Madison stiffens in his chair, then leans and spits a gout of brown juice into Richardson's brass spittoon. His eyes are small, red-rimmed, and hard for Richardson to see into.

"Did you have something you wanted to add?" Richardson asks.

"No, I do not," Madison snorts. "But that Cluverius boy, now, he's the one you ought to bring in here and question."

"Thank you for your advice, Mr. Madison," Richardson says, trying not to take too authoritative a tone with the father of a dead girl. But it bothers him that the man seems unsurprised that his daughter ended up in a reservoir. "Is there anything else either of you would like to tell me about Miss Madison?"

"She was a good girl," Madison says, "and didn't ought to end up like that." He spits again, wiping his mouth with the back of his hand. "Well, I 'spect we'd best be going on. When should we come back for her?"

"Shouldn't be more than a couple of days," Richardson says. "Let me know if you need any more help with the arrangements."

"It's all taken care of, but there won't be any stone right off." He looks square at Richardson as though challenging him. "That'll come in due time."

In the early afternoon Richardson writes out an arrest warrant and tells Officer Birney they're going on a little trip. In his late twenties, Birney has slicked-back hair and a boyish face. He speaks with a lisp, but Richardson has his eye on him for promotion to sergeant. "He's liable to be slippery," Richardson says. Birney raises his eyebrows, and Richardson says, "I mean with words. He's a lawyer. I don't think he'll run off. He's from good people down there. We'll just bring him in quick, no fanfare. If we can get him to say anything, that's fine too."

It doesn't feel exactly right to Richardson, yet he has no choice but to haul this Cluverius in. The envelope with his name on it—unless there's some other T. J. Cluverius out there—and her father's and uncle's statements point in this one direction. He'd thought he'd seen enough to last a career, but he has to admit curiosity about this fellow. The time to move is now, before the press gets any more excited and before Wren digs up something new and shows his hand. Whether Cluverius is really guilty—well, that's not for him to decide.

❧

CHAPTER EIGHT

JANE'S SERVANT, Lewis, has been with the Tunstall family since long before the war. He has slowed down in the past ten years, but every so often he likes to rise early and walk up to King and Queen Courthouse, fish in a bend in the river there, pick up Mrs. Tunstall's mail, and catch a ride home. This generally means her mail arrives early. As it does on Wednesday, along with the Tuesday *Dispatch*.

Jane has forgotten about the reservoir girl until she sees another article about her in the Tuesday paper. She runs her eyes over it, but suddenly stops at the name Fannie Lillian Madison.

At that moment Tommie is out in the machine shop telling Willie about the house he wants to buy. It's then that they hear the back porch bell ringing and Jane hollering.

"What's gotten into her waffle iron?" Willie asks.

Tommie shakes his head, afraid to move from where he sits. "She probably wants us to catch a snake. Remember that rat snake she found in Miss Hillyard's room? I thought she'd found Miss Hillyard in there with her head cut off the way she was hollering. I still don't understand how it came to be in her hatbox." Willie laughs and gives his brother a coy look. "I knew it was you all along," Tommie says.

"No, you didn't."

"And you made up that story about snakes being attracted to round places where they can nest. I ought to tell Aunt Jane right now."

"I wish you would go up there and see what the commotion's about. She doesn't sound right."

Tommie heads on up to the house. When he gets to the yard and sees his aunt on the back steps shaking the newspaper as if there were bugs in it, he begins to run. He knows what it is. He knows.

She gives him the paper and he devours the article. "They haven't said it's definitely her. Who are these Dunstans?" he demands.

"I don't know. Sounds like they were neighbors of the Madisons. But why would they say 'Fannie Lillian Madison' if it wasn't her? Tommie, I'm so worried. It just couldn't be her, could it? She was supposed to be in Point Comfort. And, Lord, I just realized something." Tommie does not take his eyes off the paper. "She was the one they said was pregnant. Dead in the reservoir and pregnant. You don't suppose she was—"

"What?"

"Lying?"

"You know she was capable of it," Tommie says. Jane nods, then shakes her head as though she is agreeing to blasphemy. So that he can get away from Jane's hysteria for a minute, Tommie says, "I'll go tell Willie." But his aunt won't let go of him. "Aunt Jane," he says, "you're pale. I'll tell Maria to come get you some aspirin. You need to sit down and catch your breath." He bounds off the porch steps, then takes his time crossing the lawn. Jane calls for him to hurry.

This had to come, sooner or later. So the story has not gone away—the headline was larger, announcing that "the case" remains cloudy. There was no mention of suicide, but neither was there talk of foul play. Yet. It's disturbing news, but not devastating. Tommie forces himself into a mildly alarmed composure—yes, Jane has a right to be upset, but we know nothing definitive yet.

Willie is lubricating the whetstone with a mouthful of tobacco juice and restarting the pedal when Tommie walks in. He glances up as he puts a scythe to the stone, sparks popping off. Tommie waits for him to stop, then goes over and puts a hand on his arm. "Well, don't you want to know what Aunt Jane was fussing about?"

"You'll tell me if it's important."

"It might be. There's an article saying Lillie was the girl they found in the reservoir."

Willie pulls the blade and sits holding it as if he doesn't know what it is. "In Richmond?"

"That's what it said."

"But her letter was written Saturday. That dudn't make sense."

"No, it doesn't, but it's got Jane in a state, as you can imagine."

Willie looks at his brother. "What do you make of it?"

"I don't know what to think. They must've made a mistake somehow."

"You didn't see her up there, did you?"

"I told you I haven't seen her. Have you?"

"You know I haven't. What are you all nettled about?"

"I'm just worried is all." Tommie picks up an oiled whipsaw and flexes the snout, the hook teeth grinning at him.

Willie waits for his brother to go on, but nothing comes. "I can't believe she'd kill herself. That doesn't seem like her. She's too lighthearted."

"You never know what women are capable of doing."

Willie spits again on the stone, then he squats down, and

Tommie sees that his brother's face has turned gray. His eyes are huge and he can't catch his breath. He's saying the name, Tommie knows he is, but he's too quiet to hear. "Lillie. It couldn't be Lillie, could it?" Now Willie looks at his brother like he's going to be sick.

"I don't think so," Tommie says, returning his brother's gaze, "but the paper says it is."

The smell of Lewis and Maria's stove curls through the afternoon air—the cooking greens and wood smoke redolent of home. Tommie looks out past the shop door, where robins dart through the softening air, full of purpose. When Tommie and his brother were younger their father pointed to a flock of blackbirds, swirling like a seine, and told them that when he was a boy the sky would sometimes go black with pigeons for days—trees would be stained white, and you could fire one time into them and get enough birds for a week. "Things change," he told them, but he didn't seem happy about it.

"We better go back up and see if Aunt Jane's all right," Willie says, and Tommie follows him up to the house. Tommie tries not to think about Lillie, but the more he tries the more she reappears in his mind, like the ghost girl along the driveway, and his head feels like it's on fire, while the rest of his body is cold and numb, a single bead of sweat sliding down his rib cage.

By mid-afternoon Richardson and Birney, dressed in civilian clothes, are making their way up the Trace from the Mattaponi ferry landing. Richardson has hired a sturdy four-seated drag with plenty of leg room for the occasion, along with two horses and a driver. Birney asks if it wouldn't be a good idea for them to stop by the courthouse in King and Queen and enlist the help of the local constable. "Jutht in cathe."

"Just in case what?" Richardson says, regarding his companion, whose scraggly mustache only accentuates his baby face.

"Jutht to greathe the wheelth."

Richardson sits back to think that one over for a while, the drag jostling over rain ruts, its wheels grinding out another mile. "Good thinking, Birney," he finally says. "He'll likely know the best way to approach these people. No point getting anybody alarmed. It's an extra couple of hours, but it's probably worth it." Birney nods, rolling a toothpick around his mouth and looking out at the greening fields.

Constable Oliver is somewhat less than happy to accompany them on account of missing the supper Mrs. Oliver has promised him—a chicken potpie. But when he hears the destination is the Tunstall place, he perks up. "She'll invite us in for a bite, sure as I'm sittin' here." He loads himself into the drag and back down the Trace they go.

"I don't think he'll make a run for it," Richardson tells Birney when they get there. "But why don't you go around the back." He winks. "Just in case."

Oliver heaves himself up the front steps and knocks on the door. Willie answers, his napkin in his hand. "Hello, Mr. Oliver," he says. "Somebody get out of your jail again?"

"No, Willie, worse than that," Oliver huffs. "He'll tell you." He thumbs to Richardson coming up behind him.

"Are you Mr. Thomas Judson Cluverius of King and Queen County?" Richardson asks.

"That's my brother, what is it—"

But Tommie is already there. "I'm Tommie," he says.

"Mr. Cluverius, I'm Justice Richardson from Richmond. I have a warrant here for your arrest on the charge of murder in the first degree." An audible gasp issues from the dining room.

"Whaa?" Tommie noises. "That's ridiculous." He looks from

Richardson to his brother to Mr. Oliver and back to Richardson. "What do you mean murder in the first degree?"

"I'm sure I don't have to tell you, being a lawyer, what murder in the first degree means."

"Now, just a minute here—" Willie cuts in, his chest puffing out.

Tommie puts a hand on his arm. "That's all right. Why don't we go sit down and sort this thing out? There's obviously some mistake that's been made."

"Who is he accused of murdering?"

"Fannie Lillian Madison of King William County." Richardson pauses, waiting for a response. The room has gone silent, the only noise a stifled sob from the other room. "I wondered why you didn't ask me that right off," he says, looking at both brothers now, as if trying to figure out a puzzle.

"I did," Tommie protests. "I asked you what the charge was." He looks to Willie for confirmation, and Willie nods.

"No, son, you didn't. I had to tell you myself."

"Yes," Tommie says, backing down, "you followed proper procedure."

"I'm going to have to bring you in to stand trial before a police court," Richardson says.

Aunt Jane has struggled to her feet, and now, ashen-faced but smiling bravely, she appears at the dining room entrance. "Gentlemen," she says in her most dignified and gracious manner, "how do you do, sirs? Whom do I have the pleasure of addressing?" Her eyes are not merry crescents but open and fearful. Richardson removes his hat and introduces himself. "I can assure you," she tells him, "that you are making an egregious error." Softening now that she has his attention, she says, "Won't you join us? We were just sitting down to supper. I'm sure we can help you with whatever you need."

"Mrs. Tunstall, I'm afraid we're going to have to take Mr. Cluverius tonight."

"Tonight?" Jane replies. "But whatever for? My nephew is the finest young man in the county. They both are. Why—" Her lips begin trembling. "You're welcome to spend the night, and if there's courthouse business you need to attend to, they'll be happy to go with you."

"We're not taking him to the courthouse, ma'am. We're bringing him to Richmond."

Jane looks stricken. She reaches for the door frame to steady herself, but, try as she might, she cannot make herself look at Tommie or Willie.

"The crime occurred there, Aunt Jane," Tommie explains.

At that moment Birney comes in, gun drawn. "Whath the matter?" he asks.

"Everything's fine, here," Richardson says. "Put that away."

"You can at least stay for supper," Jane insists.

"Well, I don't see where that would hurt," Richardson says. "We probably won't get further than the courthouse tonight anyway. Much obliged." He bows his head in a courtly way and Jane leads them into the dining room, Mr. Oliver following his belly just behind Jane.

"I'll just set some extra places," Jane says. "Mr. Richardson, you take Miss Hillyard's place, beside me. She's visiting her niece in Gloucester." The men take seats while she busies herself, passing platters of sliced ham and cucumber, biscuits and gravy. Oliver tucks into a piled-high plate, while the two officers take modest amounts. Tommie tries to finish what's on his plate, but ends up just pushing most of it around with his fork.

Aunt Jane brings Lillian's letter and hands it to Richardson. "You see," she says, "it couldn't be Lillie."

Richardson pulls out his spectacles and begins bending the wires behind his ears; he seems impressed by the letter. "Would it be all right if I took this?" he asks.

"If it'll help exonerate my nephew."

"I only want to get at the truth, ma'am," Richardson says, looking over his spectacles.

"Can I have your word you won't lose it?"

"You have my solemn word, and I'll write you a receipt as well."

"What makes you so sure it's her?" she presses.

"Her father came up and identified her."

"Her father? Ppfff—." Jane makes a dismissive noise but is disinclined to contradict a father's identification of his own daughter. "But what could you possibly have on my nephew?"

Richardson shoots a glance at Tommie, who only returns the look, with a boyish smile, before shifting his eyes elsewhere. Then Richardson meets Willie's stonewall gaze and has the distinct feeling that if the young man had a weapon nearby there would be trouble. He wonders if indeed he is not arresting the wrong brother, yet Tommie seems a little too innocent. There is something disconcerting about the whole affair, though he cannot put his finger on it. It is possible that both these young men were involved. He can only bring in one right now, but he'll come back out for the other if he has to.

Seeing the gravity and sufferance on Richardson's face, Tommie suddenly feels sick to his stomach. He glances out the window at the fleeting light of day, the pale, hopeful blue of early spring shading into evening.

Mr. Oliver keeps an eye on the plate of corn bread, and Jane— who would notice what her guests needed even if there were a dead body in the room—passes it over. He helps himself to more cold roast beef and beans. Thank God for Oliver, Tom-mie thinks, or the situation would be unbearable. These men are going to take me away from my family this very night. And then a horrible thought occurs to him. *I might never see this place again.* He banishes it from his mind, and bites his lower lip to contain his fear. He imagines excusing himself and then disappearing out the back door. He could take Willie's sorrel and be at the Clifton ferry in fifteen minutes. With luck he would beat them there, but then what? Try to hide in some barn? Richmond—that would be better. He could disappear in the city, where no one would expect him to be. He might as well announce to everybody that he's guilty. He'll tell these policemen something later—or better yet, wait and tell his lawyer. Yes, that's the thing. Meanwhile, he will have to trust God to see him through. And so he sits there waiting, trying to counter the inquisitive looks of Richardson and Birney with bland, friendly smiles.

The rest of the short-lived meal is eaten in near silence, end-ing abruptly when Richardson slips his watch from his pocket and announces that they should be leaving.

"I'll just go up and get a few things," Tommie says.

"You don't mind if Mr. Birney goes up there with you?" Rich-ardson asks.

"Not at all. Come on, Mr. Birney," he sings out, "you can help me pick out my traveling kit. Don't worry, Aunt Jane, I won't be taking much, because I won't be gone long."

Aunt Jane tries to give Richardson a five-dollar bill for the trip, but Richardson dismisses her firmly. "Ma'am, the common-wealth of Virginia takes care of our expenses."

"Very well," she says, straightening her spine, "I'll give it to my nephew."

Tommie comes down and reaches into the vestibule closet for his overcoat. Seeing mud on the one he wore in Richmond, he opts instead for a reversible coat, light on one side, dark on the other. He picks up his low-crowned gray slouch hat, but when Willie sees him fingering a tear in the crown he brings him one of his own—a brown version of the same hat. Willie leans in and says, "You take care of yourself. I'm going horseback for Mr. Evans right away." Richardson notes the whispered remarks but cannot make them out.

Aunt Jane hugs him tight, not letting go until he pulls back. "I don't understand what's happening," she says. "This makes no sense atall." He gives her what reassurance he can, and she hands him the five-dollar bill, as well as a twenty-dollar gold piece. She tries to say something, but has to stop and dab her nose with a handkerchief.

"I'll be home before you know it," he tells her.

Everything is happening so fast, Tommie thinks there must be something else he should do or say. Richardson has been keeping his eye on him like a sternly disapproving master, watching for any possible slipup, as if he can smell the fear palpable in the room like some desperate, befouled animal. Tommie already feels himself a captive, already knows that strange mixture of terror and relief.

"We've got to go," Richardson says.

And soon they are rolling north along the Trace, the drag's torchlights casting weird shadows against the dusky woods. Tommie sits beside Mr. Oliver, facing the two officers; through the little window between them he can see the road unwinding back toward where they've come. "What evidence do you have against me," Tommie says, "if I might ask?"

"I'm not allowed to say," Richardson replies. His face is a death mask, long shadows beneath eye sockets.

"Well, I can tell you now, I was in Richmond over the weekend, but I know nothing about any murder."

"You knew the episode took place in Richmond."

"Yes, I saw it in the paper."

"And you want to know what we found?"

"Looks like I'll need to prepare a defense."

"Do you want to make a statement when we get up to the courthouse?"

Tommie thinks a minute. "No," he says, "I believe I'll wait and confer with my lawyer."

"Suit yourself," Richardson says. Birney nods in a pleasant way, then looks down so as not to stare. It is a long hour, relieved only by Mr. Oliver's account of a robber who broke out because, he claimed, he hated the food so much he'd rather go back to his wife's cooking. Tommie laughs heartily at the story, Richardson watching him in the gloomy light. A nice-looking young man, Richardson thinks. And well-spoken. Could he have killed that girl? He glances to Tommie's hands, but they are hidden under a warming blanket. It *is* cold out. But Richardson has already noticed the scratches.

· CHAPTER NINE ·

TOMMIE'S VISITS to Garolami's and Lizzie Banks's became a habit. Every few weeks he would scrape together what money he had—from Aunt Jane's gifts (every week a dollar or two tucked into a letter) and what he could borrow—and went, as often as not by himself, down to Locust Alley. He rarely asked for Gretchen, preferring instead Tyler's girl from the first night, an Italian beauty named Maddalena with long legs and a flowing peignoir. He liked wrapping her silky black hair around her neck and whispering in her ear all the most vulgar desires and imagery that had burdened his mind since his last visit. Sometimes he would spend the remainder of his hour reading Blackstone's *Commentaries* or another law book—having recently switched his course of study from English to a more practical subject— with her lying prone beside him, as if to soak the dry pages in the sweet musk of sex. Or he might read to her from Keats or Poe—it didn't matter, for she understood little more than the inflection and the rhythm.

It was hard to understand why Tyler didn't want to go with him every time, nor why there was not a line outside at all hours of the day. He thought if he had the money he would certainly go every week, if not more often. And yet he wanted more. He wanted to have a regular girl he could take out for a stroll like other young gentlemen. He and Tyler would sometimes go up to the old reservoir on nice Sundays and promenade around the gravel walkway. A few men had young ladies on their arms, and it was rumored that couples sometimes sneaked into the reservoir grounds after dark for "virginal sacrifices."

Back at home on holidays, he courted Nola, but he pictured her more as a wife than a paramour, and he saw nothing wrong in having both. According to Gretchen and Maddalena, lots of men did, men with the highest reputations.

Nola was flat-chested and, most noticeably, had large slate blue or gray eyes—he could not decide which, though it seemed to depend on the light. Or perhaps she could change them as easily as she changed from a sympathetic manager of new stable hands to a businesslike purchaser of dry goods, unmoved by any salesman's story of hard times. Her eyes would linger catlike on one thing at a time before moving on, as though disapproving of what she saw. Tommie imagined that her beauty was the kind that would not last much beyond her youth—her mother had the same inquiring eyes, as well as the withered, disappointed look of a once vain woman.

Sometimes he and Nola would just walk in her shady garden and talk about their friends at school; other times they would go out to Heartquake Creek and sit on the mossy banks eating cold chicken and reading aloud to each other. They went one Sunday afternoon with Lillian and Willie down to the Mattaponi. It was a soft and warm day in early summer, just after Tommie's third year of college. Nola was reading aloud from a religious novel by Edward Payson Roe: "He wanted once and for all to satisfy himself of her vanity and frailty, to prove that goodness is accidental, only a matter of not having been tempted." A raucous heron flapped from a sycamore, and Nola stopped.

There was a little boat tied to a cypress stump along the shore, and Lillie announced that she wanted to try her hand at rowing. She claimed to have rowed many times, but she appeared unsteady as Willie handed her in. She gathered her skirts around her legs while he got in and rowed out to the middle of the river, within easy shouting distance from shore. The river was smooth and gentle and not much over head deep. Nola and Tommie watched with amusement—Tommie shading Nola with a parasol—as the others went to some pains to reposition themselves without upsetting the boat. Now Lillie took her turn at the oars. There was laughter and splashing, as Lillie, pulling too hard on one side, made the boat spin in a circle.

Willie, on his knees, tried to show Lillie how to dip and pull, his hand on the oar just below hers. Lillie seemed to lose patience and, getting into a crouch, stood as though to get back into the bow. One moment her hand was on the gunwale, steadying herself. The next moment she was falling backward into the water. She disappeared entirely, leaving nothing but a lavender hat floating on the surface. Willie jumped in after her.

What seemed like several seconds went by. Then two heads came up, and amid the coughing came Lillie's high, vibrant laughter. Willie swam her and the boat in, then carried her over to the blanket and set her down. "I guess I should learn how to swim," she said, laughing.

The young men were apologetic about not taking the proper precautions with a lady, while Nola fussed about, bundling Lillie in the blanket, and saying there was nothing to be done now except hurry home and hope she didn't catch her death. "I don't see that it's a laughing matter," she said, her eyes holding first Lillie's wet skirts and then Willie—not exactly blaming him (for how could she?) so much as asking him why Lillie behaved the way she did, laughing where she herself would have been mortified.

"Don't be silly," Lillie said. "It's warm and I'll be fine." She looked at the others as though they were crazy to suggest cutting short the outing on account of a little mishap. "Willie, you wanted to go swimming, go on. You too, Tommie. We'll go hunt for lady's slippers."

The young men stripped off their shirts and shoes and went wading out into the river. They swam to the other side before they deemed it proper to turn around, and by then the girls were somewhere out of sight. They skimmed oyster shells for a while, the day's excitement making them little boys again. Tiring of this activity, they floated on their backs and smeared pluff mud on their chests as they'd heard the Powhatan did downriver. A fish slapped the surface of the water, and Tommie was reminded of his baptism in the little pond behind the church the summer they moved in with Aunt Jane. Reverend Ryland had dunked both of them, and he had slipped out of the Reverend's grip and stayed under a moment, opening his eyes underwater and noticing the way the green river grasses fanned out like tresses of hair. Willie had asked if he'd seen angels down there.

"Remember what I told you I'd seen under the water?" he asked Willie now. It just came out. He hadn't intended to remind his brother of something they never talked about.

"Sure, I do. You said you saw Charles."

"That's right, because the river grass reminded me of how I'd thought of him, somehow gone down beneath the riverbed."

Willie shook his head in a friendly way, then dove forward and tackled Tommie into the water. They began to wrestle, and Tommie suddenly felt the need to compete with his brother. The other day he had ridden part way with Lillie to her tutoring, when he was going to see Nola. She had asked him about a scrape he'd alluded to in a letter to Aunt Jane. He had been robbed leaving Locust Alley late one night and ended up with a cut on his face. Lillian wanted details.

"It's unladylike to be interested in ugly things," he told her.

She laughed. "Mr. Proud," she said, riding off without a backward glance, posting straight-backed in her saddle.

He called for her to slow down. "Who's proud now?" But she ignored him.

Now at the river he thrashed against his brother. But within a few short minutes Willie had Tommie in a bear hug from behind.

"Lillie's a tart," Tommie said. He didn't know why he'd said it, other than to make Willie let go, though there was also something about Lillie's flouting of convention, about the idea of her disrobing in the forest like a woodland nymph, that bothered and aroused him. Willie squeezed so tightly Tommie felt his eyeballs engorging—he couldn't breathe another word, he thought his ribs might actually crack. All he could do was try to claw his brother's hands away.

"Say that again and I'll kill you," Willie said.

Then they heard a shout and saw Nola waving a handkerchief. When they got back to the shore, Nola told them that she and Lillie were going on back home. The young men made vigorous protests, but now it was Nola who was firm that they were perfectly all right walking the mile home by themselves. Lillie had a yellow primrose bud in her newly braided hair. She appeared to have yielded to Nola's bossiness—perhaps to show Nola she was indifferent about gaining the boys' attention, Tommie thought, or maybe she'd simply tired of it herself.

That evening Tommie stood out in the yard smoking a cigarette in the dark, and when Lillie came up from the barn with a pail of milk he spoke to her.

"Oh!" she cried, setting the pail down. "Look what you made me do."

She peered up at him, but he couldn't see her eyes well enough to make out what expression was in them. "Do you think I should marry Nola?" he asked her.

She thought a minute. "You've been standing out here waiting to ask me that?"

"Do you mind?"

"No, I don't mind. And, no, I don't think you and Nola should marry. Not yet. You're too young, both of you. Well, she's not. But you—you act all grown up, but you're not."

"How do you mean?"

"You're just not ready, is all. If you're in love with anybody, it's yourself."

This annoyed Tommie, and he took ahold of her wrist and said she was a sassy little thing and somebody ought to punish her.

"It won't be you," she said. "I've seen you studying me, Tommie. What are you thinking about?"

"Why can't I look at you?"

"You know good and well why. Because of your brother."

"I didn't know you'd gotten engaged. Here I was thinking you were just waiting for somebody to come along and steal your heart." He sniffed in, as though taking the words back.

"I ought to slap you," she said. She stood there breathing hard, staring up at him, seeing everything he was made of, and Tommie could feel the heat and emotion radiating from her fierce little body.

He bent over and kissed her lightly on the corner of her mouth. She returned the pressure just enough to let him know she didn't mind. "You're not at all like your brother," she said. "He's good and honest. But you—I don't know what you are. You just want what he has."

Tommie took ahold of her upper arm, gently enough that she could have pulled away if she'd wanted to. "You don't know a thing, Lillie," he said. She stood like a caught animal, but she didn't try to leave. He let go. "I can't stop thinking about you," he said. She said something about the pine trees swaying in the wind, and he said, "I don't give a damn about the pine trees. Did you hear what I said?"

"Yes, I did, Tommie. I don't know that you should've said it though. I don't think it's even true."

"I swear it is."

"You shouldn't swear. It's against the Bible."

"I don't care if it is," he said. "I wish I was in love with Nola, but I don't think I am."

"Then you should tell her that yourself," she said. She picked her pail up and hurried off into the house. The fact that he'd kissed his brother's girl didn't seem wrong—there had never been a time when they didn't use and wear each other's things, and until recently there had never been a third person who shared secrets with just one of them. He was only doing what seemed right and fair.

On another dreamy afternoon by the river, a somnolent breeze to cool them, Willie was fanning Nola with her folding Chinese fan, its mythical river and green mountain swishing up and down, up and down.

Tommie was toying with Lillie's tight sausage curls, and nobody cared because they were under the spell of "Lycidas" from Nola's reading: "He must not float upon his watery bier unwept."

Then somebody brought up Charles, and Tommie told how he imagined him going under—drawn to his own image on the dark surface of the water. He talked as they sat by the river, and it was easy, Tommie felt, for in that moment they were all in love. With each other? With life? It didn't matter. They were so young and ripe and filled with passion they could bring the dead into their sacred unity. It was as though they were drunk without drinking anything stronger than lemonade. Someone mentioned the nebular hypothesis, and they went on about how everyone was spun off from that earliest dawn of cosmic energy and some-day they would return to it.

Tommie focused on a delta of sweat on Nola's neck as she laid her head in his lap, and he thought of the river of warm blood just beneath the surface and how they were all rivers, dis-crete yet connected each to the other, and the mystery of life seemed within grasp. The rebukes and slights they'd given each other had slipped away like shed skins, and all that was left was a perfect tranquillity among them, extending outward. They were profoundly happy and in love, really, with everyone in the world. Tommie pictured Willie and Lillie together in a blissful embrace—he was happy for them and at the same time aware of his desire for her, and there was no accompanying guilt or frus-tration, only a feeling of peace and harmony. A breeze feathered the soft leaves overhead. It was as if they were afraid to move, afraid of upsetting the spell of those few happiest moments.

That evening Tommie met Lillie outside the barn, and they kissed for the first time in a month—a lingering, yearning kiss, broken off by the sound of a fox screeching in the woods. She said, "Are you in love with me?"

"No, but I love you," he said. "But maybe I'm in love with you too. Does it matter?"

She gave him a winsome look, then went up on her toes and kissed him on the mouth. "I'll turn myself into a goat-girl so you can't have me," she said. "I'll be only half yours."

"I'll have you any way I can," he said. So without her breaking off with Willie, nor he with Nola, they began to court each other in the dark, amid the pulsing trill of frogs and crickets.

Later in the summer Tommie began clerking for Mr. Evans, traveling in Aunt Jane's old rockaway buggy up to King and Queen Courthouse three times a week to help with copying documents and digging through law books. He was appointed assistant superintendent of Olivet church, and was working harder than ever and getting headaches from eye strain. "If you don't quit reading so late at night," Aunt Jane told him, "you're going to ruin your eyes."

He would ride up to Nola's once a week, usually on Sunday afternoons for garden walks, during which she would ask how his work was going and remind him to make a good impression on everybody he came across, because "the best way to get along in business, Daddy says, is to get everybody to like you."

He kissed her on the mouth once when she was being overly sententious, and when he pulled away she gave him a condescending smile and went on with her point. "I know you're a very decent and hardworking man, but you could also try to cultivate a taste in the finer things."

"That's amusing, Nola," he said, "seeing as how I studied literature in college."

"What's bothering you today, Tommie?" she asked. "You're ten thousand miles away." He reached into a paper package in his pocket and extracted a cigarette. "If you have to smoke, couldn't you smoke a cigar or a pipe like a grown man?"

He kicked the gravel with his toe and said, "I'm having a hard time pleasing you."

"I'm sorry," she said. "I'm worried over Mother's health, you know. She's been so sick, and now I'm afraid I'm taking it out on you. But I think you've become very distant lately, and I don't know why. Am I so hard to be around?"

"No, you're beautiful to look at, and I enjoy your company, same as always."

"I'm wondering if that's really true. I've been thinking, Tommie, of returning your ring to you." She twisted her ruby ring with her thumb, and lifted her thin face just so. "Isn't there someone you'd rather give it to?" She closed her eyes for a long beat and he glanced at the ring he'd given her at the beginning of the summer. He'd missed her, and since many of his friends were getting engaged to girls back at home and he too wanted to know where he stood with her, he had given her a promissory ring. Aunt Jane had told him to pick something out of her jewelry box, and he selected a simple gold band set with a small ruby. "Would you consider marrying me sometime?" he'd asked, and she'd replied that she would. It was more of a promise to become engaged than an actual engagement, which suited them both, as she had made clear she would never marry a man who was not already embarked on a career and he was still unsure whether he could be happy with her. But the thought of her returning his ring made him feel panicked.

"Who do you mean?"

"I'm not thinking of anybody. Are you?"

"I actually was thinking of somebody," he said, biting his lower lip. "I was thinking about Aunt Jane and how she used to wear her hair down her back and ride astride."

Nola smiled tolerantly and said that she was sure his aunt made quite a picture in her day. "Are you trying to tell me you want me to be improper?"

"I'm not trying to tell you anything, Nola. I just was thinking of her, and how different she was. And how it's all right for some people to be different, but not for others. Why do you think that is?"

"I don't know, Tommie. God gives us all different gifts, and you can't go against what you're made of."

"Why not?"

"It's just not right."

"Why does Ecclesiastes tell us to be not righteous overmuch?"

"Oh, Tommie, why do you think such strange things? Sometimes you worry me. If you had your brother's even temperament, you'd be the perfect man."

"And if you had Lillian's bright eyes, you'd be . . . I'm sorry," he said suddenly. "I didn't mean it, I was just flustered."

She pursed her lips tight. Then, "So I'm not as good as Lillian? What would I be if I had her bright eyes?" He shook his head. "What would I be? I'd like an answer."

"You wouldn't be so critical of me, I guess."

"I see," she said, taking off the ring. "And was there anything else?"

"No, I don't want it back."

"You take it," she demanded. He opened his hand and she dropped it in. He flung it out into the little copse of woods beyond the garden wall. Just like that. Nola stood there staring at him. "Good-bye, Tommie," she said. "Give my best wishes to your family." She crossed her arms, put her head down in a determined way, and walked briskly back to the house.

When he got home, Tommie climbed up onto the long low roof of the stable, where he liked to go when he wanted to be alone with his thoughts. From here he could look down the hill toward the Trace, or, as he did this afternoon, turn around and view the barnyard and then the cornfield and the distant trees. The chickens gathered below him, clucking as though they expected an early feeding. "I'll tell you chickens what happened," he said quietly. He raised his arms as though ready to make a speech, and it amused him that they responded with louder grousing. He got to his feet. "I'll tell you what," he told them, clearing his voice and speaking up. The chickens stretched their necks to attend. "It was a humiliation that no one should have to suffer.

"I'd be within my rights to sue for breach of contract. It'd be the same as if you were promised feed and water for an unspecified length of time—nothing in writing, mind you—and your owner up and decides not to feed you. Not that I'm anybody's chicken. The point I'm trying to make is that there is a clear case for compensation in kind—say, one hundred dollars. That would go a long—"

A high whooping laugh cut him short, and he saw Lillie emerge from around the end of the stable. She said nothing, nor did she look up.

· CHAPTER TEN ·

A T THE COURTHOUSE Richardson sleeps downstairs, leaving Tommie and Birney to share the bed upstairs. The ropes are loose and the ticking scratchy and mildewed. Birney tells him he should hire himself a detective from St. Louis or Chicago. "They have the beth," he says. "You need to prove you were at thuch and thuch a place at thuch and thuch a time, a good detective is your beth bet." Tommie tells him he'll consider it. They bid each other good night, and Birney is soon snoring, an arm flung out across Tommie's chest. Another long and sleepless night, Tommie thinks, trying to steal a few hours' rest.

In the morning Birney offers Tommie a shot of whiskey with his coffee. Tommie doesn't want to give them the wrong impression, but when he sees them each taking some, he changes his mind. "You know," he says, "it *is* mighty cold out, and that's a long ride to Richmond." So Birney adds an amber dollop to Tommie's coffee and gives him a cigar as well.

Soon they're on their way, and at first Tommie tries singing a gospel hymn. His voice quavers, so he tries whistling for a while. He loses heart and trails off, his hands tucked for warmth beneath the blanket. He also doesn't want prying eyes staring at his hurt hand, though Richardson several times looks him up and down as if trying to figure out what he might extract from him in the light of day. Tommie glances away, at one point seeing an old black man and woman waving to them from an oatfield; Tommie waves his left hand and he and the man link eyes for a moment, a brief flicker of recognition in each other's plight.

"You can see my hand if you want," he tells Richardson. "It's cold is why they're under the blanket. See, I scratched it somehow. It's not much."

Richardson looks at the hand with a critical eye. "How did you do that?"

"I don't remember exactly." He sniffs in, as though taking a quick, deep breath.

"I notice you don't wear anything on that charm link of yours," Richardson says, pointing to Tommie's watch chain.

"No," Tommie says. "I used to wear my nice watch key on it, but it got worn out. Now I just use these old steel keys." He pulls two keys out of his pocket and offers them to Richardson, who seems only mildly interested. Then Tommie shows him his gold watch. "It was a graduation present from my aunt."

They take Tommie to the second police precinct, and Birney asks him, in an almost apologetic way, to empty his pockets. Within a few hours Willie arrives with news that Crump and Crump have agreed to represent him. He has never met William Crump, but everybody knows him and his booming voice and illustrious career as legislator, commonwealth's attorney, assistant treasurer for the Confederacy. His son is no slouch as a lawyer and speaker either. God, thinks Tommie, pleased and yet scared that he may actually need the great orator.

"Is there anything you want to tell us?" Richardson asks, "before you go in front of the police court?"

"I'll wait for my counsel," Tommie says.

"That's probably a good idea," Richardson agrees.

Then Birney takes him back to a holding cell and tells him he hopes he won't have to be there too long. Tommie figures that wearing a good suit and a necktie and behaving himself like the educated gentleman he is may go a long way toward getting the whole case thrown out.

While he's trying to eat some thin soup with lumps of fat in it (Willie having gone out to find him something better), William and Beverly Crump arrive and introduce themselves. The elder Crump is the living image of Robert E. Lee, down to his neatly trimmed gray beard and bow tie. Tommie has seen this look in many men of Crump's generation; some wear it better than others, yet he feels immediately comforted by the man's warm handshake and intelligent eyes. He's hale, like Mr. Evans, but shorter, and his gestures are quick and animated. His second chin ripples as he pumps Tommie's hand. The son is quieter but equally attentive and well-mannered. They escort Tommie to a room with a table. "Mr. Evans will be handling most of the case," Crump says, "and Beverly will be assisting."

"What about the newspapers?" Tommie asks. "Once they get wind of my arrest they'll try me and convict me themselves."

"Not much we can do there, son. But we'll give you the best defense we possibly can. You just have to trust us. What do you know about this case?"

"I don't know any more than you do, sir."

"They're gonna want you to go by the almshouse to see the body of that girl. You don't have to and I strongly advise you not to, whether you know anything about it or not."

"I don't know anything about it."

"Fine, then, you'll just have to sit tight, but it may take a while."

"How long?"

"A few weeks, I'd reckon, depending on how long they can stall while they're putting their case together."

"What evidence do they have, if any?"

"Nothing much. It's all circumstantial. There's no eyewitnesses. They found a note they're mighty keen on. They claim she wrote it to you. You know anything about that?" Crump eyes Tommie, sizing him up, almost, thinks Tommie, like a lover, studying everything said and not said. Tommie has the impression that Crump has seen it all and more, and that nothing would shock him.

"Just what I've read in the paper." Tommie looks away from Crump's penetrating sea-green eyes. He could never confide fully in this man, could he? "Like I said, I was in Richmond Friday, but I never saw Miss Madison."

"I wouldn't put it past Wren to concoct something, or pay somebody to say something. But Judge Richardson says he has an envelope with your name on it, from the American Hotel, where she was staying. He's not likely to make any such thing up. How do you reckon he came by that?"

Tommie shrugs. "I wouldn't know. What does the envelope say?"

"Has your name on it, or so he says. Not too many people have your name."

Tommie thinks a minute. "There could be any number of explanations. Perhaps she was planning on sending me something sometime. Or she was just thinking about me for some reason. It doesn't mean I saw her here."

"No, it doesn't. But it dudn't look any too good. It's not signed, and it might or might not be her handwriting, but a jury might look at it and draw some conclusions." Crump waits for Tommie to respond, then goes on in a disarming way, "You should write up a detailed account of all your actions that day and evening. Anybody you spoke to or saw or even think you recognized."

Tommie wants to tell Crump everything now. Last night he told himself that this was the point at which he should make a clean breast of it, just lay it in Crump's hands. But somehow, in the daylight, he feels less afraid of the future than of Crump's judgment: How can he admit to this dignified man and his son, both members of his own profession, that he was involved in such a sordid affair? He can't do it. Anyway, the prosecution doesn't appear to have conclusive evidence. A confession now might be worse than just keeping his mouth shut.

"Tommie," Crump says, "this would be the time to tell us everything you know. We're your friends, so if you have anything to say, unburden yourself. Then we'll figure the best strategy. You know how this works."

"The truth is," Tommie says, "I went to the Dime Museum at Mozart Hall that evening, and then I walked back to my hotel." He gets up and begins pacing the little room, pausing to look out the window to the saloon and livery stable across the street. He begins chewing a nail. "I think it had to be suicide, don't you?"

"It don't matter what I think. Anyway Richardson's sent off for her trunk, and they'll be digging around in there for evidence. Are there any letters or anything that might incriminate you?"

"Not that I know of. She might've saved some I sent her, but they were just friendly. Sometimes I gave her advice about money."

"Son, do you mind sitting down—you're making me nervous." Tommie sits, but one heel goes into a sewing-machine motion. "Well," Crump continues, "once you get us a list of people who can account for your whereabouts that night, this should all go away. We just have to be prepared for what they come up with. Were you and she sweethearts?"

Tommie hesitates. "No," he says. "We were good friends. I think she wanted to be sweethearts, but I was engaged to Nola Bray, so it never came to anything."

Now Crump stands and walks to the window himself. "If this goes to a trial, they're going to have everybody who knew either of you get up in the witness box and say whether you were sweet-hearts. It sounds like at least two people are ready to swear you were."

"There's plenty of people who can swear we weren't."

"Okay, but it's awfully hard to prove a negative. For now, we'll just have to rely on proving where you were on that night. So get busy with that."

Tommie tells them he will, and, with relief, bids them thanks and good-bye. As he leaves, Crump takes Tommie's hand, and, squeezing it, looks briefly but acutely into Tommie's eyes as though for the mystery of life. Then he is suddenly gone.

That night Tommie keeps writing and erasing until a jailer comes around and extinguishes the lanterns. For the night of the thirteenth he writes that he went back to the second show-ing at the Dime Museum, then had oysters at Morgenstern's. He had seen Bernard Henley—perhaps Bernard would only vaguely remember, which would be good. "I saw him there," Tommie imagines him saying, "but whether it was during the afternoon or evening I couldn't say." He doesn't know Bernard all that well—he's practicing law now in Richmond, Tommie thinks. How precise is Bernard's memory? Even remembering the things he himself did on that important day, in their exact sequence and time, is not so easy. He knows what happened, though summoning the details and laying them out on paper is proving nearly impossible.

In the morning Birney and a superior named Sergeant Epps arrive to take Tommie to the city jail for arraignment by the po-lice court. Birney brushes his back off when he comes out of the cell, suggesting Tommie will want to look his best. "Don't mind the people out there," he warns. "They're jutht curiouth."

Tommie squints when he emerges into the morning light, and it is not until the hack is rolling that he realizes all the people gathered along the snowy sidewalk are there for him—they just want even a glimpse of him. The hack travels down Marshall to Fourteenth, then down to Franklin; Epps and Birney get out and hustle Tommie into the jail building. Mr. Wren has staked out a position close to the entrance, his bulky presence a hindrance to their progress. "Good work," he tells Epps in a knowing way, yet carefully studying Tommie as he passes. Epps nods to him in reply.

Mr. Evans is waiting for them in Judge Richardson's office. Tommie shakes his hand and has to clamp his teeth to keep the tears back. "Mr. Evans," he says, "I'm so sorry you have to do this."

"No have to about it," Evans says, glancing at Tommie's face, then away. "It's a privilege. Maybe you'll see me out of a scrape sometime." Then he leans in and in a quieter voice says, "We'll get you cleared in no time, son."

He seems to want Tommie to reassure him, but all Tommie can say is, "I know you will, Mr. Evans. You've always been very kind to me."

Evans nods, then tells Tommie it would be best not to say a word at the arraignment. "You're a good talker, but this time leave it to us."

The courtroom is packed. Tommie recognizes a number of people—young attorneys, men he went to college with, all here to feast their eyes on one of their own caught in a net. There is Sid Aylett, whom he still looks up to, now a lawyer like his father, and Bobby Valentine, and good old James Courtney, still as quiet and mild as ever. He tries to pretend he's playing a part; it's just another mock session, a refresher course. The commonwealth's attorney, a man named Charles Meredith, asks Judge Richardson for a continuance of ten days because of his upcoming cases in the hustings court. Crump objects to this length of time, but after some back-and-forth agrees to March 30. Shouts arise from outside. Someone yells, "Lynch him!" Richardson tells Crump to bring Tommie back to his office to wait for the crowd to die out. A half hour later Birney comes in and says there are more people than ever—hundreds of them, all the way down Mayo to Franklin.

"Let's go then," Epps says. "Before there's even more." With that they rush Tommie outside and into the hack, Birney holding his stick as a warning. People are yelling and hooting and pushing. Somebody spits and it lands on Birney's shoe. "Hang him! Murdering bastard!" From somewhere near the front, a woman's voice: "Why, he's only a boy." Tommie looks up to find her in the seething press of faces. But then he is in the hack and moving down the street.

Tommie was getting along well in his work with Mr. Evans, and Nola and he even patched things up enough for him to be an occasional visitor at her house. She had become engaged to a Richmond banker's son and liked confiding her concerns—the young man spent too much time at the racetrack. Tommie had every hope that, as soon as his prospects allowed, they might become reengaged. It was also near the end of that summer that Lillie announced she was going to live with her grandfather and uncle over in King William.

She came to Tommie first with the news. He was out in the garden picking a few ears of corn for their supper, disappointed with the number of worms he was finding. They'd had too much rain lately. "How about this one?" he said, handing her an especially mealy ear containing two fat green worms. He pretended not to watch her peel back the shucks.

She made a noise of disgust and dropped the ear. "You ought to be ashamed, Tommie," she said.

"Willie thinks it's because Aunt Jane makes him coat the seeds in tar," he said, "so the birds can't get them." He took a bite from a clean ear and offered it to her.

"I've decided I'm going to move in with Grandpa John." She looked up at him with such expectant eyes that he wanted to kiss her forehead as though she were a child. But she had recently told him she did not want to kiss him anymore, that she just couldn't, and after a while he'd quit trying. "They need somebody to help do for them," she said, "and I'll be close enough to home to tutor my little sisters. I've missed them."

"Have you told Aunt Jane and Willie?" Tommie asked.

"I wanted to tell you first," she said. Again she waited. "To see if you would care."

And then he understood, and yet he could not help being cruel. She missed the attention he had given her, her attachment to him growing in proportion to his very lack of attention. "Of course I care," he said. "You're like a sister to me. I'll miss you. But you'll visit, won't you?" He felt warm with pity and a kind of perverse power, and he wanted to fold her in his arms like a dog he had just kicked.

"Don't you want to know why I'm leaving?"

"You just said your grandfather needed somebody to take care of him."

She bit her lower lip and looked at him, blinking as if she were about to cry. "Willie and me are never going to get married, don't you understand that? Don't you talk to him, Tommie?"

"Not about you," he said. "He doesn't talk about you." He hadn't spoken much with Willie all summer—Willie had been away a lot, his work taking him to the far reaches of the county, and when he was home he seemed too tired and distracted for much conversation.

"I don't want to marry him," she said. She gave him a pleading look, holding her arms tight across her chest. Then she darted through the row of corn and disappeared. He stepped through the two rows that formed the edge of the garden and looked up and down the lane separating the garden from the cornfield. Then he saw the stalks moving, their high tassels clattering like paper bells. He dashed forward, calling, "Lillie!" The stalks shivered and he went plunging into a welter of greenness, the stalks and leaves and ripe ears smacking his face and arms. Then he was actually running, through tall corn, dodging this way and that, as if they were in a maddening dream of chasing, or being chased—he could feel Lillie's exhilaration and it urged him on.

He stopped and called for her again. It was quiet. There was a rustling off to his left. "Lillie?" He heard her sniffle, and as slowly as he could he came through the stalks and found her crying quietly. The sky was an almost golden blue at the end of the day, light filtering through the yellow tassels and the pale green shoots. They were out in the middle of the cornfield and he had the feeling they were alone in a vast sea at the beginning of some momentous occurrence. The pollen dust made him sneeze, and she giggled, then sniffed again. "What are you doing?" he said. She gave him a furtive glance, then bolted down an alley. He stood rooted to the ground watching her. She stopped about ten yards away, nearly hidden by the dark jade of the lower leaves like a mythical creature in a jungle. Then with one side step she melted into the next alley. He moved in an identical fashion, carefully, lest a wrong motion scare her off. Again, they regarded each other at opposite ends of a dark green hall. He tried waving. But now she backed up, inventing new rules for her little game, until she was so far down the alley he could not make out her face at all. He started slowly forward, and she turned and ran.

A breeze was up, rattling the stalks, and the air felt suddenly heavier and cooler the way it will before a summer rain. He chased Lillie until he began heaving for breath, then stopped and leaned over, letting the spots clear from his vision. When he got free of the stalks he saw her running toward a vine-covered tumbledown slave cabin between the oatfield and the woods. She glanced back, then slowed to a walk. The wind made her pink skirt wrap around her legs. The light in the west was fading rapidly from plum to liver to black as storm clouds began chasing the blue sky.

He found her sitting on the caved-in step, hands folded in her skirts. The upper corner of the open door frame at her back held a mud daubers' clay organ-pipe nest. Inside the dark cabin, slats of light fell through chinks in the pine-shingled roof to the dirt floor. He sat beside her on the coarse-grained wood. "You don't have to marry Willie," he said.

"Do you still love me, Tommie?" she asked.

He could smell her perspiration and some heavy musk that seemed strange coming from one so small that he could pick her up and carry her home. "Yes," he said, "I'll always love you. You rebuffed me, and you were right to. I'm sorry I confused you." A low rumble of thunder sounded in the distance.

"I kept waiting for you to come to me again, but you've paid me no attention all summer. Willie's a good, kind, strong man, but he's not funny and strange like you. He wouldn't dream of standing on the roof and giving a speech to the chickens. That was the funniest thing I ever saw in my life."

"Aunt Jane didn't think so," Tommie told her, not pleased that he'd made such a lasting impression when he'd thought no one had been watching.

"I could never be happy married to him, knowing that I'd turned you down. He keeps all his tools lined up in perfect order. And he talks nicely to the horses when he harnesses them. I'd trust him with my life. But—" She stopped.

"I'd trust him too," he said.

"He once saved me from a skeleton," Lillie replied. "We were out walking in the swamp and I almost stepped in it. It was a Yankee soldier, with no head. 'How do you think it got that a-way?' I asked him. And he said, 'Somebody must've cut it off.' He says funny things like that without knowing they're funny."

"But why then—"

"I don't know, Tommie. Quit asking me. I'm sitting here with you. Are you trying to make me feel guilty? He was too good for me. Now are you satisfied?"

"And I'm not as good?"

"I thought you were the more serious one, but after a while I saw that wasn't so."

"What do you mean?"

"There's something in you that's not in him. You're neat in the way you dress, but you shade your eyes with your hat."

"What are you talking about?" He pushed his hat up. "Everybody shades their eyes with their hat."

"You're very pious and moral, but I know there's a naughty streak in you a mile wide. I saw that book of dirty poems in your room."

Sid Aylett had given him a copy of *Wisdom for Girls*, a popular book with college boys. "You had no right to go snooping in my room," he told her.

"I wasn't snooping, I was looking for a pencil for Aunt Jane."

He sat back. Rain began to patter on the delicate new leaves all around, then stopped. "What about Nola?" he asked her.

"If it's me you love, you shouldn't marry her, Tommie. That's not right. You know it isn't."

He stood and looked out over the tree line to the west. It was suddenly calm, but there was lightning far away, then faint thunder. Up in the pasture the cows that had gathered under one of their favorite shade trees began moving off toward the barn. "I shouldn't have interfered," he said. "That's what wasn't right."

Now the top leaves in the shade tree, a huge gnarled silver maple, began fluttering. He saw Willie opening the pasture fence to let the cows into the paddock.

"Nola told me she wouldn't marry you if you were the Duke of York."

"Did she?" he said, watching how the tree was beginning to rock in the wind. "She only said that to test you. What did you say?"

"I told her I wouldn't either. I wouldn't marry you for all the tea in Texas." Lillie laughed, spreading her arms out to feel the breeze.

"That must be a lot," he said, laughing with her, envying her simplicity.

Lillie stood, just as a big gust came and whipped the branches of the maple. Thunder cracked much closer now, rumbling in waves all around. "I expect we'd better go," she said.

They started walking toward the house as the rain came. It began pouring all at once. They turned back to the little cabin to wait it out, taking up positions just inside the doorway. Then it commenced to spray across the roof and seep through the cracks. Soon it was running down veins in the plaster walls, exposing more horsehair, and spattering on the hard clay floor. Willie was shouting for them, so Tommie called out to him and waved. He had to jump up and down to be seen. Instead of turning back to the house, though, Willie was running toward them. "We're fine!" Tommie yelled. "Go back."

But he kept coming on. He ran across the pasture, slipping just as he got to the big tree. He picked himself up and ran for the fence and hurdled it with two hands. A shrieking boom came out of the air. The tree limbs seemed to open up, and a brilliant orange stake of electricity leaped from the tree to a jagged bolt out of the clouds. Willie went down, and the air exploded. Tommie began running to him. The entire top half of the tree was lying on the ground beside the trunk.

Willie was on all fours looking back at what had been the shade tree. "You fool," Tommie said. They were halfway between the house and the cabin.

"Lillie," Willie said. The rain and thunder were merciless. He got up and ran down the edge of the oatfield. Tommie chased after him. When they got there they were both wet to the skin. Lillie, huddling in the leaky cabin, wasn't much drier. "Are you all right?" Willie said, looking from Lillie to Tommie.

"Of course we are!" Tommie shouted over the drumming rain.

He gave Tommie another look, as if he was disappointed. Then he began walking back to the house, head down. Tommie went out and stood in front of him. "What are you doing?" he said.

"It doesn't matter," Willie said.

"Then at least run, so you don't get hit."

"I'm not worried." He tried to push past his brother.

"Willie, I'm not stealing your girl."

"It's all right," he said, moving out of Tommie's way. Tommie could have gotten in front of him again, but he knew Willie would have just pushed him or hit him.

Lillie came out and stood beside Tommie in the pouring rain. "Go on up to him," he told her. "Go!" He put a hand on her wet blouse, wanting to hold her and push her both. "Fine then," he said, "I'll go." He hurried along, turning back only once and seeing her trudging along, holding her arms tight to herself, the sky an enormous silver-gray expanse around her. He caught up with his brother and they walked quietly along together. At one point

Willie looked back and, apparently satisfied, kept going, head down. The rain was already slackening by the time they got to the tree. They paused to look at it, then continued on toward the paddock. Tommie was starting to get a chill, but he took his time coming in, letting Willie go ahead.

The tree was a slain giant, its leaves still a vivid green. In the exposed core a jagged upthrust of bright wood was charred where the lightning had struck. To the west the sky had already cleared, while in the east it was dark, and a fountain of color curved down from the clouds to the trees. He watched it as he walked back in the misting rain, wondering if it would fade or get brighter. By the time he got to the back porch, it had become luminous, full of the most brilliant color he had ever seen.

❧

CHAPTER ELEVEN

TWO DAYS AFTER Tommie's arrest, his brother receives an anonymous letter written in a crabbed, childlike hand:

> Dear Sir,
> The honor of my family has sufered due to your brother. Because of this I think it is proper that I be payed for funeral expences and something more. We can discuss the amount. If you don't come in a weeks time, I will come to you. There is no need to involve the courts in what we can settle like men. I will expect you soon.

Willie shows it to his aunt, who says he should take it to Constable Oliver right away. "He can't get away with threatening us like that, after what we've been through."

"So you think old man Madison wrote it?"

"It has to be. And anyway, it has a threatening tone, demanding money. Family honor! What family honor? They couldn't raise her and now they're trying to extort money from me. They know Tommie's innocent and he'll be home soon, so they're striking while the iron's hot. It's reprehensible."

"Well, I expect he's angry," Willie comments, "or at least he should be. But this isn't the right way to show it. Why couldn't he come over here, if he wants to settle it like men?"

"Just lazy. You know he wasn't raised right himself. His mother died when he was little and his stepmother resented having to raise somebody else's boy. She'd punish Howard by making him eat out with the dogs. Then his father died and there was nobody who cared for him atall. It was pathetic. He had a little collection of tin soldiers, and you know what she did? She put them in an iron skillet and stuck it in the oven—melted them down to sell to the junkman. Then he went and enlisted and nearly died of typhoid, and after the war he came back, and of all things, moved back into the farmhouse with his stepmother. She died not long after that, and then he married my niece, you see. The colored folks wouldn't work for him. Bad as his stepmother was, he was even worse, I guess. We joked about it at the time, wondering how his stepmother really died."

"But that was way back," Willie says. He is trying not to think about Lillie, and how she would write to her mother, but never to her father.

"It makes you wonder, though, if he didn't have something to do with this thing. There, I've gone and said what was on my mind." She crosses herself, even though she isn't Catholic, and whispers, "Forgive me."

"With Lillie?"

"If he knew she was pregnant, and didn't want the shame of it. He might've worked it someway with somebody up there. That nephew of his—Cary. Or those Dunstans. I'm suspicious, that's all."

Willie shakes his head. "It couldn't be," he says. "What kind of man would want his daughter dead?" *Could he have?* he thinks. "She got herself in trouble and drowned herself," he tells Jane. "You remember that letter she wrote before she came here? 'O, if suicide were not a sin'?"

"'O if suicide were not a sin, how soon the lingering spark of my life would vanish.'" Jane shakes her head, dabbing a tear from the corner of her eye. "I thought she was being overly dramatic—going on so about what a terror her life was and how only Jesus understood her suffering."

The following day Willie goes back up to Richmond, where he spends the next several days running errands for his brother. As in everything he does, he drives himself at a hard pace. What with keeping his business going, trying to keep the folks at home informed, and tending to his brother's needs—fetching law books, tracking down possible alibi witnesses, taking messages to and from the lawyers, and a host of other tasks large and small—there is little room in his mind for one anonymous letter.

Mr. Lucas is on his knees replacing the loose boards in the corner of the fence. He has not paid attention to the fact that the key has worked its way up his shirt and is now dangling from his neck in plain view. But Mr. Meade sees it as he comes along to inspect the work, and he sees Mr. Lucas stuff the key into his shirt. It looked like a little cross, and he doesn't want to embarrass Mr. Lucas, who seems intent on hiding the pendant. Yet he feels that a certain amount of curiosity about the people who work for him is not a bad thing. "Make it hard for them, Mr. Lucas," he says. "I don't want any more bodies in my reservoir." Lucas nods, takes another nail out of his mouth, and continues hammering. "You know," Meade tries, "I have a niece who married a Catholic boy. I'm a Baptist myself, but there's nothing wrong with being a Roman Catholic . . . What are you, Mr. Lucas?"

"Baptist same as you," Lucas says, speaking around three nails.

"That's what I thought. I thought to myself, Mr. Lucas is a Baptist. So if he wears a cross around his neck that'd be his own business, and welcome to it."

Lucas glances up, then goes on pounding, pausing on the up-swings in case Mr. Meade has something more he wants to say. Lucas wishes he would just go away, but he knows his boss to be the kind of man who wants everything the same every single day. If something's different—well, he notices it. The fact that a dead girl washed up in his reservoir hasn't set right with Mr. Meade, has kind of shaken him, and Lucas wonders if indeed his boss did forget to lock that gate. And now they've gone and arrested a man for it, and yet Lucas does not want to go up there like everybody else and see what he looks like. He can't understand why so many would, unless they feel guilty about it in some way, about a country girl coming here and getting herself killed like that in their own drinking water.

"I'm a man of science myself," Meade prattles on. "I don't have any superstitions, except that a dead body should leave the house feet first, because that's how my people did. Friday the thirteenth is no different from any other day—although for that girl it was unlucky. There are people that wear charms, even men. My father kept a railway ticket stub in his wallet—he met my mother on that trip from Baltimore. How about you, Mr. Lucas? Do you wear a rabbit's foot or any such?"

"No, I don't," Lucas says.

Mr. Meade thinks about that a minute. "I don't believe in superstition," he says. "But I do believe in the Bible where it says not to bear false witness."

Mr. Meade knows his man, and Lucas knows he knows. Lucas takes the nails out of his mouth, puts them in his apron pocket, and stands up. He removes the string from his neck and shows it to Mr. Meade. "It's not a cross, it's just a key I found. I reckon it *is* for good luck, and I didn't see any harm—"

"No harm atall," Mr. Meade says, studying Lucas's eyes. "That's a nice little key. You say you found it?"

Lucas swallows, looks at the key sadly. "Yes, a matter of fact I found it not too far from here." He hands it to Mr. Meade. "I was going to tell you about it, but it slipped my mind that first day, and then I guess I kind of got attached to it."

"What first day?"

"The day after we found that girl."

Mr. Meade looks weary. His nosiness has resulted in trouble for them both. "That's not good," he says.

"I didn't mean to cause any trouble," Lucas says. "I don't think anybody'll need it, do you?"

Mr. Meade studies the key a minute, then deliberates, stroking his neat little mustache as though making a life-changing decision. "What if they need it to convict that man?" he says.

"I don't see how one little key would make a difference."

Mr. Meade pockets it. "Still, I best take it to Justice Richardson."

"I hope you won't let me go for this, Mr. Meade. I been with you fourteen years."

"I know that, Mr. Lucas. You're the best worker I've ever had. I wish you had of spoken up about this, but I'll stand by you."

Lucas watches Mr. Meade making his way around the grounds toward the front gate. It's just a little gold watch key—what possible use could anyone find for it, even if it was the girl's? Now he'd never see it again. And he was going to have to explain himself to more than Mr. Meade. Of course they'd need it—it was her key.

Willie sees Madison first. Sees him sitting with his cronies, his hat dangling cowboy-style behind his neck, leaning over a schooner, a fist of cards clutched as tight as gold. Willie is in King William on business a week after Tommie's arrest and has stopped by the Manquin tavern for something to eat. He does not want to go out of his way to avoid Madison, nor does he wish to confront him, so he takes a seat at the bar and orders a bowl of stew. The place smells strongly of beer, cigar smoke, and damp cedar, and, built out of stone a century earlier, is always cold. But it is familiar to Willie and he likes the food and the bartender, who never fails to inquire after his family.

Willie has not been there five minutes before he feels a tap on his back. He turns and sees Madison, standing there folding his arms across his chest. He appears not to have shaved for a week, his fringe of hair sprocketed at odd angles and his small beady eyes bloodshot. Despite his appearance he manages to fix upon Willie a look of complete concentration, his head back and low as though ready for a fight.

"I was very sorry to hear about your daughter," Willie says, offering his hand.

Madison glances at the hand as if assessing its value. His thick lips spread into the suggestion of a smile. "You're late," he says. "You ready to discuss business?"

"You have something you want to sell me, Mr. Madison?"

The bartender comes in from the kitchen building and puts Willie's stew down. "Thank you," Willie says, turning his back on Madison. "Mr. Franklin, you're the second main reason I stop here." He takes a spoonful and blows on it. "And this is the first." He swallows the stew, then turns back to Madison.

"Matter of fact, I do," Madison says. Willie waits, then returns his attention to his bowl. "Come on out to the Tayloe place and we'll discuss it," Madison goes on. "Me and the boys are going up there for a hen-pullin'. Not far down the road."

"I know where it is," Willie says. "I know Mr. Tayloe quite well. I've done work for him."

"Then I'll see you there. Or at my place. Suit yourself." He goes back to his table, and Willie finishes and leaves without ever casting another glance Madison's way. He is going past the Tayloe place anyway, to trade a hatchet for a bucksaw with a man who mangled an arm in a railcar coupling and has no further use for a two-handed saw. The fact that Madison can't trouble himself to cross the river to issue a threat does not mean that he is going to forget about it. Willie knows men of Madison's stripe, old men who have room in their minds for only one or two things, usually money and how to get it. A debt such a man felt he was owed would weigh on him like the thought of meeting Jesus.

Willie decides it might be best to settle the matter now. He has become at twenty-four a man of few words, simple tastes, and unswerving reliability. If he says he'll deliver a cart of hardwood timber at ten o'clock, he will not be there at ten-fifteen with three-quarters of a load of pine, though the delivery point is three hours distant, the roads muddy, and his partner sick; that is how he stays in business and how he tries to conduct his life.

Willie turns up the narrow wooded lane that leads to the clearing where Madison and his friends are gathered. He is surprised that Tayloe allows any such foolishness on his property, but likely one of the men has some business relationship which confers hunting and other privileges—that, or Tayloe simply doesn't know. When Willie gets there two men on horseback are stringing a taut line as high as they can reach between two trees. Madison acknowledges Willie with a curt nod, then rides to the middle of the line carrying a burlap sack. He reaches in and pulls out a plump chicken that flaps its wings so hard Madison nearly drops it. From a pocket, Madison produces a piece of string, with which he binds the chicken's feet together. He then ties the feet to the overhead line.

The men now arrange themselves some thirty paces behind the line. As the first man rides forward, Madison finally turns to Willie. "A goose works best," he says, "but they're expensive. With cats you have to be careful of the claws, and it's more trouble than it's worth since you can't eat 'em." The man canters past the hanging fowl, reaching for it but only grazing a wing; the hen nonetheless lets loose a terrific squawk.

"Get in line behind me," Madison tells Willie. "And have you a turn." Willie says he'll wait, then watches as the second rider grasps the hen's head and gives it a short yank. The bird is still much alive as Madison, fourth in line, digs his heels into his barrel-bellied roan and trots forward. Gaining speed, he rises from his saddle, gives the neck a little twist, and watches over his shoulder as the hen circles the line like an acrobat. He rides back to the others, smiling as if he'd just performed at Mozart Hall.

The men go through again, the bird with its neck stretched yet still able to move a wing. The idea, Willie realizes, is not to kill the bird, which is dead by the end of the second round. "Watch this," Madison says, grinning with tobacco-stained teeth at Willie. He rides forward as fast as he can, reaches up with a practiced hand and snaps the bird's head off. The carcass bounces up and down, spewing blood, and the men cheer. One of them goes and cuts the hen down and gives it to Madison, who then pops it back into the burlap sack with a satisfied look on his face. "Thank you, gentlemen," he says, shaking hands. He excuses himself to tend to some business.

Willie rides with him a short way back down the lane. Madison reaches into the sack and pulls the chicken out and examines it. Blood is still leaking from the neck, smearing the tawny breast. "Nice clean job," he says. "I don't need this. I just come for the sport. You can have it."

Willie shakes his head. "What was it you wanted to discuss, Mr. Madison?"

Still looking at his prize, Madison says, "I reckon two hundred would do me fine."

"Two hundred what?"

"Dollars."

"Two hundred dollars for what?"

"For keeping my mouth shut."

"Keeping your mouth shut about what?"

"About your brother. I know he was with my daughter at such and such a time. I can prove it. But I don't have to say anything atall. That's up to you."

"What do you mean exactly?"

"I mean," says Madison, fixing Willie with his squinting black eyes, "I can either say your brother studded my daughter, or I can hold my tongue. I cain't do both."

Willie's horse is impatient to get moving. Willie has to lean over and try to gentle it with quiet words. He sits back up, and in nearly the same quiet, firm tone says, "First of all, Mr. Madison, there's unlikely to be a trial. And even if there is, there's no guarantee you'll be called. And even if you're called, I don't think you can prove something that isn't true."

"I know for a fact it is. You probably do too."

Willie has to wait a minute so that he will not speak in anger. He thinks of his aunt's little prayer, *Forgive me, Lord.* It's suddenly so quiet he can hear pine needles ticking softly to the ground. "The final thing I have to say to you, Mr. Madison, is that Lillie must be turning in her grave. She wouldn't hardly speak two words to you, and now I see why."

At this, Madison's face bunches into a purple mask. Then it reassumes its normal, grasping expression, the small veiny eyes working out the solution to a difficult but not insurmountable problem. He touches a nine-inch hunting knife sheathed at his belt, then lets his hand dangle. "You think you're too good for a free chicken, boy?"

"Good day, Mr. Madison," Willie says, turning his horse and starting it into a walk. He listens carefully behind him.

"I know everything about you and your brother," Madison shouts. "You're both sacks of shit, and you're gonna pay."

❧

CHAPTER TWELVE

FOR THE FIRST three months that Lillie was away Tommie was able to avoid seeing her. Although he had business that took him to King William town, not far from the house of his uncle John Walker (Lillie's grandfather), he stopped overnight in Manquin with an aging aunt. After he passed the bar examination, Mr. Evans had him represent a poor farmer against a private lender; he lost the case and told Mr. Evans he should stay closer to home. Mr. Evans told him not to be hard on himself overmuch. So back across the river he went, every two or three weeks.

Aunt Esther had a habit of asking Tommie to do unpleasant chores that hardly needed doing. It was more that she felt something was owed her for letting him stay with her and since she refused to accept money she took her payment in the form of pointless tasks. He didn't mind replacing a bad hinge or toting in enough wood for the week or painting the barn door, though she did have a man for such jobs. And her boarder, a Mrs. Eulalia Bogg, was ever, within Tommie's hearing, complaining about his appearance—"His eyes are like a bird's eyes"—and his manner—"He doesn't ask after my health," "He's too polite, I don't know if I can trust him."

Tommie decided the next time to stop with his uncle. He lived in what remained of a house that had been burned during the war. His servant, Sam, had been the property of Lillie's father, but after the war had decided to come work for her grandfather.

Sam, gone gray and rheumatic, greeted him at the door and took him back to the dim little sitting room. Uncle John was sitting on an old sofa that leaked horsehair; he tried to get to his feet with two canes, but Tommie insisted he remain sitting. He asked Tommie to repeat himself and put a little trumpet up to his ear. Then he took a pinch of snuff from a leather thumbstall around his neck—it had once protected his thumb from cannon vents, but nothing had protected his ears.

In his most stentorian voice, Tommie asked him about the price of white corn and what his thoughts were on the Chinese immigrants. Uncle John was more interested in a train that had derailed in Albemarle with a man who was on his way to be tried for murder. "Killed the prisoner. Trial by ordeal is what they used to call it. But turns out they had the wrong man. You're a lawyer. What do you make of it?"

"Clear case of mistrial by ordeal, Uncle John," Tommie said. He had to repeat it, and then the old man laughed and spat into a pewter cup.

Presently Tommie's cousin George came in, wiping his hands on his overalls. He was thin yet potbellied, and had a shaggy beard like his father. He greeted Tommie impassively and Tommie wondered if he were not taking a proprietary interest in Lillie. But George had always been quiet and somewhat backward. He stood, clutching one elbow behind his back, while Tommie filled him in on the news from Little Plymouth.

It was not until they sat down to supper that Lillie appeared. Her hair was gathered into a tight braid down her back, and she wore an apron with a floral motif along the border. She seemed more thoughtful and mature since Tommie had last seen her, more settled in her mind. Her waist was as tiny as ever, though her face seemed more angular and he noticed faint lines around her mouth when she smiled.

She was the lady of the house, treating him like an honored guest and old friend, making sure he had what he needed, ordering Sam to refill the beer and water glasses while she served and passed the food. Nola could not have done better, Tommie thought, but it was as though Lillie were playing a part. She said very little during the meal, and afterward she disappeared outside. Tommie finally excused himself and went out to the kitchen house to find her.

She was washing dishes, up to her elbows in a steel basin of soapy water. She smiled and said that she had missed him. "You could write," she said.

"I did," he said.

"One letter. After I wrote dozens."

"They weren't to me personally. They were to all of us."

"I didn't know if you wanted a personal letter."

"I expect you have plenty of young men to write to. You don't need another."

"They're just boys from camp meetings and Sunday school. They don't mean anything to me."

"You know Willie is still moping around. He can't understand why you came up here, and I'm not going to tell him."

"It's your fault. You kissed me. And you meant it."

"Well, I'm sorry. It wasn't the proper thing to do."

"Don't talk to me like a child, Tommie," she said. "You're not like that, always doing the proper thing. You pretend to be proper, with your suits and your fancy talk, but I know better. I know you, Tommie."

"What do you know?" he said. The mocking call of a whip-poor-will ricocheted through the evening air.

She pulled her hands out of the water and dried them on her apron and brushed a lock of hair from her face. "I know you're in love with me, and you don't want to be."

"I am not," he told her firmly. It disturbed him that she would stand there like a little kitchen maid and tell him how he felt, but even more upsetting was how accurate she was. He didn't like her having any such claim or power over him. He gripped her firmly by the arms, his muscles tensing so that she shook in his grip. She looked up at him with fierce brown eyes.

He went out and hurried down the yard past the coops to a meadow, and leaned against the shaggy bark of a hickory tree, silently cursing himself. The sky was darkening to indigo. She came down and stood beside him, pressing against him for warmth. "Why did you come here?" she asked.

"I wanted to see you," he said.

"I sinned with your brother," she said. She said it again, and he slapped her face. She slapped him back so hard he nearly fell down. Then he wrapped his arms around her so tightly he thought he might squeeze the life out of her. She lifted her face to his, and her rose perfume and the softness of her lips made him drunk with desire. He clung to her and kissed her hard on the mouth. At first he didn't feel the rat snake slithering over his shoes. When he looked down its tail was moving away in the grass. He held Lillie tighter, feeling as though he couldn't breathe unless his mouth was on hers.

"I'm not a pure and spotless girl, Tommie," she said. "But there's nothing I can do about it now. That's all I'll say."

The chickens and ducks were making nervous complaints, and Lillie started off to get George. "I'll do it," Tommie said. "Just get me a shovel." When she came back, he took the shovel and struck the snake as it was nosing along the coop. Lillie bent to pick up the wriggling body, then walked down to the woods and flung it. When she came back she still had the rank oily smell on her hands, and he kissed them and felt something strange working inside him. The whip-poor-will called again as the light of day winked out.

He tried not to think of her, of the gleam of her eyes when she was angry—that color, was it the color of burnt walnuts? of Heartquake Creek?—as he was drifting off to sleep with George snoring beside him. He'd decided he would try to get engaged to Nola again. Wasn't that the best thing to do? Yet then he'd picture Lillie's tiny waist and the way she went up on tiptoe to kiss him that time. It began to seem inevitable to him that they would become lovers in some way, a way that he could not clearly see—he only knew that he wanted her with every cell of his body. God, how she possessed him. He almost hated her for it. Why was God's plan so murky when it came to women? He would lie awake at night trying to puzzle it out. He tried to think about Maddalena instead, and her warm, bare skin, her hips, so much more ample and solid than Lillie's. He had a good ear for voices and music, and sometimes he would try to hear Lillie's voice and be relieved when he could not. But other times, for no reason, her voice would sound in his mind: "I do like you, Tommie." And he could hear her bright laughter, like rain on the water.

He had to get up with bowel trouble in the middle of the night and go outside, and he looked up toward her window wondering if she were still awake. In the morning he left before she was up, and he didn't come back for another two months. He kept giving Mr. Evans excuses why he should not cross the river to King William, until he worried Mr. Evans might think him lazy and lacking in ambition. It was January when he went back. He could have stayed with his aunt, but he elected to stop at Uncle John's.

He and Lillie took a blanket out to the meadow and spread it on the frosty ground. "Deer lie here," she told him. There was a nearly full moon in the early evening, and doves were still making plaintive coos.

In the spring he visited many times, often bringing little gifts for Lillie—lipstick in a paper tube, perfume from Richmond, a jar of persimmon preserves. She always had something for him as well—a bouquet of wildflowers, a tin of biscuits, or some other homemade treat. Once he brought her a curious little skull. "Randall Croxton gave it to me," he told her. "He said it was a colored baby, from the anatomy laboratory. He called it a memento mori—to remind you of mortality."

She held it at a distance, turning it in her hands. "Thank you, Tommie," she said, "but you keep it. It gives me the shivers. I don't want to be reminded of mortality."

Tommie took it back. "He said people used to keep a skull to remember how short life is and that you should eat, drink, and be merry. But I don't think I like it either, if you don't." He pulled back and threw it off into the woods.

"Tommie, no."

"It's too late."

"You oughten to've. I don't think that's right somehow." They went down to the woods looking for it, and after a few minutes Tommie suggested they go for a walk. But Lillie was determined to find the little skull and they kept looking and looking. "It'll turn up," he said, "and if not, it won't be missed by anybody."

"Don't, Tommie," she said, a hand on his arm. "Be respectful of the dead. Especially of a dead child."

"I don't believe in haints, but I'll be respectful for your sake."

They kept looking for a while, Lillie not wanting to quit. But they gave up when it was too dark to see.

In the evenings after supper Tommie would tell his uncle he was going out walking, then circle around to the meadow where she would be waiting on the blanket. Their amorous sessions were short and filled with passionate kisses and caresses. He was too polite to try to press for more. Then one night he said, "Why won't you do what you did with my brother?"

"You never asked me," she said.

"Will you?"

"I don't know."

"But why?"

"Do you think it's a sin, what we do?"

"No," Tommie said, "of course not." He kissed her and instead of sliding his hand into her blouse, this time he tucked it under the waist of her skirt. She reached down and put the hand back on her breast, then fondled him until he moaned and spent himself. He had been wrong then about her virtue all along, or else there were things that he simply did not understand about her, or possibly about all girls.

One time he got up at night, again with bowel trouble, and on his return considered going into her room, across the hall—so great was his need to be with her—but he didn't want to compromise her any more than he already had. In the morning George asked if he didn't get up at night, and Tommie told him he had. George said he thought so but he was such a sound sleeper, he wondered if he'd dreamed it.

Finally there came a time in late spring when she demanded to know if he was going to ask for her hand in marriage. "I need to know," Lillie said. They were out in Willie's buggy, which Tommie was thinking of buying if he could scrape the money together. Thrushes were fluting off in the woods, and Lillie's importunate tone gave Tommie some alarm. He asked her what the hurry was. "Nola wrote me that you were still good friends," she said, "and might become reengaged."

"I love and respect Nola, but only as a dear friend," Tommie assured her. "Compared with you she's a teacup."

"So this isn't just a dalliance for you?"

Tommie held her and told her that he would go on holding her forever like that if he could. "I mean it. I wish I could put you in my pocket and carry you with me all the time."

"Have you told Willie about us yet?"

"No," he said, "I don't see any need to."

"Don't you want to tell somebody? I want to tell somebody, but I haven't anybody to tell. I go on long walks sometimes with Uncle George and we won't say anything for five miles, and then he'll tell me he likes my dress. He's the sweetest man, and sometimes I get so lonely I tell him all kinds of things—what I want to do when I move to Richmond, the kind of house I want to live in, how many children I want to have and what I want to name them. But I don't have any friends around. There's a girl named Mary Ellen Neale I met at a basket picnic. She goes to an expensive school in Fauquier and shops with her mother at a new store in Richmond called Miller and Rhoads, where you can buy clothes ready-made. She said she would invite me to a holiday party but she never did. Oh, Tommie, I miss you when you don't come for weeks at a time."

"I'll come again soon," he told her.

"Tommie, you come here when you feel like it, you make love to me, and then you just go away. I write to you and you don't write back. Look at you, sitting there in your fancy suit." She laughed, trying to take the sting out of her words. The buggy wheels grinding over the sandy clay were the seconds when his life could have changed. He was on the point of asking her to marry him. "Let me out," she said. "Just stop and let me out, I'll walk back, I don't want to sit with you another minute."

She grabbed the reins and tugged, pulling the horse up short. Tommie told her to stop, but he couldn't get the reins away from her. She hopped down. The road was too narrow to turn around where they were, so he got out and caught up with her. "Lillian, stop," he said. "Stop this minute and look at me."

She turned and looked up at him, her face bunched with anger. "I hate you, Tommie," she said. "If you were the last person on earth I would sooner kill myself than have to say two words to you."

He had never seen her this emotional before, and he was shocked that he could have such an effect on any woman. He wondered if it was her monthly, or if perhaps he had not been attentive enough to her moods in the past. "You don't hate me," he said, grabbing her wrist. She jerked away and kept walking. He had to go back and get the buggy. Lillie meanwhile was cutting across a newly plowed field in her nice shoes, the air fresh with the smell of loam. He called once more, then sat helplessly watching her pick her way among clods of earth, her hems lifted at first, then dragging in the dirt.

He came again the next month on court Friday and spent Saturday as well, to help George put up a new fence. Lillie had cooked a roast on Friday and baked jam tarts, and she was wearing a new dress she had made of light blue jaconet. After supper he went out to the kitchen. This time she came to him, her hands wet and soapy. She wrapped herself around him and kissed him full on the mouth, prying his mouth open with her tongue and tasting him as though she were famished. "I don't care how long you're gone anymore, Tommie, as long as you keep coming back to me. You hear?" He nodded, his chin resting on her shoulder, his hands tucked beneath her bottom so that he was nearly lifting her up.

"I brought you a present," he said. He handed her an issue of *Ogelvie's Popular Readings*. "Read the one I circled," he told her. It was "A Gilded Sin," the story of Sir Jasper Brandon, "courtly, passionate and silent," whose daughter is the offspring of a secret affair; she nobly keeps her father's secret, even though it may cost her a chance for true love and happiness. "That's just for fun," he said. Then he pulled a gold watch key from his pocket and placed it on the table.

She picked it up and admired the little heart-shaped crown and the filigree around the middle. "I bought it at the shop in Centreville from a funny little foreign man. He doesn't seem to like me much, because I was impatient about getting my watch fixed one time."

"I'll wear it around my neck," she said.

"Or you could just keep it in your pocket," he suggested. She tilted her head down and nodded. He could see she was disappointed it hadn't been a ring. He had not yet made up his mind whether to ask her to marry him, because the truth was he still had fond feelings for Nola. He thought perhaps she would be the better wife for him and thus he a better husband for her than for Lillie. But he said, "It's the key to my heart. As well as my watch." She smiled a little.

Then she threw her arms around his neck. "You're a romantic, Tommie, and a gentleman. And you're my knight, and I love you." She pulled back. "But we will be engaged then?"

"As soon as I'm in a better financial position," he told her.

That night he had to go outside, and when he looked up at her window he thought he saw her white nightgown against the glass and her pale face, like a ghost moon. He wondered if he was not losing his mind over her. It felt as though she had some spell over him, and yet was it not he who was doing the corrupting? "God," he whispered, "help me do the right thing." She was a good, kind, loving person; everyone knew that. But when it came to sex she was weak—though no weaker than he was.

He spent a long hot day helping George with the fence posts, and then it was night again and he was not sure when he would be coming back. He went down to the kitchen to help Lillie, coming in so suddenly and urgently that she dropped a plate and it shattered on the brick floor. They bent down together to pick up the pieces, his hand closing over hers as she clutched a long jagged shard. He brought it to his throat. "Have you lost your mind?" she said.

"I think I have," he said. "I want you now." Her eyes grew large, like a frightened animal. "I won't hurt you."

"My monthly—"

"I don't care about that—it won't hurt, will it?"

"No, it's just—the blood."

"I don't care." He kissed her forehead, eyelids, nose, and cheeks. "Meet me down at the meadow when you're finished. I'm going up to the house for a minute." He went striding up, singing "My Grandfather's Clock," lustily so that nothing would seem amiss. George was on the front porch trimming his father's hair and beard. Uncle John sat in a chair, a white cloth tied at his neck, munching an apple. "He won't sit still," George said. "I told him Lillian can do a better job, but he's used to me."

"I could use a shave myself," Tommie said, rubbing his chin. "Lillian needed some more kerosene for that lantern and I forgot where—oh, I remember, it's back in the shed under the saw-horse, isn't it?"

"Yep, and that minds me that I need to fix that lantern. 'Tisn't lighting a-right."

"Seemed to be working fine now," Tommie said. "Just needs kerosene." He went back through the house, singing, pausing at the linen chest to pull out their blanket, then quickening his step out the back door and down to the high grass beyond the yard. The moon was just coming up, its yellow light trickling through the woods. A barred owl hooted a *hip-hurroo*, the echo giving way to the stillness of dusk and the trilling of frogs.

He couldn't see her at first. "Lillie," he called softly. "Are you there?" He waded through the hip-high grass, and listened. Lightning bugs winked secret messages across the darkening meadow. He moved toward her voice, and when he found her enfolded her in his arms. He spread the blanket and pulled her up onto his lap. She was as small and light as a child, and he felt as if he were cradling her, protecting her. He moved his hand into her blouse, she unbuttoning to help. When he tugged at her skirt, she lifted it and her petticoat and quietly undid the buttons and drawstring of her underpants. She gave herself to him as the moonlight engulfed their little nest in a pool of limpid silver. Feeling watched and cold, he held her tighter, until he quivered in relief, a timpani rumbling in his ears like distant thunder. She clung to him, her breath coming quick and shallow, and he could feel her heart thumping his chest. He kissed her, and was amazed that she tasted saltier; the evening air seemed filled with the pungent smell of her blood. The moon was in eclipse, and while they lay there it turned an angry, dark copper as though it had been swallowed by some unseen object. They both watched amazed and stricken as the shadow of the earth, stealthy and silent and unknowable, smothered the bright pale splendor of the moon. And it came out the other side and disappeared into the void and the moon shone as before.

They cleaned themselves with the blanket. Then Tommie went and got the shovel and buried the blanket out in the woods.

CHAPTER THIRTEEN

TOMMIE IS EATING breakfast in his cell when Mr. Evans comes to tell him about the new piece of evidence. "They've found a gold watch key," he says, "and they're right proud of it." He sits on the edge of the cot that Tommie carefully made only a few minutes earlier. "Apparently one of the reservoir workers found it the day after the girl was found, but he's only just now turned it over. Why he waited a week, I don't know."

Tommie is wearing a brown suit and bow tie. He takes a bite of toast and nods. "Could it have been planted?" he asks.

"Of course that's what we're going to say. It's mighty suspicious."

"What do they plan to do with it?"

"Richardson wants to know if it's yours. He's going to ask around."

"He's welcome to," Tommie says. "It's not mine. I have a fancy watch key, gold as a matter of fact. But it's at home. I'll get my brother to bring it up directly."

Mr. Evans tells him that would be a good idea. "In the meantime, I've brought a little work you can do for me—keep your mind off your troubles." He pulls a sheaf of papers from his briefcase and sets them on the little table beside the wash basin.

Willie arrives later the same day, bringing books as well as letters from well-wishers back home. Tommie tells him the news right off. "The one with the amethyst in the crown," Tommie says, "you remember Aunt Jane gave it to me? Along with my watch? It's in my room, in a little tin, with some letters."

"What about this other one?" Willie says. "What does it look like?"

Tommie glances down, then at his brother. Willie has grown a beard and he is scratching it, deep in thought like his father on the point of some momentous pronouncement. "I don't know what it looks like, because I've never seen it." He opens his mouth to say more, then stops. "But, Willie, it could be one I gave to Lillie." Willie's eyes grow large and serious. "Listen, I don't know that it is, but she was out there and they found it out there. Mr. Evans said it had a heart at the top. I'm sure a lot of keys look like that, but it could be hers and she dropped it somehow. I bought it at Bland's and gave it to her, just a gift for one of the times I was visiting."

"When was that, exactly?"

"It was last spring, around April I think, or early May."

"I see," Willie says, now studying the concrete floor instead of his brother's face. "So you were still sweet on her then?"

"Yes, Willie, I was sweet on her, but—" He gets up and goes to the gate to peer down the hall. Two officers are talking out in the office. He lowers his voice. "But I had nothing to do with this. I swear to you I didn't."

"I didn't say you did." Willie stands and leans beside some Bible verses that Tommie has copied on paper and pasted to the wall. He pulls at his beard. "I'm sorry, Tommie, I didn't mean to sound angry. Since you weren't out there, they can't prove you were. That's what makes me mad—is that you're here at all."

Tommie sighs. "Willie, I don't think it'd look good if they knew I gave her that key. There's a record of the sale in Mr. Bland's account book."

Willie takes the first train home in the morning and immediately goes out to the little village of Centreville, hauling a load of good wood in various lengths. He stops at Bland and Brothers' shop. The itinerant jeweler is not in that day, which Willie takes as a good sign. He asks the elder Bland if he could possibly check something in Mr. Joel's ledger book—he thinks he might be behind in a payment. Bland says it is an awfully bad business with his brother. He returns with the ledger book and leaves Willie at the counter while he goes out back to unload a shipment of cloth. "Help yourself to some wood out there," Willie tells him. Willie finds the page he's looking for, neatly tears it out, and folds it into his pocket. He closes the book and goes out to help Mr. Bland unload the best pieces.

Tommie's life is no longer his own. A doctor examines the scratches on his hand and makes notes. His lawyers come and go. Better meals are provided from Aunt Jane's funds, but he eats them in the solitude of his cell. On Monday he is moved from the station house to the city jail, where he takes up the routine of all the other inmates. He is housed on the lower tier of the north side, with the other white prisoners. He breakfasts at eight, takes dinner at four, then is locked into his cell at six. There are long hours when he has nothing to do except read and write—activities he has always loved, except now they are practically forced upon him. He dives into his case with all his youthful energy, his lawyers bringing casebooks and documents and newspapers. The latter he devours, looking for every scrap he can find about his case, and every day there is a front page story: "Mystery of the Morgue!" "Who Killed Her?" "The Cluverius Case Continues." He learns details he never knew about Lillie—how she had a close friend in Bath and how she supposedly told this friend she had a premonition something bad would happen to her. He finds himself fascinated and repelled by his notoriety, and cannot help reading and rereading the stories, sometimes laughing outright at how wrong they are. One claims she was his first cousin, another says he parts his hair in the middle. He wonders why it is that the papers have taken such a morbid interest in his case; he imagines that it comforts people to know they themselves are not in such a fix.

For the first week he mostly keeps to himself and stays indoors. But as the days wear on he ventures out more and becomes accustomed to the crude language and rough manners of the other prisoners. There is a Greek bricklayer who in a drunken rage pushed his wife down the back steps of their tenement house. She broke her neck and died, but the baby she was carrying lived and is now being raised by her sister. He has no other children. He's the most pathetic soul Tommie has ever encountered. He can spend an entire hour in the exercise yard weeping in a corner, or hanging on to the gate and staring dully out at the tenements across the alley.

Tommie is something of a celebrity among the prisoners. He has refined manners, and he can speak the language of the lawyers. Malachi Folger, an Irishman in for five months for disorderly conduct, says one day with a wink, "You know how I can tell you're innocent? You never ask what I think about your case."

In the meantime the coroner's jury continues its inquest. After three days they deliver their opinion: Fannie Lillian Madison came to her death on the night of March 13 in the old reservoir. Thomas Judson Cluverius was directly or indirectly the cause.

The next day, Tommie receives a visit from Aunt Jane. His conduct having always proven courteous and cooperative, he is allowed to meet with her privately in the dispensary. "I brought your Bible," she tells him. She places it and some other books and a sack of oranges and a pound cake on the examining table. "Are you getting your meals all right?"

"A boy brings them from a colored cookshop around the block," he tells her.

"I hate thinking of you here all by yourself on Palm Sunday."

"I expect I'll be here well beyond Easter, Aunt Jane. There's still no grand jury indictment." He puts his hand on hers, but withdraws it when she starts to sob. "It's not so bad here," he says. "They treat me nicely. If I was ever down on my luck, the first thing I'd do would be to get myself thrown in jail. It's very quiet, and I can do all the reading I want."

She smiles at this, and even laughs a little. "Just tell me one thing," she says. "Were you and Lillian ever in love with each other atall? No, don't tell me, I don't want to know."

He smiles and suddenly wishes she had not come. "I'll tell you this," he says. "I've always been very fond of her as a friend and cousin. But you know that." She nods, taking the words in as though they were filled with reassuring significance.

Mr. Evans visits almost daily, except when business or family matters pull him back home. Tommie's case has become his main focus, and he has taken up temporary lodgings with a Richmond relative. Tommie draws comfort from Evans's quietly methodical manner, shambling in like a friendly bear, his right eye half closed as though winking. Crump is a decade older, yet he moves like a much younger man, his gesticulations precise, his whole body jerking when he makes a good joke; he's plump and jovial, yet shrewd, not a man to be fooled with. Crump seems to want to penetrate the inner secrets of Tommie's mind; Evans simply wants to work with the available facts, and, for now, Tommie trusts him more. Yet in the courtroom Tommie is certain that Crump will be the better advocate, that his big-talking style will appeal to the jury's emotions.

"The thorny issue as I see it," Evans tells Tommie, "is how you account for yourself that day. We don't have to do that, you understand. But it's a big hole in our case." Now Evans leans in closer and assumes a friendlier, less judicial attitude. "I just need to find somebody who can verify without a doubt that you were at that play—what was the name of it?"

"*The Chimes of Normandy?*"

"Right. Somebody who saw you there that night. This fellow Henley, I can't locate him. He's apparently in New York, staying with friends. I've written to him. Is there anybody else from that night who could help us?"

"I'll have to see if I can remember," Tommie says. "This happened more than two weeks ago—I can't always remember things I did three days ago."

Evans pulls back and raps the table with his knuckles. "Well, you have to. Your life could depend on it."

The next day a grand jury indicts Thomas J. Cluverius for murder. There are five separate charges, all of them amounting to the same thing, that Cluverius "upon one Fannie Lillian Madison, unlawfully, feloniously, willfully, and of his malice aforethought did make an assault, and that the said Thomas J. Cluverius then and there, with force and arms, and in some manner and by some means to the grand jurors unknown . . . did strike, beat, and hit in and upon the right side of her face, over the right eye . . . causing one mortal blow, bruise, and wound of which said mortal blow, bruise, and wound, she, the said Fannie Lillian Madison, then and there instantly died." Another count puts it that he "did cast, throw, push, and knock the said" etc., in the old reservoir, causing suffocation and drowning. A third count has him using his fist and then drowning her; the fourth brings up the possibility of a blunt instrument; and the final charge combines the first two into one.

When Tommie sees the indictment he is upset. "How can anybody kill a person with a blow to the head and then kill her again by drowning her?"

"It's just to cover the possibilities," Evans tells him.

"But aren't they just fishing?"

"Yes, they don't know how she died any more than we do."

"Has to be suicide, doesn't it, Mr. Evans? The conductor said she told him she wished the train would run off the tracks. She could've gotten those bruises falling in, or when her body was dragged out of the reservoir. The footprints could've been anybody's—all those people wandering around the next morning."

"Have you come up with any other names?" Evans asks.

"There was somebody else at the theater that night, but I can't think of his name." Tommie considers for a moment; he has tried to fish up another face from the afternoon's performance, someone who might casually remember him. "We were acquaintances at Aberdeen. I can't remember his name. I saw him at the intermission, but I got distracted by a little boy who fell while he was holding his mother's hand." There had, in fact, been a falling boy, and some time before that Tommie had seen somebody who reminded him of a schoolmate, though he wasn't sure if it was the same person.

That night Tommie prays for strength. *I can make something worthy of my life, Lord, if you'll give me another chance.* He looks at the chipped black paint on the iron ceiling, and sees a croaking raven with a bent wing, or is the wing a woman's dress twisted at some unnatural angle? He misses Lillie. He feels her absence so deep within himself that it's a concrete, almost mathematical, revelation: He has never loved anyone nearly as much as he loved her. He doesn't know if he loved her because she desired him and held him in high esteem, or because she was so desirable herself that he melted at the thought of the smallest part of her body. Now that she's gone it seems that, whatever his life is to be, it will lack the one person who could make him happy. *Is that not punishment enough?* The wing on the ceiling is feathered and veined; it's flying over the river, its shadow gliding upstream in the afternoon light, west to the mountains and beyond.

Shortly after delivering the amethyst-crowned gold key to Crump, Willie takes the precaution of moving the little tin of letters from Tommie's trunk. He has already locked his brother's trunk and secured the key in his own. Aunt Jane and Miss Hillyard—one in fear, the other in excitement—would no doubt conduct their own private searches of Tommie's room when they could, but they would not find any letters.

After dinner one afternoon he removes the box and sits with it on his lap. A beam of light strikes through the western window, illuminating the floorboards at his feet. Cupids with bows dance along the sides of the box; the top is decorated with green and gold curlicues and the name "Antoni's Confections of Richmond." The corners are dented and worn from use.

Willie takes the lid off and flips through the letters. There are several from girls whose names he barely knows, if at all. They're filled with gushings about how sweet and adorable Tommie is and how thoughtful he was to write. One includes a lock of golden hair, bound with red thread. She writes that as soon as she turns eighteen she's going to get on a train and come right out from Richmond to see him. Another warns him that if he's writing to other girls he had "better count on losing me forever, for Tommie, I give my heart only to one boy at a time and when I do you'll know it for sure!" Another, named Georgiana Lee, mentions that he's a good kisser and she can hardly wait until she sees him again because she has some big news involving a family member. There are easily two dozen letters from five or six different girls. Only two are from Lillie.

They are down near the bottom of the tin, and Willie's heart skips a beat when he sees them. Perhaps there had been more, and Tommie destroyed them. These two were left or forgotten, or maybe were the only ones she wrote him. The best thing, Willie thinks, would be to take them out and burn them—no one need ever know their contents. It occurs to him that Aunt Jane already knows; maybe she has been reading his mail for years. If so, there's nothing damning in them.

One letter is postmarked from Manquin, April 6:

> Dearest Tommie,
> Now I know what it is to be loved now I have a purpose to my life. I have to confess, Tommie dear, that I lied about your brother—I was not with him like that but in a different way which I will explain the next time you come if you want to know. I have prayed almost all night and I have an answer this morning and that is we did not sin because we love each other and do you know as soon as I was sure of this I saw the sun coming up over my windowsill and the whole window lit up like a rainbow and I think it was a promise to me. And you won't believe this but as I sit here writing in my room the sun through the crab apple tree out my window is making a shadow on my wall that looks like a T it really does . . . When will you come back?
> Love your loving, Lillie

Willie stuffs the letter back into its envelope and crams it deep into his pocket. He can hardly bear opening the next, postmarked February 9 from Millboro' Springs:

Dear Tommie,

Please forgive my last letter being so short with you its on account of how lonely I do get out here sometimes, though I have made some jolly friends. I don't know why you would say I should marry that boy who I hardly even know I only mentioned him because we met at church and went walking on the mountain, not alone but with my friend Ella Kinney and another boy. I have to go now because little Mattie is calling for help with her ciphering. I will see you soon,

Love, your Lillie

Strange, Willie thinks, how there is no mention in the more recent letter of anything between them, just "Love, your Lillie." He folds the letter back up and pockets it. He then takes the tin of letters and returns them to his brother's trunk. For an hour he carries the letters around with him, wondering who his brother is and what he has done and not done. And when at the end of the hour he still doesn't know any more than before he found the letters, he goes into the machine shop and strikes a match and lets them burn on the dirt floor. When they are nothing but ashes, he sweeps them out and lets the wind push them toward the pasture.

That night he asks Aunt Jane if she knows of any letters anybody has written to Tommie in the past year that might be important to him. She thinks a minute, then says, "He took to having his letters held at the post office so he could get them faster. He was traveling so much for Mr. Evans, you see. It was easier for him."

Miss Hillyard, who is looking at her plate, shakes her head. "I don't see how that made it easier for him," she says, her tightly bunned hair stretching her skin so that to Willie she is a skull with eyes and a tongue.

"Rosa," Jane admonishes, "he couldn't always know when he'd be coming down here or when it would be easier to pick his mail up in King and Queen. So he told Mr. Garland to always hold it for him. What is your point?"

"Oh, I see," Miss Hillyard says. "My brain's turned to mush. I think it's the blood pills Dr. Dixon gave me." She helps herself to another of Jane's cheese biscuits and says nothing more about the mail.

It's the next day that Epps and Birney come out with a search warrant. Epps pushes his way through the house, his thick neck and beetling brow giving him a peremptory look, while Birney smiles and nods, apologetic at the intrusion. Willie gives them the key to Tommie's trunk. After going through the letters in the little tin they ask if his brother had any other letters. "Not that I know of," Willie says. "I believe he kept them all in that tin." They take the letters, as well as Tommie's two spare steel watch keys, some issues of *Ogelvie's* and other magazines with dog-eared pages, photographs of Tommie and Lillie, papers with Tommie's writing, and a penknife. "That's mine," Willie tells them. "He shaves his pencils with it."

"That so?" Epps says curtly. Birney, hands in his pockets, whistles and tries to look unobtrusive. Epps wants to take Jane's cork-handled fountain pen, but Willie convinces him it has just come from Philadelphia and nobody has used it but she. When they're finished, Jane gives them a packed lunch and wishes them a safe journey home.

CHAPTER FOURTEEN

JUDGE HILL, who at forty-three looks and acts sixty, opens the trial, telling the defense he'll tolerate reasonable delays if they need to hunt down a witness. He pauses to rearrange wisps of hair over a mottled, bald patch, a remnant of his vainer, more ambitious days. The clerk then calls on Tommie to rise. Tommie stands, steadying himself with one hand on the bar. It takes five minutes for the clerk to get through the indictment, after which he says, "What say you? Are you guilty or not guilty of the felony whereof you stand indicted?"

"Not guilty," says Tommie loudly. He lowers himself into his chair.

Tommie is asked to rise while the jury—half of whom are from out of town, so many locals were biased—is sworn and charged. Then the clerk intones, "Gentlemen of the jury, look upon the prisoner and hearken to his cause. If you find him guilty, you are then further to inquire whether it be murder in the first degree or in the second degree . . ."

Tommie listens to words that nothing in law school or private practice have prepared him for. Second-degree murder carries up to eighteen years; surely they would find a lesser degree. Voluntary manslaughter, no more than five years. Involuntary manslaughter, no more than twelve months and a fine not exceeding five hundred dollars.

". . . If you find him not guilty, say so and no more. So hearken to the evidence."

If they find him guilty of anything, Tommie decides, it will be voluntary manslaughter—no intention to kill. What keeps nagging him is whether he should break down and tell Crump everything he knows. But would anybody be sympathetic to it? The real problem, of course, is that now it would look as if he were trying to wriggle out—the public would feel justified in thinking him a depraved and despicable creature. If he gives them an opening, they'll pounce. He cannot count how many times he has lain awake at night, confessing to God, then risen in the morning feeling almost—but not quite—free of his burden.

The first day of witness depositions begins where the story began for the public—at the reservoir. Prosecutor Meredith calls Lysander Meade and asks him to describe his job and what he found on Saturday morning, March 14, at seven o'clock. Very few people know Charles Meredith yet, nor his ambition to run for lieutenant governor in the fall. But a good showing here could make his reputation. In his early thirties, he is short, barrel-chested, and has a pugnacious thrust to his clean-shaven chin.

Even Meade, his own witness, seems intimidated by him at first, but Meredith smoothly recalibrates his demeanor and continues teasing out the facts. Meade, wearing a natty little checked bow tie his wife selected for him and his navy-blue superintendent's jacket, all buttoned up and showing the double row of buttons, launches into meticulous detail on the dimensions of the reservoir. Meredith guides him toward a recital that shows off Meade's extensive knowledge, letting Meade's natural proclivity for numbers seem useful instead of eccentric. That Meade's eyesight was so bad he was still a drummer boy at eighteen during the war need never arise. Yet when Meredith asks him if he could tell right away that something wasn't right about the path,

Meade blurts out, defensively, as he has done many times over the years, "Well sir, my eyesight isn't so good, but once I was up close I saw where the walkway was rucked up right smart." Meredith quickly moves on to what Meade actually saw.

Colonel Aylett for the prosecution has a few follow-up questions. "Mr. Meade, are the reservoir's surroundings of the sort that would invite a young lady to venture there alone at night?"

"Is that not a leading question?" Crump complains.

"We withdraw it."

"But you shouldn't have asked it."

"Your Honor, I'm bound to frame my questions by my own brains, not those of the defense."

The crowd murmurs its approval. This is the kind of smart comeback they're here for, cramming themselves into every available space, one spidery man even climbing atop the stove before being shouted down by a deputy. Colonel Aylett's roots in King William County, Lillian's home, are as formidable as his oratorical wizardry. His great-grandfather was Patrick Henry; he fought in twenty-two engagements during the war; he has served numerous terms as a commonwealth's attorney. And if there is anyone who is a rhetorical match for Crump, it's Aylett. He has sharp blue eyes that need no correction and silver hair slicked back over his collar. Every inch the country gentleman, he keeps a wide-brimmed hat on his table and he wears a double-breasted coat and an old-fashioned black stock cravat. His goatee comes to a point and his twisted white mustache frames a polished set of teeth that flash like a wild beast when he talks.

On the cross-examination, Evans says, "You say your vision is imperfect, Mr. Meade. How far can you see, exactly, with your glasses?"

Meade, who has been on the witness stand for forty-five minutes, thinks, then says, "Ninety-five million miles. They say that's how far the sun is." The court erupts in laughter, and Meade enjoys his brief celebrity.

Evans then asks Meade in which direction the reservoir flows. Meade has clearly not thought about the reservoir flowing at all. "I imagine what drift there is is toward the outflow pipe, to the east."

"So something that entered that side of the reservoir wouldn't go very far, would it?"

"No, sir," Meade says, a little confused. Tommie smiles at how easily Evans has erased the picture the prosecution is trying to paint of a body being thrown over the fence on the side nearest the walkway. If the footprints indicate a struggle, and the bruises a mortal blow, then the murderer would naturally carry or drag her the shortest possible distance; carrying her all the way from the path down and around to the south side of the reservoir would make no sense.

Aylett whispers something to Meredith, then takes to his feet. "That gate in the picket fence," he says on redirect, "was it there for the public to use?"

"No," Meade says, "it was there so workers could get to a water pipe."

"Would it be difficult to find that gate in the dark if you didn't know where to look?"

"I imagine it would be. Besides which, I kept it locked."

Tommie imperceptibly shakes his head at this.

"Are the palings sharp?"

"Yes, they are."

"Now, Mr. Meade," Aylett says, "Would a woman in an advanced stage of pregnancy have a hard time climbing over a fence like that, nine inches shorter than she?"

"We object!" Mr. Crump shouts.

"Very well, we'll withdraw the question."

"But you put a question and then withdraw it," Crump says.

"I ask the court to rule on that type of question, so they won't be asked again. It's obviously an improper question."

"I thought I could please the defense by withdrawing the question. I certainly want Your Honor's views, but not in advance of any questions I might put."

Judge Hill nods, lips drawn into a tight smile—he knows Crump and Aylett quite well, and all their tricks. But though they are legends with Confederate honors trailing their names like sacred robes, he is determined to manage this trial in the proper way. The publicity it is receiving all the way from Charleston to New York worries him, and he will not let the city his father died defending, the city of Chief Justice John Marshall, be dragged in the mud in the dawn of its return to life. "The court will not rule on questions before they're put," he says.

Mr. Lucas is on the stand for only about fifteen minutes. He wears an ill-fitting gray suit, thin at the cuffs, with pants that don't reach his shoes. He is so worried about the key that he nearly forgets to take a look at the prisoner, yet today Meredith mainly wants to know about the footprints on the embankment walkway. "Yessir," Lucas says, "I took the girl's shoe up to Mr. Wren. It fit in some of the prints pretty well."

"But not the others?"

"No, sir."

"Would you say that the others were made by a man's shoe?"

"Objection, Your Honor," Crump thunders. "The witness isn't a footprint expert, is he?"

"I'll restate the question," Meredith says. "Was the other set of prints larger?"

"Yessir, they were."

Evans then proceeds to grill Lucas about the exact number and size of all the footprints. "So you think there were about ten small footprints in all?"

"Yessir, I'd guess so."

"Did you count them at the time?"

"Nosir."

"And the other ones you said were larger. How much larger were they?"

"I couldn't say, exactly. There were only a few of them, and they weren't real clear—really just the heels, because they were off more toward the grass." Lucas looks into the distance, trying to recall the day, and thinking of a girl who has so often since then appeared in his dreams—not the girl from the almshouse, whose face he doubts he would know if she were sitting in the courtroom now. He steals a glance at the prisoner—a young man with a face like a schoolboy—and he briefly wonders where the real killer is, in his imagination a big brute with a sneering pug nose.

"So, you don't know how many footprints there were, nor their size. Can you tell what kind of shoe made those larger prints?"

"What kind?"

"Well, was it a brogan, a work shoe, a dress shoe, an overshoe, or what?"

"I don't know."

"How many people were up on that walkway before you had a look at those footprints?"

"I don't know exactly. You'd have to ask Dr. Taylor."

"I intend to, but what would you say?"

"I'd say there was Detective Wren, Dr. Taylor, Mr. Meade, a newspaper man, and I don't think anybody else."

"So anybody could've made those footprints?"

"I don't think so, not in that location."

"But it's possible?"

"I suppose, yessir, 'tis."

Evans thanks him for his time and takes his seat between Tommie and Mr. Crump. To Crump he whispers, "Got 'em on the run," then winks at Tommie.

Judge Hill says, "Witness, you're dismissed," but Lucas keeps his seat until the judge says, "Mr. Lucas, please step down."

Next up is Dr. Taylor, who for more than an hour meticulously details the marks on the victim's face and head and the results of the autopsy. Evans wants to know if it's possible she could have come by the marks after entering the water. Dr. Taylor considers for a moment, then says simply, "Yes, it's possible."

"I see," says Evans, "and do you remember whether the victim was face up the entire time she was being removed from the water?"

"I believe she was." Dr. Taylor, dressed in black and clutching an umbrella, takes his time with each answer. He's proud of his reputation and confident of his findings, without which none of them would be here, and he wants to show that he is the judicious man of science he is known as.

"But you're not a hundred percent sure?"

"I'm ninety-five percent sure," Taylor says, his knowing smile undercut by his walleyed gaze.

"Thank you, Dr. Taylor, and you told the police court that you first believed that Miss Madison had killed herself. Why did you believe that?"

"That was not a medical opinion, just an individual opinion. I'm not an expert in murder or suicide."

Evans waits for the nervous laughter to die to absolute silence. "What inclined you to that opinion?"

"For one thing, as I said then, the articles scattered about looked like they could possibly have been farewell tokens. Others viewed it differently."

"I see, and what else?"

"Her advanced stage of pregnancy led me to believe she might be emotionally inclined toward suicide."

Meredith, without getting up, then asks Taylor if his opinion of two months ago has changed.

"Yes, it has," Taylor answers.

A recess is called, and Tommie turns to his brother, sitting directly behind him. They shake hands for the third time that morning, Willie seeming reluctant to let go; Aunt Jane, sitting beside Willie, beams encouragement, but the morning appears to have been more than her constitution can handle. Willie helps fan her, trying to stir the close air. "Daddy'll be up tomorrow or the day after," he says. "But maybe it'll be over by then and we'll all be on the way home."

"Can I have roast turkey and oyster pie for my homecoming?" Tommie asks, hoping to lighten everyone's spirits, his own included. He tries not to notice the eyes flickering toward him and away, the people trying to size up his character and his history and his very soul in quick glances. He wants to act calm and natural, but it's the most difficult performance of his life.

"You can have whatever you like," Willie says.

On his next visit to Manquin, Tommie and Lillie went out walking instead of to the meadow. It was Tommie's suggestion, and Lillie seemed accepting, if a little hurt. He wanted her, and now that they had crossed a threshold he thought of her in a way as his. Yet he knew he was not being fair to her—either propose or leave her alone, he told himself. But he could not make up his mind to do either. As though reading his mind, she said, "You haven't broken with Nolie, have you?"

"We talked about it."

"What did you say?"

"I asked her if she didn't think Henry Gooch or Wiley Worm-ley might be a better prospect than me. But she didn't think that was funny, even though I didn't really mean it as a joke."

"Tommie, I got a letter from her last week. Everything is fine between you two as far as she knows. I don't like your being de-ceitful, it makes me nervous."

"Deceitful? You're still writing to your cousin Cary Madison, aren't you? And half a dozen other boys?"

"Not half a dozen, Tommie. I get lonely out here. If somebody writes me a letter, I'll write them back. I'm not engaged, so why shouldn't I write letters to as many friends as I want to?" She ducked her head and folded her arms.

"I don't mind if you do," he said. Now that her passion was stirred he wanted her more than ever and he tried to take her hand. She pulled away.

"You can be very cruel, Tommie."

"What's cruel about wanting you?"

"You know as well as I do that somebody could see us now. But go on if you want to, you won't ruin my reputation around here. I'll just say you were taking advantage of me and everybody will be on my side."

In the morning she kissed him before he left and told him she was sorry for being so cross with him. "I'll be sweeter next time," she said. "And things will be different then, won't they?" She looked at him with as much concern and hope as she could muster. He nodded, and she said, "If you don't speak to Nola, I don't think I want to see you anymore, Tommie. You can stay here, but I won't be any more than a cousin to you."

It was several more weeks before he was able to return, and when he did he told her he still hadn't broken with Nola, on account of her mother's illness. What he didn't say was that he could not bring himself to turn his back on a future with the heiress to Upper Oaks estate. He promised Nola that as soon as he was able—probably within a year—he would buy a house in Little Plymouth.

And then came an evening in July when it was so hot that Uncle John suggested Tommie take his cousin down to the creek to cool off. George was in Manquin on errands. It was as though their going off alone was sanctioned by the head of the house—perhaps he even wanted to throw them together, Tommie thought. "He doesn't suspect we were sweethearts," Lillie said, when they were dipping their feet. "But he knows I've been low for a while, and company cheers me."

Tommie put his arm around her. "I've missed you, and I still love you," he said. "I think Nola and I will get married next year. I just couldn't break off with her. I don't love her the way I love you, though. I don't think I ever will."

Lillie leaned her head against his arm and held back a sob. "It's all right, Tommie. I didn't think you'd choose me." She swirled a toe out to where a water strider dimpled the skin of the creek. "Were you lying to me all along?"

Tommie thought a moment, trying to get at the truth. "No," he said, "and if I was, God will punish me."

"That's just like a lawyer, not giving a simple yes or no." She said it in a pert way, but she turned from him.

"Don't cry," he said. "Lillie? My little Lillie, can't we be friends?"

She shook her head, but she let him hold her while tears slid down her cheeks and when he kissed them she didn't try to pull away. She kissed him back a little. And then they were just looking at each other. He had a vague feeling that she was different in some way, more restless and anxious. Yet she had a certain way of looking at him—her lips tucking into a slight smile, dimpling her right cheek, a smile that said she knew things about him—that melted him entirely, and she was doing it now, giving him that secret look that was only for him, sitting there with her bare ankles crossed in the water, her skirts above her prim pressed-together knees, a long braid down her back. And then he was pawing at her blouse, and, though it had been some time, they knew just how to move for each other. So without either of them thinking the outing would go like this—but not exactly thinking that it wouldn't—they were making love again, this time to the trickling music of the little creek that ran to a larger stream and so to the Mattaponi.

She later told herself that she was mistaken, that periods were sometimes missed—though she had never missed one herself. Why now, she wondered, when he was not coming back? (For he no longer stopped with them on his visits to King William.) She wrote to a schoolmate for advice for a "poor friend" who had missed her monthly; the rest of the letter was deceitfully cheerful. She felt sick, restless, moody, and, above all, lonely. George and Daddy John worried about her, but she said she was fine, just a little melancholy sometimes. Her grandfather asked her if missing her cousin Tommie was the reason and she swore it was not, that she didn't care a thing for him. Was it some other boy then? No, she said, she just felt she was getting old and that she wanted to be moving on with her life. George nodded sadly, as though he wanted to ask her something but was afraid.

Lillie's friend finally wrote back, full of news of her family and friends, church picnics, and a trip to Baltimore and out to the seashore. She had no advice, except that Lillie's friend was probably in trouble and would just have to accept the consequences. Marriage was the only somewhat acceptable way out of such a difficulty, unless she had money for a lying-in house. There were such places in Richmond for wealthy girls who got in trouble, etc., etc. But Lillie knew all this.

She wrote to Tommie twice, but he didn't answer. In a third letter, she told him, "I simply have to see you to tell you something <u>very</u> important Tommie and it concerns you so you must come here as soon as you can and hurry because I am so lonely but that is not the reason I need to see you." He wrote that business would bring him there in ten days and he would "make it a point to stop and visit with you and George and Uncle John, because it has been too long."

In the meantime, she wrote to Mrs. Mary Dickinson in Bath County in the mountains, inquiring about teaching positions. Daddy John and James Dickinson had fought side by side when the Forty-first and Thirteenth Virginia Infantries combined at Second Manassas and Fredericksburg, and had promised to be friends for life. He had gone back to Bath and started a family, and he owned a two-hundred-acre farm on the Cowpasture River. Mrs. Dickinson wrote back to say that her grandchildren and several neighbor children were enough to make up a little school, and she would be happy to provide Lillie room and board and a little extra.

Until she could speak with Tommie, she was uncertain what she should do. Surely he would calm her fears. When he finally did come, George was out in the cornfield, and her grandfather was napping. She and Tommie sat out on the back steps with a pitcher of iced tea, talking quietly. "I've missed you, Tommie."

"I've missed you too, cousin," he said. "I've been working so hard I don't have time for my own family, it seems like. Nola sends you her love."

Lillie tightened her lips. "Tommie, I have something to tell you, so I might as well. I think I'm pregnant."

Tommie raised his eyelids as though shocked, though he really was not. For several days now, since receiving her letter, he knew that was a possibility. He had been able to put it out of his mind, except at night. He set his glass down. "And the father?"

"Tommie, there's been no one but you."

He nodded, biting his lower lip and trying to think. His nighttime fears had resulted in no plans or imagined outcomes of any sort, only vague notions of being trapped, and then praying. Indulging in these dark fantasies meant they couldn't possibly come true; besides, God had big plans for him, for why else would he be the only one in his family to go to college and become a lawyer? He suddenly felt uncomfortably hot—he loosened his cravat and ran his handkerchief over his brow.

"Tommie, what are we going to do?"

He let the ramifications of that tiny word sink in. Before, the only "we" had been a phantasmic ecstasy hidden from the light of day, and now it was oozing up from the ground where it had somehow been carelessly broadcast. "Have you seen a doctor?"

"No, I can't go to any doctor I know, and I won't see anybody by myself."

His mind was racing like a bayed fox, dodging for an opening. And then just as suddenly as the news had broken over him, he felt a calmness spreading like creek water through his veins. Sitting here on the steps with Lillian, her same lovely, if somewhat more careworn, face, the songs of birds around them, the crazed pitcher of tea, his uncle snoring inside, the chickens moving in the coop down the yard, his own watch quietly ticking in his pocket—everything in its place and reassuring of the orderliness of life—surely his world could not have slipped from its moorings. He remembered Randall Croxton telling him about a kind of pill you could take, and a malpractitioner who sometimes performed abortions because he was in debt, though it was against the law and dangerous and carried an air of squalor and degradation. "Don't worry," he said.

"What will you do?"

"I don't know, I need to talk to some people. There's some pills I might can get that will fix it, make it go away."

"And you'll bring them to me?"

"Or send them."

"I found a job teaching in Bath. I was going out there in October, but maybe I should stay here now."

"Well, I don't know," he said, not wanting to sound too eager. "No, I think it would be good for you to go. You should go on out there, and you might find there was nothing to worry about after all." The right thing to do, a voice told him, was to offer to marry her. But another, more practical voice told him there was no harm in waiting. There were girls who tried to trick boys into marrying them—probably Lillie wouldn't, but still, what was the harm in waiting to see if she really was pregnant? "You're not sure, then?" he said.

"No, but something's different. I can tell. It's like something's shifted, not just inside me, but everywhere." She touched his hand. "Tommie I'm sorry I've been so blue in my letters, but you see now, don't you?"

"Of course I do," he said. She sat beside him, knees on elbows, chin propped on her joined hands, and she glanced sidelong at him, her tea-brown eyes seeking solace. The pleats of her blouse stretched open, her narrow shoulders sloped, and he wanted to take her upstairs in his arms right then.

"You care about me, don't you, Tommie?"

He nodded.

"Then you won't leave me alone, will you?"

"No, but I need time to think what to do." He glanced at her suddenly. "How did this happen now?"

"I don't know, Tommie. It's not my fault, it's the Lord's will. I dreamed I was having a baby all by myself out in the woods somewhere and there was blood all over. I woke up sweating and so scared I almost called out."

Tommie patted her arm but had a distant look in his eyes. "I'm sorry," he said, "but we'll get through this all right." He stood and put his hat on.

"You're not staying to supper?"

"I wasn't planning to, no. Aunt Jane's expecting me home tonight."

"But you'll come back before I go off up to Bath?"

"Yes," he said, "I'll be back in two weeks, next court day."

"Try to come next week."

He nodded.

"And Tommie you must write to me. I get so worried when you don't write. I go out of my mind. Please don't let me suffer so." She gave him a pleading look and grasped his hand. "You'll come to Bath to visit if I ask you to, won't you?" He nodded again, biting his lower lip. "I'm a little bit scared, Tommie, but I think now it's all going to work out just fine." He watched her silently mouth the last few words, something she had not done in years.

Against his protests, she packed some leftover biscuits and stew beef and sliced tomatoes into a paper sack, along with a jam tart. They hugged each other and she wanted to keep holding him, but she heard her grandfather stirring in his bedroom so she told Tommie good-bye.

"Be brave," he said, meaning it as much for himself as her. And then he was gone. She stood on the front stoop dabbing her eyes with a handkerchief and watching his buggy jostle down the pine-bordered lane, then turn out onto the road. She waved her handkerchief, but he wasn't looking. She kept watching until he had completely disappeared between the fields of tobacco and tall corn.

Two weeks later a letter came from Tommie explaining that he would probably not be able to come, but that he would try to visit her in Bath County. Neither of them mentioned the problem in their letters. Yet she wished he could have said something more reassuring than "I wish you the very best" and "I'll be thinking of you and praying for you." He signed it "Love, your cousin Tommie." She felt like tearing it up, but she saved it in her trunk, along with scores of other letters and, tucked under the lining of the trunk's bottom, a dirty poem from *Wisdom for Girls*, sent by a schoolmate, who secretly copied it from her brother's book. Lillie would sometimes read it for a titillating thrill, though lately she'd forgotten it.

A month after her missed period she spent several tense days hoping and praying, but when no blood came she began packing for the trip to the mountains. Uncle George bought her a new warm black overcoat, trimmed at the neck and cuffs with fox fur. "It's from me and your granddaddy both," he said, handing it to her. He stood with his head down, one hand gripping the other wrist. Then he cleared his throat. "Miss Lillie," he said. He had such a grave look that Lillie touched his arm and asked what was the matter. "We'll get along all right here. But we'll miss you. You don't have to go away up yonder. I talked it over with Daddy, and we want to give you another dollar a week." He stood looking at his mud-scuffed work shoes.

She hugged him, and he just stood there. "Uncle George, you've both been very good to me, better than I deserve. I'll be back Christmas, I promise. I just need a change for a while."

"I expect that mountain air will be good for you," he said, repeating a formula he'd said many times the past few weeks. "You've been poorly, and that air might be just the cure."

The last few days she busied herself baking, doing the laundry, packing, polishing her shoes, giving the house a good cleaning,

and helping her grandfather hire a suitable cook and laundress.
A short letter arrived from Tommie:

> Dear Lillie,
> I have not been able to find anything to send you.
> I will keep looking. I'm sorry I will not be able to get
> up that way before you leave, but I'll write to you again
> soon. Willie says he can't come either just now, but
> sends you his best. You take care on your trip and write
> me again soon. If Jane tells you I asked why you haven't
> written me, it's because I've been taking your letters
> to me out so that she doesn't know. Please destroy this
> letter right away.
> Love from your friend, Tommie.

She read it over twice more, then threw it away.
Four days later George drove her to the station at South Point
and she boarded a train going west.

❧

CHAPTER FIFTEEN

To GIVE THE JURY a better feel for the scene of the crime,
the prosecution proposes a visit to the reservoir. The defense reluctantly agrees. Evans tells Tommie that by the light of
day the reservoir does not look at all like a gloomy, secluded place
for the commission of evil deeds. "Don't you agree?"

"I suppose so," says Tommie. "I haven't been there since I was
in college."

So the next day at the noon recess a carriage and two omni-
buses carry Tommie and his police escort, the lawyers, the judge,
the twelve gentlemen of the jury, and Willie out to the reservoir
grounds. They alight in front of the Dunstan house, Tommie not
saying a word to anyone. Willie talks cordially to a member of
the press.

They climb the embankment steps, the sun making everyone shade their eyes. Tommie stoops to pick a buttercup which
he twirls, holding his hands behind his back. He looks into the
reservoir, and it *is* unfamiliar. The water has been drawn off a
second time in a search for evidence, though nothing has turned
up, and now the bottom is brown muck, reflecting glints of sky.

God be with you till we meet again and the wheezing organ
bellows—where was that coming from? It was snowing, the smell
of coal fire from the ironworks on a frigid night, her warmth and
her naked swollen belly. She made him feel the kicking. And
later, *I could strike her and no one would hear, could squeeze the life*

out of her, because it was as though she were screaming in his ear, go on and just *do* it, Tommie, I want you to, and he felt like screaming himself.

Then it's daylight again and Willie is over talking quietly with some people, and Tommie has not seen this place since college. So there is that low picket fence around the water's edge that Mr. Meade described, and the little gate on the south end near where the body was floating, and the sloping brick walls of the reservoir. And down the other side of the embankment—there's the high board fence, and the loose board where Lillian (and her companion, if she had one) must have come through. It has been nailed back up. They go outside and around to the little smallpox cemetery, and the deadhouse where the hat was found, and the little hospital building, beyond which rises the Confederate memorial over in Hollywood Cemetery. Everything is so peaceful and green.

Tommie looks off toward the river. He could wait until the policemen seem distracted, then run for the bluffs before they have time to draw, jump down through the brambles, cross the railroad tracks, and swim the river. Hide out in farmhouses during the day and move west at night. He looks at his brother—Willie would do it, Willie would help him do it. But, no, the courtroom is more familiar, practically his home ground, and that's where he has his best chance. Anyway, what kind of life would he have running? Where would he go? The Dakota Territory? Too many Indians and too cold. California? He has no feel for those places.

Willie interrupts his reverie. "How are you feeling?" he asks.

"The fresh air," Tommie says. "It's the greatest thing in the world." He puts the buttercup under his nose. "You don't appreciate it until you can't have it."

As they are leaving the grounds Tommie hears a girl's laughter from somewhere off near the smallpox hospital. He looks over

and sees a face at the window that has a strange resemblance
to Lillie's; the girl is laughing, as though in a teasing way. She
waves, or appears to, and Tommie starts to wave back but stops
himself—the reporters, who have been watching him the entire
time, who watch his every movement except in the safety of his
cell, will make something of it—but then he decides to wave
anyway. And then he's not sure if she was even waving at him at
all, and as they pass he sees that it's really an elderly woman with
gray hair.

The trial continues with the testimony of conductor Ben-
jamin Wright, a broad-chested man with a head full of curly
brown hair. Yes, he spoke with a young woman wearing a dark
gray dress and a red shawl. She was going to Richmond to meet
a friend, but the friend wasn't at the station, so Wright went with
her on the omnibus to the American Hotel, as it was on the way
to his own hotel. Yes, she seemed preoccupied on the trip.

Evans asks him to repeat what the woman said. Wright says,
"She told me she wouldn't mind if the train ran off the tracks
and killed her."

"That's all I have for this witness," Evans says.

Aylett stands up again. "Mr. Wright, you say she was agitated?"

"Yes, I said she was preoccupied."

"What did you make of her saying that about the train running off?"

"At first I thought it was a joke. It was a strange thing for a
young lady to say."

"You thought it was a joke?"

"At first I did."

As the trial proceeds, the witnesses keep piling up their testimony, the sheer volume of it more than anything Tommie has
ever heard of. "Beats anything I've seen," Crump tells him at
one of their regular morning meetings. "I hear they're carrying

reports in London and Paris. But don't let it bother you. People are naturally curious. When the case is over, you'll be famous."

"For beating a murder charge."

Crump fixes him with a hard stare, a vein in his forehead pulsing. "You'll be free."

Tommie nods sheepishly. "That'll be enough for me." He sometimes wonders what Crump really thinks of him, but the time for a confession seems long gone. He is sure from what Willie has told him that Evans believes in his innocence, and yet Willie himself seems uncertain. Willie has never asked for the truth, nor does he appear to want to.

No matter how much Wren threatens, Slim Lane cannot seem to turn up the newsboy who brought the note for the lady in Room 21. He spent three days looking, then quietly went back to his job at the hotel and nobody said a word about it. He manages to put it out of his mind until Wren turns up again asking for him. "Well?" Wren demands.

"I axed around, but nobody seen that boy."

"I find that hard to believe," Wren puffs. He's standing arms akimbo, knuckles on his waist, staring down at Slim, who just happens to be outside of Room 21. "Mr. Dodson says you were out for three days hunting for that boy. I paid your wages for that time, and you mean to tell me you turned up nothing?"

Slim multiplies twenty-one times his own age, twenty-four, and gets five hundred and four. His eyes shift away from Wren's gaze. "Five hundred and four," he says.

"Five hundred and four? Five hundred and four what?"

Slim's mind becomes a spinning top. What does Wren want to hear? Would it please him that Slim asked five hundred and four people about the boy? That in five hundred and four hours,

exactly three weeks will have gone by, at which point he will have
earned enough money to buy a book explaining that people de-
scended from monkeys, a book his preacher said was the greatest
piece of foolishness ever written? That there are five hundred
and four cows in a field in his mind and he can see them all,
in groups of three and four and seven? Would he like to know
Psalm 50, verse 4? "He shall call to the heavens from above, and
to the earth, that he may judge his people."

"What?" Wren says. "What's the matter with you, boy?" He
shakes Slim by the shoulder. "Is something wrong with you?"

"No, sir." That isn't it, then. "They made a noration at the
church. Somebody said the boy was at five-oh-four."

"Five-oh-four?"

"Yes, sir. Five-oh-four Jackson Street."

"Who said it?"

"I don't know, sir. It was at the noration at Sixth Mount Zion."
There was a noration, though no one could come up with a name
or location for any such newsboy. It was thought that he might
have been visiting a relative and had gone back to South Hill, but
Wren would not want to hear that.

"John Jasper's church?"

"Yes, sir." It occurs to Slim that Wren might get angry after
he finds no one at that address and that he will return, wanting
more. He decides to tell him something true. "That watch key,"
he says.

"What about it?"

"I saw it in the lady's room, on her dresser."

Wren glances around, then speaks quietly, his voice tight.
"What kind of key?"

"A gold key, shiny and fancy, just like they described in the
newspaper."

"Why didn't you say anything at the police court?"

"Nobody axed."

Wren grips Slim's shoulder and stares him straight in the eyes. "You listen to me. You might've thought you saw such a thing, but I don't think you did. She didn't have any such key, you understand?"

Slim nods, remembering the little gold key when he went in with the message and waited for the lady to give him some change. But for some reason Wren doesn't want him to have seen it. "Well it looked a whole lot like a key."

"But it wasn't," Wren says. "Could've been a hinge or knob, you see. Or some coins, or a pin, or some other ladies' thingamajig." Slim nods. "If anybody asks you what you saw in there, what'll you tell them?"

"I'll say I don't remember. Unless my hand's on the Bible. Then I'll say something that looked like a key, but I don't know."

"Something that *maybe* looked like a key, but you don't know for a fact because you never held it in your hand. And that's the God's truth, isn't it, Slim?"

"Yes sir, it is."

"You're damn right it is. That girl wasn't out there alone, and it wasn't her key."

The prosecution brings Mr. Lucas back out. Meredith gets up and holds a small gold watch key in his palm. He shows it to Lucas and says, "Does this key look familiar?" Lucas studies it for a few seconds, then says that it does. "Tell us about this key." Crump objects and is immediately overruled.

Lucas has already prayed to God about this. He has put his hand on the Bible and sworn to tell the truth, so he has no choice. "I found that key at the reservoir the day after we found the girl."

"The day after, you say? And when did you report it?"

"I didn't report it until a week after that, plus one day."

"I see, and would you mind explaining to the jury why it took you so long?"

"Well sir, it's hard to explain exactly. I liked the look of it, I guess. I thought it was right pretty, and I was thinking finders-keepers, not thinking about the case. Well, that's not exactly true either. I was sort of thinking of that girl, and I didn't reckon anybody would need it."

"That's all right, Mr. Lucas. Now explain why you decided to turn it in."

"Well, Mr. Meade happened to catch sight of it around my neck and asked about it. So I told when and where I'd found it, and he said I ought to turn it in, so I did, and I hope he won't let me go, not that he would, because he's always good to me."

The audience chuckles in sympathy, while the jury passes the key around. So much chatter arises from the courtroom and out in the hallway that Judge Hill has to bang his gavel and ask for order. Then Evans gets up and tries to make Lucas change his story, quizzing him about exactly where he found the key and what his state of mind was, then repeating the questions, hoping to trip him up. But Lucas is a rock. All Evans can do is conclude, "And you swear that you found it more than a week before you reported it, and you don't know how it got there?"

"Yes, sir," Lucas says. This time as Lucas steps down he takes a better look at the prisoner. Since his last testimony he has tried to imagine the young man striking the girl, and now he is baffled seeing him there in his nice brown suit and tie. Why, that boy could no more hurt another person than he himself could.

Then George Walker is brought out. He takes the oath, looking somber and out of place, then sits and begins fidgeting with his hat in his lap and knocking his knees together. He looks more haggard than Tommie remembers, his cheeks caved in and his beard gone gray and scraggly. Two of his teeth have been pulled, and he has not bothered plugging them.

Meredith asks him when the prisoner visited his house. George has to think about it, even though Meredith has already privately gone over the kinds of questions he would ask. "The last time was around about September, but not for the night." And the last time he stopped for the night? "That was in July, I believe." Crump objects, but Meredith explains that he is trying to establish that there was an opportunity for a seduction.

"You can't prove any seduction took place," Evans shoots out. Judge Hill eyes him sharply and asks the stenographer to strike the last sentence. Evans sits back, looking chastened, while Meredith pries out the details Walker can give. Yes, the prisoner visited at various times over the course of Lillian's stay with them, and, yes, they were sometimes alone together. George explains how their rooms were situated, with his father downstairs and Lillian across the hall, and how his cousin sometimes got up at night and later complained of bowel trouble.

Meredith then asks if the prisoner was in the habit of wearing a watch key. George replies that he had a fancy one on a little chain. Asked to describe it, he says he can't remember exactly. "It was gold, I believe, and had some kind of fancy top to it. He showed it to me once—he was proud of it, and I teased him about how expensive it was." Meredith reintroduces the key he showed Lucas and asks if this is the same one. Tommie shakes his head, but George is not looking at him. "It looks like it," George says. Tommie stares at his cousin—*look* at that key, it's not mine.

"And were Miss Madison and the prisoner sweethearts?" Meredith asks.

"We object," Crump says.

"You gentlemen," Mr. Aylett calmly replies, "wanted Mr. Lucas's opinion on footprints—not exactly his expertise."

"Yes, but this is too much."

"Please, gentlemen," says Judge Hill, "proceed."

George thinks for a moment, staring into his hat for an answer. "Nosir, not as I know of."

"Didn't you tell me that you thought maybe they were?"

"Your Honor," Crump shouts, "he's badgering his own witness."

Before Hill has a chance to rule, George clears his throat and says, "I don't know for sure that they were anything but good friends." He closes his mouth and stares at Meredith as though to say he's done with answering questions.

Meredith asks him to look at the key and says, "Will you swear positively that this is his key?"

"No, I won't swear positively that it is," says George, his face gone blank with stubbornness.

"Mr. Stenographer," Crump says, "did you get that down?"

"He's got everything down," Meredith retorts.

At the break Tommie asks Evans how he thinks it's going. "Ask me when the day's over," Evans says.

"It just feels like we've turned a corner," Tommie persists. "Walker gave them nothing."

Evans is looking over notes he began working on at seven o'clock this morning. He takes off his glasses and stares at Tommie. "No," he says, "but he didn't particularly help us, either. We have to be patient, keep wearing away at them. Unless you can think of a better idea." Tommie looks suddenly deflated.

"It's going about as well as we can hope," Evans offers. "Given the information they now have, I don't believe they could connect the dots and convict. There's too much doubt. If I was on the jury I certainly wouldn't. Let's just keep working."

The clerk calls an end to the recess, and Judge Hill watches with growing impatience as the crowd fights for seats that have been saved with fans and hats. He calls the court to order and announces that to keep the rabble out he will in future be limiting the crowd to ticket holders only, and that people are welcome to stop by the clerk's office for details.

First up is a store clerk from King William named Marcellus Gateweed. He maintains that last summer he saw Cluverius wearing the watch key that was shown as evidence. Crump can see that he is a proud, easily rattled little man. He whispers to Evans that he'll do the cross-examination. "How was the prisoner's watch worn?" he asks.

"In his pocket," Gateweed replies, basking in the laughter this produces.

Crump cuts in. "Can you honestly tell the jury that from last summer until you'd heard of the case you ever thought about that watch key?"

"I can't remember," Gateweed manages. His hand goes to his tie and his hair. A juryman asks him to repeat the answer, which Gateweed does, in a sullen tone.

Crump nods sagely and takes his time now. "Mr. Gateweeeed," he says, airing the name out like an undergarment on a line, "When did Mr. Meredith show you this key?"

"I don't know," Gateweed says. "I think it was Thursday or Wednesday."

"Huh," says Crump. "Yet you remember you saw it ten months ago on July eleven?"

Gateweed nods, his lips pressed together, and Crump waits for the judge to tell him to provide a verbal response.

"Did you describe the key to Mr. Meredith before he showed it to you?"

"I said it was a small gold key."

Crump walks over and picks the key up, hiding it in his hand. "How else would you describe it?"

Gateweed now looks as though he just wants to leave. "It was fancy in some way," he says, his voice cracking. "I'm not good at describing things."

"And yet you come in here when a man's life is at stake and swear you saw him wearing a key last summer that you can't now describe?"

Aylett objects and Crump withdraws the question. "Mr. Gateweed," he says, "when was the last time you saw Colonel Aylett back at Ayletts village?"

Aylett objects but the judge tells the witness to answer. He thinks carefully, then, "It was two weeks ago, I remember clearly."

"Was he wearing the same watch chain then as he is now?"

"I don't know," Gateweed says, his face now closed into itself.

"Colonel Aylett," Crump says, "you wouldn't mind standing up like you were a minute ago to remind the witness about your watch chain?"

"I certainly would," Aylett snarls.

"Judge Hill," Crump says, "Would you please ask Colonel Aylett to stand?"

"You know I can't do that," Hill replies, studying some papers on his bench to avoid looking at any of the lawyers.

"Could the court then please," says Crump, "note for the record that Colonel Aylett has refused to show his watch chain? I'm done with this witness."

A black chambermaid named Henrietta Wimbush, wearing a bright yellow dress and a wide burgundy hat with egret feathers, is sworn in and says she saw the prisoner at the Exchange Hotel on January 5 and that he met with a lady from Room 66 and then went out with her. She did not return to spend the night. She was registered for the fifth and sixth as Miss F. L. Merton. To convince the jury she knows what she's talking about and to prepare them for the story of Tommie's return visit to Richmond in March, Meredith has her repeat the date.

Crump lights into her. "Can you swear that the man sitting here is the same man you saw all the way back in January?"

"Yes sir it is," she says. "Except he had a mustache then, and his hair was light. It *is* light," she says, looking at Tommie. "That's the man, sure as can be. And he wore a light overcoat and a black hat, and he didn't take it off in front of the lady."

"Did anybody else visit the room Miss Madison was in?" Crump asks. There is murmuring in the court, and Crump immediately realizes his mistake. As do Tommie and the other lawyers in the room. Instead of trying to correct himself, he listens politely to the answer—"Nosir"—and moves on to another question, as though he'd intentionally admitted the identification of Miss Merton. "Do you remember," he asks, "who occupied Room 66 before Miss Madison, or after her?"

"No," says the witness.

"But you're sure of that one day?" Crump says. When he sits down he whispers across to Evans and Tommie: "No harm done—just saved us all some time. Merton and Madison—just came off the tongue somehow." He flashes a look at Tommie, but Tommie only stares ahead. He hasn't talked about his alias with anybody, nor about his visit last January.

That night he has a familiar dream. Lillie is hugging his knees like a child, but she won't look up so he can see her face. She is speaking words that make no sense—she wants something from him—and then he is running through the woods, and everybody is after him—Willie, Aunt Jane, Evans, Crump, Aylett, Lucas, and other people he doesn't even know. He runs and runs, until he finds a culvert to hide in. They all go past, except one little girl with long blond hair and a white shift, and she takes his hand and leads him deeper and deeper into the tunnel until it is so dark he can see nothing.

CHAPTER SIXTEEN

IT WAS IN DECEMBER when Tommie agreed by mail to meet Lillian in Richmond. She wanted him to come out to Millboro' Springs, but he told her he was too busy for any travel other than the occasional trip to Richmond. She kept writing, two and sometimes three letters a week:

> Dear Tommie,
>   What I had feared is true. I've let my dresses out and since they don't know me well here they think I have a stout figure. Its funny because Mrs. Dickinson who is so sweet to me says I shouldn't worry about showing off my figure since many young men like stout figures. I wear my coat alot too on account of the cold, even indoors and they think its because I'm not used to the cold, which I'm not really. I have to see you Tommie. You do love me still, don't you?
>   Love, your Lillie

When he read this Tommie tried to imagine what it was like for her by herself in her condition in a strange new place. But she always made friends easily, and the fact that she mentioned other young men, even if she was only trying to make him jealous, meant she was not in despair. He did his best to put the problem out of his mind.

She wrote asking him about the pills, but all he could reply was that he hadn't found any. He had asked Gretchen what people did who didn't want babies. She told him that rubber condoms were the best thing, but that there was a negro pharmacy in Manchester that might help. Tommie went out there, and found no one in the store except an old colored woman with large, rheumy, veined eyes that watched him like a dark spirit, and he had no voice to ask for anything but directions to the bridge back to Richmond. On another visit to Lizzie Banks's, a different girl told him she knew of a negro doctor who sometimes performed abortions.

Lillie wrote: "Dear Tommie, There's now two feet of snow. I feel sad every morning but then during the day when I'm with the children things seem happier and I think I can get through this. I miss you and I have to see you soon." When no letter arrived from him after three days, she wrote again: "I'm going to come back to Aunt Jane's if I don't hear from you soon. You must write me right away. I'll take my chances with Aunt Jane you see if I don't. She was mad at me for going away without coming by to see her first and I know she would take me in and take care of me. Otherwise you have to find a lying-in house where I can be for a week or two and then I don't care what happens to me. Sometimes I can't stand the thought of something growing inside of me and I just want to tear it out and sometimes I wish I could just die."

He wrote to say that he would meet her on January 5 in Richmond and that she should register at the Exchange Hotel as F. L. Merton. Another letter from her crossed his in the mail: "Tommie, I felt it move in me today and I was so scared and surprised I thought I might yell out. I don't know if I can just give a baby away to somebody I don't even know I don't know if I can do that, but I'll try to be brave. You have to write soon."

She did as he told her in January, explaining to Mrs. Dickinson that her aunt was sick and that she would only be gone a few days. Mrs. Dickinson gave her five dollars against her next pay and told her to take as long as she needed.

On the afternoon of the fifth, Tommie entered the lobby of the Exchange and checked the register. A Miss F. L. Merton was in Room 66. He went up to her room and knocked. She opened the door a crack, then let him in. It was a small, hot room, with tall windows and brown curtains, an oblong mirror over a low white bureau, and a ceramic terrier in the corner. At first Lillie tried for a cheerful holiday mood, telling Tommie how nice the hotel was and showing him how the enunciator worked. "You can call the front desk anytime you like," she said. She gave him her shy little smile and brushed a limp wing of hair from her forehead, and he found himself wanting to take her right there on the bed. She was in a way already his to take. But he was too afraid to even touch her. It was cold and iron-gray out beyond the lace curtains, horses clopping on the street below, and life seemed a miserable prospect, endless work and trouble, and all for what?

"You haven't said two words, Tommie. Are you not feeling well?"

"Under the circumstances," he said, "I'm feeling better than average." She laughed gaily at this, but quickly changed to a serious look, waiting for him to continue. "There's a doctor I know who can help us," he said.

"At a lying-in house?"

"He'll perform an abortion," Tommie said, impatiently, then with more kindness, "and we'll save money over a place of confinement."

But Lillian was already shaking her head and frowning. "No, Tommie, I won't do that. It's illegal and it's wrong and I won't do it. The baby's alive. I think it's a girl. I thought you had already found a lying-in place."

"I've been busy," Tommie protested. "But I'm going to find you a place. Today. I promise."

She smiled tenderly at him again and touched his arm, but seeing that he didn't warm to her, she tightened her lips and simply said, "I think it's coming in April, so we ought to meet here again in March, early March just in case."

"And what if it takes a month? I don't have the money for that."

"You'll have to borrow it then from your brother or Aunt Jane, or somebody, Tommie. You'll have to."

He nodded and sat down on the bed with a city directory. He found an advertisement for a lying-in asylum called the Church Institute on Marshall Street: "All non-contagious diseases treated." Probably a euphemism for "any medical condition handled." At least he hoped so. "Public wards, in advance . . . per wk $6. Private rooms . . . per wk $15 to $25." So he would need at least fifteen dollars, which he could easily make in a good week. To Lillian he said, "I'll find the money. I'll meet you here March fifteenth."

"It should be earlier than that, Tommie, and I need another reason to be gone. I can't very well tell Mrs. D. I'm going to see about my sick aunt again. What if she were to write to Aunt Jane?"

"I wouldn't worry about that," he said.

"No, because you don't have to." She picked up her hat with the ostrich feathers.

Tommie looked up from the directory. "How about a sick school friend?"

"No, it should be a school friend's aunt. Violet Bone really does have a sick aunt. It's easier for me to fib if there's some truth in it. I'll say that Violet has to take care of her own mother, and there's no one her aunt would rather have than me."

"Of course."

"And I'll be taking her down to Old Point Comfort, where I've always wanted to go but never have."

"Well, don't look at me like that. I didn't go down there until after you'd moved out, and then it was just for the day with Willie and Aunt Jane."

"Still, it must have been beautiful out there by the sea."

"By the bay. Yes, it was beautiful. Now you should get to work on your letter." He opened the desk drawer and pulled out two blank sheets and a pencil.

"I don't know if we should use their paper for this, Tommie."

"It's already paid for. You start writing, then I can send it to you around the first of March." He watched until she had started writing the fake letter, then told her he was going out to buy them some breakfast. Twenty minutes later he was back with two cinnamon raisin buns and a little bottle of milk. He also gave Lillian a bag of candy and oranges for her trip home. She finished her letter, covering both sides of the page to save paper, while he sat eating. He read it over:

> Richmond city
> March 1885
>
>
> My dear Lillie,
> It is on business of sad importance I must write to you today—poor Mama & aunt Mary are both ill. We don't know which will die first sometimes. Mama is too ill for me to leave her at all, and the Drs. say the only remedy for aunt is a trip of a week or ten days at Old Point to take those sun bathes which are proving so beneficial to consumptives, but we cant prevail on her to go unless mama was well enough for me to go with her, which is of course out of the question as she is so

ill. She likes your gentle manners so much that when it was decided she must go to Old Pt. she begged we would get you to go . . . As we were so much in hopes of going to the New Orleans Exposition I have had a good many dresses made up and should you wish any mine are at your entire command . . .

Your loving friend, please excuse handwriting in haste. Violet Bone

"You're a very good fibber, Lillie," he said archly, "with your gentle manners."

"It's all true, in a way. And you can see I went to some trouble to make it different from my writing. And that part about her going to the Exposition—she really had planned to go . . ." She trailed off.

"Fine, Lillie," he said, taking the letter and putting it in his satchel. "I'll mail it to you in March."

"And that's it? No other letters, no visits, and I just go back to the mountains, where it's cold and snowing and I don't know anybody?"

"Lillie, I'll write to you. You know we can't risk being seen together anymore."

"But after the baby's born. What then?"

"We'll see about it then."

"Tommie, I don't know if I can give her up."

This was what he had hoped to avoid. "You never said anything before about keeping it."

"But I don't know if it's right just to give her away. What if nobody came for her? I couldn't bear to think of my baby left in an orphanage."

"You should have thought of all that—"

"What do you mean?" She stood there across the bed from him, a stranger with a swollen face and midriff. She had always been a determined, headstrong little thing, and now she was a stolid, stubborn presence, an obstacle near the door he wanted to walk through. Yet he also wanted to tear her clothes off and drive himself deep into her little dumpling of a body.

"I don't know what I mean," he said. "I just need to go now. I'll write you."

She moved toward the door, her lips pouting, her hands curling into fists. "Tommie," she said, "you'll marry me, won't you?"

He could feel the blood draining from his face, even as it rose in hers. "I'm engaged to Nola, and you know that."

"Then you'll just have to break it off. Tommie? You'll have to break it off, that's all there is to it . . . I'll tell her why you have to break it off, if you won't."

He stood there facing her like a cornered bull. "No," he said. "I'll tell her myself, when the time comes." Lillian did not move, her lips and knuckles gone white. It was impossible that his life could be ripped out from under him this way for a small mistake. He felt a rage building within him. "Okay Lillian," he said, not caring how loud he was. "I'll tell her! I'll go home today and tell her and everybody I know."

"You don't need to get angry," she said. "I'm not sure what I want to do yet. Don't act so crazy like that. It's scary. Your eyes, Tommie. Don't do that."

"I'm sorry," he said, trying to calm himself. "Of course we'll do whatever you think is the right thing. But I know we can find a good home for it, so if that's all you're worried about, just quit your worrying and leave it to me."

She smiled at him, but it was an impassive, tolerant look that said, So far, leaving it to you has accomplished nothing—there were no pills, and I had to force you to meet me here. He could see the accusation in the flat set to her mouth and eyes.

He went over and put his arms around her and said what he thought were soothing words, but she made no effort to hug him back. She patted his shoulder, as she might a child's. He said, "I promise it will all work out. I'll meet you at the American in March, and I'll have found a place for you by then." He looked down into the crown of her head, and she nodded but did not look up.

"I thought maybe you loved me, a little," she said.

"I do," he said, "of course I do."

She put his hand on her belly and he felt a rippling under the surface, as if she were performing some obscene trick. He knew what she was doing, yet he couldn't bear to leave her like this, pathetic and beautiful. He took his coat back off, and they sat on the bed together, his arm around her and her head on his shoulder. Something was breaking in him. He got on his knees and buried his face in her lap, letting her stroke his hair and smelling her warmth. His shoulders trembled, tears dampening her dress where his face lay. He reached up beneath her dress to the top of her stocking and beyond until he was stroking her crotch. Then she stood and undid the hooks and eyes at the back of her dress; Tommie undid the top button and she lifted the dress over her head. In her ivory-colored petticoat her arms were pale and thin, her shoulders narrow. She slipped off the straps and let the petticoat fall to the floor, and she stood there in nothing but her corset and drawers. He watched as she took these off as well. He had never seen her naked—she was a thing of beauty, her breasts plump and upturned above her distended middle. Then she lay back on the bed while he took off his things. He drove hard into her, augering up and in, rocking her as though to undo what they had done. After he had finished, she held him there, pushing her pelvis against his until her breath came in quick gulps and her face flushed.

"I've never loved anybody but you, Tommie," she said, "I've flirted with lots of boys, but it never meant anything. It's different with you."

"It'll be all right," he said.

He got dressed while she lay there unclothed. "I'll call for you this evening, if I can get away," he told her. He opened the door.

"If you can get away?"

"Sshh." He glanced up and down the hall. A maid was coming out of one of the rooms. Tommie yanked his slouch hat down low over his head. The maid passed by, but before she went into another room she turned and looked at him a moment as if waiting for the rest of the story. Tommie glared at her and she disappeared. "I'm supposed to meet a friend for supper," he said. "If I can break that off, I will. Otherwise, I'll come afterward." She seemed somewhat satisfied with this arrangement, and with that he headed out.

Going down the stairs he had a sudden glimpse of a future with her: He could turn now and go to her; they could get married this very day, live in Richmond and make a life together. He had seen an unpredictable power in that small frame of hers—she would take matters into her own hands if necessary—but also a vulnerability in his own character. Or was it simply good-heartedness? Was there any decision for him to make at all? He couldn't hear himself think clearly, his whole head seemed cluttered with noise.

He headed out toward Marshall and the Church Institute, pulling his coat on as he walked west, head down. Lillian would want one of the better rooms. It would be a substantial sum of money; he would have to set aside the money so he would not be tempted to spend it at Lizzie Banks's, or on a gift for Nola. He still owed money for his top-buggy, and, of course, he was saving for that house in Little Plymouth. And now he would have to part with a week's worth of money. He could always pawn his watch and gold key. He could ask Lillian to pawn the key he'd given her, but she'd feel betrayed.

When he reached the asylum he pulled out a piece of paper on which he'd written the names of the matrons and superintendent, then knocked on the door. A squat middle-aged woman, her hair in a white kerchief, opened it and stood there waiting for him to explain himself.

"I'm looking for Dr. Moncure," he said. "Is he available?"

"He might be and he might not be," the woman said, eyeing the whole of Tommie and his clothing. "Who should I tell him is calling?"

"Walter Merton," he said. "I want to see him about a cousin of mine."

"What's your cousin's name?"

Tommie had not thought about giving Lillian a name. He blurted out, "Her name is Fannie Merton. We have the same name—we're cousins, you see."

The woman continued giving him the same implacable, bovine stare, her lower lip shadowing a bewhiskered chin. She shook her head. "We have nobody here by that name," she said. "Could be she's at another house."

"No," Tommie said, flustered. "She's not here yet. I wanted to inquire about the possibility of her coming here."

"Come in, then," she said. "I'm Mrs. Paine, by the way." She moved by rocking herself left to right, using the momentum to advance the opposite leg. He followed her into the foyer, which had been converted into a waiting room. She maneuvered her bulk behind a long table which served as a desk, and into a chair. Among the papers and books scattered on the table was an open appointment book. Mrs. Paine let out a sigh and said, "What was your cousin's complaint?"

"Well, she's in some difficulty," Tommie said, shifting his weight on the sagging floorboards. "You see, she's expecting, and she needs a place for her confinement." He stopped, waiting for Mrs. Paine's reaction.

Mrs. Paine looked at the appointment book, shaking her head, as though flummoxed about the purpose of the book itself. Then she looked at him. "And who is the father?" she asked, her expression unchanged, but her eyes perhaps a little softer, more sympathetic. Or perhaps, Tommie thought, merely curious, merely in search of another example of human folly and indiscretion that she could hold up as an example for young women to avoid, or that she could gossip about in the lonely evening hours.

"That's just the problem," he said. "We don't—she doesn't know who it is, and she needs a place to be. Maybe I should wait and talk to Dr. Moncure."

"There's no need for that atall, Mr. Merton. Mrs. Harrison and I do all the admittances. We don't generally take on that kind of case. The institute is a benevolent organization, and we do all we can for all kinds of people. Mr. Paine—" (she crossed herself) "was an example of God's benevolent work on earth. Even though he took to drink and drank himself to death nearly, still he got me to promise on his deathbed that I would carry on his benevolent work here. But we do have a reputation to uphold, and if we don't know who the girl is or who the baby's father is and who their parents are, we can't just take people like that in. We did have a girl once, a shy, pretty little thing. A man said he was her father paid Dr. Moncure a hundred dollars, and after she had the baby she up and disappeared."

Mrs. Paine propped her elbows on the table, put her fingertips together, and gave Tommie another sad cow look.

"I could pay that much," Tommie said. A week's pay suddenly seemed like nothing—he'd agree to any price, and somehow find the money. "It's very important that she have a place, but she should only need it for a few days, and not until March."

"I know it," Mrs. Paine said, real sympathy in her voice now. "But we just can't help you here, young man. What did you say your name was?"

Tommie was confused at first, wondering if giving the right name would lead to the right answer. "It's Merton, Walter Merton, and I'm a good Christian, and so is she, my cousin. We're not Roman Catholic, but we go to church all the time."

"I know you do, but—"

"And we come from good family."

"Around here, you said?"

"No, but not far away—just over in New Kent."

"Oh, I have family in New Kent. You probably know the Tripp Broadnaxes?"

Tommie nodded vaguely. "I think so," he said, "I'm sure my daddy does. Gosh, if it's a matter of money, it doesn't matter how much it is, and she wouldn't think about up and running away. She just needs a quiet place for a while, because of the delicate situation."

"I know. And her daddy sent you to ask about it?"

"Yes, ma'am, well he's dead. She has no father."

"Mr. Merton, I wish we could help you, but I know Dr. Moncure would say no. Have you tried the Magdalen House?"

"No, ma'am," he said. He was beginning to feel like a mouse in front of a large, soft cat.

"Some people call it the Spring Street House because it's on Spring Street, but I've always called it the Magdalen House. It's mostly for indigents, but they might take a case like yours."

"But there are lying-in places, aren't there?"

"Oh, yes. If you have the money, there's places for anything, anything atall. 'Twasn't so when I was coming along. You couldn't just walk into a saloon on Main Street in the middle of the day, and into a house of bad repute at night. People had morals then. Now it's just sin everywhere you go. People smoking, spitting, gambling, cussing. Nosir, in my day, people didn't act thataway. They behaved theirselves, and people got along just fine, even if they didn't like each other."

"Yes, ma'am, but where would I find such a place, if I had the money? A sure enough lying-in place?"

She shook her head. "I don't know," she said. "There was a place somewhere out near Monroe Park, but I think it's gone. But seems like I heard of a place out past the college a ways. You could try them at the Magdalen House. Or ask Dr. Moncure. He'd know. But, I'll tell you, that kind of place is for the very rich only, the kind that think they can buy their way out of sin. I know some nice people that are rich, but you can't buy your way to heaven, you understand."

Tommie nodded, and Mrs. Paine crossed herself.

"You want to wait for Dr. Moncure?" she asked. "I'll go see if I can find him."

"No," Tommie said. "I'll go on to the Magdalen House and ask them." He got up to leave, thinking he had already stayed too long.

"Pray about it," Mrs. Paine was saying. "God will answer your prayers." Tommie told her he would, and she crossed herself and said, smiling sadly, "Jesus loves you."

Out on the street he started the trek down to the roughneck Oregon Hill neighborhood. Magdalen sounded like the right sort of place, even if it was for indigents—better, in fact, because it would be affordable and obscure, and he would just tell Lillian it was the only lying-in place available. Magdalen would be a good name for a whorehouse, he thought, then like Aunt Jane said a quick prayer for forgiveness. He passed Judge Crump's house with its pillared porch and corniced windows, its iron gate hiding a prim little garden—someday I'll own a house in town just like that, Tommie imagined. Or, better, something like the old John Marshall house a few streets over. That was how a lawyer should live—a plantation taking up a whole city block, with its own carriage house and stable. For those who worked hard and were blessed with God-given talent, anything was possible: A country lawyer could become chief justice of the United States Supreme Court. There would be dinner parties every week and a servant for each guest, and on outings he'd have to decide between the brougham or, for fancier occasions, the barouche.

He did not relish going down to Oregon Hill, where hoodlum sons of mill workers engaged in territorial battles in the middle of the day. He did not like the idea of going down there only to be turned away by the Magdalen House, so he was going to trust to Providence that when the time came they would take Lillian in. He would make sure she was well provided for, and then return when it was over and help her figure out what to do with the baby.

That night he had dinner with his old friend Tyler Bagby, who had married only a year ago. He sat in the little parlor talking to them, thinking of what a lucky fellow Tyler was. He lived a confined life in a small, dingy house, but he was a banker now, with a kind if not especially attractive wife, good prospects, and no baby on the way. When his wife was out of the room, Tyler, with a smile now more ironic than droll, said, "The married life ain't bad, Tommie. You should try it."

Walking back to his hotel, Tommie knew he should call on Lillian, but why risk being seen with her again? He had spent the evening with Tyler, who could vouch for him should the need ever arise, though why it should Tommie couldn't imagine. He had ten dollars in his pocket, and he suddenly decided to visit Lizzie Banks's. There was a new girl named Pauline Lacount with large breasts and a smiling leer that made him feel everything was right in his world. He sent a note to Miss Merton at the Exchange Hotel, apologizing for not being able to come by and saying he would write. He didn't sign it.

At the door of Lizzie Banks's, he lifted the knocker, then placed it gently back down. He saw Lillie as he had left her, lying there on the bed, holding him without a word. Again he lifted the knocker. He set it down and turned on his heel and headed back to his hotel.

On the train home the next morning he watched the farms flash past—the bare trees, the cattle on colorless fields under a bark-gray sky—and tried to remember the excitement of traveling to Richmond with his father eight years ago. But he could not shut out the clamor in his mind. The insistent rattling of the wheels on the track told him over and over, *Watch yourself, now, watch yourself, now, watch yourself, now.* He tried to amuse himself with an image of Pauline Lacount, leaning over him half naked, her bodice down around her waist and her soft breasts swaying toward him like big handfuls of white dough. He caught the glance of an old woman sitting opposite—she smiled politely, knowingly, and his heart raced.

❧

CHAPTER SEVENTEEN

THE AMERICAN HOTEL employees take their turns on the stand. Night clerk Julius Dodson at first seems nervous, his soft fleshy hands shaking as he describes finding the torn note. But sensing the courtroom's complete attention to his words, he warms to the limelight. Colonel Aylett introduces the torn note as evidence, asking if Dodson recognizes it.

"I strenuously object, Your Honor," Crump complains. "No one has demonstrated the relevance of this note. It has no signature on it, or identifying mark of any kind. It's not properly part of the res gestae of evidence."

"We'll prove that it is," Aylett says.

"You're putting the cart before the horse."

Judge Hill says he'll give the matter some thought, but in the meantime the prosecution may continue. Tommie sits there watching Colonel Aylett, whose nephews were his boon companions in school, doing everything in his power to put the noose around him. He has no grudge against Tommie, has never even met him, and yet he brings in people like this hotel clerk to bear witness against him. Tommie's reputation is already in tatters—what with locals dubbing him a monster, a machine, cold-blooded when he sheds no tears at court, and guilty when he so much as leans forward to look at a piece of evidence—now he's only trying to save his neck. He pictures the gallows . . . yet that simply cannot be his fate. He had a chance to come clean, yet he waited and waited—for what? God was clearly not going to give him a nudge; he had to make up his own mind to act.

"And you say you tore that note up on Saturday and didn't find it again until Monday?" Evans asks Dodson.

"Yes, but—"

"And there was at least three days' worth of trash in the cans you examined?"

"Yes, sir."

"And you glanced at the note before you tore it up, but now you think it's the same one that William Lane brought back undelivered?"

"Yes, sir."

"How many other notes were in the wastebaskets?"

"A few. I don't remember exactly."

"You don't remember? I see. Thank you. I'm finished with this witness."

Slim Lane gets on the stand and takes the oath, looking wide-eyed with uncertainty. Meredith warms him up as well as he can with innocuous questions about his job at the American and how long he has worked there. Then he asks him about March 13. Slim gives his testimony haltingly, staring mostly at a corner of the room as though reading his responses from some script posted there. On the cross-examination, he shifts to the other corner. He carefully avoids looking into the fifth pew where he knows Wren is watching, that bear with the big nose and the hole in his chin. He remembers what Wren told him, but he's afraid if he looks at him now he'll forget what he's supposed to say.

"You say you never could find this mulatto boy who supposedly delivered a note from some gentleman out on the street?" Evans asks.

"No sir."

"And how long did you search?"

"Three days at first, but then Mr. Wren told me to keep looking."

"And you never found him?"

"Nosir."

"At your police court deposition, you mentioned you had a look around Room 21 on March thirteenth when Miss Merton was there. What did you see on her bureau?"

"I didn't see much. I just got the note from the lady."

"Mr. Lane, you were under oath to tell the truth then, just as you are now. Tell us what you saw on the bureau."

Slim glances down at the Bible sitting on the edge of the evidence table. "Something gold and shiny, but I don't know what it was."

"But it could have been a key?"

"Yes I think it—I think it could've been a key."

"Thank you."

Meredith redirects. "Mr. Lane, what you saw that day three months ago might easily have been something else besides a key, mightn't it?"

"Yes sir."

"What else could it have been?"

"I think," Slim says, staring at the corner of the room closer to Meredith, "it could've been a ring, or a piece of lady's jewelry, or a brass hinge maybe."

"I see, and how long do you think you looked at the bureau?"

"Two, three seconds."

Hunter Hunt gets up and relates how a man came to the hotel inquiring after a friend of his sister's, but upon seeing the lady from Room 21 said she was not the lady he was looking for. Hunt then ushered the man into the parlor. He identifies Tommie as the man. Evans asks about Hunt's duties, then throws him a curve. "What color coat was the man wearing?"

Hunt glances at Tommie. "Dark brown, I believe."

Evans reads from a transcript. "So not light-colored, as you stated at the police court?"

Hunt is quiet for a moment. "Yessuh, I believe it was light-colored, a sort of light brown."

"So the fact that the prisoner was wearing a light coat at the police court didn't lead you to think the man you'd seen was wearing the same-colored coat?"

Hunt scratches the side of his head. "I don't remember the color. But I'm pretty sure that's the same man."

The Violet Bone letter is introduced, over Crump's vehement objection, and Violet Bone herself is brought forth. Tommie watches as a pretty young lady with blond curls comes forth—a girl with a sweet manner and a quiet confidence, a girl, the prosecution all but says, much like Lillie herself. She has been living in Baltimore and has not received any communication with the deceased since before Christmas. She does have a sick aunt, but she did not write the letter in question, though it does look something like her writing, she admits.

Meredith next produces a piece of paper containing a poem in a neatly written hand. He explains to the judge that it was found beneath the lining in Miss Madison's trunk. It is so disgusting that he cannot read it to a courtroom filled with ladies and gentlemen. The judge allows him to pass it around to the jury, each member of whom takes his time with it. Then he calls to the stand a banker who has many times served as a handwriting witness. The banker examines the poem, then the sole letter from Cluverius found in Miss Madison's trunk. The letter is dated from the time she was living with her grandfather and contains nothing incriminating—just pleasantries and a reminder that she was overdue for a visit to Little Plymouth. The banker says that the two papers appear to be from the same hand.

Crump snorts. When his turn comes, he asks, "You call your-self an expert?"

The banker is uncowed. "No sir, I never did."

"Yes, you did just now. Mr. Stenographer, read back the first question and answer." The stenographer does and there is no mention of the word "expert." Crump fumes, "You don't mind my calling you an expert then?"

"You may call me what you like, Judge Crump, but I object to your making me call myself something I never have."

Tommie is twisting in his seat. He knows the poem. It's from *Wisdom for Girls*, but how Lillie came to have a copy of it in her trunk he has no idea. Anybody could have sent it to her, and here they're claiming it's in his own hand. His teachers praised his handwriting, though a callous boy from Gloucester said it was prissy. Tommie later found an opportunity to hit him in the face.

Mrs. Mary Dickinson of Millboro' Springs takes the stand. She becomes an immediate crowd favorite with her charming laugh and mountain accent. "No," she laughs, her eyes crinkling and bosom jouncing, "I would not say Lillie was a particularly brave person. She didn't like sleeping without one of my little granddaughters being in the same room. And she had a time crossing the river by herself in the little boat." Then she grows thoughtful and quieter. "She was the sweetest thing."

"She wasn't the sort, then, to go off to a secluded place by herself?" Meredith prods.

"Oh, no sir. Not hardly."

"And when she got back from Richmond in January—who did she say she visited there?"

"She said she saw her cousin Tommie." At this, the crowd be-gins buzzing and murmuring, and Hill has to rap his gavel, not bothering anymore to explain why. Crump whispers something to Evans, then leans over and glances sharply at Tommie, who keeps his eyes on the witness.

"And before she left for Richmond in March," Meredith continues, "how did she seem to you?"

"She seemed agitated in her mind. Like something wasn't quite right. And she said a queer thing. She said she had a kind of bad feeling about the trip. And I told her she didn't have to go, but since she was going to help an elderly lady I didn't press it."

"Bad feeling about the trip? I should say so."

The parade of witnesses keeps moving through, each one questioned minutely by both sides. A streetcar driver named Loach testifies that he picked up a young couple at about nine o'clock the night of the thirteenth and drove them out to Reservoir Street, but he won't swear that the prisoner is the same man. He's also unsure whether he picked them up at Twelfth, across from the American Hotel, or farther down, around Fifteenth. The woman was short and stout and wore a red shawl.

Mark Davis, proprietor of the Davis House, relates how he chatted and ate an apple with the prisoner around midnight, nothing apparently amiss. He also states that the prisoner stayed at his hotel in early January.

Then Gretchen O'Banyon takes the stand, spreading excitement through the crowd. Tommie has not seen her for at least a year and he hardly recognizes her; she has her hair up in a way that makes her less attractive. She's thinner and unpainted and wearing a high-necked blouse and navy skirt, and looks altogether less like a prostitute and more like a working girl.

She explains that she works at Mrs. Goss's cigar store now, but did work at Lizzie Banks's house. Meredith asks her what she did there.

"I entertained gentlemen," she says, looking straight at Meredith.

"And do you recognize the prisoner?"

"Yes sir, he came and visited me and other girls several times at Lizzie Banks's."

"And what name did he go by?"

"Walter Merton."

"Walter Merton," Meredith repeats. "Are you sure?"

"Yes sir."

On cross-examination, Evans does his best to confuse and scare her, asking what she did before coming to the house of ill repute, and exactly when she saw the prisoner. "And you think you saw him there?"

She glances first at Meredith for encouragement. "I know he was there. I don't think nothing about it."

"Who did you first tell about having seen him?"

"Mr. Meredith and Jack Wren. Mr. Meredith came first, but Ada and Ella and I wouldn't tell him anything because we didn't know who he was."

"I see," says Evans. "And then Mr. Wren came?"

"Yes, and he showed us a picture of the man and I said, 'Mr. Wren, I know nothing in the world about it.' And he says, 'Uh huh, I know so-and-so.' Then Lizzie told me to go on and tell what I knew."

"What did he mean by he knows so-and-so?"

"He knew something about me that I didn't want repeated."

"What was it?"

"I'd rather not say."

"Did you used to go with Mr. Wren?"

"You don't have to answer that!" Meredith shoots out, and Gretchen, with a quick glance at Wren sitting in his customary place, claps her mouth shut. Wren gives her a smug smile and a wink—his little birds can always be counted on to sing for him and nobody else. He plans to hand the city a nice fat bill when this is all over, though the publicity alone is making it more than worth his while.

During a break Tommie and his lawyers meet in a guarded room adjacent to the judge's office. Tommie and Mr. Evans take seats, while Crump and his son stand. Crump folds his arms and stares out the window at the people across the street in Capitol Square. Tommie follows his gaze and sees a colored man with no legs dragging himself on a little wheeled board and holding out his cap. A blond-haired girl in a blue dress puts some money in and goes skipping off. Now Crump lights a cigar and turns his back to the window. "What people will do to survive is amazing," he says. "Tommie, did I ever tell you what it was like here when the Yankees came calling?"

"No, sir," Tommie says, knowing that Crump is building to some monumental chastisement.

"I was here until the last day. The lower part of the city was all smoke and fire, fire and smoke. Warships exploding in the river, mobs looting liquor stores. This was before we'd given up the city, mind you. Soldiers in hospitals suddenly discovered they could walk—they could by God run. Then the old men and boys who'd been guarding the city left with the Confederate government out across the bridges and all hell broke loose. I left too, but I'm told the prisoners in the penitentiary broke out, and got away, most of them. Just like that, their world was made anew. But Tommie, there's no war going on. So unless we have an earthquake or a flood like I've never seen in my lifetime, you're stuck in prison. When somebody like Mrs. Dickinson gets on the stand and says Miss Madison told her she saw you in Richmond last January and it's the first your counsel has heard of it—well, I don't know what to think. How can you explain such a thing? Did you, in fact, see her here then?"

"No, sir, I didn't."

"Mrs. Dickinson would have no reason to lie about that under oath. So either Miss Madison lied or you're lying now. Which is it?"

Tommie waits for Mr. Evans to say something calming, but he just sits there beside Tommie looking over some notes. Crump, his son alongside him like a shadow, stands awaiting an answer. "I don't know what reason she would have to lie," Tommie says. He is struck by his own coolness, and he begins to consider the matter from Lillie's point of view. Under what circumstances would she use his name to cover up her whereabouts? "Perhaps she wanted to throw Mrs. Dickinson off in some way," Tommie says. "What more innocent name could she use than her cousin's?"

Crump scrutinizes him. "So you were here in Richmond both times she was here, and you never laid eyes on her?"

"My business brings me here often, Mr. Crump."

"I know that, Tommie." Crump puffs out a lungful of smoke, rubs the back of his neck, and rolls his head side to side. He addresses Evans, "We'll have to go with that then." Now turning to Tommie, "Young man, did anybody ever tell you you can be infuriating?"

"Yes sir," Tommie says, a faint smile on his lips.

"I like you, honestly. But everybody out there knows now that you're no saint. If there's anything you want to tell us about you and that girl, this is the time. Believe me, it can only help. We'll work out a new battle plan."

Tommie tries to clear away the doubts that have been gathering strength. Would it be advisable even now to throw the entire matter into Crump's able hands and hope for mercy from the jury? Probably they've already made up their minds. Buried in all that testimony is a nugget of truth that the jury must have the rough shape of, even if they can't get the exact dimensions. The question is, what truth are they on to? "No sir," he says, "I don't know any more about it than you do."

During the afternoon session Tommie sits through testimony from two men employed in the nailworks on Belle Isle who claim to have seen him and a short, chunky woman with a red scarf. One of them says he heard the woman exclaim, "Oh, cousin Tommie!" Tommie has not been on Belle Isle in years, and Lillian has never called him cousin Tommie.

"You mean to tell the jury," Evans says to one of the workers, "that you have never seen the prisoner since his arrest and yet you identify him as someone you saw fleetingly three months ago?"

"Yessir."

"And how many strangers do you see on Belle Isle in the course of a week?"

"That depends, sir—sometimes a handful, sometimes maybe a dozen or two."

"Are you sure you aren't fitting your memory in with something you read in the paper?"

"I'm right sure."

On a redirect, Aylett says, "Will you ever forget the features of the dead girl out at the almshouse?"

"No sir," the worker says, shaking his head.

The star witness is saved for near the end of the prosecution's case. The jeweler Herman Joel takes his place at the head of the courtroom. He's a short man with a goatee and a heavy Polish accent, and he sometimes unintentionally makes the court laugh by mangling an English idiom. "And you sold a watch key to the prisoner?" Meredith asks.

Joel clears his throat and blinks his eyes. "Close up all day I look at jewelry. The faces not much. But, yes, I think the same man it is."

"And is this the key?" Meredith shows him the gold key.

Here Joel takes out a pair of eyeglasses, tucks the stems methodically behind his ears, and examines the key.

Again he rapidly blinks his eyes, then says, "I believe it is a key on which I replace the barrel and selled, yes, to the gentleman."

"How would you know for a fact if it was the key?"

"I take apart the key and see it is my work, or, no, it is not."

"Judge," Meredith says, "could Mr. Joel be permitted to open the key up and see if it's his work?"

"I object to this proceeding," Crump says. "We haven't even identified it yet, and here you are wanting to destroy it."

Hill rules that unless both sides agree, the key cannot be tampered with. When Crump's turn comes, he asks Joel if he has any proof he sold the key to the prisoner.

Joel runs air across his vocal cords. "Records of my works and sales I keep in Bland's store. But page is missing."

"That's convenient for you. You say the page for that day is gone?"

"Yes sir."

"What happened to it?"

"I don't know." Joel blinks once.

"You come in here with a story before twelve bearded men, men of brains representing the commonwealth of Virginia, and you can't back it up in any way whatsoever? Who did you first tell this story to?"

"I speak with detective. Now I think the less talk the better it is. I should speak with a cat tongue." The audience titters.

"I should say so," Crump fumes. "That's all, Your Honor."

Crump sits down in a huff. At the break, Crump and Evans confer about this as if Tommie doesn't exist. Then Evans turns to Tommie. "This could be what tilts the jury, Tommie. It's little things like this. Suppose we let him open it and he claims it's his work, then at least we've taken the mystery out of it. We can always point out that one jeweler's work is similar to another's, and, anyway, just because it looks like his work that doesn't mean it's the same key he repaired for you."

"He didn't repair a key for me. He recognizes me because he repaired a watch for me. He took his time getting it back to me and I got upset with him, and that's why he's so happy to come in here now and perjure himself. It's good publicity."

"I'm sure all that's true, but what about letting him open it up? The jury has a picture of you crawling through the fence and snagging your watch key. We need to change that picture."

Tommie thinks about it for a moment. "What do you think, Mr. Crump?"

Crump rubs his beard, becoming the contemplative jurist he does not show in front of the court. "I don't know, son. Mr. Evans could be right. On the other hand, Joel's hardly going to back down now, even if the file marks and whatnot he finds inside that key aren't what he expects."

Both wait for Tommie's decision. "I think for now we don't let them open it," he says. "Maybe they'll forget about it once they've heard our defense."

Crump and Evans exchange looks. "Maybe," Evans says. "But the prosecution will remind them."

Richardson and Birney take their turns on the stand, recounting the details of the arrest, Richardson from time to time glancing at Tommie as though trying to square in his mind the young man he met in Little Plymouth with the murderer the prosecution has pieced together. The hours Richardson and his men have spent tracking down leads, interviewing people who have some connection or other with the case, and then sorting through all this evidence, have accumulated to where he hardly knows his home anymore. He has attended some of the trial, when he could find the time, because people keep asking him his opinion about

Tommie's aunt, his brother, his parents, Lillie's home life, and all kinds of things the newspapers have gotten onto. He doesn't have answers for most of them, nor can he quite fathom what it is people are after. Do they just want to be entertained by the downfall of a fellow human being? Do they feel pity for Cluverius? Or is there some deep-seated anger at a fellow who gets too big for his britches and comes here to visit an unspeakable act upon a girl—who could have been one of their own daughters—and is so lacking in honor and decency that he tries to hide it, taking what he wants like a carpetbagger and then running off?

Richardson answers the questions both sides put to him, but only one question really bothers him and it comes from Aylett: "In addition to the torn note, what made you decide to arrest the prisoner?"

"The testimony of the victim's father," Richardson says, and as soon as he does he sees weeks of work by scores of people adding up to nothing but a weak chain leading from the American Hotel to the reservoir. He still thinks he arrested the right man—there is a mountain of proof. Yet none of it is solid. The only truth, as he has long known, is what you can get people to believe.

And then, after ten days and seventy-seven witnesses, the torture is nearly over. The commonwealth says it has one more witness.

Howard Madison has been noticeably absent for most of the trial of his daughter's accused killer. He takes his time walking to the witness box as though he's ten years older than he really is. Willie studies him, wondering if he hasn't primed himself with a drink or two. His hair is slicked back and he's wearing a wrinkled black bow tie and a gray Confederate jacket with brass buttons and the number of his unit stitched to the shoulder.

Aylett tells him he knows how difficult it must be to have to come here and discuss the murder of his daughter, and that he doesn't have many questions. He then asks if Madison's daughter and the prisoner were romantically involved. Madison replies that Fannie Lillian told him she was in love with her cousin Tommie and that he had promised to marry her. Willie stares hard at Madison, almost daring him to look his way. He has not laid eyes on the man since their encounter at the Tayloe place, and now he's sure that Madison is lying—and enjoying himself in the process.

On his cross, Evans asks Madison, "When exactly was it that she told you this?"

Madison screws up his brow, shakes his head. "It was 'long about July."

"Early July? Late July? When exactly?"

"I don't know. What difference does it make?"

"It makes a great deal of difference, Mr. Madison. The timing is crucial, as is your memory of it."

"I think it was early July."

"And where exactly were you at that time?"

"At my place. We were out in the barn. I was mending an axle on my hay tedder, and she come in and says, 'Pa, I need to tell you something,' like it was real important."

"Go on, what were her exact words?"

"She said, 'Pa, me and Tommie are gettin' married. He's promised me.' I said, 'What's the rush?' and she said, 'We just have to.' Those were her exact words, 'We just have to.' And then she went off up to the house."

"Mr. Madison, is there anyone else, your wife, for instance, to whom she might have said the same thing?"

"She might've."

"And yet you're the only one who has come forward with this unsupportable hearsay. Don't you think that's strange?"

"Objection, Your Honor," Meredith says.

"I don't mind," Madison says. "No, I don't think it's strange atall. Mrs. Madison is a quiet woman who minds her own business. I had to speak out, though."

"And yet," Evans says, "she didn't marry him. In fact, she went off to Bath to teach. And there was never another mention of her marrying Mr. Cluverius?"

"Not as I know of, no sir." The tension has gone from Madison's face. Before he steps down he takes a moment to glance over at Tommie and Willie. Willie catches the look, sees the smirk ripple across Madison's features like a breath of wind on the water.

❧

CHAPTER EIGHTEEN

THE DEFENSE BEGINS.

Tyler Bagby swears to the good character of Thomas Cluverius and says that on the night of January 5 Tommie had dinner with him and his wife. Martin Harrison is a well-spoken young lawyer who says he talked with the prisoner at Schoen's on March 13, and Bernard Henley saw him at the Dime Museum later that day. Crump tries to plant a subliminal idea. "So you saw him at the intermission of the evening performance—how did he seem to you?" Henley says they only waved across the lobby, but that Tommie seemed fine. "And he was alone?" Yes, he was alone.

Meredith spots the trick and on cross-examination clarifies: "When you say evening performance you mean you saw him at the *afternoon* performance, is that not correct?" Henley says that it is. "So you never saw him that night after five o'clock?"

"No sir, I did not."

A handful of friends come forward to say what an outstanding citizen Tommie is, how they've never known him to have anything but a sterling character. The Aylett brothers have, of course, not attended the trial, their father sitting on the side of the prosecution, but Randall Croxton stands up and avers that no matter what anybody says, Tommie is "a true-blue friend who couldn't think a harmful thought if he tried." At this, Tommie begins to tear up and has to fight to stop the flow. The prosecution doesn't bother much with these witnesses. They have no evidence, and the jury knows they're standing by their friend and kinsman.

The next day Jane Tunstall takes the stand for the defense. She wears a black dress and veil, but the heat is such that after a while she takes the veil off. Her eyes are grief-worn, but she tries to smile. Crump asks her about Tommie's watch keys. She says that the one with the amethyst had been her husband's and that she gave it to Tommie when he went off to college. Then Crump wants to know about the nature of the trouble Lillian had with her parents.

"I didn't understand it exactly," Jane says. "They thought she was out of control someway, so I let her come live with me. They didn't have the money to send her to private school and I did, so I didn't see anything wrong in that. But they seemed to resent me after that. I sent a dress to her one time, when she went home for a holiday, and they sent it back."

Crump then has Jane identify a letter written to her by Lillian shortly before she moved out of her parents' house. He reads aloud, "'It is my prayer tonight that the sun of tomorrow may shine on me a corpse. O if suicide were not a sin, how soon the lingering spark of my life would vanish.' I realize she was very young when she wrote that, but she appeared to be capable of high-strung emotions. Would you agree with that?"

Jane looks torn for the first time. "I loved my grandniece very much." She dabs her eyes. "But, yes, she could be very flighty, and, as you say, high-strung."

On cross-examination Aylett asks, "Didn't you think, ma'am, you might be spoiling Lillian? Making her unfit to be happy in her own home?"

"No," Jane says, quietly, fanning herself. She smiles, batting her eyelashes at Aylett. "She was just as unhappy there before she came to me as after."

"But by educating her at your own expense," Aylett persists, "weren't you giving her high aspirations and enabling her to move in a different circle from what she had been born and raised in?"

"Yes, I suppose so."

"And so weren't you teaching her to be disobedient to her own flesh and blood?"

"No sir, I was not. I'm her own flesh and blood."

"How many children do you have?"

"None that have lived."

"By taking Lillie in weren't you able to strike at her parents over her shoulders?"

Jane cannot stifle a little laugh. "No, I don't believe I was."

"Does that furnish an amusing idea to your mind?"

"No, but it sounds funny." When she has finished, she takes her place behind Tommie; she doesn't touch him, but sits there watching her own hands, wondering what happened under her own roof that she might have been the cause of. It is too impossible to imagine, so she closes her eyes and sees her husband, sitting in a carriage waiting for her, his hand outstretched to help her up.

Tommie's brother comes to see him that evening at suppertime. He fills up the cell doorway with his broad shoulders and wide-brimmed straw hat, and Tommie feels a twinge of resentment at his brother's health and freedom. No matter what happens, however careworn his face is now, he'll go on and raise a family and live a full life.

Willie takes off his hat and comes in. "Are you eating enough, Tommie?" he asks.

"Yes, fine." The truth is, he feels weaker than he ever has in his life. The lack of exercise and sunlight, the strain of the trial, are beginning to take a toll. He wakes up nights, his heart banging in his ears, his eyes sand-filled sockets searching the darkness for

what woke him—a dream? a terrified outburst down the hall?—
and then he lies awake for hours, afraid to go back to sleep.

"I want you to think about something," Willie says, sitting
down. "You know I was awfully keen on Lillian. I'd like to—I
want to take your place, Tommie. You have the bright future; I'm
just a laborer, always will be."

Tommie shakes his head. "I don't know what you're talking
about."

"That could have been my child she was carrying."

Tommie eyes him sharply, waiting.

"I mean it may have been. How do you know it wasn't? She
wrote me asking for some help back in February."

"I don't believe you. You weren't intimate with her. Not like
that." And yet he's not sure, and it seems that this rope his brother
is throwing him may be real enough to grasp.

"She did write me," Willie insists. "She asked for money. She
said she was in trouble. She didn't say what kind, but she said she
wanted to see me."

"Did she mention me?"

"Not a word."

But Tommie can tell by the way he tongues his lower lip and
shakes his head that his brother is, at least in part, lying. "I still
have the letter," Willie says. "It's proof I was involved—I can
bring it to you. I can give it to Colonel Aylett and make a confession. There'd be nothing you could do about it."

"I'd say you were lying. I'd confess myself."

"Would you?"

They look at each other. The guard at the end of the hall coughs;
somewhere nearby a spoon scrapes against a metal bowl. Tommie
glances at Forney's *Anecdotes of Public Men* in his stack of books,
and an old image of himself addressing the general assembly flick-
ers in his brain. "I honestly don't know what I'd do," he says.

"I've thought about it," Willie says. "I could take my chances. I'd be out in ten years, at the most. My whole life ahead of me. I could survive in here. I don't know if you can."

"Ten years," Tommie says. "Is that what you think I'll get?"

"I think you'll walk out of here. But why risk it?"

"You can't save me, Willie. There's nothing you can do anymore, except what you've been doing."

"It's not too late for me to get up there. I want to do it."

"No," Tommie says, but he won't look at his brother, because Willie will see that he desperately wants to say yes.

"But it's not right. You didn't do this. She killed herself. God knows it, and he won't let you be punished for it. I know he won't, Tommie. I'm going to confess."

Tommie puts a hand on his arm. "No, you're not. You wouldn't get away with it. You can't prove you were in Richmond. You'd just look like a liar, like you're trying to cover up my tracks."

Willie considers a minute, then nods. "All right, then. Are you sure there's nothing you want? Do you have enough blankets?"

"It's not cold anymore. A little more light would help, but they won't let you bring a lantern in."

Now Willie leans in and whispers, "I could help you get out of here. It wouldn't be that hard—nobody expects you to run. I've studied the walls, and there's a place over in the southwest corner where the barbed wire sags. You can't tell from inside the yard. You'd have to figure out when the guard is watching. The bars in here are practically rusted out at the top. We'd pick a dark night in the rain. I'd throw a rope over at your signal and a piece of saddle leather so you won't cut yourself. We'd go down by the creek, and get you on a freight train."

Tommie smiles. "You have it all figured out."

"What about it?"

"Well, it hasn't come to that yet, but it'll give me something to think about at night."

Willie goes and looks up and down the corridor. "Listen, Tommie, there's something I've been meaning to tell you," he says. "It's about Mr. Madison." Tommie looks alarmed, and Willie wonders if his brother already knows. "He threatened to get up in that box and say you and Lillie were involved if I didn't pay him two hundred dollars. I can't prove that he said it, but he did. I want to get up there and tell the jury."

"They'll think you're lying to protect me."

"So what if they do? Isn't that better than letting him get away with a real lie?" Willie looks at his brother, trying to pry out what might be hidden there.

"He wanted money?" Tommie says. He gets up and grips the bars on his gate. He turns and squats, facing Willie. "He's crazy, Willie. He's liable to do anything."

"I know it. He was mean to Lillie, and now here he is trying to extract money for her sake." Again, Willie regards his brother, trying to figure if he wants to say something else. "What do you mean, he's liable to do anything?"

"I don't know. Just don't give him any money."

"The only thing he'll get from me is a fist in the face if he ever speaks to me again on this earth."

"Willie, if I don't get out of here . . . well, there's some things you should know. I don't want to tell you everything now, but there's some important things you should know."

"What are you talking about?"

"Not everything is as I've told it. There's some missing pieces that I can't talk about. You're the only one I'll tell, but not yet."

"What are you waiting for, Tommie? If there's something that can save you, what could you possibly be waiting for?"

"I can't say that either. The jury doesn't want to hear things. Nobody wants to hear certain things, because nobody can believe certain things even if they hear them. There's strange things that happen in the world sometimes, I've come to understand that, and they don't fit in with the rest of our lives. These things, they're like a burl in a tree, Willie—they don't belong there. They get in somehow and the tree has to work around it. Or else die."

"Burls won't hurt anything. Some people think they're pretty. Mighty hard to work with though."

"Okay, Willie, but my point is that not everybody thinks they're pretty."

Willie rises from the little fanback chair. "You get some sleep. Things are going to turn around, I can feel it in my marrow."

In the morning Willie takes his turn. Tommie can hardly bear to look, and for the second time in as many days he feels his eyes welling. He has never been prouder of his brother, sitting there in the witness chair looking so confident and friendly—the man Tommie has always looked up to, and, as he once told Lillie, would trust with his life. He answers Evans's questions in an unhesitating, forthright, clear voice. No, it was not strange that Tommie went out the night he was arrested wearing his brother's hat—there was no effort to conceal anything. No, he never wore a mustache. Tommie traveled to Richmond March 12 on business pertaining to a land suit in a bankruptcy court, representing Mr. Bray. He often went to Richmond for such matters.

"Tell the jury," Mr. Evans says, "whether Miss Madison was able to swim."

"She couldn't swim to save herself," Willie says. "She fell in the river when we were out boating and I had to jump in and rescue her."

"So if she had thrown herself into the reservoir she couldn't have changed her mind and gotten out?"

"I don't see how."

Evans shows him a gold watch key similar to the one found at the reservoir. It's an inch-long gold cylinder, but the top is inset with a hexagonal amethyst. "Do you recognize this key?" Evans asks.

"It's my brother's," he says.

"Did you bring this to your brother after his arrest?"

"Yes I did."

"Why did you do that?"

"He sent word he needed it, to clear his name."

"And where did you get it?"

"From his desk at home where he left it. It didn't work well, so he was using his steel keys."

"I see." Now he shows him the reservoir key. "Have you ever seen this key before?"

Willie studies it. "No, sir, not before it was shown in this courtroom."

Aylett then gets up and says, "Your Honor, it might be instructive to the jury to see how well this new key fits on the prisoner's watch." Hill nods his assent, and the clerk brings out Tommie's pocket watch. Aylett offers to let the defense try it.

"This is your show," Crump says.

Aylett inserts the key and attempts to wind the watch. "Well, it's not turning anything, it's just spinning." He shows the judge as if asking for help.

"Our witness just explained it was worn out," Crump says. "Of course it doesn't work."

"Could we try the reservoir key while we're at it?" Aylett says, casually, as if he had not been awaiting this moment. Since there is no objection, he inserts the heart-crowned key. It fits but the watch will not wind. "It appears to be fully wound already," Aylett says, looking around and raising an eyebrow at his law clerks.

Crump's belly bounces in mirth. "Must've been back there trying out a bunch of keys," he says audibly to his team. "I don't know what keys they were using."

Aylett quickly moves on. He asks Willie if he was aware of his brother's private life.

"I knew that on occasion he had paid to lie with a woman."

"Did you know that he sometimes went about as Walter Merton?"

"No."

"Did you know that he was a frequenter of Richmond taverns?"

"I object to all this," Evans says, genuinely annoyed. But Judge Hill rules that since these points have already been testified to by other witnesses, Willie has to answer.

Willie considers. "I don't think he went frequently anywhere, except to church and to visit his parents."

A dog fight erupts out in the hallway, nearly drowning out the end of Willie's statement. Evans says, "I couldn't hear that. Would the witness mind repeating it?"

When Willie sits down he catches his brother's eye, and there's a faint smile between them. Willie has considered the possibility that Tommie never gave Lillian a watch key, that Tommie himself lost a gold key out there . . . that, in fact, he was with her at the reservoir. But the thought sickens him, so he pushes it out of his mind.

Tommie's father has not been able to come back since that first week. Mrs. Cluverius could not be by herself for so long. She sent a message saying she would come and get up on the stand for him, but he wrote back more than once telling her not to worry—that he was innocent, had the best lawyers in the state, and that he was confident of a successful outcome. But here his father is standing up for his son on the final day of testimony. He is sparer even than three weeks ago, as though he'd been drained, his beard a scrap of Spanish moss. His suit hangs on him like a scarecrow's—he looks like a good wind could blow him all the way back to King and Queen. Yet his face seems as unlined as on that first trip to Richmond.

Meredith wants to know about the marks on the prisoner's hand. "We have witnesses we can bring in here who'll swear you said he got them on a fence rail. Do you stand by that story?"

"I do," Cluverius says, looking straight at Aylett. Tommie almost wishes his father had stayed home. Detective Wren dug up this confabulation of his father's and the prosecution now claims they have witnesses to verify that he went around telling it. Tommie has no idea how his father came up with it, nor why, unless he felt his son guilty. Crump and Evans have offered no alternative to the prosecution's witness, a medical examiner, who maintained the scratches on his hand were from some curved object like a curette—or a fingernail. When Crump asked Tommie about the scratches, all Tommie could say was, "I don't remember what happened or what I said. They didn't seem important." Both Crump and Evans thought it all right, then, if Mr. Cluverius came out with his story.

"When did that happen?" Aylett asks, stretching his mouth so that his teeth flash beneath his waxed and curled mustache.

"The day he got back from Richmond."

"The day he got back from Richmond? And how exactly did it happen?"

"Well sir, I met with him at the store that afternoon, and we went a little ways off to talk. Tommie leaned against a fence. He slipped and scratched his hand on a knothole."

"What kind of fence was it?"

"A stake-and-rail fence."

"And how was he standing?"

"With his back to the fence, arms stretched out along it."

"How many rails did the fence have?"

Cluverius ponders this for a hidden trick. "I believe three or four."

"How high was it?"

"I don't know, I didn't measure it. I reckon as high as a man."

"And how was he standing?"

"I already told you that, with his back to the fence."

"Did you notice the knothole then, or later?"

"What do you mean? I noticed it then."

"Who did you tell about the accident?"

"I didn't tell anybody, it wasn't a big scratch."

"Yet you saw the cuts on his hand?"

"Yes, I did."

"You mean to tell me that you took his hand in yours and he a grown man?"

"My children are as dear to me as babies."

"How come other people who saw him that day claim he said he caught his hand in his watch chain getting on the train?"

"I don't know why they would say a thing like that. I never heard it."

"Did you know he tried to hide his hands from the police and then told them he thought he had a skin eruption?"

"It was cold," Cluverius snaps. "They gave him no gloves, he had to keep himself warm someway." Meredith keeps pressing him for details. Finally, Mr. Cluverius has had enough. "Before I answer any more questions, I'd like to ask you some," he says.

"Your business is to answer questions, not ask them."

"I reckon I have as much right to ask a question as you do."

Judge Hill, in a low, polite voice says, "Mr. Cluverius, if you wouldn't mind just answering his questions." Cluverius thinks about it a minute, then glances at Crump, who winks at him. Meredith softens his tone, and asks him to draw a picture of the knothole.

Aylett takes a look at the finished drawing and says, "That looks more like a rose potato than anything I can think of."

Having called thirty-four witnesses in four days, the defense has no one left. By law, Tommie is not allowed to testify on his own behalf. The prosecution again asks that Joel be allowed to take apart the watch key. Evans objects, and Hill sustains him.

Willie touches Tommie's back. "We're almost there," he whispers.

CHAPTER NINETEEN

JUDGE HILL INSTRUCTS the jury: "Before you can convict the accused you must be satisfied from the evidence that he is guilty of the offense charged in the indictment beyond reasonable doubt. It is not sufficient that you believe his guilt probable. The evidence must be of such character and tendency as to produce a moral certainty. If you entertain a reasonable doubt as to whether the deceased came to her death by violence committed by herself or by the hands of another, you must find the prisoner not guilty."

Tommie and his counsel wrote and rewrote the last sentence only that morning, adding to the draft presented by the commonwealth. It seemed fair that the final word to the jury should emphasize their responsibility—if they had serious misgivings—to let the accused go. But Tommie wanted further reassurance. How reasonable were the twelve men deciding his fate? Evans asked Crump to argue for some changes.

So when the morning session opens, Crump requests that the jury be sent out. Then he asks the judge for some clarification of the phrases "reasonable doubt" and "moral certainty." Cannot these be made clearer? Could not the court instruct the jury to treat the evidence as though it pertains to a person they hold dear?

Hill mulls this for a moment or two, then says, "I think the phrases are clear enough. Clerk, please call the jury back for closing arguments."

This is the theater that everyone has been waiting for, and the streets around the courthouse are again jammed. Headlines announcing "Evidence All In," "Final Arguments Begin Tomorrow," have brought people out in droves, hoping just to get close to the courthouse so that they can be a part of the city's biggest spectacle in years, part of the chain that will relay the news up and down the streets even before the newspapers. Policemen have been dispatched to keep order, but with the sidewalks all but impassable the street is the only place for actual movement. Several people have sold their own tickets for a dollar, even two dollars, apiece, and now the buyers have no way to get into the building—one of them yells that he's been defrauded.

Tommie is wearing a new dove-gray suit that Willie brought him, with a navy bow tie, ends tucked under his collar. Willie, sitting behind, puts a hand on his brother's shoulder, leans in close, and says, "We'll be home tomorrow, Wednesday at the latest." He threads a white carnation bud into his brother's buttonhole and sits back beside Aunt Jane, who is fanning furiously; Willie takes over for her.

Aylett will lead off, leaving to Meredith the job of raking the defense. He stands, and every eye is riveted, his dignified person commanding attention and respect as he waits for silence to fill the room. Suddenly it is so quiet Tommie can feel his heart jumping in its cage; his calves tighten and his arm hairs stand on end.

"May it please Your Honor and gentlemen of the jury," Aylett says, "I approach the end of this cause with a feeling of awe. Little was I aware when I took this case on at the request of the commonwealth's attorney and yielding to the voice of the people of my own county, where this young woman was born and lived—people to whom I owe almost everything I am—that I should see and hear what I have in the last few weeks. Nor that the faces we have seen here would become as familiar to me as those of my intimate acquaintances. For what we have witnessed, gentlemen, in these weeks is nothing short of an age-old drama of man. It is a tale of lust, seduction, and, finally, deceitful, cold-blooded murder. Thank God, gentlemen, that the hideous nightmare we have all endured will, so far as I am concerned, soon be ended.

"You are charged to return a guilty verdict only if you are convinced beyond a reasonable doubt. What is a reasonable doubt? Why, it's a doubt you can find a reason for. If you cannot find the evidence that will remove that doubt—if you cannot tell whether it was a case of murder or suicide, then you must give the prisoner the benefit of your doubt. But if the evidence drives the doubt from your minds, then you must find him guilty.

"A moral certainty is not a mathematical certainty; it is not a proposition from Euclid. Rather, it is a certainty satisfactory to your mind and conscience. Doubt may still be there, because all human affairs are matters of doubt. People every day trust to circumstantial evidence. We may not see the rain fall at night, yet when we arise and find the streets wet we know that it rained. We act in life more on circumstantial evidence than on direct testimony.

"Gentlemen, first we must ask ourselves has a murder been committed? And secondly, who committed it? Dr. Taylor has told us that in his expert opinion the blows to Miss Madison's head can only mean that she was struck prior to drowning in the reservoir. The footprints show that a man and a woman were at the reservoir on the night of March thirteen. The prisoner at the bar was the only man known to be a sweetheart of Miss Madison. He seduced her at his uncle's house, and got her with child. He was already engaged at the time to a young woman of some means in King and Queen County, and as an ambitious young man he was not about to let his mistake alter his path to success. He conspired to meet with Miss Madison twice in Richmond, luring her all the way from Bath County, six hours away by train. On the second occasion, he took her with him to the most desolate place he could think of, a place where he thought his dark deeds would go unnoticed. There he struck her and threw her unconscious body into the reservoir. He may have thrown her over the picket fence, or he may have walked around to the gate and opened it and then thrown her in. Gentlemen, these are technicalities which the defense may choose to dwell on, but the fact remains that she ended up in the reservoir and drowned there . . ."

Aylett continues laying out the case against Tommie, who now feels himself so far away he can hardly hear the words. Most of the previous night he spent lying on his back praying, and seeing in his mind the shore at Point Comfort, where the gray-green waves keep rippling and rippling onto the sand. And now he can practically hear waves hissing across the sand, and see the sun sparkling on a limitless horizon.

At one point he hears the cries of a baby from the open windows. Aylett pauses to let the laughter die out, then plays into the moment. "Judge, have you no jurisdiction out there?" Hill says he's afraid not, but he'll send the sergeant out to try to quiet the crowd. "I don't know if a baby constitutes a crowd," Aylett says, "but it can make a lot of noise." Having mastered the interruption, he pauses once again, stands erect, goateed chin out, as though summoning the spirit of his great-grandfather, who a hundred and ten years earlier stood up in a church a mile east and rallied his countrymen to liberty or death.

"And what does the prisoner do to defend himself against these charges? He brings in a few friends and relatives to testify to his character. Gentlemen, could not eleven men have testified to the good character of Judas Iscariot the night before he betrayed our Savior? Could not George Washington have testified to the good character of Benedict Arnold before he betrayed his country, and later came to this very city and burned it? The prisoner puts his friend Henley on the stand to testify that he saw him at the Dime Museum—at the *afternoon* performance, mind you. But that does not bring him to safe ground. Of his whereabouts between the hours of eight and midnight, when the murder took place, we are not vouchsafed a word.

"A key was discovered at the reservoir, yet the prisoner will not let Joel open it to ascertain whose key it was. Why will he not? A note in Miss Madison's handwriting, directed to the prisoner, was found at the American Hotel, where she was registered under the name Merton, a name the prisoner used on his frequent visits to houses of ill repute—a prisoner, by the way, who was careful to maintain a saintly reputation at home. A letter in the prisoner's handwriting was found in Miss Madison's trunk, as well as several envelopes in the prisoner's handwriting. But the most damning thing of all is an abominable piece of so-called poetry, in his hand, of such a lurid, despicable nature that I wish I could forget it. But I cannot, gentlemen, for it lays out in the foulest language imaginable the seduction of a young woman.

"Witness after witness has come forward, gentlemen, to say they saw the prisoner and Miss Madison here together. A trail leads directly from the American Hotel out to the reservoir. And there the trail ends for not one, but two people. For the prisoner killed two people that lonely night, leaving his unborn child there to die within its mother's womb. Since then he has done nothing but lie about his crime.

"And they ask for mercy! Great God, gentlemen, have we not shown him mercy enough? Turn him loose for his progeny to plague and vex mankind? I have seen too many of our brave and loyal soldiers laid to rest in the cemeteries around our fair city to heed cries of mercy from such a quarter. Last night as I pondered what to say to you, I took a stroll among the peaceful graves of Hollywood Cemetery, shouting distance from the old reservoir where this horrible crime took place. And I thought about those lately tenanted soldiers who breathed their last amid the smoke and carnage of battle, young men like the prisoner before you. But unlike him, men who did not think of themselves first, but of their duty and honor to their families and the commonwealth of Virginia, and of the daughters, sisters, and mothers they protected and revered unto death.

"Do we not owe it to those brave young soldiers to stand like men and uphold the law? If the victim in this case were a strong man, killed perhaps in a fit of jealous passion, we might feel a measure of pity for the prisoner. But, gentlemen, this was a petite, defenseless woman, soon to be a mother. The blood boils at the very idea. Gentlemen, we can feel compassion toward a fellow human being, but as honorable men we must do our duty by meting out justice. We must protect the commonwealth against immorality, selfishness, and evil. To return a verdict of anything less than guilty of murder in the first degree is not to show mercy, but to perpetuate and condone the practice of evil. The greatest mercy we can grant the prisoner is to show the same mercy he showed his cousin and companion."

Aylett stands for a moment, his thunder cracking the air, the tension building like the sudden pressure dive before the cloudburst. He waits . . . waits another moment . . . and then calls forth a ghost:

"The truth in this case, gentlemen, could not be clearer if one final witness were to burst the bonds of her grave and come before the court in her cerements, pointing and saying, 'That is the man!'"

The room is hushed and strained as Aylett takes his seat. Instead of exploding in cheers, which they desperately want to do, people cough into their hands, and more than one spectator wipes away a tear. Mr. Lucas, who was given a ticket by Mr. Meade, feels himself trembling, having never heard any speech so moving in his life. Judge Hill calls for a break, and the murmuring approval of the packed courtroom spreads into the streets, where snatches of the speech dart like lightning across town.

After the noon break, Evans gets up and delivers a long, winding speech, peppered with anecdotes and legal precedents. He carefully picks apart the prosecution's case, pointing out every inconsistency and every leap to conclusion, until the whole thing appears to be nothing but a rag held together by a few thin threads:

"A maid, Henrietta Wimbush, claimed upon the stand, and never before, that she saw them in the Exchange Hotel. That was an afterthought, probably made at someone else's suggestion to suit the necessities of the case. It is impossible she carried the face of the prisoner in her mind from that day to this, considering the vast number of faces she encounters in a day. And so it is with the other supposed witnesses who claim to have seen the prisoner at the American Hotel in March. Witnesses have been manufactured to order."

"Do you mean that for me, sir?" Meredith bursts out.

Evans's voice goes up a notch as he replies, "No sir, I do not."

"I hope you don't mean me then," Aylett says, an amused look on his face.

"We let you speak without interruption," Evans rejoins. "Why won't you let us?" Getting no reply, he goes on. "As for the unfortunate young woman, she left home at an early age, a home that was a cruelty and misery to her. It's absurd to suggest, as my friend for the commonwealth does, that the education her aunt provided made her unfit for the home of her parents. If that were the case, no parent in Virginia should educate their children. She wrote to and received letters from numerous young men . . ." He continues for more than two hours, yet with less emotion than Aylett, and by the end the jurymen are shifting in their seats.

On the following day William Crump rises slowly, with much shuffling of papers and clearing of his throat. He has used this trick for years to disarm a jury, appearing disorganized and unprepared before launching into a brilliantly crafted piece of rhetorical magic. "Gentlemen, it is with great assurance in your integrity and collective wisdom that the defense is confident the prisoner at the bar will not be convicted upon argument clothed in the beautiful figures of rhetoric, roving among the vales of fancy and hyperbole with the likes of Judas Iscariot and Benedict Arnold. I will endeavor in the remarks I shall make not to soar aloft on wings of such plumage, but to come down upon plain and solid ground, and scratch that ground to see what those facts really mean. Nor will you find me strolling among the graves of the Confederate dead looking for reasons for a verdict in this cause. I only seek to walk with you step by step up that rugged stairway to the temple of justice, within whose vestibule Truth sits enthroned.

"When I am reminded of the powerful forces aligned against the prisoner—the full police force of the city of Richmond, the representation of commonwealth's attorneys, the zealous detective service of Jack Wren, and the sympathies of the men and women of Richmond—it is with pleasure that I address a Virginia jury who remember the obligation they assumed when upon their voir dire they declared that they were above the influences of the surrounding community, and that they were prepared to hear impartially and to decide impartially as between the commonwealth and the prisoner.

"He came here in January on business, to see the auditor for his aunt and attend a meeting of Dwight Moody, the evangelist. You may say it's a strange coincidence that Lillian Madison was here at the same time, but where is the proof of their meeting here? He had dinner that night at the home of his friend Tyler Bagby, a stalwart citizen . . ."

After an hour or so, Crump wipes his perspiring forehead and holds the bar. Aylett, seeming genuinely concerned, half rises to offer him a glass of water. Crump waves him off, but accepts a glass from his son. "And now," he continues, "we come to the strangest business in this case. The finding of that key. We are asked to believe that all day Saturday that glittering, bright key lay in the grass, while person after person combed the entire reservoir grounds. If it was there, someone would've seen it as sure as there is a God in heaven. Nor did any key turn up on Sunday, nor the rest of that entire *week*, until the following Monday. Then a laborer comes before the court claiming he found it—*eight days earlier*. Gentlemen, this is too much to believe. That key was never in the possession of the prisoner. It is alleged that the prisoner was carrying it on his watch chain and that it snagged as he crawled through the hole in the fence. With his overcoat buttoned on a cold night, how could he have snagged his key? Accept the testimony of Mr. Lucas if you will—he seems an honest man. But whether as a prank or in deliberate malfeasance, someone placed that key there later.

"In a remarkable development, the defense brings forth a note allegedly written by the deceased to the prisoner. Her signature is nowhere on the scrap of paper. The only eyewitness to the sender of a possible previous note cannot be found. A bellboy named William Lane says he received it from a mulatto boy, who has mysteriously disappeared. I don't believe that for one minute. He has certainly been secreted. Surely the detective hired by the commonwealth, a man who knows every sewer in this city and every rat in it, could find that boy. Instead, he produces a woman of ill repute, with whom he has had a liaison, to impugn the character of the prisoner.

"The only letter found among the belongings of the deceased written by the prisoner is of an innocent nature. The prosecution will have you believe there was a lively correspondence between these two. But where is the proof? There were plenty of letters from others, but not from him. The old legal maxim declaring that that which does not exist shall be held never to have existed is simply inverted. What kind of argument is that to address to twelve gentlemen sworn to act upon the facts of this case? They produce some blank envelopes and say he was scheming with his paramour. This is the sort of proceeding where you try a man at the crossroads, you convict him with a shout, and hang him with a hurrah."

Having brought his speech to a climax, Crump, florid-faced and sweating, decides to take a break, leaving the jury poised for act two.

Lucas slips out now—he was already pushing his luck with Mr. Meade by asking for more time off. He is grateful to Mr. Crump for saying he was honest, but now he feels ashamed for ever thinking that young man capable of killing the girl. The whole trial has been a mistake and he wants no more part of it.

Willie goes outside for a smoke, a habit he has recently developed. He walks around to Rum Cut Alley and leans against the brick front of a grocer's, watching people and staring a "mind your own business" at strangers who appear to recognize him. The odors of horse manure and coal smoke mix with those of nearby gardens and women's perfume to make a not unpleasant smell. But the noise is something he has never gotten used to: the constant tread of carriage wheels and hooves, the shouts of grocers and newsboys and truant children, the clanging and banging of buildings going up or coming down. It's all right for a few days, but he cannot understand how Tommie would like it here so much. Sometimes it's all one can do to keep from being run over by a speeding carriage or wagon. At home there are no blaring fire-engine horns and no eye-stinging fumes, no ladies with red paint eyeing you greedily, no sad old men with stumps for legs sitting on stoops, caps held out for coins. Only the smell of growing things and wood smoke and that clean fertile scent of the river as the tide shifts, and the quiet that lingers in between the song of the thrush and the bobolink and the bittern. In the city it is as if you are walking on the graves of a thousand thousand people—all stone and concrete and the ghost of an older city that was built, in turn, upon some earlier version of itself. At home you walk on land that feels cleansed by the tide and the rain and the dew, the earth opening like a hand to feed you, if you know how to coax it.

Willie finishes his cigarette and throws the butt into the street, then turns back toward City Hall. He takes his place beside Aunt Jane and squeezes her hand. Crump rises to continue his speech. It is brilliant, everything you could want, Willie thinks, but as he studies the motionless faces of the jury, he doesn't know if it will be enough. Did Tommie make a mistake he could not live with? Willie thinks back to the mistake he himself made when he was six years old, and how he will have to live with that for the rest of his life.

Crump is drawing to a close. "My friend on the other side says the people of Virginia should rise up as one man to demand the conviction of the prisoner at the bar. But we are not here to carry out the demands of the people of Virginia. Demands of that sort are unreasonable and unjust. Such demands may result in the sacrifice of the innocent. Since the day that the maddened mob cried at the heels of the Savior, 'Crucify him! Crucify him!' no reliance is to be placed upon the demands of the impassioned mob. Prejudice runs away with them.

"But, gentlemen, I shall detain you no longer. My physical strength has been exhausted, and I shall conclude my remarks by reminding you that to violate the living temple which the Lord hath made—to quench the fire within a man's breast—is an awful and a terrible responsibility, and the verdict of 'guilty,' once pronounced, is irrevocable. Speak not that word lightly; speak it not on suspicion, however strong, nor upon moral conviction, nor inference or doubt. I tell you that if you condemn that man lightly, or upon mere suspicion consign him to death, the recollection of the deed will never die within you."

Crump takes his seat, the hush of the crowd hovering like the uneasy, conscience-stricken silence in church. Tommie can feel the tide turning in his favor and he glances over to the jury—certainly they're impressed by Crump's overpowering logic and wisdom. Even if they wanted to convict him, how could they in good conscience now? Mercy and truth appear ready to triumph over bloodlust and ignorance.

But Crump has spoken for so long, and the exhaustion in the courtroom is so palpable, that Meredith requests they reconvene tomorrow so he can have a chance to condense his speech. Crump scoffs under his breath, "Hmmpf. That's a good one. He wants fresh ears. But it's his prerogative." The jury agrees to the adjournment, and Hill says Mr. Meredith can commence his argument in the morning.

Tommie cannot force himself to eat that night. He decides to fast, to purify himself for what lies ahead. Tomorrow either he'll be a free man or his troubles will be just beginning. He thinks of Lillie's line, "O if suicide were not a sin." To have the ordeal over with now, out of the public eye, would be a blessing. But by what method? The idea of hanging himself turns his stomach, and it brings to mind the picture he has successfully banished, except on the worst nights—the rope dangling from the gallows. But there it is again—the wooden frame, the rough hemp around his neck, the barbarity of it. He tries to tamp down the fear by imagining it in detail—the fibers scratching his soft skin, the moment of hot pain, the air beneath his feet, a knot that slips, his feet perhaps his last sight on earth, and then the release. Into what? Would it at least be quick? And again the darkness of his cell smothers him, and he breathes loudly just to hear his body working. He puts his hand on his heart to feel its life. A tear rolls down his cheek. Isn't he too young to die? "God," he whispers, "please, I beg of you to spare me. I'll devote my life to your service."

He dreams again he's standing beside the ocean, which is vaster than anything he has ever seen, excepting the night sky, the waves a perfect green scroll unfurling at his feet and withdrawing like the ceaseless inbreathing of the earth. He stands alone before the sea, and, despite its incomprehensible depth and breadth, there is no deeper mystery than the very fact of his own existence there at the edge of the infinite and the eternal. Then farther down the shore he sees a girl with long brown hair and bare feet. She begins walking into the water, her white dress clinging to her legs, and she doesn't have to turn for him to understand she's beckoning. All he wants to do is follow—it seems so easy—but he's afraid. He's anchored to the shore, and she keeps moving out into the sun-rippled water.

"I thought today of all days you'd be awake, sir," says the guard.

So he wakes to the final day of his trial, and dons a new gray serge suit. He eats a little breakfast so that he won't faint, and he tries to keep that picture of the vast sea in his mind on the way to the courthouse. But then he remembers the girl, and a strange feeling of both terror and peace spreads through his body. He clears his head and watches the people pointing at his carriage along the way.

Meredith takes the floor for the final speech. He speaks elegantly, without the bombast of Aylett or Crump, and as confidently as if he were addressing the general assembly. His voice is oddly warming, and Tommie imagines if not for the sense in them the words might have given him strength.

"I venture the assertion," he says, "that not a man among you did not have in his heart when this case began the earnest hope that the young man who stands at the bar might come forth acquitted. I do not censure you for it. But I submit now that the day for hope has passed . . ." Tommie drifts away, finding his place again beside the sea.

"Gentlemen, the defense has tried to frighten you with cases of circumstantial evidence that have resulted in miscarriages of justice. I could undertake to cite case after case where men have been unjustly hanged, not upon circumstantial evidence, but upon direct evidence. Is it because men err that men shall not do justice and do the best they can according to their judgment and their consciences? The wheels of justice are necessarily imperfect, but for this reason are they to stop turning? Because a man dies in a factory explosion, are we then to shut down all factories? As in battle, innocent people sometimes die for the common good.

"Yes, there have been cases of wrongful conviction. But let me assure you, this is no such case. Seventy-eight witnesses have been produced by the commonwealth, and the character of not one has been attacked legitimately.

"The defense would have you believe Miss Madison committed suicide, but why would she come all the way to Richmond to kill herself? And why go out to the reservoir to do it? She could have committed suicide easier from a hundred other places.

And you are asked to believe that a woman in her condition—a woman but nineteen inches higher than the fence—could have gotten over the fence. Possible, but improbable. How much easier it would be with someone—a larger and stronger person—to assist her. Mr. Crump said she could have opened the latch on the picket fence gate—also possible, but so could some other person carrying her . . .

"In regard to Mr. Jack Wren, I have here a letter endorsing him, signed by every bank president in the city and many of the leading businessmen as well. As for him going into the sewers and ratholes of the city—he does it so that others may keep their hands clean. Do you expect him to find criminals in church congregations? Of course he receives pay for his work. Lawyers who stand up in court to defend murderers also receive pay for their services.

"We have before us a prisoner, who at least a week before coming here last March, plotted to take the life of a young woman. He mailed her the fake letter that she, in her innocence, believed would unite them here in Richmond. It did unite them, but for what sinister purpose she was unaware. He had the motive, the means, the conduct, and the opportunity to murder her on the night of March the thirteenth. And so, gentlemen, as difficult as I know it is, you must not now shrink from your duty.

"Gentlemen, the commonwealth does not seek revenge, nor ask for outrage and anger; the commonwealth simply seeks to find an answer to a crime and to deal with it justly. There is no one else remotely suspected of the crime, and every circumstance laid down for your guidance points clearly and directly to the prisoner. We have contended for murder in the first degree, and if you should find such, we ask that you return a verdict of guilty of murder in the first degree."

Again a hush overhangs the courtroom, but this time the crowd cannot contain itself, and the tension that has built up for weeks bursts forth like a dam in clapping and shouting and foot stomping. It is quickly taken up outside, where men are standing on tables and chairs for a closer ear on the proceedings. Hill, his face flushed with the heat of the room, turns to the officers, who begin shouting for order. Aylett rises and shakes hands with Meredith as he resumes his seat, and after a minute or two order is restored. A deputy sergeant brings in two bouquets, one for Mr. Aylett, the other for Mr. Meredith. A card in a flowery hand is attached to Aylett's: "With thanks for his beautiful oration in defense of the dead Lillian."

Tommie comes back from the edge of the sea, applause receding around him like wavelets slapping the shore. He asks Evans for some water, and drinks an entire glass. It seems as if his soul has separated from his body and is lingering above the back of the room, watching in detached curiosity. Behind him, Willie swishes his fan over Tommie's neck. Why did he not let Willie take his place? All he can do now is hope and pray for mercy at the hands of twelve men who won't meet his eyes.

CHAPTER TWENTY

I<small>T'S ALREADY</small> getting close to day's end, but Hill wants to gallop on to the finish line if he can. He sends the jury out to see if they can come to a decision before too long. Evans and Tommie go to the judge's waiting room. "If we can get past the one hour mark," Evans says, "it's a good sign."

"But what's your feeling now?" Tommie wants to know.

"I don't see how they could convict on the evidence they have, Tommie. I really don't." He looks at his young charge with sad eyes. "I think we've done nearly all we could."

"I know you have, Mr. Evans, and I want to thank you for it, and I'm sorry you've had to take so much trouble over me. I hope after this is over, we can go on where we left off."

"I don't see why not, as long as you change your name." Mr. Evans smiles and grips Tommie's shoulder.

Outside, the crowd steadily grows thicker and louder, and twice officers have to go out and request quiet so that the jury can have some peace. Willie looks in on his brother. "I'm going out and wait in the carriage," he says. He won't say what he's thinking—that he can't bear to sit in the courtroom for this part.

"Go on," Tommie says, "I'm fine. Take Aunt Jane with you, if you want."

"She'll wait in there." Willie thumbs toward the courtroom.

Inside the courtroom, Crump has gone over to speak with General Imboden, who has been attending the trial regularly, his place reserved right behind Colonel Aylett. Imboden stands and clasps his old friend's hand. "Not a more valiant effort in twenty years," he says. "This Mr. Meredith is something, isn't he?" Crump agrees, and they laugh about what a good rat chaser Wren actually is, then turn to other topics of the day and their mutual friends.

A full hour has not quite gone by when the sergeant comes in and, in a solemn voice, tells Evans that the jury is ready. "Not good," Tommie says. He feels hollow and strangely light as he stands and follows Evans back into the courtroom. When they have taken their seats, Hill calls the jury in.

A few minutes later the jurors are standing in two rows with expressionless faces. The clerk calls each of their names, and each answers. Then the clerk says, "Thomas J. Cluverius, please stand up." Tommie pulls his hand away from his aunt and rises.

"Gentlemen of the jury," says the clerk, "look upon the prisoner. How say you? Is he guilty or not guilty of the felony charged in the indictment?"

In the three seconds before the foreman can clear his throat, Tommie's mind leaps back nearly twenty years. He's following his brother down the creek from their old house upcounty, before they moved in with Aunt Jane. There had been a storm and the water was high, and they wanted to keep walking and exploring. Their little brother, Charles, had tried to tag along, but they'd made him go back. Willie told Tommie that the creek joined with the Mattaponi River and that there were Pamunkey Indians living somewhere down there. Even then Tommie thought he would remember this day when he was old, as old as his father.

The woods began growing thicker and darker, and in places it was hard to stay with the creek because of the tangles of vines and roots along the bank. At one point the bright oval leaves

of a pawpaw tree caught the sunlight, and the boys peeked between limbs onto the creek. There had been soldiers marauding
as recently as last summer, and their mother was not convinced
that there were not still stragglers, deserters, vagabonds, and
cutthroats—Union or Confederate—abroad in the countryside.
"I'm hungry," Tommie announced.

"We'll find more berries and keep going," Willie decided.

Tommie wanted to go home now, though he wouldn't say it.
He was afraid of a lot of things—at the moment, snakes. To go
on would mean crossing another creek, more of a swamp, where
there were certain to be snakes. They started in and were soon
up to their calves in rusty water, their feet squishing the bottom.
Tommie stepped up on a cypress knee and thought maybe he
could cross on just roots and knees and that if he fell and hurt
himself they could go home. But then he heard his little brother
crying somewhere behind them. Now everything was all right,
because they would have to take Charles home.

"We'll never get to the river now," Willie said. Charles was
sitting in a patch of brown sand at the edge of the creek, crying
quietly to himself. His legs were covered with scratches, and the
two older boys saw that their own legs were also scored and torn
by brambles they had hardly noticed. Tommie wasn't worried
about getting in trouble, because if they were punished Willie
would take the larger share.

At the bend in the creek where Charles sat, the water moved
more swiftly than in the straight parts, and there were little ed-
dies whirling and shifting as if guided by some unseen hand beneath the surface.

The creek whispered and murmured.

What was it murmuring? Why did it keep whispering the
same silvery phrase over and over? There was a little island of
trees and shrubs out in the middle, and Willie started wading

toward it without a word. Tommie went in after his brother. They could tend to Charles later.

Willie and Tommie reached the island without hearing the plop of their brother going under. They looked back to see if he had noticed their triumph and to figure out a way to get him there as well. Willie was the only one who could swim—he'd learned to dog-paddle at the edge of their neighbor's pond that summer. Tommie wanted to learn so that he could fly out across the river on the rope swing.

But Charles was not where they last saw him. Willie began shouting. "Must of went home," he said. Tommie shook his head, because his brother said it wrong, not the way his mother would. Still, he liked the sound of his brother's voice, its confidence and hopefulness, like a wise old frog.

When they realized their brother was gone, they headed back, thinking to overtake him around every twist in the creek, every stand of shrubs they broke through. With each failed sighting, they picked up their pace. At home the first words from their father's mouth were ones Tommie knew all along he would say: "Where's Charles?"

And then they had to go all the way back, both of them, with their father and a colored man named Cato, while their mother ran for help, and they were tired and it was after noon and they hadn't had their dinner. Willie didn't seem to care about any of that—he was suddenly like one of the grown-ups.

When Tommie imagined it later, he saw Charles looking into the flat dark water, drawn to his own silhouette and the way the overhanging limbs of trees were painted upside down on the top of the creek. There was something about it that made him want to test the perfection of it, to break up the ghost of the trees by planting his foot in the middle of the scene. When he was standing in the water up to his knees, he noticed his brothers wading in above their waists to an island downstream. He started to the island as well, but within a few steps the sandy bottom dropped away and he found himself falling. The last thing he knew was the blue-white flash of a kingfisher darting downstream, into a liquid sky. His last breath broke the surface of the copper water, and the rippled mirror flattened again and the trees were repainted in perfect order, as if nothing had disturbed their timeless tranquil image.

The rest of the episode fractured into little pieces that settled on the bottom of Tommie's mind, where they occasionally stirred to the surface—how the men came and found Charles caught against the submerged trunk of a tree just downstream of the island, how they tried to blow air into his lungs. And how for days and days his mother cried, and that before they took Charles away she dressed him in clean Sunday clothes that Tommie himself had once worn. And how Willie was never the same after.

"Is he guilty or not guilty of the felony charged in the indictment?"

The foreman steadies his voice. "Guilty," he says.

Then each member of the jury in turn says, "Guilty as charged."

After the last juryman has spoken, a tremendous and awful silence expands within the courtroom. When the verdict had been relayed to the crowd outside, a shout goes up. People lean over to congratulate the prosecutors. But almost as quickly as it arises, the clamor dies, and the crowd, having heard what it came for, begins to disperse.

There's a buzzing in Tommie's ears that won't stop. That's it then? No discussion of a lesser charge? It does not seem as though he is really here, in his own body.

Evans has an arm around his shoulder. "That's just the first inning," he tells Tommie. "There's still a long way to go. We have more tricks to pull."

Aunt Jane cannot open her eyes to look at her nephew, nor can she even rise to her feet. Tommie leans over and kisses her. He wants to tell her it's all right, but his mouth has gone dry and nothing comes out. She seizes his hand and focuses on it, her body beginning to shake with sobs. Two jurors come by and tell Tommie they had no hard feelings, and Tommie nods politely and says, "I understand." Then he shakes hands with Evans and the Crumps. "You did all you could," he says.

Out in the police carriage, Willie sits waiting for his brother. He hears the triumphant shouting in the street. "Guilty!" And all he can think is—my brother, my brother, my brother. When Tommie gets in beside him, the only thing Willie can manage is a glance through blurred eyes.

"It's all right," Tommie says, avoiding his brother's eyes. "It's not over. We're making a motion for a new trial tomorrow. And, failing that, there's a writ of error, appeals, pardons."

Willie nods, but his shoulders convulse and his face runs with tears. He's embarrassed to look up.

The silence is too awful, so Tommie takes it upon himself to talk. "It could be worse," he tries, with a grim little laugh. "I could've been lynched . . . I wonder what's for supper tonight?"

Officer Birney, whom Richardson has recently promoted to sergeant, has volunteered to drive Tommie the past few days. He says, "I think they were making beef sthew over at the cookhouth today. I'll go ahead and thend out for thome if you'd like."

"I think beef stew does sound good." Tommie realizes how hungry he is, after eating almost nothing the past twenty-four hours. "I can't help thinking of robin pie," he says. "We used to have it this time of year, but I haven't tasted any in I don't know how long."

Birney laughs. "I don't know if I can thcare you up any robin pie, but I think it would be all right if your brother wanth to thtay to thupper with you thith evening."

"That would be fine," Tommie says. "And send out for some Trixy cigars, would you, Sergeant? And a tin of caviar? Maybe a bottle of Christian and White's old blackberry wine, and a tub of Antoni's ice cream? I'm planning quite a party."

"Well, I don't know about all that, but we might find you thome orangeth and a bottle of lemonade."

Tommie disappears inside himself momentarily, the forced levity costing him too much pain. Willie takes up the slack and says, "If you want ice cream every day, I'll see that you get it."

When they are back in Tommie's hallway, other prisoners come to their barred doors, and even though they know what his return means, one of them asks, "So how did you fare?"

"They found me guilty of murder in the first degree," Tommie sings out, almost laughing at how absurd he sounds. Willie, coming behind, offers to clean the man's plow, but Tommie quiets him down.

At his cell, Tommie turns to his brother and offers his hand, but Willie reaches his strong arms around him and holds him to his chest for a moment, until Tommie can feel the beating of his brother's heart against his own.

"I have to tell you something," Tommie says, "but you have to promise never to repeat it." Willie agrees and he sits on the edge of Tommie's cot, watching his brother pace back and forth, five steps up and five steps back, over and over as he spills his tale.

· CHAPTER TWENTY-ONE ·

ONE SUNDAY AFTERNOON in February, I went over to visit
Ma and Pa. Pa was out offering advice to a friend about a
horse. It was just as well, because what I really wanted was Ma's
opinion on premarital pregnancy. The fact is, Lillie had told me
she was pregnant, and, Willie, I'd been with her—only twice, but
it doesn't take but once. Anyway, you know Ma had been starting in on the jug earlier and earlier in the afternoons, and I was
counting on her being in a tipsy haze and not making any hasty
conclusions—she'd probably forget about it later.

She was quite merry, singing a tune and actually doing some
housework. She was cleaning the front window, and she saw me
coming and gave me the brightest smile I'd seen in some time.
After she'd hugged me, she began talking a flood tide, and I was
thinking she could've been a preacher if she'd been a man. She
was telling me about her relatives, about her half-brother and her
niece, Lillie's mother. This niece, you know Hannah Walker, had
always looked up to Ma, asking her advice on clothes and boys
and even whether she should marry Howard Madison. Ma had
said no, but Hannah went ahead and married him, and for some
time afterward was estranged from our family. Yet later she asked
Ma whether Lillie ought to go live with Aunt Jane.

She went on at some length, and I was wondering if there was
a point to it and whether I'd get a chance to ask what I wanted to.
Clearly something was on her mind, but it seemed only mildly

interesting. Then she went out back to get me some chicory root for my coffee, even though I said I didn't want any. I stood and looked around at the projects she'd started and left unfinished— the hemming work on the table, the polishing rag on the andiron. There was a book on the mantelpiece lying on its side, spine out. *Pilgrim's Progress*. I picked it up, and it opened on a folded piece of foolscap—a letter dated the previous week and addressed to Ma. I scanned it, and the phrases leaped off the page:

> Dear Aunt Eliza,
> I write you with a heart heavy with sorow . . . know how we sent Fannie Lillian to live with Aunt Jane because of her difficult nature? Well the truth is that I wanted her to go . . . said if he lifted his hand to her one more time I would call out the sherf and I didn't care if he hit me for doing it . . . He was at her for some time, ever since she became a woman. It is a horible crime against nature and his own flesh & blood and I know I stand to be judged for letting it go on for so long . . . I thoght it had stopped but last summer when she was over here to teach the girls I chanced to go out to the barn looking for a length of string to tie up my beans and I saw something Im ashamed to write about. They were over in the corner behind the hay bales where it was dark but I know it was them laying together I saw there legs . . . I like to have died . . . scared of God's jdgmnt on all of us . . . don't know if I will send this or burn it . . . never ever tell a living soul . . . say a prayer for us, Eliza, could you? . . . I feel so blessed that finelly that girl is far away living on her own & maybe now we will have some peace.
> Much Love, Hannah.

When Ma came back in and saw me holding the letter, she stopped short. "Where did you get that?" she said. "You weren't supposed to see that." She took it from me and was on the point of dropping it into the sputtering little fire she had going. "Did you read all of it?"

I nodded.

"Well you have to forget you ever saw it." She dropped it on a tongue of flame and watched the edges curl.

I later wondered if Ma hadn't left the letter out on purpose, so that I might find it and lose all interest in Lillie. But by then it was far too late.

Tommie pauses in his story, trying to gauge his brother's reaction, but Willie will not take his eyes off the concrete floor. When asked if he wants to hear the rest, Willie nods slowly, his broad shoulders lifting and falling with his breath.

Lillie was supposed to arrive in Richmond on Wednesday, March eleventh, so I could take her to a lying-in house. I didn't know it, but she'd missed her train. I'd gotten there on Thursday and decided to stay an extra day just to make sure, though I was hoping she'd changed her mind and simply wasn't coming. So on Friday morning, I headed out of the Davis House at nine-thirty and went down to the *Dispatch* office, opposite the American Hotel.

I got a newspaper, looked around to see if I recognized anyone, then crossed the street and stepped smartly into the hotel. Scanning the register, I came across the name I didn't want to see: F. L. Merton, Roanoke City. It was just like her to pick a place she liked the sound of.

I exited the hotel and crossed Main again and took from my jacket pocket an envelope containing a note I'd written in my room that morning: "Meet me at the post office at eleven o'clock." That seemed like a busy enough place that no one would take notice of us. I wrote "Merton, Room 21" on the envelope and spotted a thin, light-skinned negro boy leaning against the wall. "I've got a job for you," I said. The boy was wearing a clean white long-sleeved shirt and brown corduroy pants; he looked casually at me. "Take this across to the American Hotel over there and hand it to the clerk at the desk," I told him. The boy looked at me as though he didn't speak English. "I'll pay you," I said, trying not to be impatient.

"I'm waiting for my uncle," the boy said. "He a Knights of Labor man. We're going back to Washington today. The climate doesn't suit us here."

"I don't blame you," I told him. "You folks were right to complain about those hotels. It's a real shame."

The boy, who I guessed was fourteen or fifteen, hitched up his pants and put on a countrified accent, rolling his eyes. "Now boss, what was that task you hiring me fo?" I gave him the envelope and the boy made a show of ambling, elbows out, across the street. When he got back I asked if he'd done as I told him, and he shook his head and said, "Nawsuh. I tried to, but a bellboy stopped me and said he'd take care of it."

"That's fine," I said, handing the boy a nickel. He shook his head, eyeing the coin as though he wanted to take it. I'd never seen anything like it, but I didn't wait for him to change his mind. "Well, good luck to you then," I said, pocketing the nickel and heading up the street.

At the Planter's Bank I withdrew ten dollars, making now thirty-six dollars in my pocket—it would have to do. I continued, stopping in at Lumsden & Sons jewelers to ask about a breast pin

Nola had sent with me several weeks before for repair—I always enjoyed doing these little favors for people back home, and that day they served as convenient stops. No, the pin was not ready, nor were Aunt Jane's shoes up at Griggs'. I still had twenty minutes, so I stopped at Schoen's for a mineral water and a smoke. A college mate named Martin Harrison came in and we said a few words of greeting, nothing out of the ordinary.

At the post office I inquired about receiving a money order from King and Queen. If Magdalen House—where I was planning to take Lillie—required a substantial down payment, I figured I could wire Aunt Jane . . . or you . . . to send me money, saying it was for a diamond ring for Nola. Finding that King and Queen couldn't send money orders, I decided to simply wait for Lillian. I wondered how many people who knew me had already spotted me, and whether that was good or bad. The important thing was that I had not been seen with her. I'd always thought of the city as an anonymous place, and now not so.

And there she was, walking up the street, wearing a black overcoat and red shawl, like a fat red-winged blackbird. She smiled as though she was on holiday. "Let's go," I said, stepping out onto the sidewalk. "Have you eaten?"

"You have a way with words, Tommie," she said. "Yes, I had breakfast at the hotel, and it's great to see you, too. You needn't walk so fast."

"We should keep moving," I said. "And if you could put your veil over your eyes—"

She did as I said. "Don't be cross with me," she told me. "If I'm smiling, it's because I'm trying to keep my spirits up, not because I feel happy. I came exactly what time you told me to, and now you could at least tell me where we're going."

"There's a house on Spring Street that can take you in," I said, though I didn't know for sure if that was true.

She wanted to know how far away it was, and whether we could take the streetcar. "I get tired easily these days," she said.

I told her it was about a mile and since the streetcar didn't go that way we could walk slowly. I wanted to know what had happened to her and told her I had been worried when she hadn't showed up.

She moved closer to me on the sidewalk, her hand brushing against mine. She told me she'd missed the train and felt terrible, with no way to reach me. And then last night the train was six hours late. It was after three in the morning when she got in. "I thought maybe you would meet me at the station," she said. I told her I didn't even know if she was coming, and she said, "What did you think I was going to do, Tommie?"

I winced at her raised voice. We went on another block in silence, and then I told her about the place we were going to and how nice it was (though, of course, I didn't really know). "They may not be expecting you yet," I said, "but I know once they see you it'll be fine."

"You mean you haven't spoken to them?" she asked. "What kind of place is this?"

"It's a very respectable lying-in establishment recommended to me by the director of the Church Institute." That was completely true.

"But you're not coming in too?"

"They don't want to see me, they want to see you. They don't want couples, you see, just unmarried women, and if I went in with you it might look—well, just not right."

"Oh, Tommie, no," she interrupted, "I won't go into a place like that by myself. I couldn't do it."

I wished I were anywhere in the world but there then, any other person in the world, even an old gray-haired negro I saw pushing a cart of vegetables down the street. I could tell her what

I knew about her father right then. We would have a scene right there on the sidewalk, but I wanted to try to do the right thing by her first. I swear I did. And, besides, I didn't know how she was going to take what I had to tell her. "I'll walk you right up to it," I said. "It's better if you go on by yourself."

"I won't do it," she said, and I recognized the firmness in her voice—that determined, iron-willed little spirit inside that small body I'd once found attractive.

We turned onto Spring, the tower of the penitentiary looming on a knoll not far away, its weather vane pointing east—some weather coming in. Down the block a scrape involving about ten boys was in progress. A rock went whizzing a few feet from our heads. I held up my hands and in my most authoritative voice said, "Could I ask you boys where I might find the Magdalen House?"

One of them pointed it out, his companions making rude noises off to the side. I thanked him and the boy touched his cap, and then they all went on trying to put each other's eyes out.

The building was a three-story brick pile, with dormer windows and a double veranda on the side. I knocked and a matron of about thirty-five years greeted us. Her hair was hidden nurse-style in a kerchief, but she had a demure face and manner. It was my last real hope and I hesitated. The matron smiled politely and introduced herself as Miss Pilcher—her soft brown eyes reminded me of Lillie's, and I wondered if she had ever been in the same predicament.

"My cousin here is in the family way," I said, "and we—she was wondering if she might stay here through her confinement." I took the place in at a glance—even though it was in a bad neighborhood, it looked pretty nice. Just off the receiving room was a friendly dining room, with the smell of bread baking and a ceiling fan hooked to a belt and pulleys. A needlepoint "As for me and my house we will serve the Lord," hung in the hallway, along with a benefactor's portrait.

"Yes," Miss Pilcher said, "unmarried mothers are welcome to stay here until they can be out on their own."

I felt the rope around me loosen just a little—I thought there might yet be an escape. "That's just fine," I said. "I'll bring her things around later."

"Oh, I'm sorry," she said. "We don't have a bed just now. We had one yesterday. But there should be one this evening. We'll need a letter of reference from a family member, preferably in the Richmond area, and a deposit of twenty dollars for the stay. Of course, you're welcome to give more, since we depend on charitable donations. Or, if you can't afford it, we have a work program."

Lillian stood there apparently neither embarrassed nor concerned, waiting for me to speak. But now Miss Pilcher addressed her. "Would it be possible for one of your parents to come tomorrow to work out the details?" Her expression was so kind and serene it reminded me of something I couldn't remember just then. "I know Miss Elder would prefer that."

"That's not possible," I blurted out. "They're dead. So, no, that wouldn't be possible."

Miss Pilcher kept smiling encouragingly at Lillian, who was now pouting. "If you're under age we'll still need a reference from your nearest of kin."

"She's twenty-one and I'm her nearest of kin," I said. I almost added that I was a lawyer, but I decided it was best not to press her.

Miss Pilcher studied Lillian's face but was apparently too polite to say that she looked younger than twenty-one. "Well, that should be all right then," she said. "If you'll wait here, I'll see if Miss Elder can speak with you now."

She disappeared down the hall, and Lillie said, "I won't stay where I'm not wanted."

"But they do want you," I said, "and this is a nice place." If only her train had not been late, she'd have a bed and be settling in now.

"It's for poor people, Tommie. I don't like it here. It smells funny, and I don't like the way she looked at me."

"We are poor," I said. "And I think it smells good."

"You're not the one having a baby." She pressed her lips together and folded her arms.

I told her there was no other choice and that she was being unreasonable. Then I suggested we could find a boardinghouse somewhere, and when the time came get her a midwife. "Would you like that better?" I asked.

Without another word she turned abruptly and walked from the office and then out onto the street. All I could do was try to keep up.

"I don't think I can go through with that," she said, "not knowing what's on the other side."

"What do you mean?" I said.

"I want to get married first, and then it doesn't matter what you do. The baby will have a father, and then I can decide whether I want to keep her."

I admit I was irritated with her. "Quit calling it her," I said, "you don't know what it is, or if it'll even be alive."

"Hush, Tommie, that's horrible. I know she's alive. She's kicking in me right now. Do you want to feel? Here, put your hand—" She took hold of my wrist but I pulled away.

We kept walking to the end of Spring Street, and then down along Hollywood Cemetery toward the river. We crossed the railroad tracks and proceeded to the bridge to Belle Isle, but then Lillian stopped. If I close my eyes I can see the whole thing like it was right in front of me. The day had not warmed up at all—the sun was frozen behind a thin blanket of clouds. But there was

a promise of spring in the tight little balls and buds of the bare
sycamores and shrubby trees lining the shore. A pair of geese
were flying downriver, one scolding the other, and the sound carried over the noise of the falls and the nailworks on the island.

We stood there for a time looking into the river, its jumble of
rock slabs like giant stepping-stones you could almost cross.

"Tommie," she said, "what are you thinking now?"

"I was thinking what it would be like if we were married. Do
you think we would be happy?"

"I think we would be happier than we are now." She pulled her
shawl closer around her neck and took my hand. "I'd be a good
wife for you. You'd be a good father. I know neither of us wanted
this now, but we'll make do and someday we'll look back and it
won't seem so bad. You'll see."

Something about the way she said, "You'll see," the almost ar-
rogant certainty of it, made me pull my hand away.

"I'm tired and hungry," she said. "I don't know why we've
come all the way out here."

"I was just following you," I replied, but a distracting idea had
come into my mind. It was unformed and didn't present a picture
that made any sense. A hole in a wall. That was the image that
kept popping into my mind—a hole in a wall, through which
I could crawl to freedom, like being born anew. It didn't bear
dwelling on, because there was nothing before or after it, just an
escape to freedom—and yet now the idea had lodged in my brain
it wouldn't go away. I'm ashamed to admit it, but there it was.

I turned and headed back toward the railroad, letting her fall
in behind me. "We'll get some dinner," I told her, "then you'll go
back to your hotel and rest and I'll tend to the final arrangements."

She followed along in silence for a while, but as we started
uphill, she said, "What are we going to do then?"

"I haven't decided," I said, going on.

"You won't get away with it." At that, I stopped and turned. A cold breeze off the river wrapped her dress against her legs. "If you don't marry me, you'll be sorry," she said. "You know God sees everything we do. You know what I think? I think we belong together forever." Now whispering, "Forever and ever, amen."

"How do you know it's my child?" I said.

She stared at me, not moving a muscle. Her rosy cheeks were drained of color. "I told you, Tommie, there's been no one but you."

"Hasn't there?"

"What do you mean?"

I had to tell her, I couldn't hold it back any longer. I said, "I know everything, Lillie. Everything you've been hiding. Your mother wrote my mother. Everybody knows."

"Everybody?" her voice quavered and she glanced around. She suddenly looked as if she were about to faint. "Tommie, I swear it's yours. I can tell by the timing of it."

"I don't believe you." I said. "I don't think you know at all. You lay with your own father, and now you want me to take responsibility. I won't do it, I tell you."

She collapsed in a heap, right on the side of the road, one leg sliding out toward the ditch. Just down the road was a gray clapboard workmen's tavern, and across the way a few flat-roofed wooden shacks, but no one was about. "Go on," she told me. "Just go on."

"I'm not going to just leave you here," I told her. "I thought you were hungry."

"I don't need anything," she said. She was so quiet I had to ask her to repeat herself. "I don't need anything. I'm an abomination."

"Lillie, nobody knows but my mother and me, and she would never tell anyone."

"But no one will ever want me."

"That's not true."

"You don't want me. It might have a tail and cloven feet. I'm afraid, Tommie, I'm so afraid."

"That's ridiculous," I said.

She looked up at me with hurt eyes. "It might be yours, you know, I think it is. She's yours, Tommie, I know it." I looked away, trying to figure out the best way to get her up and moving. "You were in love with me in January," she said, "you can't deny it."

I took her hand and she let me pull her to her feet, but when I tried to let go, she flopped down again as if she had no bones. "You have to help me here," I said. This time I supported her with my arm around her waist and we began slowly walking up the hill again. "I've decided I'm going to kill myself, Tommie," she said.

"No, you're not." I had to keep thinking, trying to soothe her, before she turned this into an obscene drama. There were people up on Byrd Street. It would not do to have her in this state.

"My life is ruined," she said, "why shouldn't I?"

"Suicide's a sin."

"I don't care about that. I've already sinned."

"God'll forgive you."

"But nobody else will."

"Hush now," I said. "We should get you something to eat." She put her head down and walked along beside me up to Main, then down to Delarue's lunchroom. I asked for a table near the back and ordered. Then I drank a glass of pilsner and smoked while she quietly ate her dinner.

"So what are you going to do?" she asked.

"I think the best thing is to get you into the Magdalen House after supper this evening."

She nodded. "I don't mind."

In my mind's eye I saw Miss Pilcher's face in a painting. "The Madonna," I said.

"What?"

"That's who Miss Pilcher reminds me of—the Madonna in St. Peter's. She looks so patient. Have you been there?" She shook her head. "It has a basin for holy water. You can dip your hand in water that's been blessed by a priest. I think it counts even if you're not Catholic. You have to cross yourself with it." I was really saying the first thing I could think of, something to calm us both down, but it didn't work.

"I don't think it counts if you're not Catholic," she said.

Some tomb from out whose sounding door she ne'er shall force an echo more. Why those lines from Poe should've come to mind like some taunt I couldn't say, except that I did want to seal her out of my heart forever. When she had finished eating I told her I wouldn't see her to the hotel door. I reminded her to use the ladies' entrance and said that I would be back for her that evening as early as I could.

When she had gone I paid the bill and left fifteen cents for the waiter. Then I walked up to Mozart Hall, where the Dime Museum was presenting *The Chimes of Normandy* at two-thirty. I paid my ten cents and entered the hall and took a seat near the back. The story was about Germaine, a beautiful young woman raised by a cruel man claiming to be her uncle. As a little girl, she was rescued from drowning by a mysterious marquis who later returns from exile. At the intermission, I said hello to Bernard Henley, a college friend. In the final act the marquis fell in love with Germaine and claimed his title to the Castle of Corneville, and the story ended in laughter and happiness.

Sitting in a theater with a happy crowd, you see, living for a while in another world, was just the diversion I'd needed. I took a deep breath and headed out. It was now after five o'clock. The sky was gray.

I thought: Soon this'll all be over.

Leaving the Dime Museum I began walking quickly, yet with no direction. I went down to Canal Street and looked onto the looming smokestacks of the ironworks and beyond to the bridges that crossed the river over the falls. The sky wept tiny crystals of snow. I looked up, and stray pellets stung my face and found a hole in my hat. Where was a sign from God? I had never been more uncertain about anything in my life.

The noise of the river seemed to grow louder, and a strain of happy music from the operetta drifted through my mind. I turned away from the river and began walking back up to Main. I didn't know why, but I felt as if I were in a current, like when I wanted to go to Lizzie Banks's. Once I had resolved to go, nothing could deter me.

I walked slowly back into the heart of the city. Random noises came and went from open doors—music, laughter, shouts, clapping. "O dem golden slippers" drifted from a window. A stray thought: *Murderers and whoremongers shall have their part in the lake which burneth with fire!* I began whistling, and a tremor went through my body. *He shall come in judgment!*

I trudged across Capitol Square, where several men, black and white, were sitting on benches clustered around a gray-haired negro; as I drew near, I recognized the preacher John Jasper, a man who seemed to collect a crowd wherever he went. Jasper said, "The day's comin' when the sun will be called from his racetrack, and his light squinked out forever; the moon shall turn to blood and this earth be consumed with fire. Let 'em go. Won't scare me, nor trouble Gawd's elected people. For the word of Gawd shall endure forever."

The old man's voice was powerful and frightening, and I hurried away. But the voice dogged me. "A city on a hill cannot be hid," Jasper shouted. "Go on, shout the Lord's praises as you go! And I shall meet you in the city of the New Jerusalem, where we shan't need the light of the sun. For the lamb of the Lord is the light of the world."

The muscles in my arms felt tight with strain and I was out of breath. I looked around and found myself well past my hotel. It was nearly dark now and the lamplighter was making his way up the sidewalk. Grains of snow were falling, dusting the coats of passersby. I sniffed the air, flipped my collar up, and hurried along. Back in my room, I put on my overshoes, then headed to the American Hotel. I decided not to bother with a messenger—someone might remember me. Instead, I stepped swiftly into the lobby, hat tilted over my face, and went straight up to Room 21.

She let me in and held me with a sob. "Thank God you're here," she said. Her eyes were red-rimmed, but she was dressed and ready to go, her hair gathered in back with a piece of shoe-lace. That clothes bag of hers sat on the bed, its green linen embossed with a wheat-sheaf pattern. "I'm ready," she said. "Are we taking the streetcar?"

"To Belvidere," I said. "It's only a few blocks from there." Even then, I wanted to put my arms around her, to lay her out on the bed and cradle her. I thought of her father. "I'll be waiting for you over at the *Dispatch* office," I said.

"I've written a note to Aunt Jane," she told me, looking me full in the face, as though she wanted me to say something. "I've told her I had to meet a friend's aunt in Richmond, and I'm going on with her to Old Point. I dated it the fourteenth, because I may be too busy to write tomorrow and for some time, and I didn't want her to worry."

"That's fine," I said.

She began reading some aloud, then laughed in an oddly coy way, as though this were all a lark and we were conspiring as we had back in January. "You can read the rest if you want to."

"No, go ahead and seal it." She seemed unusually animated and fidgety. It made me nervous while I was trying to think, trying to anticipate what we would do if Magdalen House turned us away.

"Everything will turn out all right," she said, as though reading my mind. "You'll see. You'll be fine, and we'll both be happy. I just know it."

I took her letter and left the room, then headed down the corridor. A colored man in uniform doffed his cap and asked if I'd found the lady I was looking for, apparently confusing me with someone else. It caught me by surprise, but, the Violet Bone plot coming to mind, I quickly said, "No, I was looking for a lady who went to school with my sister." I regretted this immediately. I should've told the man to mind his own business. Instead, I found myself being shown to the parlor, where men were supposed to wait for unescorted women. Pretending to be ignorant of the practice, I handed the man a nickel and thanked him for his service.

I took a seat in the parlor and read the newspaper for a minute or two. There was an advertisement for baby carriages, and one for a liniment called Mother's Friend, "to be used after the first two or three months." To be used how and for what, after the first two or three months of what, it didn't say. I turned the page and saw a short notice about men in England who, when they tired of their wives, sold them for sixpence or a quart of beer.

Checking my watch, I feigned a sigh and went outside and across to the streetcar stop, where I deposited the letter in a mailbox. A few minutes later Lillian arrived, carrying her bag and wrist satchel. I reached over and pulled her veil down to cover her face.

Presently a streetcar came along, pulled by two stoical, blinkered horses. The elderly negro driver nodded once as Lillian and I got on. We went around to the left side and sat together, quietly, near the front. As the car proceeded up Main, a few other people got off and on, but they all sat facing the right side. From an open doorway at one stop a half dozen voices sang, "God be with you till we meet again." The open front of the streetcar let in cold night air as we moved on, now with no fellow passengers. Flakes of snow melted on the window.

"Let's keep riding," Lillie suddenly said. "I don't want to get off just yet."

"But our stop is coming up," I said.

"I'm not getting off. You can if you want to."

"How far do you plan to ride?" I wanted to know.

"To the end of the line." She was now drawn into herself, her face a frozen mask.

Fine, I thought—only a few extra blocks. The problem now, though, was that she might do anything. I stood and asked the driver what street we were on and how much farther to the end of the line.

"Coming up to it in five minutes, boss," said the driver. "Reservoir's the end of the line. I been twenty years driving this route, ever since the war ended, and Reservoir's always been the end of the line." He glanced back, saw that we weren't interested in the life of an old negro streetcar driver, brushed the snow from his eyebrows, and turned back to his work. I thought, Oh, the burden of always being oneself.

Lillian and I disembarked at Reservoir and began walking south. "Why don't we go over to the reservoir?" she said.

I looked at her, confused. "Whatever for?" I asked her.

"Because I'm frightened of the river."

That made no sense to me. "What are you talking about?" I said. "It's cold out here, and I don't know how late we can turn up. They might not answer the door after nine."

"That doesn't matter," she said. "I think it's a nice cool evening for a walk and I haven't been up there in a long time. I don't know when I'll get another chance. It's so beautiful and peaceful, and you can think and nobody will bother you."

I told her there was nothing to see there at night. "We'll turn left at the next corner," I said.

"No," she said, stepping out into Cary Street. "I went strolling up there with Cary Madison." I followed behind, hooking my arm in hers and trying to turn her left. She slid her arm out and kept going straight. "Does that make you jealous, Tommie? I was up here with another boy. I kissed him—on the mouth. How many girls have you taken up to the old Marshall Reservoir? Isn't it the most romantic place?"

"I can't force you to go anywhere, Lillie," I said. "But I don't have to follow you."

"Oh, are you still here?" she said, laughing, looking over her shoulder. She tucked her chin into her shawl and began to trot along. "It was just a silly flirtation," she said, "there was nobody serious, not even your brother. Nobody until you."

I caught up to her and put myself in front of her. She reached up and brushed the snow from my collars. "I couldn't help it with my father," she said. "He has things over people and he gets what he wants. He could tell I'd been with you, he could tell I wasn't his anymore. I thought he might kill me. He called me out to the barn and he got that look, that silly grin, and he put his arm around me and smelled my hair and called me his little girl and I was afraid to pull away from him. That smell of his—like green tobacco and whiskey—his scratchy cheek on mine, and I wanted him to hold me so I wouldn't be afraid, even though it was him I was afraid of."

"It's all right," I said, holding her, feeling love for her, even as I tried not to.

"I've ruined my life, haven't I?"

"I don't want you going out to the reservoir by yourself. For my sake will you just not do that?"

"There's nowhere else to go." She went on, I following, and we passed a small tenement house she must've remembered from a visit long ago. Hardly knowing what she was doing, she took her shawl off and dropped it on a bush, as though marking her trail. "The Dunstans live there," she said absently.

"Who?" I said.

"Nobody. Some friends of my parents. They visited us once." She looked around, then quickened her step. The farther we walked, the fewer houses and lights there were. Lillian walked so that she was brushing up against me.

In another block the street ended at the Clarke Spring property, where the old smallpox hospital is. There was a bar on the corner of Reservoir and Ashland—we could hear voices and lights penetrating the night, and Lillie wanted to hurry by, back into the safety of the dark.

"Let's rest here," I said. "You must be tired."

Stray flakes of snow drifted from a pale sky and across the yellow rectangle of light from the bar window.

"No," Lillie said. "It's too cold to stop. We should keep moving. Have you ever seen the reservoir at night?"

"No, and I don't want to."

"You can see everything from up there—the river, the city." She began moving again, down to the end of the block. "It's not much farther," she said. "See—there it is." To the southwest a dark mound loomed above fields and trees—a huge, flat-topped mass arising like an ancient earthen temple from out of a dream. I could see that to Lillian it was a destination, its size and gravity compelling her to find a way in and up. Since she didn't know the way in, I began leading her.

We walked along a tall fence to the gate. I tried it, but it was locked. "There's a hole," I said, and we continued around the corner and down the long side of the earthen mound. "I'll show you there's nothing to see, then we can go."

She twisted her ankle on the uneven ground, and she held my arm while she wiggled her foot. "I think it's all right," she said.

We continued on, and finally, along the south fence, I found the loose board, which I pushed aside. I crawled through, then held the board for her. But while she was waiting for me she turned and noticed the few rows of white wooden headboards jutting from their little plot like bad teeth. The clouds were scuttling fast across the sky now, veiling and unveiling a bone-white moon on the wax, and all she could do was just stand there staring at the crooked graves.

"What is it?" I asked, peering back through at her legs.

"Graves."

"It's only the smallpox cemetery," I told her.

She stood for a moment looking at the sad little graveyard. "You're cold and alone in your beds," she said. "Someday, you will all awake and be happy again." She sounded half crazy, but by then I honestly was carried away by the spell she was under. Then with me holding the board, she hunched down and was able to stoop through without getting on her knees. I began walking ahead of her, up the grassy embankment to the top of the slope. She started after me and caught her dress beneath her foot, and when she stumbled I held out my hand for her.

She said, "I'm walking to the top of a temple, Tommie. It's like the earth mounds back home, and I'm an Indian princess. Daddy John said they were built by people before the Powhatan. That's all so long ago, it's like a dream, Tommie. Daddy John is like a dream, and you are too." The snow had stopped and the clouds were thinning, and beyond them stars winked in the blackness of the heavens. She continued to the top, compelled by the slope and the certainty of her hand in mine.

We came out on a wide pathway which forms the rim of the reservoir. The lights of the city glowed to the northeast, the smoke of factories billowing even darker than the night sky, while down below ran the churning river. In the distance somewhere a train chuffed along. What drew Lillian's attention now was the basin dropping away at her feet—she was staring at it, as if into a void whose dimensions were impossible to fathom.

"Tommie," she said, barely audible, "hold me. I'm shaking." It seemed we had arrived at a point of embarkation. I dropped her bag and put my arms around her. A dog barked, and the train grew fainter.

She shuddered at how deserted and gloomy the place was at night. "Tommie," she said, "is there a God?" She sat down, her limbs lifeless. "I can't see anything," she said. "I can't breathe. Where are you?"

"I'm right here in front of you," I said. "Now we've seen the reservoir, let's go." She said something in a childlike voice that I couldn't understand. "Lillie!" I said. "You're cold. We have to go now. Lillie! We have to go, get up."

"There is a God," she mumbled, "but it doesn't matter." She took off her hat and gloves.

"Lillie! Let's go. It's cold here. Get up now." I pulled her hand, trying to make her stand up, but she was inert.

"Get up!" I said. "Lillie! Lillie! I'm going to leave now."

She held my hand tighter and tried to pull me down to her, and I cried out at the suddenness of her movement. Then I heaved her to her feet, drawing her in to myself, and when she yelled I put my hand over her mouth. I just did it without thinking—her voice was so shrill in the dark. I told her to be quiet. She twisted in my arms, but I gripped her tighter. "We're going to leave now,"

I said. "Do you understand me?" But she only struggled the more, and I was afraid to take my hand off her mouth. She was hurting me in some way—my hand hurt, and she was kicking me.

"Stop it," I said. Then for a moment she was still, and I took my hand away from her mouth, waiting for the scream. There was nothing but her ragged breathing. "Let's go," I said. "Before it's too late."

But now she was moving away from me. "I've kept your key close to my heart," she said. She opened her coat and drew the gold key from her pocket, then threw it toward the outer fence. "You want me out of the way, I'll go." She headed down toward the water.

"Don't be foolish, Lillian," I said, following.

Not turning around, she said, "There's no other choice."

She made her way down to the low picket fence at the edge of the water, then walked around to the end, as though trying to find a way in. Halfway along the south side there was a little gate. She fumbled with the latch.

I came and squatted on the slope just above, afraid now to touch her. "What are you doing, Lillie?" I said.

"Something I should've already done."

The gate opened and she stepped onto the little grassy ledge, a border about a foot wide between the fence and the reservoir. She held onto the gate to steady herself, and it swung to and relatched.

"You might as well come back up here," I said, not believing she would jump in with me sitting there.

"I can't, the gate's closed."

"You got it open, and now you're just putting on a stunt."

She turned to face the water. The side of the reservoir sloped away, the water level a couple of feet below the grassy verge— she'd have to jump out. From where I sat, even I could feel the chill of the water. The footing was slippery from the snow, and as she turned back—and I think she'd decided now it was a foolish gesture after all—her foot went out from under her and she fell sideways, reaching for the fence.

She splashed in with a little yelp. I jumped up and called her name. But she wasn't moving—all I could think was that either she was pretending, or she'd struck her head on the bricks lining the side. One doesn't simply fall into the water and die.

I tried to open the latch as Lillian had done, but my hands were shaking and I couldn't make it work. I would have to climb over—or run for help. She was only stunned, I told myself. She could not be dead. But what was I to do? If I went for help, it might be too late anyway—I might even be accused of murder. I stood watching her float, just beyond reach. I would have to get in the reservoir myself to save her—assuming it was still possible to save her. She looked so peaceful there. This was not supposed to happen. I was crying, and calling her name out into a black void. Then I staggered back up the slope.

I left her there.

CHAPTER TWENTY-TWO

W HEN TOMMIE has finished talking, his brother looks at him and asks, "Why? Why did you let all this happen, when you could've just walked away? And why didn't you tell me or somebody before now? I'll go tell Mr. Evans tonight, Tommie, we'll get you a new trial. I'll get Ma and Hannah Madison in here to testify what they know."

"It won't work, Willie. It'll just bring shame on the family and you'll be accused of perjury for things you've already said. Ma's in no condition to come. Aylett will paint her as a drunk old lady who can't remember anything straight, and Hannah Madison—you know she won't say such things about her husband. And who would believe her if she did? They'd say we put her up to it. I tell you we have a better chance on appeal. Don't make me sorry I've told you."

"Then why did you?"

"I don't know." Tommie presses his hands against his head as though to stop the noise inside. He leans headfirst against the wall. "Do you honestly think it would stand in court?"

"I think we should at least run it by Mr. Evans."

Willie is able to get Tommie's permission to talk to Mr. Evans, and the next morning he meets him at his hotel before he has had his breakfast. He tells him there's a new development in the case. They go to Mr. Evans's room, where for more than an hour Willie lays out his brother's story, during the recital of which he sits, then stands, then sits again, his foot jiggling while he talks.

When Willie has said everything, Mr. Evans shakes his head in disbelief. "Why now?" he demands. "Not that it would've gotten him off. But it might've saved him from hanging. *Might've.* Of course, he's got no proof of any of it. The best thing for you and me to do is forget about it." He thinks for a minute. "Unless. How well do you know this cousin of yours, Hannah Madison?"

"Enough to know she's timid as a mouse and would rather die than get up in front of a crowd and say anything against her husband."

Evans nods. "If we could get a signed affidavit from her it could help. But even were Hill to believe her, he'd be unlikely to throw out three months of work, given the fact that it still doesn't clear your brother."

"But all the rest—her slipping on the snow and—"

"I know, that's in his favor, but there's no proof of any of that, and, again, there's the problem of him leaving her there."

"I think maybe I shouldn't have told you any of this," Willie says, hanging his head.

"Of course you should. I would've in your position. I'll speak to Mr. Crump about it, but I think he'll agree with Tommie— our best bet now is to hope for leniency down the line. I don't believe that's a long shot."

Now Willie goes back to the jail to report to Tommie, and finds his brother in no mood to talk about anything. He doesn't want to talk about Evans, Crump, Hannah Madison, their mother—none of it seems to matter. Yet he's cheerful, ready to go to the courthouse for his sentencing, as if he knows something that no one else does. And again, Willie has confidence in his brother, even though he knows he should not.

The crowd is thinner this morning at the courthouse, but there is growing concern about what's going to happen to Tommie— as people are calling him now, instead of "the prisoner"—and whether it's right. A lingering doubt still hangs in many people's minds about whether Tommie got a fair trial after all, and whether he really deserves to die. He seemed like such a nice young man at the trial, not a mean snake—just a frightened boy, really. And that girl, she certainly was no innocent virgin. What really happened out there that night in the hearts of two young lovers, people want to know, and why were we so quick to pass judgment?

Inside, it's not impossible to get a seat anymore. Tommie notices a few familiar faces—the stalwarts of the trial, including an old lady who has a sympathetic face and reminds him of his mother. She sits there with her knitting, and when he catches her eye, she smiles sadly. And there's Wren, sitting beside Gretchen, as though proclaiming he doesn't care whom he is seen with; he laughs at something she says, his high voice carrying through the room.

When the court is in session again, Crump makes a motion for a new trial. It being Saturday, the judge says he'll come to a decision on Monday. Meredith says he has no interest in arguing right then against such a motion. Instead, he says, "We would appreciate it if Your Honor could go ahead and fix a sentencing date."

Tommie sits motionless, staring out the window, while powerful men calmly discuss ending his life. When they're done, he again thanks Evans and Crump, and Evans takes him aside and shakes his hand. "How are you holding up?" he says, his palsied eye now seeming less conspiratorial than disdainful.

"Better than you might expect," Tommie replies. "I still have hope."

"That's good, son, that's good. Your brother gave me your declaration."

"Do you think it could help?"

"It's late in the game, but it could still save you. I've canceled my plans to go home today. I'm going to meet with Mr. Crump and we'll discuss it in detail. You need to write up a statement."

"But if I change my mind?" Tommie locks eyes with his mentor. "I don't know if I want a confession like this to be out in the public."

"It's too late for that, Tommie. People will find out. I won't tell them, nor would Mr. Crump. But things have a way of getting out. As your counsel I have to advise you to present this statement."

On Sunday, then, Tommie meets with his lawyers in the jail's dispensary. No one beyond the four men in this room and Willie have any idea of the turn the case has suddenly taken. A confession is what the public is now clamoring for, to ease their doubts about the verdict. And a confession is exactly what Tommie most wishes to avoid.

Crump is stony-faced, his son offering a smile and handshake for both of them. Evans greets Tommie with his usual inquiries after his health. They take seats around a small deal table that has been moved in for the occasion. Crump Junior is the only one preparing to take notes, his stack of writing paper squared in front of him and his sharpened pencil in hand. A guard comes in and reaches up on a high shelf for a roll of bandages. Evans nods to him, and the guard says he'll leave them undisturbed unless he needs anything else.

When the door has closed, Crump says gruffly, "Let's see your statement." Tommie slides over the pages he has worked feverishly on since yesterday. There are fourteen sheets of Tommie's tight, precise handwriting. Crump glances through them, occasionally rubbing his face or puffing through his nose. After a few minutes he hands them on to Mr. Evans. "So the only thing they were wrong about was the way she died?"

"They were wrong about lots of things," Tommie begins. "The key, the poem, the Belle Isle business, the letters, I don't know where to begin—"

Crump cuts him off. "The only *important* matter they were wrong about was the manner in which the girl died. And the possibility that you were not the father. Is that correct?"

"Yes, sir, it is."

Crump nods, his grave expression unchanging. "Son, I'll just tell you that when Mr. Evans told me about this, I thought the best thing for me to do was to drop this case. Can you tell me why I shouldn't?" Before Tommie can articulate a word, Crump goes on. "You hoodwinked the court. You made fools of your counsel. And, worst of all, you probably sank your own case." Tommie's jaw unhinges as if he has been socked, and Crump takes pity. "Maybe you didn't sink it, but you didn't help it any."

"I'm sorry, Mr. Crump," Tommie says. "Especially for making a fool of you."

Crump laughs at this, glancing to the other two. "It's certainly not the first time that's happened. I just don't like being left in the dark, goes against my nature. Hoodwinking the court—now, that's all right, as long you don't make an occupation of it. But in all seriousness, I declare I think we're better off at this point sticking with what we've got. Our whole case is built around the flimsiness of theirs. They have no solid proof that you struck or drowned Miss Madison. But you have even less proof of your statement here." Crump slaps the pages that Evans has laid down. "This Mr. Madison business is a serious charge, and if you had left it at that—"

"I wanted to tell Willie the whole thing," Tommie says, "but I wish I hadn't."

"Be that as it may, you stated to the police that you never saw her here. To go back and change that now . . ." Crump shakes his head, rubs the back of his neck.

"Tommie," says Mr. Evans, "we're going to study this, but there's not much we can do to put off sentencing tomorrow. We might can buy us a day with a motion for arrest of judgment. Beverly's preparing the bills of exception, but they'll take a few days. I do think we've got a good chance on appeal. In the meantime, we'll just have to see what sort of mood Judge Hill is in."

Crump makes a little laugh. "I wasn't aware of Judge Hill having moods."

On Monday Judge Hill overrules the motion for a new trial, much as Crump and Evans expected, and Crump makes a motion for arrest of judgment. "Well, it buys us another day," Crump tells Tommie. "Try to get some rest, and take care of that cold." Tommie nods. He caught a chill the night before, even though it was not a particularly cool night, and today his head is fogged and cloudy.

Willie has been seeing to some business back down the country, but Jane continues to visit the jail twice a day. Now that the trial is over, only Tommie's lawyers can see him in private; all other visits are attended by an officer.

"I wrote a letter to the judge," Jane tells Tommie. She alternates between black and dark blue dresses; today, feeling more optimistic, she wears dark blue, and a black velvet hat with a veil. "I think he's a fair man, and I think he'll overturn the verdict once he reads it. I told him what a dear, dear boy you are and that you could not possibly have seduced, much less harmed, your own sweet cousin. I know in my bones it was her father that was responsible for naming you in the first place."

Tommie raises his eyebrows, wondering if Willie has hinted anything to her.

"I've told Willie this," she says, "and I hardly want to repeat it to you." She glances over to the guard, who is standing just outside the dispensary with an inattentive expression. "I've sometimes wondered . . . if he didn't engineer it all some way himself. There, I've said it, and God forgive me, but I might as well say as think it. It's good to get it off my chest."

"You think he—?"

"He was ashamed of her," Jane says. "And if he found out that she was—expecting, and maybe she told them, poor thing . . . I just don't know. They were so jealous and spiteful, I just don't know what they might do. Oh, Lord, what am I saying? Of course, it was suicide. It just had to've been." She pauses to blow her nose, not bothering for reassurance from Tommie.

"And I see you have an admirer," she says, smelling a bouquet of flowers in a vase.

"A man from Alexandria sent them," Tommie tells her. "I'd never heard of him. And look at all these cards and letters."

"Are they all nice?"

"Mostly. There's some that want me to roast in hell, but I've learned to spot them. Here's a nice one: 'In your time of tribulation, trust in the Lord to break the bonds that you so unjustly wear.' And here's one from a Pennsylvania woman. She says I was framed, and 'I have important information for you.'"

"What does she mean?" Jane has a credulous, hopeful look.

"Probably she's crazy, but I'll give it to Judge Crump."

"Of course you must, right away. I'll take it to him directly I leave here. Let me sort through all those, Tommie. You know I'll do anything for you, don't you?"

Tommie hands her a stack of letters. "If I didn't know that by now, there'd be something wrong with me. But this has been too much for you, Aunt Jane. And you've spent far more than you should've."

"I don't care if it takes every penny I have. I'm going to get you out of here." She averts her face and blows her nose again. "It was all going to be yours anyway. Yours and Willie's. You're my boys." She seems unable to find anything more to say, so he asks her for the news of Little Plymouth. She's all right until, without thinking, she says, "Nola Bray's gotten engaged to a lawyer from Richmond." She suddenly goes blank and white, her storytelling hand floating like a wounded bird back to her lap.

Tommie pats her arm. "I'm happy for her, Aunt Jane, and I'm glad to hear about it. I know it was hard for her to have her name mixed up in this thing." Tommie had written to her, and received no reply.

The next morning the heat and humidity of summer have settled in like a fat, sedentary cousin from the Deep South, the effluvia of the sluggish canal filling the pores of the city and plastering shirts and blouses onto sweaty backs. Tommie attends to his toilet—shaving, putting on his suit, oiling and combing his hair—as though he were meeting with potential clients.

Again a crowd has formed along Tenth and in the alley behind City Hall, just to catch a glimpse, to gape openly as he emerges from the carriage, as though he were an exotic animal or mythical creature. There are black people as well as white people, young and old, and they are mostly quiet, content just to stare, and he is content to look as ordinary as he can for them, an unassuming young man whom they might see anywhere—in the haberdasher's, in church, on their own street—and think nothing of.

The burning question of the day is whether he'll confess, and what he'll say if he does. Won't he give them some word of explanation? Surely he can explain his relationship to the girl. A few words and they can go home, at peace in their hearts. Won't he at least give them that? And so they have gathered to see if now he'll open his mouth and say something. Anything—even the sound of his voice could be a clue. He catches a glimpse of his old friend Tyler Bagby, explaining something to a young lady wearing a blue shade hat, and for a moment he can picture himself in Tyler's place, standing there telling what he knows about Tyler and how sad it was that he got caught up in such a mess and how you never can tell about people. Tommie now tries to avoid looking at faces, fearing he'll see someone else he knows.

The little courtroom is overflowing, people wedged into the jury box, around the bar and the clerk's desk, the incessant rattle of hats and fans louder than the voices outside. Some people who have gotten in now try unsuccessfully to get back out; a few of the more supple bodies climb out the window and drop eight feet to the sidewalk into another mass of humanity.

Back in the sergeant's office, Tommie meets with Crump and Evans. "You know, Hill ruling for an arrest of judgment is the longest of long shots," Evans warns. Tommie nods. "Just so you're prepared."

"How are the bills of exception coming?" Tommie wants to know.

"Don't ask," Crump tells him. "Beverly's chained himself to his desk. There's seven bills, probably over five hundred pages. Wouldn't have delayed the sentencing anyway, I don't think. But I'll see if we can stall."

In the courtroom, then, the first thing Crump does is bring up the issue of the bills. He asks the judge, "Since it will take a full day to read them, could not the court adjourn until the day after tomorrow?"

And now Meredith says, "Your Honor, the defense is the best judge of that, and I would be in favor of it if it could possibly benefit the prisoner in any way. But tomorrow is the last day of term and suppose Your Honor were taken sick?"

Hill then says he can just as well read and sign the bills after the sentencing as before. "Mr. Crump," he says, "do you have anything to say about the motion for the arrest of judgment?"

"I have no further evidence at this point," Crump says. "But clearly there was insufficient evidence to convict, as one of our bills explains at length. On that alone, an arrest of judgment could, I believe, be made."

Hill nods politely, then says, "I overrule the motion in arrest of judgment."

"Thomas J. Cluverius," the clerk says, "stand up." Tommie stands, his hand going immediately to the bar. He just wants it over with.

"Do you have anything to say why the sentence of the court should not now be pronounced?" Hill asks.

The courtroom has gone so dead quiet Tommie can hear his watch ticking in his pocket. He wets his lips and says, in clear, ringing tones, "I would only say, sir, that you are pronouncing sentence upon an innocent man." He had not planned to say more, but now he wonders if he should continue, saying that his side was not adequately heard, that there were mitigating factors to be taken into account. But what would be the point of arguing with the judge in this way? The spectators would love to hear him argue, but he won't oblige.

"Anything more?" Judge Hill says.

"No, sir."

Hill glances down at a sheet of paper, then up. "Thomas J. Cluverius, you have been indicted for the willful, deliberate, premeditated murder of Fannie Lillian Madison, your companion and cousin, whom you had, betraying her confidence, treacherously seduced. Twelve of your fellow men, selected for their intelligence and impartiality, have patiently and attentively listened to the evidence in this cause. Witness after witness has been examined, and day after day consumed in an endeavor to arrive at the truth. Exceedingly able counsel have done all that learning, eloquence, skill, and experience could accomplish on your behalf. You have had a fair trial, and the jury, in the faithful discharge of their duty, have pronounced you guilty, and that verdict has been approved by the court. I shall not harrow your feelings by referring at length to the enormity of your crime, every step in the perpetration of which must be deeply engraved upon your memory. To a man of your intelligence, no good could be accomplished by so doing. I commend you to the suggestions of your own better thoughts. I do not deem it my duty, therefore, to do more than pronounce upon you the sentence which the law affixes to the crime of murder in the first degree, upon which you stand convicted.

"Thomas J. Cluverius, you shall be taken hence to the city jail, and there kept securely until the sixteenth day of October next, on which day, between the hours of nine in the morning and six in the evening, you shall be removed to some convenient place of execution, and, in the presence of such officers of the law as may be necessary to see this sentence carried out, be there hanged by the neck until you are dead. And may God in his infinite goodness have mercy upon your soul."

A fly lights on Tommie's brow; he brushes it away. It is as though he has just awakened from a dream of startling clarity. So this is what his life was about. All along—it was to be this.

At the door of his cell he stands a moment uncertain what they are asking of him. "Mr. Cluverius, you have to step back, please, so we can close the door." But once the door is closed, he won't be able to leave. He is to be locked in his cell now for the duration of his time here, and all visits will have to be in this nine-by-ten-foot chamber. And as he stands on the threshold facing outward he cannot take that one more step backward. Malachi Folger is calling out something from his cell. "Don't you give a care, Tommie," he says, "I'll come round and see you every day."

Then the barred door is closed and bolted, and his world is now his cell and the dingy gray hallway with the few other cells he can see.

That evening Willie is late with Tommie's supper, and Tommie is hanging on the bars waiting and hungry when his brother comes storming in. Willie sets the box of food down and says, "There's stories going around at home, Tommie." He has a wild look in his eyes.

"Stories about what?" Tommie says, eyeing the box. He wants to eat, but Willie seems impatient to talk.

"About Madison. How he intimidated witnesses. He told that Gateweed if he didn't smear you he was going to regret it, and the same with Joel. And there's others. You wouldn't believe what I've been hearing. The two counties are ready to fight each other. We've got a real case for a mistrial, Tommie, if we can get those people to come back in and tell the truth. I've a mind to go find them and threaten them myself."

"They'll read it for a bluff, Willie. They know you're a God-fearing Christian."

"They know I'll by God back up my words," he says, balling a fist.

"Do what you have to, Willie, but don't let your business suffer."

"I'm not doing this for nothing," Willie tells him. "I aim to collect from you soon as you're out." He punches his brother in the shoulder.

"I believe it," Tommie says, managing a smile. He opens the

box and begins greedily eating the eggs and ham, yet he finds
that he is quickly full. "You brought too much," he explains.

"No, you don't eat enough."

"Whose leg are you trying to pull? I've been getting soft and
fat in here. Would you give the leftovers to Malachi in number
nine? He'll hand around what he doesn't want."

Willie nods, boxing up the remaining food. "Everybody back
home wants you to know they're pulling for you," he says. He
takes a letter out of his jacket, signed with good wishes by every
willing person he could find in Little Plymouth. "And Aunt
Jane wants to do something for you. She told me about a singer
named Frank Cunningham. He's supposed to be good, and he
hires out."

"I heard him sing once, in church," Tommie says. "Well, if we
don't like him, Malachi can throw him out."

Willie sits there wiggling his foot, trying to think of something comforting, but he feels the constraint of the solitary confinement. If he had to stay in here even for a day, he would go
half mad, but to be locked in with no chance of walking again in
the woods, hearing birdsong on a bright morning, feeling the sun
on his face as he hefts his ax . . . And yet he knows if he could he
would change places with his brother.

He stands and paces, until Tommie tells him to sit back down.
The guard is at the end of the hall, and Willie leans into Tommie's ear and whispers, "It's not too late to get you out of here.
It'll be harder, but I'll figure it out someway. You could take sick,
and they'd drive you to the hospital—I'd meet you there."

Tommie smiles at the picture, then shakes his head. "No,"
he says, "I really think I'll get another trial on appeal. Plenty of
folks are saying I will. Right now, Judge Hill is probably sitting
up reading these bills of exception. I've only skimmed them so
far, but I know Crump and Crump are the best legal minds in

Virginia. Look here." He flips through the pages of a preliminary copy for his brother's benefit, and Willie watches Tommie's face to see if he's trying to humor him.

"Look," Tommie says, "it's not just folderol—most of it. The trial was full of technical errors. We could have brought up any number of them."

When Tommie has finished explaining the legal processes for his brother, who is sitting there chewing his lip and jiggling his foot with a dazed, half-credulous look, he says, "One more thing you might do." And Willie immediately comes to attention. "You could find out if Reverend Hatcher at the college could come around and visit me sometime." He lowers his voice. "It's not as though I need any more spiritual guidance than before, or unction, or salvation, or any such thing. I won't be able to attend chapel services now, you see—"

"Of course," Willie interrupts.

"No, wait, just let me tell you. They want me to break down, but I won't do it for them. They expect me to confess, and I won't do that either. I have nothing to confess. I only want to talk with Hatcher about private matters, and listen to what he has to say."

"Who are you talking about? Who wants you to break down?"

"Just the people out there who can't wait to see me—"

"You don't have to explain," Willie says. "I'll get Hatcher and anybody else you want. "You want John Jasper, I'll get him in here to preach a stem-winder of a sermon. I'll get Henry Ward Beecher himself in the flesh right here. Knock me over with a feather if I don't." He gets a little chuckle from his brother, the creases around Tommie's mouth and eyes evident when he breaks into a smile, as if he has aged a decade in the past three months.

"When people find out what really happened," Willie says, growing quieter and more serious, "they'll be lining up to apologize."

"It's all a lie anyway," Tommie says. He stands and puts his hands in his pockets. "None of it happened like that, you know. The fact is, I hit her on the head with a blackjack that I stole from the closet at Lizzie Banks's." Tommie's voice has become flat and matter-of-fact—the way it will, Willie knows, before he goes into a crazy outburst. "I threw it in the river along with Lillie's bag. It sank. If I had put it in the bag like I almost did this would've been over weeks ago. I probably would've confessed, knowing I didn't have a chance."

"I don't believe you, Tommie."

"It's true, I picked her up and carried her to the gate in the picket fence and I laid her down there and opened the gate—it wasn't locked. I would've thrown her over anyway." He is talking faster, his eyes focused on something far off.

"That's a lie, Tommie. Why are you doing this?"

"Because I want you to know. I got her to go out there with me, telling her a coach was meeting us at the end of the streetcar line to take us to Hanover to get married. And we went up to the top of the reservoir to have a look around before it got there, and then I hit her."

"All right, when did you conceive such an idea?"

"I had it all along," Tommie says, talking faster, "way back in January when we wrote that fake letter together—yes, I met her here and we wrote that together. I was working on the idea even before that, but I didn't have it fully formed in my mind until just before I came here in March."

"Stop it! You did no such thing." Willie feels his heart thumping wildly in his chest. He wants to get up and beat his brother until he can no longer speak any words. A guard walks past the cell and glances in, then disappears down the hall.

"You're right, Willie, I did no such thing. But do you really believe everything I told you the other night? Because sometimes

I don't myself and I have to tell it to myself in the dark to know what's real and what isn't."

"Of course I believe it, Tommie. I can tell when you're fibbing. I know you."

"Do you? Do you really? Give me your hand." Tommie takes his brother's hand and puts it to his chest. "Do you feel that? It's a heart, and it beats just like yours. But it's different, different from everybody's. You don't know what's in my heart any more than I know what's in yours. Sometimes I don't even know my own heart from one day to the next. Do you?"

"I think I do," Willie says. "I know that I forgive you for what you did and I want to try to help you out of this." Yet he is not at all sure if he really forgives his brother.

"But you wouldn't have done it. You'd have gone in after her."

Willie tightens his lips but doesn't say a word. He can picture himself jumping in the reservoir just as he did in the river, without a moment's hesitation. He wishes he were there now, so he could pull her out and reverse this whole thing. When he thinks about it, which is almost all the time, he feels bad for not having seen what was happening with his brother and Lillie. Why had he not said something encouraging, or discouraging, either way? He wanted Tommie to get hurt by her, just as he had been—he *wanted* his brother to suffer just as he had suffered, so when he saw how his brother was mooning about over her he had not warned him off. He had said nothing.

"I'm going to find out what Madison's been up to," Willie says. "He doesn't know whose tail he's jerking."

"Just be careful," Tommie tells him.

A week goes by, and with Jane's influence and Crump's assurances, Tommie is again allowed to move about the jail and yard from noon to four, and to receive visitors up in the dispensary. Anyway, the afternoon hours have been the worst for strangers snooping around for a look at the prisoner, some of them trying to get in a nasty word about applying for the hangman's job, until it has become more a nuisance for the guards to have him in solitary confinement than out with his fellow prisoners. One day there's a stir when a young man claims to have seen Tommie at the Dime Museum on the night of March 13. This lifeline is quickly withdrawn when it turns out that he's a drifter hoping for remuneration. The loss of a potential alibi puts Tommie in a foul, half-desperate mood for days.

What sustains him in the darkest hours is an evolving idea of his transfiguration into something better and more innocent than even the most innocent of children. He doesn't picture himself as a martyr, because he cannot bear to think of his end, his life extinguished, and the humiliation of a public hanging. It simply cannot be. He prays several times a day now for guidance, for a sign showing him how to act and what to think and say. He prays every day for Lillian, and he asks God how guilty he is and whether he deserves to die. He listens for an answer and tries to make out word sounds in the rain spattering the roof, or wind fingering the chimney flue. But the words are indistinct, and the voice inseparable from the one in his own head.

He desperately wants to speak with Reverend Hatcher because he cannot keep doubts out of his head. If God is out there, why will he not answer? Tommie lies on his cot, staring up at the raven's wing, afraid of his own doubts. If there's no God, the end is just a void: October 16, four months away. A void. But if there is a God, he'll punish me for losing faith. And then what? Flames? Anguish? Eternal suffering and damnation? The worst pain imaginable—a stomach illness, a burn, a deep cut— multiplied times a hundred and never stopping? Why would the universe be devised in such a way? What purpose could that possibly serve? Should I confess and save my soul, or is confession just a trick to make desperate people exonerate the public? On the other hand, my giving them something—isn't that a final act of mercy and contrition I could show? Crump and Evans have yet to decide what strategy to take. But is there now a moral obligation beyond legal maneuvering?

He thinks about Willie, chopping wood in a forest where birds are singing, and he begins drifting off. But then he finds himself thinking of Lillie, standing there waiting, just beyond Willie's hearing. "I did it," he whispers. "I killed her. I killed her!" He sits up, wide awake, panting and sweating. Had he spoken out loud? How loud had he said the words he can hear even now? All is quiet again, and he lays his head back down and prays, "If there is a heaven, God, I know I don't deserve to go there. But why would you create a hell? Wouldn't the void be better for people like me? Please help me, God." He feels a weight on his chest, a sense of desperation, as after days of cloud cover when all you want is a hole of blue to pin your hopes on, or just the song of a sparrow in the morning.

· CHAPTER TWENTY-THREE ·

TOMMIE'S HOPES rise and fall on the faintest glimmerings of news—from visitors, from his lawyers, from bits of overheard conversations which he later, in the endless hours, tries to reconstruct and interpret. When the newspaper carries no story of his case he feels abject and lonely and forgotten—anything, even a report of a North Carolina spiritualist who can divine the truth by communicating with Miss Madison, means that attention is still being paid his case.

Tommie gets out of jail only to make application to the state supreme court of appeals for a writ of error and supersedeas to the judgment of the lower court. The court decides to hear his case, but not until October. And so, with a simple stroke of the pen, he is granted another few weeks of life.

Reverend Hatcher has been on vacation, but when he returns he makes a visit one afternoon to the city jail. He is still the affable, ingratiating, youthful man Tommie remembers—slightly unsure of himself, never overtly religious. His appearance is of a young man disguised as a middle-aged Baptist minister, with white beard and hair and a way of studying one's face as though he wants some deeper level of friendship than one is prepared to offer. Tommie had warmed to the man's intelligence and his lack of utter confidence in himself, which was so very different from Reverend Ryland's dullness and studied gravity.

And yet when Hatcher comes into Tommie's cell, he seems older and more cautious, not unfriendly, but cognizant that there is now a border which his former congregant has crossed—he can only shout encouragement from the opposite shore. Tommie offers him the chair, then sits on the edge of the cot.

"I thought you might call for me," Hatcher says, "and I'm glad you did, my friend. I didn't want to press myself on you, in case you had another spiritual counselor. And if you do, that's fine with me. I should tell you right off that I come to you expecting nothing other than what you ask of me. I've ministered to many men in jail." He stops a moment. "Never to one in your situation. But I think I can give you comfort, and, if you should want it, guidance. I'll pray with you, sit with you, talk with you."

"About?"

"About whatever you like. About your case, if you care to."

"Is that what you want to talk about?"

"I'd be happy just to sit and pray quietly with you, or just sit."

Tommie mulls this over, and then stands and paces. "Have people asked you about why you've come?"

"A few. Not many know I'm here, other than my family. They'll find out, and, yes, they'll want to know. People are curious. But I want you to understand that whatever we say here is in the strictest confidence."

Tommie waits for Hatcher to go on, but the minister seems uncertain and so Tommie, not wanting him to feel awkward, says, "God has always been an important part of my life. Maybe you've read that in the papers. Some people have mocked it as false piety." He takes a seat again, gripping the edge of the cot.

"Never mind about the newspapers. And lawyers, as you know, say what they have to to win cases."

"Yes, well, I don't think I could have stood what I've gone through without the words of Jesus." Tommie holds up his Bible, its leaves marked with slivers of paper. "But . . ." He hesitates, because he is not sure what Hatcher really means by "strictest confidence." Yet Hatcher's face in the half-light of the cell is so young and honest-looking, and he feels himself so much older by comparison that it is as though he were talking to a person from the distant past, or some out-of-joint time. "I guess I've lately felt unsure—about what comes after."

Hatcher clears his throat, and Tommie can see that it's hard for him to remain natural and relaxed under the circumstances. "These doubts," Hatcher says, "are ones that everybody has from time to time."

"Yes, it's just that I've never expressed them to anybody. Except maybe to my brother."

"Tell me about these doubts."

"I suppose you're right," Tommie says. "They're nothing out of the ordinary. Nothing that a man on his deathbed or on the battlefront doesn't face all the time, everywhere. It's just that I didn't expect to face them so soon."

"Remember that our Savior faced doubts, more troubling than any of ours. He asked God, his father, if the cup could not be taken from him, but it was the cup of salvation and he knew that he had to drink it. And then on the cross he cried out that he was forsaken. But he was not."

"But he wasn't an ordinary mortal."

"In that sense, I think he was. He suffered what we suffer. He felt the pain of mortals. He prepared himself in the wilderness for what he knew lay ahead—his own death—and he was tempted by doubts."

"That's some comfort, I reckon, but I'm not part of any grand scheme or prophesy like that."

"But we all are, Tommie. We're all part of the grand scheme. Christ played his part, just like we all play ours. He could have run off, but he did not. He stayed and was executed as a common criminal. And, Tommie, you must understand that he did that for you and me. We're sinners, and he offered to take away our sin, to bear it himself, and so to wash us clean with his forgiveness and love. That's what he was doing up there on the cross—taking our sins. It was hard and it was humiliating and it was painful. And of all the miracles he performed, you'd think he could manage that of leaping off the cross. But God had a higher purpose for him. God wanted him to suffer and die, just like we all do. And you know why, of course."

Hatcher leaves the question hanging, but Tommie is thinking about the public, horrible death that Christ chose, instead of the quiet deathbed, and wondering how he himself would handle it. He nods vaguely.

"He had to die so that he could come back to life. That was the ultimate, unexpected miracle. Not saving himself, but giving himself over to God to save him. And through his son, God showed that we too have eternal life."

"But as he was dying, Christ didn't trust God," Tommie says. "He lost his faith, even at the last minute."

"I don't think so," Hatcher says, "and I don't think you should be troubled by that anyway. Why don't you turn to Luke and see what his last words were? He says to one of the robbers beside him, 'Today thou shalt be with me in paradise.' And then in a little while, 'Father, into thy hands I commend my spirit; and having said thus, he gave up the ghost.'"

Hatcher gives Tommie some other Bible verses to read, then promises to come back whenever Tommie needs him.

Willie in the meantime has been making inquiries back at home. One day he makes a visit to the home of Marcellus Gateweed, a small man who has a small, invisible wife and no children. They live in the village of King William in a tiny house with a vegetable garden in front and a horse and a donkey out back. Willie knocks on the door at dinnertime, and Gateweed answers, napkin tucked under his chin as though to point out the fact that he has been interrupted. "Mind if I have a word with you?" Willie asks.

Gateweed squints at him, his trim mustache nearly sliding off his face. He reaches into his vest pocket for a monocle. "I don't believe—"

"You know who I am," Willie says, stepping in. "Brother of Tommie Cluverius. I only want to know if somebody put you up to it." Again Gateweed squints at him, but also glances nervously out to the dining room. His hand goes to the napkin at his neck. "Did Madison ask you to say you recognized that key as my brother's?"

"I think you should go," Gateweed says, trying to shut the door with Willie in front of it.

Willie doesn't move a step. "If he did, you can sign a statement. If there's a perjury charge, I'll pay—you won't likely go to jail. I'll find out either way, so the best thing for you to do is sign a statement."

Gateweed's wife is calling him back to the table. "I don't know anything about this," Gateweed says, again trying to shut the door on Willie's immovable foot.

"I think you do, Mr. Gateweed, and believe me, whatever threat Madison issued is nothing compared to what's coming from me."

"I'll send for the sheriff if you don't leave now," Gateweed says, his voice trembling. "I think Mr. Madison is the person you want to see."

"I aim to." Willie stands there eyeing Gateweed's frightened fox face.

"Look, Mr., uh, Cluverius. I run my shop and mind my own business. Madison came in two months ago and asked me if I knew anything about this Tommie Cluverius. I said, 'Of course I do, I read the newspapers same as anybody.' So he says, 'The man ought to hang for what he did.' And I told him, 'Every man deserves a fair trial.'"

"You said that?"

Gateweed nods rapidly. "Yes, I did, I said words very much to that effect, and then he asked if I knew the suspect. I told him the truth. I knew him by sight—he'd come to my store many times on court days. Well sir, he leans his knuckles on the counter and looks at me and says, 'You know he wears a gold watch key?' I told him I had noticed such an item. And he says, 'Well then you'll recognize it as this key, won't you?' And he slaps a picture from the newspaper down, and I looked at it and nodded because it did look like it and the way he said it made me feel uncomfortable. And he wanted to know what I'd say if anybody were to ask me about it, so I told him of course I'd say I recognized it. What would you have said?"

Willie shakes his head, thinking it was no wonder that Madison came hunting for such a man. Joel had no doubt the same cowardly soul, but he'd deal with him later. "Go on then," Willie says, "write up what you just told me and put your name to it. And put that you were wrong about the key, that it wasn't my brother's."

"Well, the truth is that I don't really know which was which."

"Then put that down!" Willie shouts, growing impatient with Gateweed's sudden finicking over the truth. "I'll wait here."

Gateweed goes out and says something to his wife, and a few minutes later comes back out with a piece of paper and a feather pen that he seems to have no ink for. "And you a shopkeeper," Willie says. "You can use my pencil."

Gateweed laughs nervously. "This could take some time, and I don't know if it will stand in court."

"I'll trouble with that," Willie assures him.

When he has the document secured in his leather pouch and slung across his chest, he mounts his horse and rides for home. He can hand it to Crump first thing in the morning. What troubles him is whether one coercible witness will do any good now.

Malachi is released in the middle of August, around the same time a telephone agent with a hunted look is brought in for killing a Kentucky gambler he suspected of sleeping with his wife. The word around jail is that he'll get off with no more than five years. With Malachi's departure, Tommie is offered the yardmaster position, but he gratefully declines—he has all the privileges he needs, and he's afraid that the goodwill of his fellow inmates might turn to resentment if he held any authority over them.

The weeks of anxiety and waiting until the court of appeals hears Tommie's case are nonetheless weeks that he is alive and has hope. Then the counselors present their sides of the case to the court, going over much the same ground as before. Tommie is not allowed to attend. They have decided, after much thought and consultation and late-night pencil chewing, not to introduce Tommie's latest version of events.

During the entire week of the arguments there are torrential rains across the state, like nothing people have seen in years. Is it a sign? Tommie wonders, watching the rain fall like spilt nails across the prison yard and blow in whickering cold waves against the walls. Even inside, you can hear it, pelting interminably on chimney flues and ceaselessly murmuring in many tongues on the gray slate roof. Not since the freshet of 1870, people say, has there been such a flood. That was the year Jeter Philips was hanged for killing his wife, and no one knew he was even married.

By Thursday, the day Crump speaks for three hours, the rains are continual and the river has risen to perilous heights, rising as the waters of a thousand and more streams swell its banks. It rises and rises, four inches an hour, then six inches, until it's running two feet beneath the Mayo Bridge. In the afternoon a tremendous log comes smashing into the bridge, threatening to destroy it. Sawyers come and cut away enough planking to let the log pass. Then the gasworks gives out, and except for the few electric lights of downtown, the city falls into darkness. Candles and oil lamps flicker on here and there as in olden times. Down at the warehouses, sweaty-faced men load hogsheads of tobacco into drays and drive the cargo to higher ground, while up near the jail Shockoe Creek is spilling from its banks. The prisoners can sense that something is on the verge of happening, something beyond even the control of the officers. A little closer and they could be free . . .

Finally the waters recede, and in the days before the supreme court issues its decision, Tommie goes about his life as before, giving no one any trouble and maintaining a pleasant disposition from morning to night. His routine is unvarying, and there are no complications other than the arrival of new prisoners. He mostly avoids making new friends. The great majority are in for a much shorter stay; already the telephone man has been convicted and sent to the penitentiary for seven years. Everything Tommie needs is provided, and nothing whatsoever is expected of him except good behavior. The only real source of disquietude is the uncertainty ahead. Sometimes he finds himself thinking that if he knew for certain he was going to die, he would find more peace. But the hope of life, of walking out and going anywhere he likes, doing whatever he wants, running down to the river and leaping in if he feels like it, keeps him agitated from one day to the next. These are private thoughts, shared only with his brother, and sometimes Evans or Crump, and it's always a relief to unburden himself of these fantasies. "When you get out," Willie tells him, "we'll get you a new suit, made to order at Carter Brothers."

"No," Tommie replies, "first thing I'll do is go over to Schoen's and have a smoke and a drink. Then I'm going to Lumsden's and buy presents for you and Aunt Jane, Ma and Daddy, everybody— the most expensive things I can find, borrowed against what I'll earn later. Then we'll see about that suit."

And then afterward, by himself, he's still smiling, and he goes over the scene again, putting a woman in somewhere after the suit, almost feeling the softness of her skin against his. Then the image dissolves and there above him is just the black iron ceiling and the raven's wing.

✦✦

CHAPTER TWENTY-FOUR

THE SUPREME COURT of appeals rules three to two against Tommie. To get a rehearing he needs only one of the three who ruled against him to agree. Crump tells Tommie this to cheer him up. What he doesn't say, and they both know, is that if the high court denies a rehearing the only remaining hope is a pardon or commutation from the governor.

From now on Tommie is to live a restricted life in a larger room on the second floor where a guard will be with him night and day, lest he attempt to escape or harm himself. "I'm sorry we have to do this," one of the guards tells him.

"I don't mind," Tommie says. "You've always treated me fairly."

The new room is altogether better. It's larger and better ventilated and has two south-facing barred windows overlooking the city stables and the colored jail yard, from whence often rise tattered bits of work songs and spirituals. The room's brick walls are painted white, and there's an iron cot, a table, a nightstand, a trunk, and two chairs. The two officers who take turns at the watch have a poorer arrangement—they sleep or sit just outside the room. Often they leave the heavy wooden door ajar, but when it is closed they can check on him through a wicket. After Aunt Jane tells them that the potted geraniums she brought are for the two of them, as well as her nephew, they take it upon themselves to water them.

Tommie dresses nearly every day in a suit and cravat, or a necktie and gold pin. His health and appetite are good, but the strain begins to show in his face. Strands of gray appear in his hair, and lines become etched around his eyes and mouth; for lack of exercise he puts on some weight, so Willie buys him three new suits.

He begins writing a treatise on the death penalty, and why he opposes it: Convicts could repay some of their debt by hard labor; life in prison is often harsher punishment; the death penalty goes against the teachings of Christ; and, most important, mistakes are sometimes made. Reading the whole thing over, he thinks it would be seen as too self-serving and decides against sending it to the newspaper. Instead he mails a copy to the governor; he also shows it to Hatcher on his next visit.

"You are using the mind God gave you to a higher purpose and that's good," Hatcher says, "as long as you're not putting your faith in things of this world to save you. There may not be much time, you know. You need to prepare for eternity, Tommie. Even your innocence won't save you—only your trust in Jesus. I beg you not to cling to any hope of release."

"I don't want to," Tommie says. "It's the hope that makes me suffer."

Hatcher nods, trying to understand where his lost sheep is leading him. "Tommie, I say your innocence won't save you. But your guilt, if you are guilty, is a terrible burden to bring before God unconfessed. If you're to be saved, you must confess and do it without fear of the gallows. But even a confession won't save you without your faith in Christ as your redeemer."

"I have nothing to confess," Tommie says. "I am not guilty of the blood of Lillian Madison."

Hatcher nods gravely, but the tightness around his eyes relaxes and he seems a little less burdened. "Very well then, I accept that as a true statement."

"It's just the shame—the gallows. Why does it have to be so cruel? I—" He looks away, unable to go on.

Hatcher tries to speak, but his lips have gone dry and he fights away tears.

"Reverend Hatcher," Tommie says, "do you think a soul could be corrupt by nature?"

"No, I don't think so," Hatcher says. "Why do you ask?"

"I just wondered if some people are born bad and have to fight to be good."

"I don't think anybody is born bad. But, yes, it is harder for some people to do the right thing. Men with much greater minds than my own have even said that man is fundamentally prone to evil. Saint Augustine thought that, but I don't. I do know one thing, though—the devil is loose in the world, and it's hard to get through life without facing him. Some people are more sorely tested than others—I don't know why. But only those with the most trust in God can survive the test." He waits a moment, then says, "Is there anything else you want to talk about?" Tommie shakes his head, and Hatcher seems almost relieved.

When he is alone again, Tommie thinks about Willie and Jane and all the men here, going on with their lives after he's dead and gone—most people will forget about him. Sometimes drifting off to sleep he can see her floating lifelessly on the unruffled surface of the reservoir, her white face and hands the only things visible in the blackness of the universe, her eyes open and staring into the depthless sky. Was it his desire only that was to blame? Of course not—she had wanted him as much as he had wanted her. They had cleaved together.

Evans comes to tell him how they ruled on the rehearing. Tommie knows right away that this penultimate prop has been pulled out from under him. He feels his face flush as Evans tells him how sorry he is.

"But, Tommie," he says, "the governor has the final say and public opinion is turning. He's pardoned plenty of people." He can see that Tommie's in no mood to talk about pardons. "How's your brother getting along?"

Tommie tells him that Willie is supplying timber for the Richmond and Chesapeake company, and that if the new railroad is built he stands to make quite a profit. They talk about other news of the day, about the new trolley system being installed and how things are changing all the time. Then Evans says he'll come back up as soon as he can. There is no need to say the obvious, that his work for Tommie is essentially over. They stand and shake hands.

The judgment of the supreme court is certified, and again Judge Hill is given the task of scheduling an execution date. He settles on Friday, December 11. Crump and Evans then write up petitions to the governor both for pardon and for commutation of sentence, and hand them over to Willie, who takes immediate charge. He brings them to a printer and has twenty-five copies made in booklet form so that signatures can be appended on the following pages. Then he travels around to everyone he knows in any position of influence and collects the names and addresses of people around the state and beyond who might be sympathetic to their cause. He enlists the help of a lady friend, then has more booklets printed up and mails those out as well, stressing in a covering letter that the matter is urgent. He discovers that his brother is about as well known as any man in the country. The petitions are circulated among Baptists, Quakers, Methodists, Presbyterians, Catholics, Jews, and reform societies as far away as Boston and Charleston.

And they begin pouring back in—from Fauquier and Fluvanna, the Northern Neck, Baltimore. The little town of

Chester, Pennsylvania, returns a petition signed by twenty-four people; one hundred twenty-seven citizens of New York City send back their own engraved petition. Northerners seem more sympathetic, or perhaps, Tommie and Willie conjecture, quicker to decry the apparent mob mentality of Southern justice.

The petitions pour in from the remotest corners of the land, a steady flow of voices pleading mercy for a man the signers have never seen. Willie is determined to keep sending petitions, even to the most unlikely places, until Governor Lee has made his decision. By the end of November, five jurors, all from Alexandria, have signed petitions for commutation. Three of them complain that they were not aware they could find for anything less than murder in the first degree. Now they begin to speak out: If they had known of their power, surely they would have voted for second degree. This prompts the hustings court clerk to defend himself, saying he gave them clear instructions at the beginning of the trial.

Other contrite voices speak up on behalf of the prisoner, citizens who have changed their minds—they're no longer so sure, they think suicide was as likely as murder, they heard the jury had been unduly influenced.

Now it seems probable that Governor Lee will at least commute the sentence. He'll show the same wisdom and compassion as his uncle, the greatest general in the nation's history. Armed with over three thousand signatures, then, Crump and Evans call on him in the capitol, and Fitzhugh Lee—the dashing, bushy-bearded cavalry commander—welcomes them and says he has read every scrap of information about the case and will be pleased to hear their petition. They spend most of the afternoon with him, pointing out the weaknesses in the commonwealth's murder theory. Lee listens politely, attentively, and with no attempt to hurry them along.

Willie planned to make his own appeal to the governor on the same day, but he has decided, without telling anyone, to travel back home and call on his mother. Things are out of balance, and a reckoning is coming due. Yes, Tommie had become scared and had left Lillie there, but he doesn't deserve to die for it. Willie has anyway convinced himself that she was already dead, that there was nothing more Tommie could have done for her. The scales have to be righted in some way. Aylett and Meredith and Hill—they were only doing their jobs. The jury—it was partly to blame, but they had been swayed by all the witnesses Richardson and Wren and the others had dug up, and probably they were afraid of their reputations if they went against the tide. It was wrong, but Willie found it hard to be angry at twelve men he didn't know. Everybody had a hand in it—the court of appeals, Governor Lee, Herman Joel.

But the person who most often surfaces to mind, bubbling up like gas from a rotting log on a pond bottom, is a criminal far worse than his brother. Lillie's words, which he'd long ago put out of his mind, come back again and again: "He made me feel dirty." Willie remembers telling this to Tommie—could it be that his brother was now embellishing from that? Or was it that Lillie had not told him the entire truth? Or did something happen later between her and her father? He feels his universe coming unhinged, and all he can do is direct his considerable energy on Madison. Whatever happened in the past, the man deserves jail, if not hanging, and yet he is allowed to walk free, to laugh and drink and grow old, while Tommie will turn cold in his grave before his twenty-fourth birthday. It isn't right. But first Willie has to see about something.

He has to know for sure.

He walks in without knocking and finds his mother doing needlework by the light of the western parlor window. She drops it in her lap and looks up at him, haggard and confused. "Son? I thought you were in Richmond to see the governor. Did you forget the letter?"

"No, I have it, Ma," Willie says. "I'll see the governor tomorrow and I'll give it to him."

"Your Pa wrote it, and I cried a-reading it. If that doesn't move the governor, he's made of stone. Nothing but stone." She takes a long sip from a blue ceramic mug of coffee and bourbon. "I wanted to take it myself, but I wasn't feeling good, and the roads have been so bad with the weather. You know I write your brother every day. I just don't know if I can bear to see him there."

"That's all right, Ma," Willie says. "Does he ever write about visiting you here before—before Lillian died?"

"He visited me all the time."

"Ma, he told me all about it. I know about the letter. I just want to know if you think Hannah would give me a statement. It's time her husband was behind bars."

"Statement? What do you mean?"

"Mother, you don't have to pretend with me. I know what she wrote you."

"Who wrote me?"

"Hannah Walker Madison, your niece, Mother, for God's sakes!" Willie is beginning to lose his patience. He eyes his mother's afternoon libation. "I'm sorry, Ma, I didn't mean to shout."

"That's all right."

She looks hurt now, and he tries a gentler approach. "Tommie told me about the letter Hannah sent, about how her husband had used Lillie."

"I believe you, son. It's just that I don't remember it. You see, I don't remember things like I used to. Your father still has a very good memory, he can remember everything he said and the day he said it. He says my memory's fine, but I know it's not so."

"Ma, this is very important," Willie says. He suddenly feels himself panicking, picturing his brother at the reservoir. "It is crucial that you remember some piece of this. You had a letter, it was in a book on the mantelpiece. *Pilgrim's Progress.*" He gets up and strides to the fireplace where a little fire is going. The only items on the mantelpiece are two candles, a pewter cup filled with paper lamplighters, a box of cascara quinine tablets, and a photograph of Tommie and himself as boys standing outside their old house in Sunday clothes. "And he read the letter and you took it and threw it in the fire."

"I believe we had a copy of *Pilgrim's Progress,* but I don't know where 'tis. It's your father's book."

"No," Willie says, adamant. "The book was up here." He slaps the top of the mantelpiece and dust flies up. He has to get out of here before he says something he'll regret. He has to get outside where he can breathe, where the world isn't turning upside down.

There is no time now, he tells himself, to visit Hannah Madison even if he wasn't afraid to—he has to hurry back to Richmond to see the governor first thing in the morning and hope that Lee will meet with him after Willie failed to present himself today. There is no time to take the evening train. He'll have to leave his horse at his parents' house—going up to Aunt Jane's would only waste more time—and then hire a carriage and driver. To hell with the expense.

Willie is kept waiting for nearly two hours outside the governor's office. Important men come and go, and still he waits. He cannot remember sleeping at all last night, though he must have slept some for he remembers a dream of running to catch a train, his legs unable to coordinate into a dash.

Now a black man in a tailcoat tells him the governor is ready to see him. He enters a small office where a pretty young woman, her hair in a bun and her eyeglasses down her nose, is pecking away at a Remington typewriting machine, her fetching profile visible from the door. "You can go on in," she tells him. Willie thanks her, and moves past her desk into another, larger office, where the governor sits behind a big mahogany desk in his shirtsleeves and tailored vest. He wears silver cuff links and has a gold watch chain that disappears into his vest pocket. The office is oak-paneled and furnished with three or four plush leather armchairs, shelves of neatly arranged books, a globe on a large brass stand, and a Confederate battle flag hanging above a sheathed dress sword, everything bespeaking order and respectability.

The governor stands and greets him warmly, shaking hands across the desk. Willie starts to give him a speech he'd rehearsed, but his lips keep quivering, and seeing this the governor tries to put him at his ease. "Have a seat, son," he says. "Would you just look at that? Half a foot of snow in the first week of December." Willie glances vaguely out the window and nods, the letter from his parents clutched in his hands.

"Son, I have the greatest respect for how you've stuck by your brother. You've shouldered this burden heroically. Did you have something you wanted to tell me?"

Willie blows his nose into his handkerchief and apologizes, smiling. "I didn't think I'd be here begging for my brother's— I didn't think it would come to this, you see. He's innocent, I know that, but I don't know how I can make you see it. He was almost a stranger here. That's why he can't find anybody who remembers seeing him at the theater that night. It's much easier to make a conjecture about where somebody was than to prove it, which he now finds himself having to do. And it should be the other way around—there is no proof he was at the reservoir, and no proof that my cousin was murdered there. Here is a letter from my parents. They beg you, and I beg you to . . . spare . . ." Willie swallows and tries to go on.

The governor takes the letter and smiles in a sad, not unkindly way. "Mr. Cluverius," he says, "I don't want you to get your hopes up. I'm looking into it, but you know I have a grave duty in this office. Three tribunals have pronounced your brother guilty. The most venerated jurisprudential body in the commonwealth has meticulously reviewed this case. Their learning and wisdom in these matters far surpasses mine. For me to overturn their ruling would require something extraordinary—some convincing new evidence, which so far has not come to light. I have great sympathy for your brother, you understand, and for your whole family, but I'm above all a servant of the commonwealth here."

"Five jurors have changed their minds," Willie says.

"I received their petition today," Lee replies.

"And we have an affidavit coming from a gentleman who saw Tommie at the theater that night."

Lee nods. "Mr. Crump informed me you might have something of that nature."

"Yes, it's a solid alibi." Though Willie knows it is anything but—likely another derelict in need of money. "And you have Marcellus Gateweed's retraction?"

"Yes, I do. It's curious he would do that."

"Yes, sir, people are rethinking this. I don't believe the real culprit in this case has been revealed. It's my opinion there's a family member involved."

"Oh?"

"Yes, sir, there is. I just don't know how to get any evidence against him."

"Mr. Cluverius, if there is any important new evidence, I'd be happy to consider it. I plan to review everything. I'm even going out to take a look at the reservoir." But there is now a distance in the governor's voice and demeanor, signaling that the meeting is over, and Willie leaves the capitol feeling that he has somehow failed his brother.

He begins walking along in a daze, and Tommie's story comes flooding to mind—the letter, the hole in the wall, Poe, Reverend Jasper, the snow, the streetcar to the reservoir. How had he put it? A void whose dimensions were impossible to fathom. Such pretty language—Tommie was meant to be an orator . . . It all meshed together with the stories from the trial like a tongue and groove, but made something different.

The reservoir. That's where he has to go, and without thinking he finds himself striding west out Main, then down toward a place he has tried to put out of his mind. The reservoir, and then to that house on Spring Street—Magdalen House. Did such a place even exist? And if it did not, what would he say to his brother? Would he tell him how much he himself misses Lillie, how he remembers stroking her hair and her face, and how soft and sweet she was?

When he gets there, it's mid-afternoon, and a light snow has begun to fall, sifting through the trees and disappearing into the blanket already on the ground. *It was such a time as this,* Willie thinks, and he reaches for the handle on the tall wooden gate. The door opens and he walks in. The mound, its slopes rising higher than the cottages along the street, is quiet and white, and as Willie begins climbing the stairs, he can see them—Tommie and Lillie here that night, hand in hand as they ascend the embankment, Tommie leading the way. But it's *Tommie* who has brought *her* here, not the other way around, Tommie whose idea this whole thing was. Tommie knew about the reservoir; why would Lillie want to come out here on a cold night to kill herself?

Willie can hardly catch his breath when he reaches the top. There's a tall, stoop-shouldered man down the path, clearing snow with a shovel. He's wearing no hat, and his ears protrude like wings from the side of his head. He looks up and lifts a hand in greeting, and Willie recognizes him as Mr. Lucas from the trial. Willie walks slowly along the cleared pathway, stopping a few feet from Lucas and turning to the reservoir as though admiring the view. It's now a dark rectangle in a white frame, and farther out, way beyond a line of snowy trees, the river curves its way west.

Lucas nods hello. "Mighty nice out," he says, chuckling. "And I don't mean that for a joke. I like how it covers things up, makes everything clean and white. Just like brand new." He leans on his shovel, glances at Willie as though he can't quite place him. "But this one won't last. They say warm weather's a-coming."

"That so?" Willie says. He leans and finds a pebble about the weight of a gold key. "Okay if I throw this?"

"It's your water," Lucas replies. Willie wings it out and watches it splash. He reaches for another pebble and turns, eyeing a spot well behind Lucas, trying to gauge how far it is from here to the corner of the outer fence. He's sure he cannot throw it that far, but, then, *they* were farther along the path. What can he say to Lucas? "Do you think I could throw this over the fence?"

Lucas tilts his head, confused by the question. "I don't know that Mr. Meade would approve of rock-throwing like this," he says, hesitating. "Suppose somebody was on the other side of that fence?"

"What? In this weather?" Willie says. "There's just graves over there." He's now walking along the uncleared path ahead of Lucas, because he is going to throw this one more stone and then he will leave and never come back. He finds a spot he judges to be about right. The corner boards have been replaced with new slats, but he knows the place. Right here. And he flings the rock out, hard, but not too hard, because she was a girl and was only trying to make a point. The rock disappears into the snow halfway to the fence. Not even close.

He goes back to Lucas. "Where did you find that key?" he demands. "Was it all the way at the fence?"

Lucas shakes his head slowly, staring into Willie's eyes. "Who are you?" he says.

Willie tries to calm himself. He stares up into this strange man's face as if the man has an answer that will make everything okay. But Lucas only looks wary and slightly annoyed. "It wasn't really at the fence, was it?" Willie pleads. "It was out there somewhere, wasn't it?" He points toward the middle of the snowy grounds. "It's okay if it was. I won't tell anybody, I swear to you I won't."

But Lucas has become a pillar of stone, leaning on his shovel, mute and impassive, his mouth open but unmoving, as flakes of snow dust his gray head and melt on his winged ears. Willie brushes past him. There is no answer. Lucas has forgotten, or maybe he lied about the whole thing from the beginning— finding that damned key, keeping it for his own private reasons, then turning it in. Of course he forgot. What difference does it make anyway? *What difference does it make?* And he can hear Evans as if he were right beside him: *It makes a great deal of difference, Willie.* But why do they want to kill him? Willie shakes his head to get the noise out, and he hurries down the steps as though flying from the reservoir.

CHAPTER TWENTY-FIVE

FOR TWO DAYS Tommie awaits the governor's decision. Life cannot be over, he thinks—if ever there was a case calling for executive clemency, this surely is it. Looking down the tunnel of years that awaits him if the governor chooses life in prison, Tommie can hardly bear it. Yet he dare not hope for under twenty years. Twenty years! He'd be forty-three years old, and starting out again with nothing—life would practically be over. But, of course, there would be a chance for parole. Everyone said he was the best-behaved prisoner they knew . . . But what should he reasonably hope for? Many were now calling for a life sentence, as though that were an act of mercy. After all, life in prison is at least life, with the chance of a pardon from a later governor. But surely Governor Lee would not be so hardhearted. Twenty, then, it would be twenty—just over a seconddegree sentence, which would satisfy everyone.

He hears visitors. If it's good news, it'll be Willie.

There is Crump's voice, speaking low, and Evans's. Perhaps Willie was held up, has gone to tell Aunt Jane the news, or out to buy flowers. Tommie stands and paces in front of the window. The snow is turning into a muddy slush, and from the buildings in the lower part of town chimney smoke rises into a leaden sky. It's too somber a day for the way he's feeling, almost giddy with anticipation—today the burden will be lifted. The work is finally over; there's nothing more to be done.

Crump enters first. Tommie decides to ignore the seriousness on his face and on Evans's. "Where's Willie?" he asks. "Shouldn't he be here?" He can feel the wind being sucked out of him.

"He'll be around later," Crump says. "Tommie, I'm sorry. The petition was denied."

"For a pardon?"

"And for a commutation."

Tommie waits. There is always one more card to play, some word of encouragement or comfort. He himself has often been a step ahead of his own counsel. He takes the letter from Crump's hand and his eyes swim across the page: "Gentlemen, I have had the honor of giving your statements, papers, and petitions about Thomas J. Cluverius careful consideration and attention . . . With the greatest sympathy for those upon whom this blow must fall, I now write to inform you that I have not been able to reach a decision different from that held by the courts . . ."

"So what does this mean?" he says.

Crump looks at Evans, then says, "I think the governor will probably grant you a reprieve. For a few weeks. It's probably best if the request comes from your minister. I'll see to it with Reverend Hatcher."

Evans comes over and takes Tommie's arm and guides him to a chair. Tommie suddenly feels himself sweating all over. His vision goes gray and spotted; he leans over to keep himself from fainting. And then as clear as day he can see his little brother going under the water, and he recognizes the vision from countless dreams—in the dreams it was himself as a little boy, but now it's Charles, towheaded and round-cheeked, and he's waving.

Tommie gets hold of himself and says, "Do you think he might change his mind?"

"No, I don't," says Crump.

Tommie nods. "All right, then," he says quietly, yet there's a bitterness of gall and ashes in his gut. He quickly composes himself and tells his counselors again how much he appreciates everything they've done for him. "Pray for me," he says.

He cannot eat more than a few bites of his dinner that afternoon. He sits at his desk and, with tears in his eyes, writes the governor the most servile letter he can:

> Dear Governor Fitzhugh Lee,
> I hereby humbly present to you my final petition, that you will in your mercy grant to me a respite of sixty days that I may have a suitable time to prepare for my inevitable end. This I solemnly feel is most important for me in my sad condition, all earthly hope being now cut off.
> Your servant,
> Thomas J. Cluverius

When Reverend Hatcher comes by, Tommie says he'll feel more like talking after he has heard the governor's response. Hatcher goes away, then returns within two hours with the news that the governor is giving him until January 14. Tommie thinks a moment, then brightens, and with a faint grin says, "Thirty-seven days. It's less than sixty, but it's the best news I've received in some time."

He slumps to the edge of his cot and stares at his shoes; Hatcher takes a seat on one of the chairs. "It's not so much for myself," Tommie says. "I'll be gone, but the others will take it hard. Willie and Aunt Jane and my parents—and to have to live with this stain the rest of their lives."

"They'll be forgiven."

"I can't help thinking that there's still a chance. It's a good sign, this reprieve—wouldn't you agree?"

"Tommie, please, don't keep putting your faith on getting out of prison. Now you have to look to God only—not to save you from death, but to redeem your soul for everlasting life. That's enough, isn't it?"

"I never said it wasn't."

Hatcher smiles a little sheepishly. "Tommie, you just have to believe that in the end we're none of us much different from the other. It's all stripped away—the good and the bad—and we come away like newborns. At least, that's what I think."

"But you don't know."

"I feel that it's true." Hatcher places a hand over his heart. "But, no, I don't know."

Tommie looks away, then says, "I pray all the time, and I read my Bible. But I'm still here facing the gallows, so you can see I have doubts about whether God is listening."

Hatcher goes to the window and looks out. "I'm going to ask you something a wise man once asked me," he says. "Supposing this window were open and a man down in the yard yelled for you to jump and he would catch you. Would you jump?"

"Of course not."

"No, but if it were Jesus, would you?"

"If I knew it was Jesus, I wouldn't hesitate. I wouldn't even ask why."

"I wish I could help give you absolute trust in Jesus, Tommie. But I can only go with you a little ways. You have to make the leap yourself, over and over."

When it appears that Tommie has no more to say, Hatcher stands, then hesitates. "I've struggled with something myself lately," he says. "If you were to decide to make a confession, I would keep it a private matter for a long time. But eventually I might come to think that people had a right to know the truth. I tell you this, Tommie, because it would trouble me greatly knowing I'd deceived you in any way."

"So you think I'm guilty of murder?"

Hatcher stands quietly, until the distant clanking-shut of a cell door breaks the silence. "No, I don't," he says.

Willie doesn't arrive until that evening. To steel himself, he has stopped at a tavern on the way up, and his head is light, his tongue loose. Yes, he'll comfort Tommie again, and go on doing it, but now he needs some answers.

A bulb-nosed guard named Dunn lets him in and he puts Tommie's supper on the table, where his brother sits writing. "Mr. Evans told me," Willie says.

Tommie nods, without looking around. "I'm writing a little book about my life and trial. Maybe you can sell it later and give the money to Aunt Jane?"

Willie waits until Tommie has scraped his chair around and is looking at him. "Mother has no recollection of any such letter from Hannah," Willie says.

"Does that surprise you?" Tommie asks.

"I don't know what to think, brother. I believe you told me the truth. I don't think you could've invented all that in your head."

"I've had a lot of time to do nothing but think."

"Then what is the truth?" Willie demands.

"The truth is just like I told you."

"Which time? The first time, about you not seeing her here atall? Or the second time, about her leading you up there and slipping? Or the third time, about you hitting her? Or is there another version you want to tell me now? Which is it, Tommie?

Maybe now you want to say you never came to Richmond that day, or maybe you want to tell me somebody else killed her but you can't prove it?"

"Nothing can hurt me anymore, Willie. I'm nearly a shade now. Look, can't you see right through me to the wall? Can you read that verse behind me? 'Neither death, nor life, nor angels, nor principalities—' " ·

"Shut up, Tommie."

" '—nor powers, nor things present, nor things to come shall be able to separate us from the love—' "

"I don't know who you are anymore."

"Did you ever? Did you ever really know me, Willie? I don't think you did. I don't think I ever knew myself."

Willie can see it's no use trying to reason with his brother. He goes to the window and looks out toward the warehouses, between which he can make out the masts of schooners and a wedge of the river, glimmering in the low sun. "When you get home, you'll be right back to normal."

"When I get home, I'll be in a box. Could you do me a favor and bury me out in the Tunstall plot, under the cedars beside Uncle Samuel? Can you see to that with Aunt Jane? I don't fancy going into a church cemetery somehow—vandals might get to my grave."

"There's still hope, Tommie."

"Yes," Tommie says. "I'm sorry I haven't been acting myself lately. I want you to do me a favor, though. When this is over, I want you to take a trip to Washington and New York and see the sights—the Capitol and the President's House and all that. Would you do that for me?"

Willie nods.

"What I'll miss the most," Tommie says, "is the beauty all around. When you're out there trying to make your mark on the world, don't ever forget how beautiful it already is."

"I won't." Willie watches a late-arriving ship, its sails lit by the sun, just before they're furled.

"If I could do one thing different," Tommie goes on, "it would be to love a little more. Willie, you can't undo the wrong you did. You can only do other good things. I wish I could explain that. Everybody ends up paying with their life for what they did wrong."

Willie nods, his lips pressed together.

"Ma's been writing me all along." Tommie shows Willie a bundle of letters. "And she said a curious thing. She said, 'I didn't come to love your father for a long time. Some people don't learn to love right off.'" He looks at his brother for a response.

"You were always her favorite. She likes telling you things." The visiting hour is nearly over, yet how little time remains to spend with his brother. He has put so much of himself into saving Tommie that he hasn't given much thought to the real possibility of losing him. Eternity is not something he thinks much about, nor heaven either for that matter. But he feels an invisible force pulling them farther and farther apart, like roots plucked from the ground—and his brother, sitting there opposite him, may soon be nothing but a lifeless body. He is so startled by the idea that he has to get up, and, ashamed of himself, tell Tommie that he has to go now.

❦

CHAPTER TWENTY-SIX

Bᴜᴛ ᴡʜᴀᴛ ᴀʀᴇ thirty-seven days? The waking hours Tommie spends in feverish activity—there is his life's story to write, endless reading, and a stream of visitors, any one of whom might be the key to his salvation. The two pretty girls from Philadelphia who are curious—he lets them come by and talk for a few minutes. Perhaps one of them will see somebody who is friendly with the governor . . . He knows he should be concentrating more on his spiritual life, but while he is alive there is still hope.

Willie is now writing letters to every state legislator—a hundred and forty in all—asking them to request of the governor a further reprieve until the February session of the general assembly, at which time that body might recommend a further stay. He is also trying to get the Honorable John S. Wise to consider taking the case to the United States Supreme Court, and he has another meeting scheduled with the governor, at which he plans to ask him to personally visit his brother.

Then at night, all the ceaseless activity and clamor of the day dies away and Tommie is again alone in the dark, faced with the void. What is the point of sleep, when there is work to do, when he will most likely awaken sweating and terrified? Some nights he can fall right into a dreamless, uninterrupted sleep of several hours. But as one week is chipped away, and then another, he finds this harder to do. His head will pop up after what seems hours. Then he'll lie back down and listen to the coils of the furnace hiss and rattle, and after a while all will be quiet again. Only his breathing for company and nothing to stop the image of the noose, dangling there in the darkness.

So many times in his life he has wanted things to come quickly—the trip to Richmond with his father seemed like it would never come, but finally it did. Going off to school and college, sleeping with a girl, with Lillian—with what a voracious, impetuous appetite he had craved these things and more. There was so much he wanted to see and do, and yet now it is all running out of his grasp. Only twice in his life has he wanted the clock to reverse itself: After the reservoir the days had spun out of control, and so had the hours after his little brother drowned. But now he finds himself in a carriage careening down a steep hill, a mad blindered horse galloping hell-bent for whatever lies at the bottom. His life can seem so paltry and insignificant, then suddenly so dear, and then he prays to God for peace in his heart.

Letters of support pour in during these last weeks, far outweighing the voices of those who say hanging is too good for him. Yet only twenty-four state legislators respond favorably; a few others write letters of sympathy, but say the case is out of their jurisdiction. The governor is disinclined to make a visit to the prisoner.

For his Christmas dinner Tommie eats heartily of roast turkey and ham, sweet potatoes, and plum pudding. The silver-tongued tenor Captain Frank Cunningham calls on Tommie that afternoon and entertains him with ballads and sacred songs. He sings "Annie Laurie" and "Home of the Soul," and they seem to Tommie the most beautiful music he has ever heard. Cunningham is a tall, broad-shouldered, handsome brick of a man with flashing blue-green eyes and a firm handshake. Tommie shakes his hand for a long time, not wanting to let go.

"Please come again," he says. "I want you to know that whatever anybody else says, I'm not guilty, and one day we'll meet in
heaven, and you'll know it." He wants to say more, but Cunningham seems more comfortable when he's singing.

Then the days slip by, and it is the final week. And even those
days dissolve away like snow falling in the river. Tommie's parents
want to come, but an ice storm makes the journey too hazard-
ous. Out in the jail yard men are at work finishing the scaffold.
Most of it has been constructed in a workshop in another part
of the city, but the pieces have to be assembled on site and so the
knocking and buzzing of hammers and saws carries up to the
room where Tommie stands looking out at the shifting clouds.
The colored prisoners below sing more fervently, drowning out
the hammers with their own unleashed lament. Fights break out
as the work goes on, and guards have to disperse the men back
to their cells.

On Wednesday Cunningham calls again and sings for Tommie until late into the night. Jane comes for a final visit the next
day, but can do little more than sit beside Tommie on the cot,
holding his hand and looking at it as if to sear it on her memory.

"You've stood right by me, Aunt Jane," he says. "And the Lord
knows it."

"What they're doing is wrong, I don't care if you're guilty or
not, it's just wrong wrong wrong. But I won't hold it against
anybody, and, Tommie, hard as it is, neither should you." That is
as much as she can get out before the sobs constrict her throat.

"I don't, Aunt Jane," he says. "I can't repay you, but will you
take some of the money from the sale of my book and fix up the
best garden you ever had? With lots of flowers? I'm sorry I won't
get to put one in for you this year."

"I don't need any garden, Tommie, but I'll put one in if you
want."

"I'm giving my clothes and books to Willie, though the clothes probably won't fit. I'd say give them to Ma and Daddy, but they'd just be sad. Willie finished paying off my buggy, so it's his. I don't have anything else much except my watch, which you can have back. Or find somebody to give it to."

She seems relieved when Willie comes to take her back to her hotel. She kisses Tommie again and says she loves him, and then Willie holds her to keep her steady as she makes her way out of the room and down the steps. When Willie returns he says that he's putting her on the early morning train.

For a long while Willie just sits beside his brother on the cot, as Aunt Jane had done. It's much easier than having to look at each other. Finally Willie speaks. "I'm going to see the governor again this evening. And in the morning."

Tommie makes no response. Then, "You get that contract with the Richmond and Chesapeake company?"

"Yeah, project could last two years."

"I expect you'll be wanting to get married."

"What makes you say that?"

"Oh, I've heard there's a young lady you're awfully fond of."

"You have, huh? I haven't heard much about that." Then, in a serious tone: "Her name's Clara, Clara Allan. Her father's a Presbyterian minister over in Manchester. She's forming a unit of the Salvation Army. She's been so helpful to me these past weeks, more than just about anybody. I'd've brought her around today, but she didn't want to be in the way."

"No, no, don't bother her with me. I'd only scare her off. What a terrible way to meet a girl."

"I've heard of worse."

"Tell me."

"Well," Willie laughs. "Well, maybe not."

"Willie," he says, "do you know Romans 8?"

"Remind me."

"'There is therefore now no condemnation to them which are in Christ Jesus, who walk not after the flesh, but after the Spirit.' That's been a big comfort to me. But there are some things I need to tell you."

"I'll hear whatever you want to tell me and I'll take it to my grave, and no matter what you say I'll always love you."

"I know that. But listen. I've always wanted more things than you, ever since we were little, so maybe you won't understand me exactly. I wanted—I don't know how to explain. I wanted everything and I wanted it right away, and when things didn't go according to plan I had to blot it out, as if it wasn't there, and then go on. When Charles died I just blotted him out of my mind, but I don't think you did. And then you fell in love with Lillian, and I'd already been with women before but not in love and that made me want her. I think that was it at first, but then I did fall in love with her, but I hated myself for it at the same time. And when she got—when she got in trouble and moved away I tried to blot her out of my mind, but she wouldn't let me go."

"I've had a good life, and I'm about ready to go. It's just—"

"What?"

"It seems unfinished. I was looking out at the clouds before Aunt Jane came. They were sliding away to the east toward home, changing shape, and the sky was so blue I just wanted to fall into it and float away. I think I'll be there in heaven waiting for you, Willie. I've prayed and prayed on it. Sometimes I'm scared, but I'm not scared to die, even if it hurts for a while. It'll all be over soon—"

"There's still hope," Willie says, his jaw clenching. "It's not over yet."

Tommie puts his arm around his brother. "You did everything possible," he says. "You're going to be more successful than I ever could've been. I see that now. You're like an ox—you just keep plowing on, and no stump gets in your way."

"I've failed you though, brother."

"No. I failed you."

Willie shakes his head but will not look at his brother. Out in the yard, the hammering dies away, and the black voices are lifted on the wind and carried beyond the prison walls, heavenward. Neither of them speaks for a moment.

"Could you do me one more favor?" Tommie asks. "Tomorrow—I don't want you to be there at the end. I don't want you to see me like that."

CHAPTER TWENTY-SEVEN

D UNN COMES IN LATE on the last night and offers Tommie
a dram of whiskey; they sit together for an hour or so
drinking and smoking cigars, Tommie mostly listening to Dunn
talk about his wife and sons, one of whom has gotten into some
trouble. Tommie has polished off a plate of beefsteak, cabbage,
and slaw, followed by some ginger snaps, and still he finds himself not satisfied. Dunn sends out for more food; presently a boy
returns with a plate of macaroni and grated cheese, with rolls.

"I feel alive again," Tommie says. "I think I could eat an entire
turkey right now."

"Shall I send out for more then?"

"Only if you'd share it with me."

Dunn, who often eats Tommie's leftover desserts, says, "If
they'd send up some of those pastry puffs I think I could oblige."

Before Dunn finally leaves for the night he lingers at the door
of Tommie's cell. "Sir?" he says.

"What is it?" Tommie asks.

"When I was first to come out here, my wife told me to bring
along a pistol because you might give me some trouble. After I saw
what a small, well-mannered fellow you was, I went outside and had
a right good laugh. I don't think they gave you a fair trial atall, sir."

After Dunn goes out Tommie tries to stay awake praying.
Lord, not as I will, but as thou wilt. He falls asleep for an hour or
two, but wakens before dawn and waits for the light to come once

more to his window. He eats a few bites of bread and butter, then shaves and combs his hair and dresses in the black corkscrew twill suit that the jail has provided for him—a simple straight-back jacket and pants. Outside a gray mist is rising, giving way to a cold and clear morning, with bright blades of sun touching the snow and the rooftops and the distant hills.

Reverend Hatcher arrives, looking more careworn and depressed than Tommie has ever seen him. He asks if there is anything in particular Tommie wants to talk about. "I'd just like to pray with you," Tommie says. "Until it's time. And if you could give me a prayer to say on the gallows, that would be a big help."

"I think you could say, 'Lord Jesus receive my spirit.'"

Tommie nods and repeats it a few times. Then Willie arrives and says that the governor turned him down last night. "But I had the feeling he was seriously mulling it over in his mind," he says. "I told him Judge Crump would come back in the morning. When he gets here I'll see if he thinks I should go over there myself. Mr. Crump thought it was best not to apply too much pressure today, let him come to a decision on his own."

Then he takes a closer look at his brother. "Where did you get that suit?"

"They gave it to me to wear."

Willie's brow furrows. "All right, then, dammit, if it has to be a black suit, I'll send out for one. You don't have to wear that." An hour later a man comes back with a diagonal-weave black suit with a cutaway coat.

Meanwhile, friends new and old come by and shake hands with Tommie, until he begins to feel as if he were going on a great trip. But the person he most wants to see is Crump, with news of a reprieve.

Suddenly it's noon, and Tommie thanks everyone for coming and asks if he can be alone now with his brother and Reverend

Hatcher and Captain Cunningham. He gets down on his knees on the bare wood floor, facing the window, Willie kneeling alongside him. Hatcher comes and stands with his Bible on the other side of Tommie. Cunningham positions himself near the door, singing softly.

"Blessed are they that mourn," Hatcher says, "for they shall be comforted. Blessed are the dead which die in the Lord." And Tommie opens his eyes and sees the sun edging around a cloud and glinting in through the top of the window so brightly he has to shut his eyes again, the afterimage a purple orb pulsing beyond the bars.

"Be thou faithful unto death, and I will give thee a crown of life."

Tommie feels afraid, for the first time, of the pain. Would it end? A cold sweat trickles from his armpits. *Lord Jesus receive my spirit.*

"God shall wipe away all tears from their eyes; and there shall be no more death, neither sorrow, nor crying, neither shall there be any more pain." Then Hatcher touches Tommie's shoulder and says, "We humbly beseech thee, Lord, to look upon thy servant now in this his hour of supreme affliction, and grant him thy tender mercy when human friendship and sympathy is unavailing. O God, we commit his spirit into thy hands."

At twelve-thirty, Crump returns with word that the governor has declined to interfere. Willie gets up. He embraces his brother one more time and says simply, "Good-bye." Then he hurries from the jail and strides briskly, not seeing anything, back to his hotel room, where friends are waiting.

Crump takes his leave. Then Dunn comes in and asks Tommie if he doesn't want to relieve himself one more time. "I think that's a good idea," Tommie says. When he's finished, Dunn and Hatcher and Cunningham step back in, and presently an officer comes to the room. Tommie holds his hands out while the sergeant ties them at the wrists. Only now does he notice that his knees are, and have been, trembling violently. Then Dunn places Willie's black derby on Tommie's head and they start off.

At the stairs they're joined by two deputies, and the procession moves forward, past the other prisoners, locked in their cells. Tommie bids many of them farewell, though most are new to him since his confinement on the second floor. "Rock of ages," Cunningham sings, "cleft for me, let me hide myself in thee." When they are out in the yard, he shakes Tommie's tethered hand and leaves.

A few steps on, a great shout arises from a flock of thousands, as they catch sight of the prisoner. The hanging is supposed to be closed to the public, but scores have talked their way past the guards, claiming one special privilege or another. In the jail yard, Charles Meredith mills with cronies, making the most of a final chance for a boost from the Cluverius case into the lieutenant governor's office. And on the hills and housetops beyond the walls, multitudes have gathered as though for a miracle. Lithe young men have staked out perches in trees; others, affixing spurs to their shoes, have clambered up telegraph poles. Standing room on rooftops is sold out, the roofs sagging dangerously under the weight of gawkers passing telescopes and field glasses.

Tommie turns his eyes on the ground, and, when he looks up, it's to the sun. There in the middle of the yard is the platform— from the crossbar hangs the rope that has been waiting for him all his life. As though he has rehearsed it, he walks steadily behind the sergeant, toward the steps. Someone says something about olive oil, and a cold knot slipping better with grease, but the words are strands of gossamer.

He and the sergeant climb up, Hatcher and Dunn following. Dunn comes forward and takes Willie's hat, and the sergeant begins placing a black silk cap over his head. "I'd prefer to wear my own hat," Tommie says. The sergeant hesitates, then shrugs and puts the derby back on.

Life is so futile, he thinks. But there had been moments of such startling beauty that the veil of the eternal had briefly slipped and you could see that heaven was real. A frog, a brilliant green gem with ruby splotches on its back—he had caught it and watched its eyes, its pulsing throat, he put it in a bowl with some greenery that might be its food and covered it. But the next day it was dead, its lustre gone—he was sorry now he had captured it.

It's all a trick to make me confess. I'll step onto the trapdoor, and just before they pull the bolt the sergeant will announce I've been given a stay.

The sergeant reads the death warrant, after which Hatcher begins praying, but Tommie cannot make out the words. There is a roaring larger than life coming from inside his head—a river in flood crashing into the ocean. And then there is perfect stillness and clarity.

"For his anger endureth but a moment," Hatcher says, "in his favor is life; weeping may endure for a night, but joy cometh in the morning . . ."

Tommie is standing now over the square door, looking at his feet. He had meant to take a final look at the sun, but he can feel it on his back. In the sky above, a buzzard circles—then he sees it's a gas balloon, as if from a dream, and he imagines it's there to bear him aloft. All the people out there—they've gathered not just to gape, he realizes, but so that he won't have to die alone. There is nothing more they can do for him. Hatcher finishes his prayer, and the sergeant asks Tommie if he has anything to say.

Tommie pauses, then leans to Hatcher and whispers in his ear: "Tell them I bear no ill will toward anyone in the world." He sniffs in.

Hatcher clears his throat and repeats the words to the people assembled in the yard.

"Is that all?" Hatcher asks Tommie.

"Yes," Tommie says. And in a voice that only Hatcher can hear he says, "Please try to comfort those at home, and give them my love."

"God bless you," Hatcher says.

Then Tommie bows his head again and waits. His legs are bound together below the knees. He looks out and sees, on the hill outside the yard, a little yellow-haired girl in a white dress, standing, watching, waiting for him. He thinks of Lillian once more, smiling up at him with love. *We belong together forever and ever.* The rope is placed over his head, the noose tightened. *Thy will be done.* There in the yard is Justice Richardson, standing at attention in his blue uniform and tall derby, looking at Tommie with an expression of grave certainty. Tommie closes his eyes.

A wind whips over the prison walls, swirls through the yard, and snatches at Tommie's hat. He can sense a hand upon his head, the hat secured, and Dunn's voice: "Good-bye, sir."

Now he wishes his brother were there to make sure he is all right. He doesn't want to suffer. But it's too late for that.

Lord Jesus receive my spirit.

The door springs open and Tommie shoots through space. He bounces, spins around to his right, then to his left, then back again, as the rope stretches. His weight not enough to jerk the knot tighter, he hangs as much by his chin as his neck, the loop up around his ear on one side and digging into his neck on the other. His hat tips over his eyes. He kicks and kicks, trying to launch himself into the next world, his feet nearly touching the ground. But nothing happens. Minutes go by, hours. The world weeps. Aunt Jane, his parents, himself a boy on a journey away from home—all watch through frosted glass, waiting, hoping, the pale winter sun unmoving. Then he kicks furiously against the fire in his lungs, the exquisite pain in his loins, the release, birds fluttering up around him, his blameless heart racing against itself and the insult to its strength, his throat struggling under a fence in a far field, the weight of his life hanging from him, his head dying to explode. Somehow unable to break through. *Willie leaning over him, waiting, waiting . . . Lift me up, Willie . . . Save me . . . Pull me out . . .*

And then he is free somehow, the rope loosened, his breathing restored, and the water of the river lapping over him is cool, the most beautiful feeling in the universe, carrying him downstream toward home, the green trees overhead and beyond them the deepest sparkling blue sky he has ever known . . .

CHAPTER TWENTY-EIGHT

I N THE AFTERNOON Willie collects the body of his brother, but he will not lift the black silk hood to look at his face. He watches the undertaker nail the lid on the coffin and helps him load it into the hired carriage.

Aunt Jane has already had a hole dug out beside her husband, and the following day Willie and Lewis lower the box on ropes. Reverend Ryland refused to come read from the Bible on account of the damage it might do to his reputation in neighboring counties, so Willie does the reading himself. It's just Aunt Jane, Lewis, Maria, his parents, and himself. His mother throws in a sprig of holly with red berries, but can't bring herself to say anything. Nor can Willie say anything other than the words written on the page.

And then he has a pressing matter to attend to over in Manquin with Mr. Howard Madison. Perhaps he should have already attended to it, but now it's urgent. He goes horseback to the Clifton ferry, crosses the river, then heads up the road to the Madison place. He wants to sing to honor his brother, like the Powhatan of long ago, but his voice quakes—he doesn't have his brother's talent. There is no promise of spring on this still, gray day of bare trees, no heat nor movement except that of small birds in the thickets by the sides of the road. The horse moves steadily along, one mile after another.

The Madison place is as it has always been, the house bearing loose scabs of whitewash, the porch sagging into a hideous grin, skirts of weeds around the outbuildings. A muddy boy is crawling beneath the house (black or white, Willie can't discern), and the odor of rancid meat is everywhere on the property, as though it were a charnel house. Steaming vats of bluing indicate there is at least a woman who cares about clean laundry.

Willie hears a rhythmic thumping over in the barn and turns his horse that direction. To the left of the building a slit-open hog hangs by its heels from a tree, its guts cooling on a table beside a greasy, foot-long meat cleaver. A scraper lies on the ground beneath the hog, whose bristly neck suggests the task has been simply too much bother. A kettle of boiling water stands off to the side, though, Willie thinks, still a little too close to the barn.

He slides down and steps into the dusty gloom. The smell of moldy hay strikes him. The barn is a chaos of ill-kempt equipment and random feedbags tucked wherever space is available. From one wall peg hangs a halter, from which depends a sickle. On a workbench lies an assortment of tinsnips, mallets, a sawed-off grubbing hoe, and a coffee grinder. A rabbit gum is suspended by twine from the hayloft—to preserve space? Or did Madison believe he could catch flying rabbits in his barn? There is no rhyme nor reason to any of it as far as Willie can fathom. In one corner is a John Deere grain binder, or a rusting carcass that once represented such a machine. Perhaps Madison bought it secondhand thinking to fix it up, but at any rate there he is thrashing grain on a low platform with a grain flail. At this kind of work, he is quite expert for an old man, raising the staff so that the thongs flick the stick back, then forward, letting the stick land with a punishing smack against the stalks. Over and over, grunting each time it lands.

He stops suddenly and jerks around. "Cain't hear good no more," he says. He turns back to finish the pile he's working on. After a few strokes, he pauses. "Thresher's broke," he says, "but this does just as good for the horses. Used to have a nigger to do it, now I just pretend I'm beating that selfsame nigger." He laughs and works with renewed energy.

Madison is not one to appreciate the subtleties of a thoughtful gesture, and yet he knows when he is being challenged. He has developed an instinct for it, just as he knows when it is time to kill a hog that has gotten too ornery, same with a dog. He'll say, "Mr. Hog I've took all the shit from you I'm gonna take. I'm going up to the house for my gun." And the hog will know that something is different and trot away with a grumble across the mud and up against the slats of its pen, its snout pushed out, and regard the man walking with the long stick in his hand and a crazy happiness on his face. Madison will take his time, letting the hog trot from one side to the other; he is too old to turn it out into the pasture the way he used to—he's liable to slip in his excitement.

When he is done with his grain pile he turns around. He spits, frowns. "What can I do for you, Mr. Cluverius?" He wears a long-sleeved out-at-elbows undershirt and baggy overalls held up by one suspender and stuffed into an ancient pair of brown riding boots. His thin fringe of hair hangs to his neck, a week-old beard hiding caved-in cheeks. The one thing not disheveled about him, Willie observes for the first time, is his strength—from his thick neck down to his trunk he looks to be a mean and unbending thing of muscle.

"I came to ask why you lied about my brother."

He regards Willie with red-rimmed eyes that are heavy, milky, and unmoving. His face is downturned, made of melted wax and years of rage. "I didn't lie and I'll thank you to get off my property."

"You got up in the witness box and swore before God that Lillie told you she was carrying Tommie's baby. I know that's a lie. I just want to hear you say it, and then I'll go away."

"Say it for what?" Madison tightens his grip on the flail, his neck going to cords.

"Because I want you to. You started this, and now you're going to end it. I know you won't apologize, I just want to hear you say you put your hand on the Bible and lied to God."

"I won't do any such a thing."

"She didn't speak more than two words to you the last years of her life."

"Why, you boy. You're just a nothing. I won't do anything for you. You and your people are trash. Your aunt Jane with her nose in the air thinking she's too good to give me a nod nor a grin. She ruined that girl, and you and your brother too. Your mother's a four o'clock drunk. But, your daddy now. He's good for something. For making words come out of his mouth all day long, and none of them add up to more than a pile of hog's innards. Just like out yonder." He points his flail over Willie's shoulder to the killing table outside.

Willie tenses his jaw, his hands flexing of their own accord. He tries to think how it is that people like Madison come to be in this world. He wants to jump on him, to beat him until he takes back what he has said, and he feels himself leaning forward on the balls of his feet.

The restraint seems unnoticed by Madison. "Your brother got what he deserved," he says. "'Cept I wished I could've done it myself. You wasn't there so I'll tell you how it went."

"You won't say another word to me as long as you live. I promise you that." He stares hard at Madison, who returns the look with flat, uncomprehending eyes. Willie turns then and begins walking back to his horse.

"What was it you wanted to promise me, boy?" Madison says. His breath comes out in hard bursts, turning to mist in the cold air. He raises the flail and brings it down, whizzing in front of Willie's face and torso.

"She wasn't your property to do with as you pleased," Willie says.

"You shut your mouth, boy."

Tears are now sliding down Willie's cheeks as he backs away, stumbling. "You think you're above the law," he says. "You think the law doesn't apply to you."

"Who are you talking about?" As Madison lunges, Willie trips and nearly falls. All he can do is watch as Madison steps forward, his Adam's apple pulsing like a blind animal trying to free itself. "Your brother choked to death. Rope didn't break his neck. He strangled, died gasping for breath. It was right fitting."

Before Madison can raise the flail again, Willie bursts upon him and catches him in a bear grip. Madison manages to get his arms around Willie's, and they struggle, trying to unbalance each other. Willie is stronger, but Madison has more heft to him, and he is using it to try to maneuver Willie toward the boiling kettle. They go lurching up against the hot iron rim, scattering coals with their feet, Madison trying to force Willie over into the water. The rim is nearly waist high and the effort to side-bend Willie is sapping Madison's strength.

But the fight begins to turn on experience, and despite Willie's youth and years of working in the woods he cannot equal Madison's penchant for bitter struggle. Madison grappled hand to hand for his life on more than one occasion during the war, and it comes back naturally to him. Yet Willie is able to twist Madison around to his weaker left side until they bang into the killing table, then fall scrabbling to the ground. Madison is now able to get his hands around Willie's throat, and Willie cannot dislodge them. The meat cleaver spins on the rattling, grease-slick table and falls on the ground. Willie sees it. His hand reaches out and takes it, like a tool, with the business end toward Madison's head.

In an instant Willie can see where it is going: the blade landing neat along the temple and jawline, cleaving meat and bone, the rivulets of blood darkening the cruel Adam's apple as it bobs one last time, blood raining on the ground as Madison falls in a ruined heap, half his face torn away. As the blade swings through the air, Willie twists it so that it slaps flat as an iron skillet against Madison's cheek. The man falls away insensate, his features gone suddenly gentle as a child's, his breath blown back into him like a corpse restored. Willie gets up and drops the cleaver and brushes himself off, stunned by what has just unfolded. He regards the crumpled figure of Madison, lying on his side.

"Is he dead?" says a woman's voice.

Willie looks up and sees Mrs. Madison standing on the side steps, a little girl peering from behind her apron.

"No," Willie says, "just stunned." He looks at Madison again, sees his chest rise and fall; he feels his own lungs filling and refilling.

Mrs. Madison nods, her dimpled chin tucking up toward a permanently downturned mouth. "Well—," she replies. Her faded brown hair has come loose and falls across her cheek. She bears a strong resemblance to Lillie—she's small like Lillie, but stouter and beaten down, her eyes showing fear. She steps to the ground, her arms crossed. "What made him to come after you that a-way?" she says.

"Cousin Hannah?" Willie says. "Do you recognize me?"

"You're Aunt Eliza's older boy, Willie Cluverius."

Willie nods. He starts to tell her what happened, but she cuts in, "You don't have to tell me. I saw it." The girl comes from around her mother now. She has long limp brown hair, a small face, and wide dark eyes that study him—she looks even more like Lillie than her mother does. Willie cannot keep from staring at her.

"I don't know what you came for," Mrs. Cluverius tells him, "but I know you didn't ought to be attacked. You've had your share of misery."

Willie waits a minute, then ventures, "You and my ma were close at one time. You wrote letters and such."

"We still do from time to time."

Willie tucks his lower lip into his teeth. He tries to think how to frame the question.

Hannah is looking thoughtfully at her prostrate husband. "He's not much of a man, my husband," she says, sniffing in and pulling herself erect for the first time in years. "Something's not right about him. I don't know how to describe it."

"You don't have to," Willie says. He doesn't want to hear any more. Faith alone, he thinks—the not-knowing rather than the knowing. He wants to say something that he only partly understands—that it doesn't matter what he believes, that the only thing you can count on in faith, as in love, is that the ground is going to shift under you, just like it does on the shore. But they would be sure to misunderstand.

Madison tries to mumble something, saliva oozing from his cracked lips, his bruised and swelling jaw unable to work. A rooster crows off in the yard, then stops mid-cry for some reason known only in the world of roosters.

"I came here to ask him a question," Willie says, "though he couldn't answer me."

"He don't answer to nobody, not even to—" Mrs. Madison clamps her lips together as she glances up, then over to her husband, who begins trying to right himself, getting on all fours.

"I'mon kill you, boy," Madison croaks. His heavy eyes open slowly, then close, then open again. He makes another attempt to move, but his limbs will not coordinate themselves, and all he can do is make another feeble threat, mewling in incoherent, impotent fury.

Willie regards the girl—he has not seen her in years and cannot think of her name. "Cousin Hannah," he says, "you send your girl around to Aunt Jane and me if you want. We'd be proud to look after her schooling and such." Mrs. Madison nods briefly, glances at her husband. "It wouldn't be a bother," Willie goes on. "Jane gets lonely, you see, she likes young people around." He stands there looking at Mrs. Madison and her daughter, watching them as their eyes dart beyond him and grow suddenly large. A moment stretches into perfect stillness, and no act of violence or reconcilement can unbalance it. Willie turns and sees Madison, grasping the cleaver, rise to his knees, his eyes trained on Willie's midsection and, at the same time, on something so distant that Willie could think on it for the rest of his life and never know what it was.

Madison sees his daughter's accusing eyes. His single overalls strap has broken so that the bib hangs below his waist, his dirt-smeared, sagging undershirt revealing the pale breast of an old man. He tries to say something to Willie, but his jaw is locked, his throat a dry streambed. He drops the cleaver.

Willie turns to his cousin. "I'd best be leaving if I'm to catch the ferry." He picks up his hat where it fell, slaps it on his thigh, and mounts his horse. "Good-bye," he says, lifting his hat for Hannah, the same hat Tommie wore that day in Richmond—a gray slouch hat with a tear in the crown. He rides slowly up the hard-packed dirt of the drive, its stripe of high grass leading him out to the road. "Come back here," Madison says, his voice hollow, gone to nothing but wind along the ground.

The smell of wood smoke and green cedar bites through the cold of a January afternoon. A little farther down the road and he finds he does feel like singing after all. He wets his lips, and softly, jostling along, he hums songs he remembers his brother singing.

After a while the cloud cover begins lifting, the sun edging out of the western sky, and he sees what looks like a formation of geese. But as he watches it grow closer, he realizes it's a balloon. It's the strangest thing he has ever seen in his life. A balloon in King William County—who would have thought? It grows larger, a giant sea-green teardrop, and he can see people in the wicker basket, waving their hats. He waves back as they go silently floating over the trees, riding beneath their own world. How strange life is, how filled with wonder and amazement. "Did you see that, Tommie?" he says. "Damnedest thing. I miss you, brother. God be with you."

He looks up and beholds at the edge of the clouds the deepest blue sky he has ever seen, with the evening star shining like a little fire in the west. "Till we meet," he sings quietly, "God be with you till we meet again." Two brothers gone—it's just himself now. "The world is upside down, Tommie," he says, "and I can't make it any righter."

He pushes his horse into a trot. With luck he'll be home in time for a late supper.

A Note on the Sources

This novel is based on an actual court case, *Commonwealth v. Cluverius*. A paragraph in a book on Richmond history got me digging deeper. I found copious newsprint dedicated to what became a sensational trial; it was wonderfully detailed, but it gave no clear idea of who the participants were, where they had come from, and why they ended up doing what they did.

I continued to dig up as much as I could about the case, while doing general research on the period. Though most of Richmond's early buildings have fallen to the wrecking ball, a good sample from various periods remains. Finding Lillian's grave early on—which took more effort than I'd thought it would—gave me a tangible link to the story and made me feel committed to telling it with as much passion and honesty as I could.

I soon realized that I was going to have to imagine most of the story. By this point I felt so connected to these long-dead people that I thought I owed it to them to get it right, which in fictional terms meant that the story would have to rise up out of the facts like a holographic image from a flat screen.

But the question remained: What *was* the story? I was lucky in that the events of the case suggested a rough plot line, as all interesting court cases do. There was a real Tommie, Lillian, Willie, Jane Tunstall, Richardson, a shadowy character on whom Nola was based, and so on. In my research I came across key pieces of evidence, carefully preserved for more than a century:

letters, photographs, and, most interesting of all, a watch key and a torn note. I integrated much of this into the story, though not always exactly as it appeared in the actual case.

While I have done my best to keep the novel true to its historical period, I have tailored the facts to suit the story's dramatic purposes. Most of the pre- and post-trial story is of my own creation. For the trial itself I borrowed freely from the transcripts, employing the standard writer's tricks of cutting, adding, and moving. Time was collapsed in some places—Tommie, for instance, spent much longer in jail than he does in the novel; the lawyers are composites, and minor characters have been added as necessary; events such as Hatcher's visits were filled out; and so forth. The details of the case, then, were the fence posts on which I hung the story. The tragic love triangle at its heart was my invention, but it was suggested by the facts.

As to Tommie's guilt, the record remains tantalizingly unclear. One can pore through pages of material and be convinced one way, then sift some more another day and completely change one's mind.

The following sources were invaluable: The *Richmond Dispatch*, *Chataigne's Richmond City Directory* (1885), *Cluverius: My Life, Trial and Conviction* by Thomas J. Cluverius (Richmond: S. J. Dudley, 1887), *Houses of Old Richmond* by Mary Wingfield Scott (Richmond: Valentine Museum, 1941), *Old Richmond Neighborhoods* by Mary Wingfield Scott (Richmond: Whittet & Shepperson, 1950), *Richmond: The Story of a City* by Virginius Dabney (Charlottesville: University Press of Virginia, 1990), *Celebrate Richmond* edited by Elisabeth Dementi and Wayne Dementi (Richmond: Dietz, 1999), *Richmond: A Pictorial History from the Valentine Museum and Dementi Collections* edited by Thomas F. Hale

(Richmond: Whittet & Shepperson, 1974), *American State Trials* edited by John D. Lawson (St. Louis: Thomas Law Book, 1936), *Along the Trail of the Friendly Years* by William E. Hatcher (New York: Fleming H. Revell, 1910), *John Jasper* by William E. Hatcher (New York: Fleming H. Revell, 1908), *William E. Hatcher* by Eldridge B. Hatcher (Richmond: W. C. Hill, 1915), *Old Houses of King and Queen County Virginia* by Virginia D. Cox and Willie T. Weathers (King and Queen County Historical Society, 1973), *Old King William Homes and Families* by Peyton Neale Clarke (Baltimore: Genealogical Publishing, 1976), *The Architecture of Historic Richmond* by Paul S. Dulaney (Charlottesville: University Press of Virginia, 1968), and *General Fitzhugh Lee: A Biography* by James L. Nichols (Lynchburg: H. E. Howard, 1989).

Archivist and Southern gentleman Minor Weisiger at the Library of Virginia was extremely helpful and gracious; he is, coincidentally, the great-great-grandson of one of the lead reporters on the Cluverius case. In general, the Library of Virginia was essential; particular thanks goes to map specialist Cassandra Farrell. I received good advice from professor W. Hamilton Bryson, expert on Virginia legal history; King William County historian Steve Colvin; professor James A. Bostwick; and Richmond Circuit Court Assistant Chief Deputy Supervisor Ed Jewett. I'm also deeply indebted to Alderman Library and the Albert and Shirley Small Special Collections at the University of Virginia.

Acknowledgments

I'm unutterably grateful for the extraordinary talents of editor Katie Henderson, who pulled me across the finish line and made this a much better book; the keen insights of Judith Gurewich; and the generosity of Paul Kozlowski, Sarah Reidy, Marjorie De-Witt, Yvonne E. Cárdenas, and the rest of the Other Press staff. I bow as well to Alanna Ramirez and Ellen Levine for their encouragement and unfailing support. For reading, listening, locating graves, and showing me what a meat cleaver can do, thanks also to Chris Tilghman, Caroline Preston, Henry Wiencek, Donna Lucey, Tom Whitehead, Sue Hart, Steve Keach, and Ricky Weeks. Finally, thanks to my wife, Margo Browning, who has been with this novel every step of the way—helping me see where to go, again and again.

JOHN MILLIKEN THOMPSON is the author of *America's Historic Trails* and *Wildlands of the Upper South*, and coauthor of the *National Geographic Almanac of American History*. His articles have appeared in *Smithsonian*, *The Washington Post*, *Islands*, and other publications, and his short stories have been published in *Louisiana Literature*, *South Dakota Review*, and many other literary journals. He has lived in the South all his life. This is his first novel.